CRITICAL ACCLAIM FOR STEVEN SAYLOR'S NOVELS OF ANCIENT ROME

LAST SEEN IN MASSILIA

"Accurately depicts Roman society. . . . characters are believable and well-delineated. . . . this is recommended." —*Library Journal*

"Saylor knows his material well enough to make the ancient world come vividly alive." —*The Anniston Star*

"Saylor is as much historian as he is weaver of suspense. . . . a rich, enriching series." —*Christian Science Monitor*

"In *Catilina's Riddle*, the aging of the main character parallels the maturing of Saylor's talent as a novelist. The plot is richer and more dramatic; the stakes are higher, and the situation is in Rome itself more desperate." —*San Francisco Review of Books*

"A spacious, provocative portrait." —*Kirkus Reviews*

RUBICON

"Saylor makes Ancient Rome come alive. . . . a gripping read that's as intense as it is satisfying." —*Booklist*

"This is a brilliant portrait of a chaotic time. . . . Saylor has the rare ability to make history comprehensible but also entirely personal and therefore terrifying" —*The Sunday Oregonian*

"Saylor's books are delightfully rampant with fact-founded ribaldry, political treachery, and arcane social prejudices, all of which make you wonder why the hell you didn't pay more attention to Roman history in school." —*Seattle Weekly*

MORE . . .

CATILINA'S RIDDLE

Steven Saylor

St. Martin's Paperbacks

CATILINA'S RIDDLE

Copyright © 1993 by Steven Saylor,

Map copyright © 1993 by Steven Saylor.

Library of Congress Catalog Card Number: 93-24282

ISBN: 0-312-98211-9
EAN: 80312-98211-9

Printed in the United States of America

St. Martin's Press hardcover edition / September 1993
Ballantine edition / October 1994
St. Martin's Paperbacks edition / February 2002

St. Martin's Paperbacks are published by St. Martin's Press, 175 Fifth Avenue, New York, N.Y. 10010.

10 9 8 7 6 5 4 3

To the Shade of My Mother

CONTENTS

NOMENCLATURA

THE Latin name Catilina is sometimes spelled Catiline, especially in older texts, just as the Latin Pompeius is more familiarly rendered Pompey and Marcus Antonius becomes Mark Antony. Scholars nowadays tend to prefer original Latin spellings, which I have followed in the case of Catilina, if only for its euphony. The stress falls on the third syllable, which has a long *i*.

I have also used contemporary Latin names for a number of cities. Some of these (with their more familiar names) include: Faesulae (Fiesole), Arretium (Arezzo), Massilia (Marseille), and Florentia (Florence).

Dates are given according to the Roman calendar before it was reformed by Julius Caesar. These are the months of the year (with English names and spellings, if different, in parentheses, along with their number of days): Januarius (January, 29 days), Februarius (February, 28 days), Martius (March, 31 days), Aprilis (April, 29 days), Maius (May, 31 days), Junius (June, 29 days), Quinctilis (July, 31 days), Sextilis (August, 29 days), September (29 days), October (31 days), November (29 days), and December (29 days).

The Romans did not reckon the days of the months by consecutive numbers, as we do, but by their positions in relation to certain nodal days, namely the Kalends (the first day of the month), the Nones (the fifth or seventh day), and the Ides (the thirteenth or fifteenth day). The day of the month was reckoned by counting backward from these days. I have tried to conform to this system in most cases.

The story begins on the first day of June (the Kalends of Junius), 63 B.C.

Embossed upon the shield Aeneas saw
The stony halls of the netherworld, the domain of the damned
And the punishments they suffer. There Catilina clings to the
edge of a sheer
Precipice, cringing in terror while the Furies beat their wings
about him . . .
VIRGIL, *The Aeneid*,
VIII: 666–669

How haue we chang'd, and come about
in euery doome,
Since wicked CATILINE went out,
And quitted *Rome*?
One while, we thought him innocent;
And then w'accus'd
The *Consul*, for his malice spent;
And power abus'd.
Since, that we heare, he is in armes,
We thinke not so:
Yet charge the *Consul*, with our harmes,
That let him goe.
So, in our censure of the state,
We still do wander;
And make the carefull magistrate
The marke of slander.
BEN JONSON, *Catiline his Conspiracy*,
ACT IV: 863–878

What is truth?
PONTIUS PILATUS

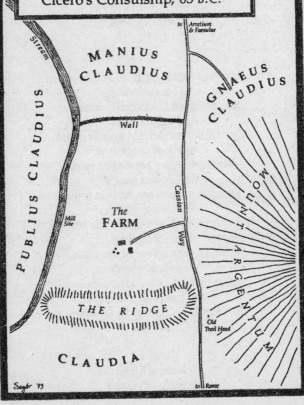

The
CLAUDIAN ESTATES
in Etruria, together with maps of
Rome & Northern Italy at the time of
Cicero's Consulship, 63 B.C.

Stream

to Arretium
& Faesulae

MANIUS
CLAUDIUS

GNAEUS
CLAUDIUS

PUBLIUS CLAUDIUS

Wall

Cassian Way

Mill
Site

The
FARM

MONS ARGENTUM

THE RIDGE

Old
Trail Head

CLAUDIA

Saylor '93

to Rome

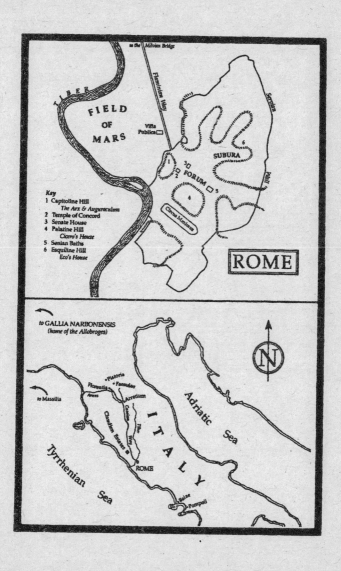

to the Milvian Bridge

Flaminian Way

TIBER

FIELD
OF
MARS

Villa
Publica

Subura Way

SUBURA

1
3
2
FORUM
5

4

Circus Maximus

Key
1 Capitoline Hill
    The Arx & Auguraculum
2 Temple of Concord
3 Senate House
4 Palatine Hill
    Cicero's House
5 Senian Baths
6 Esquiline Hill
    Eco's House

6

ROME

to GALLIA NARBONENSIS
(home of the Allobroges)

N

Pistoria
Florentia
Arnus
Faesulae
Arretium
Clanis
Tiber
Cassian Way

ITALY

Adriatic Sea

to Massilia

Tyrrhenian
Sea

ROME

Baiae
Pompeii

PART ONE

NEMO

ONE

"ACCORDING to Cato . . ." I said, and paused, squinting at the scroll. Bright summer sunlight from the window glared across the parchment, obscuring the faded black letters. Then again, at forty-seven, my eyes are not what they used to be. I can count the leaves on an olive tree fifty feet away, but the difference between *O* and *U*, or even *I* and *L*, is not as clear as it once was.

"According to Cato," I began again, holding the scroll at arm's length and reading silently. "Well, this is ridiculous! Cato clearly says that the haymaking should have been done by now, yet here it is, the Kalends of Junius, and we haven't even begun!"

"If I may interject, Master . . ." Aratus, standing at my elbow, cleared his throat. He was a slave, not yet fifty, and had been foreman of the farm since long before my arrival the previous autumn.

"Yes?"

"Master, the blooms are not yet off the grass. It is not uncommon for the crop to be late. Why, last year it was just the same. We didn't harvest the hay until almost the end of Junius—"

"And I saw how much of it went bad in the barn! Bundles and bundles rotted away during the winter, so there was hardly enough left to feed the oxen during the plowing this spring."

"But that was because of the storm damage to the roof of the barn last winter, which let in the rain and so spoiled much of the hay. It had nothing to do with the late harvest last summer." Aratus lowered his eyes and compressed his lips. His patience was near its end, if his subservience was not.

"Still, Cato is explicit: 'Cut the grass crop when the time comes, and *take care that you are not too late* in cutting it.'

Now, Marcus Porcius Cato may have been dead for almost a hundred years, but I don't suppose the ways of nature have changed in that time." I looked up at Aratus, who pursed his lips tightly.

"And another thing . . ." I shifted through the scroll, seeking the passage that had leaped out at me the night before. "Ah, here: 'The chickpea is poisonous to livestock and thus should be pulled up when found growing among the grain.' And yet, only the other day, I saw one of the slaves take the burnt portions of chickpeas from the kitchen and mix them in among the oxen's feed."

Did I catch Aratus rolling his eyes, or only imagine it? "The *herbage* of the chickpea is poisonous to livestock, Master, not the bean. Poisonous to men, as well, I suspect," he added dryly.

"Ah, well. Yes, that explains it then." I closed my' eyes and pinched the bridge of my nose. "As you say, if the bloom is not yet off the grass, I suppose we shall simply have to wait to begin the haymaking. The vineyard has begun to come out in leaf?"

"Yes, Master. We have already begun to trim the vines and tie them to supports—just as *Cato* says to do. And since, as *Cato* advises, only the most skilled and experienced slaves should be engaged in the task, perhaps I should go and oversee the work."

I nodded, and he left.

The room seemed suddenly stuffy and hot, though the hour was not quite noon. I felt a throbbing in my temples and told myself it was the heat, though it was more likely from squinting at the scroll and arguing with Aratus. I walked out into the herb garden, where the air was cooler. From within the house I heard a sudden shriek—Diana screaming, and then Meto shouting, "I never touched her," followed by a maternal scolding from Bethesda. I sighed and kept walking, through the gate and onto the path that led to the goat pens, where two of the slaves were engaged in mending a broken fence. They scarcely looked up as I passed.

The path took me alongside the vineyards, where Aratus was already busy overseeing the tying of the young vines. I kept walking until I came to the olive orchard and paused in the cool shade. A bee buzzed by my head and flitted among the tree trunks. I followed it up the hillside to the edge of the orchard, to the ridge where a patch of virgin forest stood. A few naked stumps at the periphery showed where an attempt had once been made to clear the high land, and then abandoned. I was glad the ridge had been left wild and wooded, though Cato would have advised clearing it for crops; Cato always seemed to prefer high places to the lowlands where mist might gather and ruin the crops with rust.

I sat on one of the stumps and caught my breath beneath the shade of a gnarled, ancient oak. The bee buzzed by my ear again—perhaps it was drawn to the almond-scented oil that Bethesda had rubbed into my hair the night before. How gray my hair was becoming, half gray or more, mixed in with the black. Living in the countryside, I did not bother to have it cut as often as in the city, so that the loose curls lapped onto my neck and over my ears, and for the first time in my life I had grown a beard—that also was half gray, especially around the chin.

Bethesda, too, had been growing grayer, until she began to dye her hair with henna; the tint she had concocted was a deep, rich red, like the color of a bloodstain. How beautiful her hair still was, thick and luxurious. As I had grown more careless with mine, she had grown more elaborate with hers. She never wore it down anymore, except for bed. During the day she wrapped it into coils and pinned it atop her head, as haughty as any Roman matron—though her Egyptian accent would always give her away.

The thought made me laugh, and I realized that my headache was gone. I looked down on the valley and breathed in the smells of summer in the country: the odor of living beasts, of grass rustling in the dry breeze, of the earth itself dozing beneath the hot, baking sun. I studied the plan of the farm, like a picture laid before me: the red-tiled roof of the great house, hiding the bedrooms, kitchen, library, and dining room within; the higher roof that showed where the baths were installed; the formal courtyard just within the front door, with its fishpond and flowers; the second courtyard where the wine was fermented, with its kettles and vats; the third courtyard with its paved threshing floor open to the sky; the herb garden appended to the library, from which I had come. Close by the house were the sheds and pens and the well and the little house that held the olive press. The surrounding land was divided into various uses: fields for grains and other crops, vineyards, olive orchards. The boundary was marked on my left by a wooded stream, on my right by the road from Rome—the wide, paved Cassian Way—and in the far distance directly before me, beyond an expanse of cultivated fields, by a low stone wall that ran from the stream to the road. Stream to the left, road to the right, wall in the distance; and the fourth boundary was the ridge on which I sat. It was an idyllic setting, worthy of a poem or even of crusty old Cato's praise, I thought. It is the dream of every Roman, rich or poor, to have a farm in the countryside, to escape the turbulence and madness of the city. Against all expectations, I had done so at last. Why, then, was I not happy?

"You don't belong here, Gordianus."

I gave a start and swung around. "Claudia! You startled me."

"Good! Startled is better than bored and unhappy."

"And how, from behind, could you tell that I'm bored and unhappy?"

My neighbor put her hands on her ample hips and looked at me askance. "Feet and knees apart," she observed. "Elbows on knees, hands cupped together, chin on hands, head cocked to one side, shoulders slumped. If you were thirty years younger, Gordianus, I'd say you were miserably in love. In your case, it's what I've told you before: you simply don't belong in the countryside. Here, let me join you on this neighboring stump and show you how someone who truly loves the country surveys such a magnificent scene."

She sat down on the stump, which was apparently a bit lower than she thought so that she bumped it with her well-padded bottom and let out a good-natured laugh. She spread her legs, slapped her palms on her knees and beamed at the vista before her. Had we been sitting on the opposite slope of the ridge, looking down on her own farm, she could not have looked more pleased.

Claudia was the cousin of my late friend and benefactor Lucius Claudius, from whom I had inherited the farm. In appearance she was as much like him to have been his sister, and indeed in many ways seemed a female incarnation of Lucius, which predisposed me to like her from the first day she had come over the hill to introduce herself. Like Lucius she was sausage-fingered, plum-cheeked, and cherry-nosed. She had considerably more hair than Lucius, who had grown quite bald before his death, but like his, her hair was orange-red (faded with age and mixed with strands of silver) and of the same wispy, frazzled texture; she wore it atop her head in a careless clump from which stray tendrils escaped to waft about her friendly, round face. Unlike Lucius, she did not care for ornamentation, and the only jewelry I ever saw her wear was a simple gold chain around her neck. She disdained a woman's stola as impractical for farm life, and instead wore long woolen tunics in rustic colors, so that at a distance, given her general bulk and plain dress, she could be mistaken for a man, or even for a male slave, an ironic circumstance considering her high patrician blood.

Her farm was on the other side of the ridge; when I say that it was hers, I mean it quite literally, for she owned the property outright without recourse to father, brother, or husband. Like Lucius, Claudia had never married, but had somehow contrived to live independently and on her own terms. This would have been a notable feat even for a wealthy patrician matron in the city, but for a woman in the tradition-bound countryside it was nothing less than remarkable, and bespoke a strength of character and resolve of which Claudia's soft, round features gave no indication.

How she had wrested her particular plot of land from the Claudian fortunes I did not know. Her farm was only a small part of the family's holdings in the region. Indeed, I found myself surrounded by Claudii on every side. Over the ridge from me to the south was Claudia's small farm, which was generally held to be one of the poorer tracts, given the rocky nature of the slope and the lowness of the valley, plagued in winter by those mists so dreaded by Cato. Across the wooded stream, to the west, were the holdings of her cousin Publius Claudius; from my high vantage I could just glimpse the roof of his massive villa above the treetops. Beyond the low wall to the north was the property of another cousin, Manius Clau-

dius; because of the distance I could see little of his land and
nothing of his house. Across the Cassian Way, to the east,
the land became steep and rocky at the base of the mountain
the locals called Mount Argentum, whose upper reaches were
wreathed by a dark forest. This property was owned by Claudia's cousin, Gnaeus Claudius, and was said to be prime land
for hunting boar and deer. There was also, drilled somewhere
into the heart of the mountain, a deep silver mine. The mine,
however, was said to have been exhausted long ago. I could
clearly see the winding trail that led up the mountain's side
and disappeared over a pine-studded shoulder; where once
many slaves must have trekked in continuous labor, the way
had become disused and overgrown and was now a path for
goats.

Of all these properties, it was generally agreed that that of
Lucius Claudius, my benefactor, was much the best, and Lucius, by his will, had left it to me. The Claudii, in the name
of young Gnaeus and represented by a veritable legion of
advocates, had contested the will, but to no avail. I had had
my day in a Roman court, and the farm was mine. Why was
it not enough?

"Truly, it's a beautiful place," said Claudia, gazing down
at the red tiled roof and the cultivated earth. "When I was a
girl, it was quite run-down; Cousin Lucius took no interest at
all in the place, and let it fall to ruin. Then, oh, about fifteen
years ago—just after he met you and you had your first adventure together—he took a sudden interest in the place and
began to come here quite often. He purchased Aratus and
installed him as foreman, planted new vineyards and olive
orchards, brought in new slaves, refurbished the house. He
turned the farm into quite a lucrative enterprise, as well as a
retreat from the city. We were all amazed at his success. And
distressed at his sudden demise last year, alas," she sighed.

"And disappointed in his choice of an heir," I added quietly.

"Now, Gordianus, you must not bear a grudge. You can't
blame my Cousin Gnaeus for bringing that suit against you;
Lucius *was* his cousin, and we all expected Gnaeus to inherit,
since his own property is good only for hunting, not for farming, and the silver mine was long ago exhausted. Alas, Cicero

put your case quite brilliantly, as usual—you're very lucky to have had access to the great man, and we all envy you. Swayed by Cicero's arguments, the court in Rome ruled that Lucius's will was valid, and that was that. Lucius's fortune was not small; he had many other wonderful possessions, which he settled among his blood relations. I myself inherited his mother's jewelry and his town house on the Palatine Hill in the city. To you he gave his Etruscan farm. We have all reconciled ourselves to the fact."

"I know that *you* have, Claudia, but I'm not so sure about your cousins."

"Why? Have they been harassing you somehow?"

"Not exactly. I haven't seen either Gnaeus or Manius since our day in court, but each of them sent a messenger to tell my foreman to be sure to keep my slaves off their property—that is, unless I cared to have a slave returned to me with a limb missing."

Claudia frowned and shook her head. "Regrettable. How about Publius? He's the oldest and has always had a level head."

"Actually, Publius and I may be going to court soon."

"No! But why?"

"There seems to be some disagreement about the stream that marks the boundary of our two farms. The deed I inherited from Lucius clearly indicates that I have the right to use the stream and anything in the stream as I wish, but Publius recently sent me a letter in which he claims that such rights belong to him exclusively."

"Oh, dear!"

"The lawyers will sort it out eventually. Meanwhile, yesterday some of my slaves were washing some clothes downstream from some of Publius's slaves, who deliberately stirred up the water so that it was full of mud, which prompted the women on my side to hurl insults at the women on the opposite bank, until more than insults were hurled. The two foremen finally arrived to stop the altercation, but not until one of my women had been struck on the head by a flying rock."

"Was she seriously hurt?"

"No, but there was plenty of blood, and the wound will

leave a scar. If I had a litigious nature I'd demand that Publius buy me a replacement."

Claudia slapped her hands on her knees. "Intolerable! I had no idea that such provocations were being imposed on you, Gordianus. Really, I will have a word with my dear relatives and see if I can't intervene on behalf of good neighborly relations, not to mention common sense and law and order!"

She was so dramatically outraged that I laughed. "Your intervention on my behalf would be most appreciated, Claudia."

"It's the least I can do. Really, constant litigation and neighborly ill will may be the rule in the city, but here in the country such unpleasantness has no place. Here, all should be tranquillity, fertility, and domesticity, as Lucius himself used to say."

"Yes, I remember his using those very words once, when he was making ready to leave the city for the farm." I glanced down at the stream and then above the treetops to the roof of Publius's house, felt a vague uneasiness, then looked away and resolved to think of something else. "You saw Lucius often when he visited the farm?"

"Oh, I never missed seeing him whenever he came. Such a sweet man—but you know that. We would come and sit on this very ridgetop, on these very stumps, and gaze down on the farm, and make plans for the future. He was going to build a little mill house down by the stream. Did you know that?"

"No."

"Yes, with a great waterwheel, and one set of gears for grinding meal and another set for grinding stones dug out of Gnaeus's mine. It all sounded very ambitious and complex, but Lucius thought he could design the workings himself. A pity he died as he did, so suddenly."

"Suddenly is best, I think. I've known many men who were less fortunate."

"Yes, I suppose it would be worse to die slowly, or alone. . . ."

"Instead, Lucius died very swiftly, with hundreds of people around—crossing the Forum, where he was known and liked by just about everyone. Laughing and joking with his entourage—so I was later told—when he suddenly gripped his chest and collapsed. He died almost at once; he suffered only a little. The funeral was quite an affair—so many loving friends, from all walks of life." I smiled, remembering. "He had put his will into the keeping of the Vestal Virgins, as many rich men do. I had no idea, until I was called to see it for myself, that he had left anything to me at all. And there it was, the deed to his Etruscan farm, together with a worn copy of Cato's *On Farming*. I suppose he must have heard me daydreaming from time to time about retiring to the countryside, escaping all the madness in Rome. Of course, those were only idle dreams—what man of my means could ever afford to buy a decent farm, with all the slaves necessary to run it?"

"And a year later here you are, with that very dream realized."

"Yes, thanks to Lucius."

"And yet I find you brooding up here on the hilltop, like Jupiter looking down on burning Troy."

"Blame the behavior of certain of my neighbors," I said ruefully.

"Granted, but there is something else that troubles you."

I shrugged. "This morning Aratus and I almost came to blows. He thinks I'm an impossible, pompous ass from the city who knows nothing about farming and only wants to get in his way. I suppose I must look rather ridiculous to him, fussing about details I only half understand and quoting to him from Cato."

"And how does he look to you?"

"I know that Lucius thought highly of him, but it seems to me that the farm is not run nearly as efficiently as it could be. There's too much waste."

"Oh, how I hate waste!" said Claudia. "I never allow my slaves to throw anything away if I can possibly make use of it."

"Well, between Aratus and myself it's been one battle after another ever since I arrived last fall. Perhaps I *am* a pompous ass from the city who knows nothing about farming, but I do know waste when I see it, and I can read Cato. And beneath that, there's something about Aratus I don't trust. Perhaps I'm simply not used to owning so many slaves and having to manage them all, especially not a slave as strong-willed and sure of himself as Aratus. I gather that Lucius generally gave him the run of the farm, so that my arrival was a great inconvenience to him. He looks on me as a thorn in his side. I look on him the way you might look on a horse you don't trust; you must have the beast to get where you're going, but secretly you suspect he'll throw you. I find myself sniping at him constantly. He reacts by acting surly and impertinent."

Claudia nodded sympathetically. "Ah, a good foreman is always hard to find. But the joys of farm life far outweigh the travails, or so I've always found. I think more than Aratus is bothering you, Gordianus."

I looked at her sidelong. Her probing was beginning to touch on tender spots. "I suppose I should confess that I miss my elder son."

"Ah, young Eco. I met him when he helped you move in last fall. A fine-looking young man. Why is he not here with you?"

"He's taken over my house on the Esquiline Hill in the city and seems quite content there. Well, you can't expect a young man of twenty-seven to choose the tranquillity of country life over the distractions of the city. Besides, he's newly married; the girl no doubt prefers to run her own household. Can you imagine a young bride competing with Bethesda for command of a household? I shudder at the thought. There would be no tranquillity in that! Also, his work is there. He does the sort of things that I used to do—dangerous, and I worry. Rome has become a dreadful place. . . ."

"One must let them go their own way eventually. Or so I've heard. And you still have children at home."

"Yes, they were at each other's throats when I left the house. Meto is old enough to know better. He'll turn sixteen next month and put on his toga of manhood. He has no business fighting with Diana. She's only six. But she does delight in tormenting him. . . ."

"Diana? Is that what you call her for short?"

"Well, Gordiana is too big a name for such a small girl, don't you agree? Besides, the name of the goddess suits her; she loves wild things. She's happy here in the country. I have to be careful that she doesn't go wandering too far on her own."

"Ah, how big the farm must seem to a six-year-old. This ridge must be a mountain, the wall a great fortification, the stream a mighty river. And Meto, does he like the country?"

"He grew up away from the city, down in Baiae, on the coast." Claudia looked at me oddly. "Adopted, like his older brother," I explained. I did not add that Meto had been born a slave; others might discover that fact, but not from me. "So country ways come naturally to him. He was happy enough in the city, but he likes it here as well."

"And your wife, Bethesda?"

"There are women who have the power to remake whatever corner of the world they occupy to suit themselves; she is one. Besides, all places pale when compared to her native Alexandria. Rome could not match it, so why should the Etruscan countryside? But in truth I think she misses the big markets and the gossip, the smell of fish at the waterfront, the crush of the Forum on festival days, all the rush and madness of the city."

"And you?"

"What about me?"

"Do you miss those things?"

"Not for a moment!"

She looked at me shrewdly, but not without sympathy. "Gordianus, I have not been the sole mistress and overseer of two generations of conniving slaves, not to mention the customer of every cunning auctioneer and merchant between here and Rome for the last forty years, without learning to discern when a man is being less than honest with me. You are not happy here, and the reason has nothing to do with quarreling neighbors or missing your son in the city. You are homesick."

"Nonsense!"

"You are bored."

"With a farm to run?"

"And lonely."

"With my family around me?"

"Not bored because you have nothing to do; bored because you miss the unexpected adventures of the city. Not lonely for lack of loved ones, but lonely for new strangers to come into your life. Oh, the loneliness for strangers is nothing new to country dwellers; I have known it all my life. Don't you think I grow weary of my little circle of Cousin Publius and Cousin Manius and Cousin Gnaeus and their slaves, and long for a new face to appear in my world? Which is why I like talking to you, Gordianus. But I was raised in the country and you in the city, so it must be much worse for you, this boredom and loneliness."

"Well, there may be some truth in what you say, Claudia, but you can't say that I miss the city. I couldn't wait to leave it! It's all right for younger men, or those who are driven by their vices—there is no place like Rome for a man to satisfy his ambition for power or his lust or greed, or to die in the pursuit. No, I've turned my back on all that. The fact that Lucius died and left me this farm was the will of the gods, smiling on me, showing me a way out. Rome has become unlivable—filthy, overcrowded, noisy, and violent. Only a madman could go on living there!"

"But your work—"

"I miss that least of all! Do you know what I did for a living? I called myself a Finder. Advocates hired me to find proof of their enemies' crimes. Politicians—may I never see another!—hired me to uncover scandal about their adversaries. I once thought that I served truth, and through truth, justice, but truth and justice are meaningless words in Rome. They might as well be obliterated from the Latin tongue. I discover a man is guilty of some heinous crime, only to see him acquitted by a bribed panel of judges! I learn that a man is innocent, then see him convicted on spurious evidence and hounded out of the city! I discover that the scandal attached to powerful man is true enough, but for all that he is a sound and honest man who has only the same failings as other men; even so, the scandal is all that anyone cares about, and he is expelled from the Senate, and the true reason is some political maneuvering by his enemies, whose true agenda I can only guess at. Meanwhile a total scoundrel charms the mob and bribes their leaders and gets himself elected consul! I used to think that Rome was growing worse and worse, but it was I who changed. I've grown too old and weary to stomach such beastliness any longer."

To this tirade Claudia made no answer. She raised her eyebrows and shifted a bit uncomfortably at such an outburst of passion, then joined me in gazing silently at the view. A plume of smoke ascended from the kitchen. The muffled pounding of mallets, swung by the slaves repairing the goat pen, echoed up from the valley, along with the bleating of a kid which had wandered through the breach and was lost in the high grass of the hayfield. A young slave had gone looking for it, but was headed in the wrong direction. Over on the Cassian Way, coming down from the north, was a train of wagons, their contents battened down and covered by heavy sheets of canvas. To judge by the retinue of armed guards, the contents were quite valuable—probably a shipment of vases from the famous workshops at Arretium on its way down to Rome. Heading north on the road, about to meet and pass the wagons, was a long file of slaves with heavy loads on their backs, driven by men on horseback. Their chains were new and glinted in the noonday sun. Beyond the road, up on the slope of Mount Argentum and just across from our high vantage point on the ridge, a herd of unattended goats negotiated the winding path that led to Gnaeus's abandoned silver mine. A faint bleating, barely audible, echoed across the hot, still air.

"And yet . . ." I sighed.

"Yes, Gordianus?"

"And yet . . . do you know what this makes me think of, sitting here and gazing down on the scene?"

"Of Rome?"

"Yes, Claudia, of Rome! The city has seven hills, and every hill affords a different view. I was thinking of one in particular, on the Quirinal Hill, just up from the Fontinal Gate. You can see all of the northern quadrant of Rome. On a clear summer day like this, the Tiber sparkles beneath the sun as if it were on fire. The great Flaminian Way is thronged with carts and men on horseback. The Circus Flaminius looms up in the middle distance, looking enormous and yet like a toy; the crowded little tenements and shops cluster around it like sucklings to their mother. Beyond the city wall lies the

Field of Mars, hazy with dust from the racers in their chariots. The sounds and odors of the city rise up on the warm air like the breath of the city itself."

"You miss the city, Gordianus."

"Yes," I sighed. "For all its danger and corruption, for all its meanness and squalor—still, I miss the city."

We looked down again in silence. The slave had found the kid, which bleated and kicked at being dragged through the high grass. A kitchen girl brought a draft of water to the slaves at the goat pen, and their mallets fell silent. In the stillness I could hear Aratus shouting in a shrill voice at one of the slaves in the vineyard: "Wrong, the whole row is wrong! Redo them, every one!" Then all was quiet again, except for the buzzing of bees in the woods behind us.

"Actually, Gordianus, I was hoping to find you here on the ridge today."

"Yes, Claudia?"

"As you know, election time is close at hand."

"Don't remind me. After last summer's farce I never care to witness another such disgusting spectacle."

"Nevertheless, some of us have kept our civic spirit. Next month the election for the two consuls will be held in Rome. It's a tradition for our branch of the Claudii—the Etruscan country cousins, we call ourselves—to gather beforehand, decide which candidate to support, and choose a representative to send to Rome to vote. This year it falls my turn to play hostess to this little gathering. Never mind that my house is modest and I haven't the household slaves to properly provide for such a conclave; duty is duty. The gathering will be at the end of the month. It would help tremendously if I could borrow your cook and some of your kitchen slaves for the occasion. I'd need them for only a couple of days beforehand, to help prepare the feast, and then on the day of the gathering itself to help serve. Three days in all. Would it be too great an imposition, Gordianus?"

"Of course not."

"I shall repay you somehow. You never know when you'll need to borrow an ox or some bundles of hay. It's the way that country neighbors should help each other, yes?"

"Yes, indeed."

"And I trust that you won't instruct your slaves to slip a bit of poison into the feast—that would be too drastic a solution to your troublesome neighbors, eh?"

It was a joke, of course, but in such bad taste that I winced instead of smiling. In Rome I had encountered more cases of poisoning than I cared to remember.

"Come, Gordianus, don't cringe! Seriously, I'll take the opportunity to have a word with my relations about their uncivil treatment of you."

"That would be appreciated."

"Any advice on this year's slate of candidates? Your friend Cicero seems to be having quite a successful year as consul. We bear him no grudge, of course, even though he represented you in the case of Lucius's will. You must be proud to have such a friend. As consul, he's turned out better than any of us expected—too bad he can't serve two years in a row. At least last year he kept that wild-eyed madman Catilina out of office. Now Catilina is running again this year, and appears unstoppable, or so says—"

"Please, Claudia—no politics!"

"But of course; you're sick of all that."

"Quite. I may miss Rome, but I don't miss—"

At that moment I heard a high voice calling from the valley below. It was Diana, sent by her mother to fetch me for the midday meal. I watched her step from the library doorway into the herb garden. Her long hair was uncommonly thick and black for a child, glinting almost blue in the sunlight. She was dressed in a bright yellow tunic with her arms and legs bare. Her skin was tanned to a dark bronze, the gift of her Egyptian mother. She ran through the gate and skipped quickly along the path, passed the goat pens and the vineyards, and disappeared in the olive orchard at the foot of the hill. Through the foliage I glimpsed the yellow tunic approaching and heard her laughing: "I see you, Papa! I see you, Papa!"

A moment later she was rushing into my arms, giggling and out of breath.

"Diana, do you remember our neighbor? This is Claudia."

"Yes, I remember her. Do you live up here in the woods?" said Diana.

Claudia laughed. "No, my dear, this is only where I come to visit your father from time to time. I live down in the valley on the other side of this ridge, on my own little farm. You must come and visit me sometime."

Diana looked at her gravely for a moment, then turned to me. "Mama says you must come at once or she shall throw your food into the pen and let the goats eat it!"

Claudia and I both laughed and rose from the stumps. She said farewell and disappeared into the woods. Diana wrapped her little arms around my neck and I carried her down the hillside all the way to the house.

After the midday meal, the day grew even warmer. Everyone—animals, slaves, and children alike—found a shaded place and dozed in the heat. Everyone but me. I went to the library and took out some parchment and a stylus. I began to draw wheels with notches that fit into other wheels, trying to imagine the water mill that Lucius Claudius had planned to construct down on the stream.

All was peace and contentment, yet I was not bored at all. I had been mad, I decided, to tell Claudia that I missed the murderous intrigues of the city. Nothing and no one in this world, neither man nor god, could ever persuade me to return to such a life.

TWO

I was contemplating the problem of the water mill again ten days later when Aratus brought the cook and his two young assistants into my library. Congrio was a heavy man; what good cook is not? As Lucius Claudius had once remarked, a cook whose creations are not so tempting that he stuffs himself with stolen delicacies is not a cook worth having. Congrio was not Lucius's best cook—that post had been reserved for Lucius's house on the Palatine Hill in Rome, where he entertained his friends. But Lucius had not been a man to stint himself of culinary pleasures no matter where he went, and his country cook was more than skillful enough to delight my palate.

In the heat of the morning Congrio was already sweating. His two assistants stood to each side and slightly behind him, respectful of his authority.

I dismissed Aratus and asked Congrio and his helpers to step closer. I explained my intention to lend them to Claudia for the next few days. Congrio knew Claudia, because she had dined with his late master from time to time. She had always been pleased with his work, he assured me, and he was certain he would please her again and give me cause to be proud of him.

"Good," I said, thinking it might help to smooth matters with the Claudii to render them this favor. "There is one other thing. . . ."

"Yes, Master."

"You will do your best for the Claudii, of course; you will obey Claudia, and Claudia's own cook as well, since you will be serving in her house."

"Of course, Master; I understand."

"And also, Congrio . . ."

"Yes, Master?" He wrinkled his fleshy brow.

"You will say nothing to embarrass me while you are in Claudia's service."

"Of course not, Master!" He seemed genuinely hurt.

"You will not exchange gossip with the other slaves, or trade opinions of your respective masters, or pass along what you may perceive to be my opinions."

"Master, I fully understand the proper behavior of a slave who has been lent to a friend of his master."

"I'm sure you do. Only, while you keep your mouth closed, I want you to keep your ears open."

"Master?" He inclined his head, seeking clarification.

"This applies more to your assistants than to you, since I assume you may not leave the kitchen at all, while they may assist in serving the Claudii at their meal. The family will mostly be discussing politics and the upcoming consular elections; about that I care nothing, and you may ignore whatever they say. But if you should happen to hear my name mentioned, or any other matter concerning this farm, prick up your ears. Indicate no interest, but note what is said and by whom. Do not discuss the details among yourselves, but remember them. When you return, I will want to hear any such details, faithfully recounted. Do you understand, all of you?"

Congrio drew back with a sudden look of self-importance and nodded gravely. His assistants, watching him for their lead, did likewise. What makes a slave feel more warmly wicked than to be commissioned as a spy?

"Good. About the instructions I have just given, you will say nothing, not even to the other slaves. Not even to Aratus," I added. They nodded again.

After I sent them on their way, I stepped to the window and leaned out, breathing in the warm fragrance of mowed grass. The bloom was finally off the grass, and the slaves had begun to make hay. I also noted the figure of Aratus walking quickly alongside the house, his back turned to me, as if he had been standing by the window and listening to everything I said.

It was two days later, in the afternoon, when the stranger arrived.

I had taken a stroll to the stream and had settled on a grassy slope, my back against the trunk of a spreading oak, a wax tablet on my knees and a stylus in my hand. In my imagination a mill began to take shape on the bank of the stream. I tried to draw what I saw in my mind, but my fingers were clumsy. I smoothed the wax with the edge of my hand and started again.

"Papa! Papa!" Diana's voice came from somewhere behind me and echoed off the opposite bank. I stayed quiet and continued to draw. The result was no more satisfactory the second time. I rubbed the tablet clear again.

"Papa! Why didn't you answer me?" Diana stepped in front of me, putting her hands on her hips in imitation of her mother.

"Because I was hiding from you," I said, beginning a fresh mark in the wax.

"That's silly. You know I can always find you."

"Really? Then I hardly need to answer when you call, do I?"

"Papa!" She rolled her eyes, imitating Bethesda again, then collapsed on the grass beside me as if suddenly exhausted. While I drew, she contorted herself into a wheel and pulled at her toes, then lay flat again and squinted up at the sunlight that filtered through the oak canopy above. "It's true that I can always find you, you know."

"Can you? And how is that?"

"Because Meto taught me how. Meto says that you taught him. I can follow your footsteps in the grass and always find you."

"Really?" I said, impressed. "I'm not sure that I like that."

"What are you drawing?"

"It's called a mill. A little house with a great wheel that dips into the water. The flowing water turns the wheel, which turns other wheels, which will grind corn, or stones, or a little girl's fingers if she isn't careful."

"Papa!"

"Don't worry, it's just an idea. A problem, if you like, and probably too complicated for me ever to solve it."

"Meto says that you can solve any problem."

"Does he?" I put the tablet aside. She squirmed and rolled on the grass and laid her head in my lap. The broken sunlight spangled her hair, jet black in shadow and shot through with lustrous rainbows, like oil on water, where the light struck it. I had never seen a child with hair so black. Her eyes were also black, very deep and clear as only a child's eyes can be. A bird flitted above us. I watched Diana follow it with her gaze, amazed at the beauty of her least movement. She reached for the tablet and stylus, stretching her body awkwardly, and held them above her.

"I don't see a picture at all," she said.

"It's not very good," I admitted.

"Can I draw over it?"

"Yes."

She did a thorough job of obliterating my tentative lines with her small hand, then set to drawing. I stroked her hair and studied my imaginary mill by the stream. At length, across the water, two women emerged from the woods. They were kitchen slaves carrying clay jugs. They saw me and gave a start, conferred for a moment with their heads close together, then disappeared back into the woods. A little later I glimpsed something farther down the stream and saw them stepping down to the water's edge at a less convenient place. They dipped their jugs into the current, hoisted them onto their shoulders, and struggled up the steep bank and into the woods. Had Publius Claudius told them I was a monster who would eat them?

"This is you!" announced Diana, turning the tablet about and thrusting it toward me. Among the squiggles and curlicues I could barely make out a face. She was an even poorer draftsman than myself, I thought, but not by much.

"Extraordinary!" I said. "Another Iaia Cyzicena is among us!"

"Who is—" She stumbled over the unfamiliar name.

"Iaia, born in the city of Cyzicus, on the Sea of Marmara far away. She is a great painter, one of the greatest of our day. I met her down in Baiae, when your brother Meto first came into my life."

"Did Meto know her?"

"He did."

"Will I ever meet her?"

"It is always possible." Nine years had passed since the events in Baiae, and Iaia had not been so very old. She might yet live long enough for Diana to know her. "Perhaps one day you and Iaia may meet and compare your drawings."

"Papa, what is a Minotaur?"

"A Minotaur?" I laughed at the abrupt change of subject. "So far as I know, there was only ever one, *the* Minotaur. A terrible creature, the offspring of a woman and a bull; they say it had a bull's head and a man's body. It lived on a faraway island called Crete, where a wicked king kept it in a place called the Labyrinth, a great maze."

"A maze?"

"Yes, with walls like this." I wiped the tablet clean and set about drawing a maze. "Every year the king gave the Minotaur young boys and girls to eat. They would make the children enter *here*, you see, and the Minotaur would be waiting for them *here*. This went on for a very long time, until a hero named Theseus entered the Labyrinth and slew the Minotaur."

"He killed it?"

"Yes."

"Are you sure?"

"Quite."

"Completely sure?"

"Yes."

"Good!"

"Why do you ask about the Minotaur?" I said, anticipating the answer.

"Because Meto has been saying that if I'm not good, you'll feed me to it. But you've just said that it's dead."

"Ah, so it is."

"So Meto is wrong!" She rolled out of my lap. "Oh, Papa, I almost forgot! Mama sent me to fetch you. It's important."

"Yes?" I raised an eyebrow, imagining some dispute with the unskilled slaves who were overseeing the kitchen in Congrio's absence.

"Yes! There's a man who's come to see you, a man on horseback all the way from Rome, all covered with dust."

It was not one man, but three. Two of them were slaves, or more precisely bodyguards, to judge from their size and the daggers at their belts. The slaves had not entered the house, but stood outside with their horses, drinking water from a jug. Their master awaited me just inside the house, in the little formal courtyard with its fishpond and flowers.

He was a tall, strikingly handsome young man with dark eyes. His wavy black hair was trimmed short over his ears but left long on top, so that black curls fell carelessly about his smooth forehead. His beard was trimmed and blocked so that it was no more than a black strap across his chin and upper lip, accentuating his high cheekbones and red lips. As Diana had said, he was dusty from his journey, but the dust did not hide the fashionable and expensive-looking cut of his red tunic or the quality of his riding shoes. He looked familiar; a face from the Forum, I thought.

A slave had brought him a folding chair to sit on. He stood up as I entered and put down the cup of watered wine from which he had been drinking. "Gordianus," he said, "it's good to see you again. Country life agrees with you." His tone was casual, but it carried the polish of an orator's training.

"Do I know you?" I said. "My eyes fail me. The sunlight is so bright outside, here in the shade I can't see you clearly . . ."

"Forgive me! I'm Marcus Caelius. We've met before, but there's no reason you should remember me."

"Ah, yes," I said. "I see you more clearly now. You're a protégé of Cicero's—and also of Crassus, I believe. You're right, we've met before, no doubt at Cicero's house or in the Forum. Memories of Rome are so irrelevant here, I sometimes have a hard time recollecting. And the beard fooled me. The beard is definitely new."

He reached up and stroked it proudly. "Yes, I was probably clean-shaven when we met. You've grown a beard, as well."

"Mere laziness—not to mention cowardice. At my age a man needs every drop of blood he has to keep his bones warm. Is that the fashion in Rome these days? The way you trim it, I mean."

"Yes. Among a certain set." There was a trace of smugness in his voice that put me off.

"The girl has already brought you some wine, I see."

"Yes. It's quite good."

"A modest vintage. My late friend Lucius Claudius was rather proud of it. Are you on your way from Rome to some point farther north?"

"I've come from Rome, yes, but this is my destination."

"Really?" My heart sank. I had hoped he was merely passing through.

"I have business with you, Gordianus the Finder."

"It's Gordianus the Farmer now, if you don't mind."

"Whatever." He shrugged. "Perhaps we could retire to another room?"

"The courtyard is the coolest and most comfortable place at this time of day."

"But perhaps there's another place more private, where we might be less likely to be overheard," he suggested. My heart sank again.

"Marcus Caelius, it's good to see you again, truly. The day is hot and the road is dusty. I'm glad I can give you a cup of cool wine and a respite from your horse. Perhaps you require more than a drink and a brief rest? Very well, my hospitality is not exhausted. To ride all the way from Rome to my door and back again in a single day would challenge even a man as young and fit as you appear to be, and so I will gladly offer you accommodations for the night, if you wish. But unless you want to talk about haymaking or pressing olive oil or tending the vine, you and I have no business to discuss. I have given up my old livelihood.".

"So I've heard," he said amiably, with an undaunted glimmer in his eyes. "But you needn't worry. I haven't come to offer you work."

"No?"

"No. I've come merely to ask a favor. Not for myself, you understand, but on behalf of the highest citizen in the land."

"Cicero," I sighed. "I might have known."

"When a duly elected consul calls him to duty, what Roman can refuse?" said Caelius. "Especially considering the ties that bind the two of you. Are you sure there's not another room that might be more appropriate for our discussion?"

"My library is more private . . . if hardly more secure," I added under my breath, remembering my glimpse of Aratus skulking away from the window two days before. "Come."

Once there, I shut the door behind us and offered him a chair. I sat near the door to the herb garden, so that I could see anyone approaching, and kept an eye on the window above Caelius's shoulder, where I had caught Aratus eavesdropping. "What have you come for, Marcus Caelius?" I said, dropping all pretense of pleasant conversation. "I'll tell you right now that I will not go back to the city. If you need someone to spy for you or dig up trouble, you can go to my son Eco, though I hardly wish it on him."

"No one is asking you to come back to Rome," said Caelius soothingly.

"No?"

"Not at all. Quite the opposite. Indeed, the very fact that you are now living in the countryside is what makes you so appropriate for the purpose Cicero has in mind."

"I don't like the sound of that."

Caelius smiled thinly. "Cicero said you wouldn't."

"I'm not a tool that Cicero can pick up whenever he

wishes, or bend to his purpose at will; I never was and never
will be. No matter that he's consul for the year, he's still only
a citizen, as I am. I have every right to refuse him."

"But you don't even know what he's asking of you." Caelius seemed amused.

"Whatever it is, I won't like it."

"Perhaps not, but would you refuse an opportunity to serve
the state?"

"Please, Caelius, no empty calls to patriotism."

"The call is not empty." His face became serious. "The
threat is very real. Oh, I understand your cynicism, Gordianus. I may have lived only half as long as you, but I've seen
my share of treachery and corruption in the Forum, enough
for ten lifetimes!"

Considering his political education at the side of men like
Crassus and Cicero, he was probably speaking the truth. Cicero himself had trained him in oratory, and the pupil did his
master proud; the words that poured from his lips were polished like precious stones. He might have been an actor or a
singer. I found myself listening to him in spite of myself.

"The state stands poised on the brink of a terrible catastrophe, Gordianus. If it steps over that brink—or is pushed,
against the will of every decent citizen—the descent will be
more abrupt and harrowing than anything we've known before. Certain parties are determined to destroy the Republic
once and for all. Imagine the Senate awash in blood. Imagine
a return of the dictator Sulla's proscriptions, when any citizen
could be named an enemy of the state for no reason at all—
you must remember gangs running through the streets, carrying severed heads to the Forum to receive their bounty from
Sulla's coffers. Only this time the anarchy will spread un-
ceasingly, like waves from a great stone cast into a pond.
This time the enemies of the state are determined not to reform it, at whatever bloody cost, but to smash it altogether.
You own a farm now, Gordianus; do you want to see it taken
from you by force? It will happen, most certainly; because in
the new order everything already established will be usurped
and thrown down, ground into the dust. The fact that you no
longer live in Rome will provide no protection to you or your
family. Bury your head in a haystack if you wish, but don't

be surprised when someone comes up behind you and cuts it clean off."

I sat for a long moment in silence, unblinking. At last I managed to shake my head and suck in a breath. "Well done, Marcus Caelius!" I said. "For a moment there, you had me entirely under your spell! Cicero has taught you exceedingly well. Such rhetoric could make any man's hair stand on end!"

He raised his eyebrows, then his lids grew heavy. "Cicero said you would be unreasonable. I told him he should have sent that slave of his, Tiro. Tiro you know and trust—"

"Tiro I sincerely like and respect, because he is such a kind and openhearted man, but I would have beaten him back with words at every turn, which is no doubt precisely why Cicero did not send him. No, he did very well to send you as his agent, Marcus Caelius, but he did not count on the depth of my disgust with Roman politics, or the strength of my resolve to steer clear of any involvement with his consulship."

"Then what I've said so far means nothing to you?"

"Only that you've mastered the skill of making insanely exaggerated statements as if you sincerely believed them."

"But every word is true. I exaggerate nothing."

"Caelius, please! You're a Roman politician in the making. You are not allowed to speak the truth, and you are absolutely required to exaggerate everything."

He sat back, momentarily rebuffed but regrouping, as I could see from the glimmer in his eyes. He stroked his narrow beard. "Very well, you care nothing for the Republic. But surely you at least retain some vestige of your personal honor as a Roman."

"You are in my house, Caelius. Do not insult me."

"Very well, I won't. I will argue with you no longer. I will simply remind you of a favor you owe to Marcus Tullius Cicero, and request on his behalf that you pay back that favor now. Having faith in your honor as a Roman, I know you won't refuse."

I shifted in my seat uneasily. I glanced over my shoulder, through the doorway into the herb garden, where a wasp was buzzing among the leaves. I sighed, already sensing defeat.

"I assume you refer to the case that Cicero argued on my behalf last summer?"

"I do. You inherited this estate from the late Lucius Claudius. His family, quite reasonably, contested the will. The Claudii are a very old and distinguished patrician clan, whereas you are a plebeian with no ancestry at all, a dubious career, and a most irregular family. You might very well have lost your case, and with it any claim to this farm where you have so comfortably retired from the city you claim to loathe so much. For that you can thank Cicero, and don't deny it—I was in the court that day and I heard his arguments myself. I have seldom witnessed such eloquence—excuse me, untruths and exaggerations, if you prefer. It was you who asked Cicero to speak for you. He might well have declined. He had just finished a grueling political campaign, and as consul-elect he was pressed on all sides with obligations and requests. Yet he took time to prepare your case and to present it himself. Afterward, Cicero asked no payment for his service to you; he spoke on your behalf to honor you, acknowledging the many occasions on which you have assisted him since the trial of Sextus Roscius, seventeen years ago.* Cicero doesn't forget his friends. Does Gordianus?"

I looked out at the herb garden, avoiding his gaze. I watched the wasp, envying its freedom. "Oh, Cicero trained you well indeed!" I said under my breath.

"He did," Caelius acknowledged quietly, with a crooked smile of triumph on his lips.

"What does Cicero want from me?" I growled.

"Only a small favor."

I pursed my lips. "You try my patience, Marcus Caelius."

He laughed good-naturedly, as if to say: Very well, I've bested you and will toy with you no longer. "Cicero wishes that you should play host to a certain senator. He asks you to open your house to this senator whenever he wishes and provide a haven for him, a safe retreat from the city. You should understand the need for that."

"Who is this senator? A friend of Cicero's, or someone to whom he owes a favor?"

Roman Blood (St. Martin's Press, 2000)

"Not exactly."

"Then who?"

"Catilina."

"What!"

"Lucius Sergius Catilina."

"Cicero wishes me to provide a safe haven for his worst enemy? What sort of plot is this?"

"The plot is Catilina's. The point is to stop it."

I vigorously shook my head. "I want no part of this!"

"Your honor, Gordianus—"

"To Hades with you!" I rose from my chair so abruptly that I knocked it to the floor. I stepped out the door and crossed the herb garden, waving the wasp out of my way, and strode through the gate without looking back.

I turned toward the front of the house, then remembered that Caelius's bodyguards were loitering there. The sight of them would only make me more furious. I spun around and circled toward the rear of the house. An instant later I glimpsed a figure crouching beneath the library window. Aratus, I thought, spying on me again!

I opened my mouth, but the curse died stillborn in my throat. The figure turned toward me—and it was Meto, not Aratus, who looked me square in the face. He put a finger to his lips and backed cautiously away from the window, then scurried to my side, looking not the least bit guilty for eavesdropping on his own father.

THREE

"A son should not spy on his father," I said, trying to be stern. "There are some Roman fathers who would beat their sons for such a crime, or even have them strangled."

Up on the ridge, Meto and I sat side by side on the stumps and looked down on the farm. In front of the house, Caelius's bodyguards sat beneath the shade of a yew tree. Caelius himself had stepped into the herb garden and was peering toward the stream with one hand shading his brow from the westering sun. He had no idea where I was.

"I wasn't exactly spying," Meto said, chagrined.

"No? Spying is the only word for it."

"Well, I learned it from you. I suppose it's in the blood."

This last was absurd, since Meto was the son of slaves and had not a drop of my blood in his veins, but I was touched by his fantasy. I couldn't resist reaching out to muss his hair, and none too gently. "I suppose you blame your willfulness on me, as well?"

"I give you credit for all my outstanding qualities, Papa." He smiled crookedly. The clever, charming little boy I had adopted had grown into a handsome and soft-spoken youth. His face became pensive. "Papa, who is Catilina? And why do you bear such a grudge against Cicero? I thought he was your friend."

I sighed. "These matters are very complex. Or not complex at all if a man does the sensible thing and turns his back on them for good."

"But is that possible? Marcus Caelius says you owe a personal favor to Cicero."

"True enough."

"Without Cicero, we wouldn't have the farm."

"*Might* not have the farm," I corrected him—but the guilelessness in his soft brown eyes compelled me to acknowledge the truth. "Very well, without Cicero there would be no farm. Without him to represent me, the Claudii and their lawyers would have eaten me alive in court. I owe him a great favor, like it or not. But what use is this farm if I must pay for it by allowing men like Caelius to bring Rome to my very doorstep?"

"Is Rome truly so awful? I like the farm, Papa, but sometimes I miss the city." His eyes lit up. "Do you know what I miss most? The festivals, when they have plays and chariot races! Especially the races."

Of course you miss them, I thought. You're young, and youth craves distraction. I shook my head, feeling old and sour.

"The festivals are only another form of corruption, Meto. Who pays for festivals? The various magistrates elected each year. And why? They will tell you they do it to honor the gods and the traditions of our ancestors, but in truth they do it to impress the crowd, for their own personal aggrandizement. The crowd gives its support to the man who can put on the most splendid games and spectacles. Absurd! The spectacles are only a means to an end. They impress the voters, who in turn give a man power. It's the power which ultimately counts—power over the fates and property of men, over the life and death of nations. Time and again I see the people, impressed by games and shows, give their votes to a man who then proceeds to legislate against their interest. Sheer stupidity! Point out this betrayal to the citizen in the street and he will answer: But, oh, what a splendid spectacle the man put on for us! Never mind that he emasculated the people's representation in the Forum or passed some invidious property law—he brought white tigers from Libya to the Circus Maximus and hosted a great feast to inaugurate the Temple of Hercules! Who's more to blame for such wickedness—the cynical politician without a shred of principle, or the Roman citizens who allow themselves to be so easily duped?"

I shook my head. "You see how it affects me to speak of it, Meto? My heart begins to race and my face turns hot. Once I accepted the madness of the city without question; such was life and there was nothing particularly wrong with it—there is a fascination, after all, in the dealings of men, no matter how vile and corrupt. More importantly, there was nothing I could do about it, and so I merely accepted it. My livelihood took me deep within the councils of powerful men, and showed me more of the truth than most men ever see. I was growing wise in the ways of the world, I thought proudly, but what good is such wisdom if it only leads to a knowledge of how helpless one is to change this world? Now, as I grow older, Meto, I grow less and less able to tolerate the stupidity of the people and the wickedness of their rulers. I have seen too much suffering created by ambitious men who care only for themselves. Unable to affect the course of events, I turn my back on them! Now Cicero would force me into the arena again, like a gladiator pressed to fight against his will."

Meto considered this in silence for a moment. "Is Cicero a bad man, Papa?"

"Better than most. Worse than some."

"And Catilina?"

I remembered my recent conversation with Claudia, whom I had cut off when she began to talk of Catilina's bid for the consulship. "Our neighbor on the far side of the ridge calls him a wild-eyed madman."

"Is he?"

"Cicero would say so."

"But what do *you* think, Papa?" He frowned. "Or should I not press you to talk about it?"

I sighed. "No, Meto, press on. Since I manumitted you and made you my son, you are a Roman citizen, no more or less than any other Roman, and soon you will put on the manly toga. Who else should educate a boy in the ways of Roman politics except his father, even if I must bite my tongue to do it?"

I paused for breath and looked down on the farm. Caelius's men were still idle, while Caelius himself had withdrawn from the heat of the herb garden back into the cool of the library; he was probably looking through the few modest volumes I had acquired over the years, many of them from Cicero as gifts to sweeten his payment for my services. The slaves were busy at their labors; the beasts were drowsing in their pens. I could stay on the ridge all afternoon, but eventually the sun would set and Bethesda would send Diana to fetch us for dinner. I would be compelled to offer hospitality to Marcus Caelius. He would press me again to honor my debt to Cicero, and how could I refuse?

"I've often thought, Meto, that the death of my friend Lucius Claudius was somehow providential. Oh, I'm not so vain as to think that the gods would strike down a good man merely to make my life more bearable, but in many odd ways the Fates sift out the details of our lives to unseen ends and, if we're fortunate, to happy coincidence. Just when I felt that I could no longer stand living in the city another year, the dream of a retreat from the city became real. The election campaign last summer was the last straw. Consular campaigns as a rule are crude, vicious affairs, but an uglier campaign I've never witnessed.

"Candidates all run against each other," I explained, "and the two who garner the most votes become joint consuls for the year. If the two consuls are of the same political persuasion, they can reinforce one another and have a very effective year in office. If they're of different stripes, the Senate quickly learns which is the more dominant of the two and which the more easily led. In some years rivals are elected, and the stalemate as they try to outdo one another can be spectacular—literally. The year you came to live with me, Crassus and Pompey shared the consulship, and it was one feast after another, festival upon festival, from their inauguration in Januarius up to their valedictory addresses in December. The citizens grew fat and saw some fine chariot races that year!"

"Can any senator run for the consulship?" asked Meto.

"No. There is a prescribed sequence of offices that must be held first. The praetorships, the quaestorships, and so on, all last a year and have their specific functions. A politician goes up the ladder rung by rung, year by year. An electoral defeat means he sits out a whole year, and men in a hurry quickly grow bitter."

"But what keeps a man from holding the same office over and over?"

"No man may hold the same office two years in a row—otherwise the same tiny handful of the most powerful men, like Pompey and Crassus, would be consul over and over. Besides, the consulship itself is yet another stepping-stone. The whole point of attaining the consulship is that it entitles a man to a year as governor of a foreign province. A Roman governor can become fabulously rich by bleeding the locals white with taxes. The whole ugly enterprise is fueled by endless corruption and greed."

"And who votes?"

"Every citizen but me, I suppose, since I gave it up years ago. Nothing will ever be changed in Rome by voting, because not all votes are equal."

"What do you mean?"

I shook my head. Having been born a slave, Meto had no

grounding from infancy in the inherited privileges of citizenship; having been raised in my household, his subsequent education in such technicalities had been sorely neglected, due
to my own growing apathy. "The votes of a poor man count
less than those of a rich one," I said.

"But how?"

"On election day the citizens gather on the Campus Martius, between the old city walls and the River Tiber. Eligible
voters are divided into what are called centuries. But the centuries have nothing to do with the number of voters in them.
One century might have a hundred men in it and another
might have a thousand. The rich are allotted more centuries
than the poor, even though there are fewer rich men than poor
ones. Thus, when a rich man votes, his vote counts much
more than a poor man's vote.

"Even so, the poor man's vote is often needed, since the
candidates all come from the rich or high-born classes and
split those centuries among themselves. So common citizens
are not neglected; they are wooed, seduced, suborned, and
intimidated in all sorts of legal and illegal ways, from promises of favoritism, to outright bribery, to gangs set loose in
the streets to beat up a rival's supporters. During the campaign the candidates tell pretty lies about themselves and hurl
hideous accusations at their rivals, while their supporters
cover the city with slanderous graffiti."

" 'Lucius Roscius Otho kisses the buttocks of the brothel
keepers!' " quoted Meto, laughing.

"Yes, one of the more memorable slogans from last year,"
I agreed glumly. "Yet Otho was elected praetor nonetheless!"

"But what was so unusual about last year's campaign?"
asked Meto earnestly. "I remember hearing you rage about it
to visitors in your library, but I never really understood."

"Only that it was so dirty and disgusting. And the fact that
it was Cicero, of all people, who plunged the tone of the
campaign to such depths. And the things that Cicero has done
since the election . . ."

I shook my head and started again. "There were three leading candidates: Cicero, Catilina, and Antonius. Antonius is a
nonentity, a wastrel and a scoundrel, with no political pro-
gram at all, only a desperate need to get his hands on a pro-

vincial governorship so that he can bleed enough taxes from the unfortunate locals to pay off his debts. There are those who say the same things about Catilina, but no one denies that Catilina has charm to spare and a keen political sense. He comes from ancient patrician stock, but he has no fortune; just the sort of aristocrat who backs radical schemes for redistributing wealth, canceling debts, democratizing public offices and the priesthoods—and the conservative ruling class do not like to hear *that* sort of talk. Even so, within the old ruling classes there are plenty of patricians who have fallen on bad times and are desperate for a way out, and there are plenty of rich men who think they might use a demagogue for their own purposes, and so Catilina was not without substantial backing, despite his radical posturing. Crassus himself, the richest man in Rome, was his chief financial backer. Who knows what Crassus was up to?

"Then there was Cicero. None of his ancestors had ever held elective office before—he was the first of his family to hold public office, what they call a New Man. And no New Man had managed to get himself elected consul in living memory. The aristocracy turned up their noses at him, despising his political canniness, his eloquence, his success with the crowd. Cicero is a glorious upstart, a comet that came from nowhere, and immodest as a peacock. In his own way he must have appeared as much a threat to the order of things as Catilina. And he might have been, had his principles not proved to be so flexible.

"Catilina and Antonius formed an alliance. From early on they were both favored to win. Catilina never ceased to needle the aristocracy with reminders of Cicero's common origins (though Cicero was hardly born poor!), but to his own supporters he began talking up the kind of radical schemes that give property owners gray hair and sleepless nights. The rich were in a quandary—Cicero they could not stomach, but Catilina they truly feared.

"As for Cicero, his campaign was managed by his brother Quintus. After the election, one day when I had business at his house, Cicero pressed me to look at a series of letters that he had exchanged with Quintus, discussing the progress of the campaign; he was so proud of them that he was actually

talking about making them into a pamphlet, a sort of guide
to successful electioneering. At the very outset Cicero and his
brother decided to stop at nothing to destroy Catilina's character. Slander is the accepted style in any election campaign,
but Cicero set new standards. Some of the accusations were
whispered from ear to ear; others were made by Cicero outright in his speeches. In the thick of it I dreaded setting foot
in the Forum, knowing I would have to hear Cicero harangu-
ing the crowd. Even when I could avoid the Forum, the graffiti and the gossip were everywhere. If only half of what they
said about Catilina is true, the man should have been strangled in his mother's womb."

"What was he accused of?"

"A whole catalogue of crimes. There were the usual accusations of corruption, of course, such as buying votes and
bribing elections officials; those accusations were probably
true, considering the financial backing that Catilina was re-
ceiving from Crassus—what good is so much money in an
election except for bribes? When Roman voters know a candidate has money, they run to him with their palms up.

"Cicero also dredged up old charges of corruption from
the days when Catilina was an administrator in Africa. A few
years ago Catilina was tried on those particular charges—and
Cicero himself considered defending him! Catilina was found
innocent, for what it's worth. Lodging such criminal charges
is just another tool that Roman politicians use to embarrass a
rival and disqualify him from running for office. Both the
charge and the verdict are purely political; any link to truth
or justice is purely coincidental.

"Then there were the more serious accusations and innu-
endoes—rumors of sexual scandal, incest, murder . . . but perhaps all this talk of politics is beginning to bore you."

"Not at all!" Meto's wide eyes showed I had his full attention.

I cleared my throat. "Very well. They say that back in the
terrible days of Sulla the dictator, Catilina served as one of
his henchmen, killing Sulla's enemies and bringing in their
heads for the bounty. They say he got away with murdering
his own brother-in-law that way; Catilina's sister wanted the
man killed and Catilina did it in cold blood, then made it

legal by listing the man as one of Sulla's enemies."

"Is it true?"

I shrugged. "Men did terrible things in Sulla's time. Crassus made himself rich by buying up murdered men's estates. When murder is made legal, you see the true capacity of men for wickedness. Perhaps the story about Catilina is true, perhaps not. He was brought to trial for one instance of murder, twenty years after the fact, and found innocent. Who knows? But these were only the first of his alleged murders.

"A few years ago, when he came back from Africa, Catilina took a new wife. They say the woman refused to wed Catilina if there was already an heir in his house, so he murdered his son. As for the young bride, she happens to be the daughter of one of Catilina's former mistresses—there are even those who say she's Catilina's daughter!"

"Incest!" whispered Meto.

"Cicero himself never said that word aloud, he only made the innuendo. And that is only the beginning of the list of Catilina's alleged sexual crimes. They claim he corrupted one of the Vestal Virgins in a great scandal ten years ago; about that I happen to know a little, because I was summoned to investigate the matter in secret. It's the only time I've ever had personal dealings with Catilina, and I found him a puzzlement—utterly charming and utterly suspicious. Cicero likes to remind his listeners of the scandal, but only to a point, since his wife's sister was the Vestal accused of fornicating with Catilina! Oh, in some ways Rome is quite a small town."

"And did they? Catilina and the Vestal?" Meto was positively glowing with interest.

"That I don't know, though I have my suspicions. I'll tell you the full story some other time. At any rate, both Catilina and the Vestal won acquittal—which, as I told you, has little to do with guilt or innocence."

"It sounds as if Catilina has spent most of his career defending himself in court, or else murdering people!"

"And the rest of the time he fornicates, if you believe the stories. His circle in Rome is said to be utterly dissolute; he charms the bright young men of Rome by pimping for them, and charms rich, aging matrons by guiding the same young men into their bedrooms; they say he occasionally takes the

best-looking of the young men and the richest of the matrons
for himself. Certainly a contrast to Cicero! Say, do you want
to hear a joke about Cicero that was going around during the
campaign?"

"Yes."

"Keep in mind this probably came from Catilina. You have
to know that Cicero has a daughter who's thirteen, Tullia, and
a son who's barely two, Marcus. Well, they say that Cicero
hates sex so much that he's tried it only twice in his life.
Tullia came of the first time, but he hated it as much as he
thought he would. Eleven years later his wife nagged him
into trying it again, and he agreed, just to be sure that it was
as bad as he remembered—and the outcome was Marcus!"

Meto winced.

"Well, I suppose it's a rare boy who laughs at his father's
jokes. But you should have heard them laughing in the taverns
when they told that one on election day. But after the votes
were counted, it was Cicero who laughed."

"Did Catilina just tell jokes about Cicero, or did he try to
defend himself against all those accusations?"

"Oddly enough, he didn't try. Perhaps the rumors are true,
or true enough that he didn't care to repeat them, even to
refute them. And then, Catilina is a patrician, and Cicero is
a New Man—I think that Catilina was too haughty to step
into the gutter with someone he considers so far beneath him.
That's another tactic of Roman politicians, especially from
old families—they wrap themselves in their dignity. But Catilina's haughtiness proved a cold garment. On election day
Cicero was the clear winner by an overwhelming majority. It
was a tremendous personal triumph for a man without ancestry, who created a political career by his own canniness and
perseverance. The consulship is a pinnacle few men attain.
Cicero has reached it. This is his glorious year, and no one
can say he didn't earn it."

"And Catilina?"

"Trailing far behind Cicero in the votes was Antonius, the
nonentity. Catilina was a very close third, but third means
nothing in a race for the consulship. In previous years one
lawsuit after another kept Catilina from running. When he
finally had his chance, Cicero trounced him. This year Catil-

ina is running again. He was said to be heavily in debt when he ran last year. How much further into debt will this race drive him? He must be a desperate man, and if one can believe even a small part of the rumors, a man easily disposed to murder. Not the sort of man I would care to have as a guest under my roof."

"I suppose not," said Meto gravely, "even to return Cicero's favor." We sat for a while in silence, looking down on the farm. Suddenly Meto made an odd noise and began to shiver. He clutched himself so violently that I was alarmed—but he was only laughing, so uproariously that he rolled off the stump onto the grass, hugging himself.

"What in Hades—"

"Now I get it!" he gasped. "Only twice in his life—and tried it the second time just to make sure it was as bad as he remembered!" He laughed so hard his face turned red.

I rolled my eyes, but couldn't help smiling. The law and society might say that he was almost a man, but it often seemed to me that Meto was still very much a boy.

FOUR

DINNER that night was not a success. Bethesda is not a bad cook, but cooking is among the least of her skills; cooking was certainly not the reason I bought her at the slave market in Alexandria those many years ago. A slave no longer—when she became pregnant with Diana I manumitted and married her—she was quite skillful in managing the labor of others, and to her I could leave the running of the household with complete confidence . . . except in the matter of the kitchen, where the egos of cooks were always colliding with her own. With Congrio lent to Claudia, Bethesda had taken advantage of the opportunity to exercise full sway in the kitchen.

Alas, her genius, so far as it went, was with simple foods such as she had served me in my leaner years (leaner in every

sense), and particularly with fish, which were always to be
had in quality and abundance at the markets in Rome, either
freshly caught in the Tiber or brought upriver from the sea.
At the farm good fish were harder to come by, and so, with
a guest from the city to entertain, Bethesda had chosen to
attempt something extravagant with the provisions on hand.
She had overreached herself. The celery and calf's brains with
egg sauce was not up to Congrio's standards, and the aspar-
agus stewed in wine might have succeeded had she chosen a
less assertive vintage. (Such pretentious judgments about food
I learned from the late Lucius Claudius.) The carrots with
coriander were passable, and the potted peaches stewed with
cumin at last provided a triumph I could sincerely compliment—which was a mistake.

"Congrio potted the peaches," she remarked tersely. "I
merely instructed one of the slaves to simmer them with the
olive oil and cumin."

"Ah—and your instructions were impeccable," I said, kissing my fingertips. Bethesda raised a dubious eyebrow.

"I'll take some more," said Meto, gesturing to the serving
slave.

"Actually, the whole meal was delicious," insisted Marcus
Caelius. "There aren't many Roman matrons who could personally oversee every course of such an ambitious meal in
the absence of their cook. To find such culinary excellence
here in the countryside is a delight." The words sounded false
to my ear, but Bethesda was suddenly glowing; it was the
fancy beard that charmed her, I thought. "But you need not
strive to impress Catilina when he stays here," added Caelius.
"He's a man of adaptable tastes. He can discriminate between
two vintages of Falernian wine blindfolded, or drink from the
jug kept for slaves with equal relish. Catilina says, 'A man's
palate was meant to experience every possible flavor, or else
a tongue is good only for talking.' "

This struck me as vaguely obscene; Bethesda must have
caught the implication as well, for she now seemed even more
charmed by our guest. Was it this that irritated me, or the fact
that Caelius seemed to take my acquiescence for granted?

"I think we should retire to the library," I said. "We still
have business to discuss, Marcus Caelius."

Meto looked up expectantly and began to rise from his couch. "No," I said, "stay and finish your peaches."

"You have some very fine works in your collection," said Caelius, trailing his eye over the scrolls in their pigeonholes and fingering the little labels that hung from them. "I see you're particularly fond of collecting plays. So is Cicero. I suppose on occasion he passes on his duplicates to you. I had plenty of time to look through your library this afternoon, and I was impressed by all the volumes inscribed, 'From Marcus Tullius Cicero, to his friend Gordianus, with warm regards—' "

"Yes, Caelius, I'm well acquainted with the contents of my own library. I remember where each volume came from."

"Books are like friends, are they not? Steadfast, unchanging, reliable. There's a comfort in that. Pick up a volume you put away a year ago, and the words will be the same."

"I take your meaning, Caelius. But is Cicero really the same man now that he was a year ago? Or seventeen years ago, when I first met him?"

"I don't understand."

"The news from Rome arrives here sporadically and secondhand, and I listen to it with only one ear, but it seems to me that Cicero the consul has turned out to be rather more reactionary than was Cicero the aspiring advocate. The man of the people who bravely spoke out against Sulla now seems quite at home serving the interests of the same handful of rich families whom Sulla served."

Caelius shrugged. "This is all beside the point, isn't it? I thought you were sick of politics. That's why I chose to talk about friendship, instead."

"Caelius, even if I were eager to do as you ask, I would hesitate. How old are you?"

"Twenty-five."

"Quite young. I take it you have no wife and children yet."

"No."

"Then you probably don't understand why I hesitate to allow a man like Catilina into my house, no matter what the circumstance or pretext. I left Rome partly because I was sick of the constant violence and danger. Not because I feared for

my own safety, but because there are others I must consider
and protect. Before I adopted him, my elder son Eco was a
child of the streets; he could always fend for himself, and
now he's a man and on his own. But my younger son Meto
is quite different; clever and resourceful, yes, but not nearly
as canny or resilient as Eco. I've shared as little of the dangerous part of my life with him as I could. And you've seen
my little girl, Diana. She needs protection most of all."

"But we're not asking you to do anything dangerous, Gordianus, only—"

"You sound as sincere now as when you complimented
Bethesda's dinner."

Caelius gave me his heavy-lidded look. I think he was used
to getting his way by using charm alone and could not quite
account for my obstinacy.

I sighed. "What precisely is it that Cicero wants of me?"

To his credit, Caelius showed no hint of smugness at this
concession. His face became quite grave. "I spoke to you this
afternoon of a looming threat to the state. You discounted my
words as mere rhetoric, Gordianus, but the facts are plain
enough. The threat is Catilina. You may despise the pomposity and corruption of what passes for politics in Rome nowadays, but believe me, the anarchy Catilina would bring
would be far more terrible."

"You're beginning to speechify," I warned.

Caelius smiled grudgingly. "Stop me when I do that. To
be clear, then: Catilina, as you know, is running for consul
again. He cannot possibly win, but that won't stop him from
trying, and from stirring up as much trouble as he can, using
the campaign as a vehicle to foment disorder and discontent
in the city. He has two plans. The first is predicated on his
victory. If he should win the consulship—"

"You just said that was impossible."

"I was speechifying, Gordianus; I told you to stop me if I
did that. On the very slight chance, then, that Catilina should
win the election, it will be taken as a sign that the electorate
is irreparably fragmented. Cicero's consulship will have been
a momentary respite of sanity before the storm. The Senate
will erupt. There will be riots and murders in the streets. Very
likely there will be civil war; the various politicians and great

families are already aligning themselves. In such a conflict Catilina will inevitably lose, if not quickly, then when Pompey brings his troops back from the East. And if Pompey has to be called back to restore order, what is to stop Pompey from becoming dictator? Consider that possibility."

Against my will, I did. After Catilina, Pompey as dictator was the ruling oligarchy's worst nightmare. Such an eventuality would mean either the end of the Republic or yet another civil war; men like Crassus and the young Julius Caesar would not let power elude them without a struggle.

"And if the only possible thing happens, and Catilina loses the election?" I said, hating to be drawn into the argument.

"He's already begun planning his revolt. His supporters are as desperate as he is. His military support is concentrated among the veterans settled here in Etruria, farther north. Within the city he has a small but devoted coterie of powerful men who will stop at nothing. There is already evidence that he plans to murder Cicero *before* the election."

"But why?"

"Chiefly because he blames Cicero for stealing the election from him last year, and longs to see him dead. How it fits into Catilina's overall scheme, I'm not not sure; perhaps he simply wants to spread chaos and fear before the polling, or to cancel the election altogether."

"How do you know all this, Marcus Caelius?"

"There was a meeting of the conspirators earlier this month—"

"*How* do you know this?"

"I'm telling you: there was a meeting of the conspirators earlier this month, and *I was there*."

I paused to absorb this. If only it could have been Aratus seated across from me, discussing how many oxen to buy at market this year, or Congrio telling me we would need more provisions for the month ahead. Instead I was confronted with one of Cicero's smoothest protégés, listening to him pronounce dire warnings of conspiracy and revolution.

"This is all too much, Caelius. You say that Catilina is hatching a conspiracy to murder Cicero, and that you yourself sat in on his secret proceedings?"

"I'm telling you too much, Gordianus, more than I intended to, but you're a difficult man to convince."

"This is your way of convincing me to help you? I tell you I want no danger to this house and you tell me stories of assassination and civil war!"

"All of which can be prevented, *if we work together.*"

Why—in spite of all my protests, my clearly reasoned judgment, all the resolutions and promises I had made to myself, the great daily satisfaction I took in turning my back on the madness of the city—why in that moment did I experience a shiver of excitement? Intrigue is an intoxicant more powerful than the headiest wine. Secrecy casts a spell over the workaday world and turns common, drab existence into the stuff of plays and epics. A man eats of such stuff and only feels hungry for more. Even so, such a diet makes a man feel alive. That shiver of excitement was something I had not felt since I left the city.

"Tell me more about the meeting you attended with Catilina," I said slowly.

"It was at Catilina's house on the Palatine; a splendid, rambling mansion that his father built, and the only thing left of his inheritance, besides his name. It began as a dinner party, but after the meal we withdrew to a room deep within the house. The slaves were dismissed and the door was shut. If I told you the names of the senators and patricians who were there—"

"Don't."

Caelius nodded. "Then I'll only tell you that the gathering ranged from the respectable to the notorious—"

" 'Taste every flavor.' So Catilina says."

"Exactly. He coins a memorable phrase, as you see. You flatter me by calling me an apt pupil of Cicero's, but I tell you Cicero has nothing on Catilina when it comes to passionate speeches. He dwelt upon the common distress of the men gathered there and pointed to the wealthy oligarchs as the cause of all their misery; he promised them a new state consecrated by the blood of the old; he spoke of canceled debts and confiscations from the rich. When it was over he produced a bowl of wine and compelled every man to make a cut on his arm and squeeze a tickle of blood into the bowl."

"And you?"

Caelius held forth his arm and showed me the scar. "The bowl was passed around. Every man drank from it. We all took an oath of secrecy—"

"Which you're breaking right now."

"An oath against Rome is no oath at all to a true Roman." Even so, he lowered his eyes.

"Then Catilina accepted you as one of his own, despite your connection to Cicero?"

"Yes, because for a time I was truly under his spell. I convinced him of my loyalty because it was real, at the time. Until I suddenly saw through him, until I learned that he planned to murder Cicero. Then I went to Cicero with all I knew. He told me to remain in Catilina's confidence and said that I could be more valuable to him as a spy. I'm not the only one who watches Catilina for him."

"And now he wants me to spy for him as well."

"No, Gordianus. He merely wants you to play passive host to Catilina. Catilina's movements are watched, but he has ways of getting out of the city unobserved. His principal ally outside Rome is Gaius Manlius, a military man up in Faesulae; Catilina needs a secret place of refuge between Faesulae and Rome, not one of his known supporters' farms, but a place where his enemies would never think to look."

"And that place is with me? If he doesn't know already, anyone could tell Catilina that I've done much work for Cicero in the past, and that Cicero helped me hold on to this farm."

"Yes, but I've told Catilina that you've had a serious falling-out with Cicero—that's easy enough to believe, isn't it?—and that you're disgusted with things as they are in Rome, and sympathize with him. That you know how to be discreet is accepted without question; you do have a reputation for that, Gordianus. Catilina doesn't believe that you're an ardent supporter, only that you're willing to offer him hospitality and to keep your mouth shut. That's all he'll expect from you—a safe retreat when he needs to get out of the city, and a way station on the road to Faesulae."

"How do I know there won't be secret meetings in my house, with bowls of human blood passed around?"

Caelius shook his head. "That's not what he wants from

you. He wants a refuge, not a meeting place."

"And what does Cicero want?"

"An accounting of Catilina's movement, through me. Of course, if Catilina should happen to confide something of importance to you, Cicero trusts you to use your judgment in passing on vital information. They say you have a way of drawing out the truth from men, even when they hope to conceal it."

I turned my back on him and looked out the west-facing windows, beyond the herb garden to the land sloping down toward the stream. The treetops were gilded with moonlight. The night was quiet and peaceful, pleasantly warm. The air smelled rich and sweet, a mixture of animal dung and cut grass. Rome seemed very far away, and yet inescapable.

"I would deal only with you, then, and with Catilina? With no one else?"

"Yes. Cicero himself will be only a phantom, never seen. Any message you need to send you will send to me, in the city. Catilina will find nothing suspicious in that."

"It can't be as simple as you claim. Is it because of your youth and inexperience that you can't see all the terrible things that could go wrong? Or are you intentionally trying to coddle me?"

He smiled. "My teacher Cicero would say that one should never respond to a question of either/or if both answers are damaging. One should change the subject instead."

I begrudged him a smile in return. "You're positively wicked, Marcus Caelius; too wicked for a man your age. Yes, I do believe you could fool Catilina himself into trusting you. If I agree to do as you ask, I must have some way of protecting myself; I can't be seen as an ally of Catilina's if he comes to ruin, as he probably will. A letter from Cicero would be useful, acknowledging my help ahead of time."

Caelius grimaced. "Cicero foresaw such a request. It's not possible. If such a communication were to be intercepted, it would spoil everything, and put you in immediate jeopardy, besides. Put your mind at ease. If a crisis comes, Cicero will not forget you."

"Still, I'd like some assurance from Cicero himself. If I came to Rome—"

"He couldn't see you, not now. Catilina would know, and all would be ruined. Do you not believe me, Gordianus?"

I considered for a long moment. The shiver of excitement I had felt earlier was joined by a prickle of apprehension. I felt like the man who cannot control his drinking and so abstains, but who picks up a cup intended for someone else and accidentally swallows a mouthful of warm wine. "I believe you," I finally said.

But later that night, as I lay beside Bethesda, a doubt took shape, grew and hovered over me like a gray mist in the moonlit darkness. Caelius had offered no proof that he came from Cicero. Might he have been sent by Catilina, instead? Even if he had come from Cicero, might not Catilina have seen through their plan? Where did Caelius's true allegiance lie? The same charming young man who claimed to have fooled Catilina might just as easily be able to fool Cicero, not to mention an unreformed intriguer name Gordianus the Finder, who thought he had sworn off politics forever.

Bethesda stirred. "What's wrong, Master?" she whispered. She had ceased to call me Master on the day of our marriage, but occasionally she slipped in her sleep; to hear her call me that reminded me of days long ago, before the world became so weary and complex. I reached out and touched her. The familiarity of her body—firm, warm, and responsive—dispelled my hovering doubts like ragged mists beneath the sun. She rolled toward me and we folded our bodies together. For a while all apprehensions were forgotten in the animal act of love, and afterward I slept the sleep of a country farmer, dreaming of endless fields of hay and the musical lowing of oxen.

FIVE

THE next morning Marcus Caelius was up before I was. I found him in front of the stable, fully dressed and readying his mount for the ride back to Rome. His bodyguards emerged from within, rubbing their eyes and brushing straw from their hair. The sun was not quite above Mount Argentum, and the world was lit by a thin blue light. A trail of mist hovered over the stream and crept into the low places. From Publius Claudius's farm to the west, a faraway cock began to crow.

"Weren't you able to sleep, Caelius?"

"Quite well, thank you."

"The bed was too hard, wasn't it? I knew it would be. And the room was too stuffy."

"No. . . ."

"Alas, as you've seen for yourself, my home is wholly unsuitable for distinguished guests."

Caelius caught my meaning and smiled. "They say that Catilina is like a good general; he can eat and sleep under *any* conditions. Your accommodations will be more than adequate."

"I still haven't said yes, Caelius."

"I thought you had."

"I'll need to consider it."

"Which is the same as saying no. Time presses, Gordianus."

"Then *no*," I snapped, suddenly tired of bantering with him.

He clucked his tongue. "You'll change your mind as soon as I'm gone. Send a messenger to me." He mounted his horse and ordered his bodyguards to get ready.

Bethesda emerged from the house, dressed in a long-sleeved stola with her hair down. The black and silver strands cascaded in splendid waves down her back, and there was a dreamy look in her eyes, for which I felt partly responsible.

"Surely, Marcus Caelius, you're not leaving us without eating first?" She positively purred. "I had planned something special for breakfast."

"I prefer to start a long ride on an empty stomach. I've looted some bread and fruit from your larder, for the road." He turned his steed around a few times while his bodyguards mounted their horses.

"Wait a moment," I said. "I'll ride with you as far as the Cassian Way."

As we set out, the sun crested the mountain and lit up the world, casting long shadows behind us. Birds began to sing. We passed by vineyards on one side and a mowed field of hay on the other. Caelius breathed in deeply. "Ah, Gordianus, the smell of a country morning! I see why you prefer it to the city. Yet the city does not cease to exist, merely because you turn your back on it. Neither do a man's obligations."

"You are nothing if not persistent, Caelius," I said, shaking my head ruefully. "Did you learn that trait from Cicero, or from Catilina?"

"A little from both, I think. There's something else I learned from Catilina: a riddle. You must like riddles, Gordianus, being so adept at solving mysteries. Do you want to hear it?"

I shrugged.

"It's a little riddle that Catilina likes to pose to his friends. He told it on the night of the blood oath. 'I see two bodies,' he said. 'One is thin and wasted, but has a great head. The other body is big and strong—*but it has no head at all*!' " He laughed quietly.

I shifted uneasily on my mount. "What is the point?"

Caelius gave me his heavy-lidded look. "But it's a riddle, Gordianus! You must figure out the answer for yourself. I tell you what: when you dispatch your messenger to me, use a code. If you'll play host to Catilina, if your answer is yes, then say: 'The body without a head.' But if no, then say: 'The head without a body.' But don't wait long; once set in motion, events will move very swiftly."

"They always do," I said, reining in my horse. We had reached the Cassian Way. Caelius waved to me, then with his men turned onto the stone-paved surface and gathered speed.

For a moment I watched their capes fluttering behind them like pennants, then turned back toward the house, more uncertain and apprehensive than ever.

I was in my library that afternoon, sketching fanciful plans for the water mill, when Aratus announced that Congrio and his assistants had returned.

"Good, show them in. I want to see them. Privately."

Aratus narrowed his eyes and withdrew. A few moments later Congrio and the kitchen slaves entered. I put aside my tablet and stylus and gestured for them to shut the door.

"Well, Congrio, how did things go with the Claudii?"

"Quite well, Master. I'm sure you'll receive no complaints about our service. Claudia gave me this note to give to you." He handed me a rolled scrap of parchment sealed with wax on which Claudia had impressed her ring. Her seal, I noticed, was an abbreviation of her name, with the letter *C* enclosing a smaller *A*. It was clearly her own seal, neither inherited from her father nor taken from a husband, but invented by herself. This was unusual for a Roman matron, but Claudia was an unusually independent woman. I broke the seal and unrolled the letter.

> To Gordianus:
>
> Greetings, neighbor, and my gratitude for the loan of your slaves. They have comported themselves admirably, most especially your chief of the kitchen, Congrio, who has lost none of his skill since the days when he served my cousin Lucius. I am doubly grateful because my own head cook fell ill in the midst of preparations, whereupon Congrio proved to be not merely a great help but utterly essential; I should have been distraught and desperate without him. I will remember this when calculating the favor I owe you.
>
> On a different subject, and confidentially, I want you to know that I did my best to put in a good word for you in the family council. We Claudii are a stubborn and opinionated bunch, and I cannot say that I immediately swayed anyone toward a more moderate view, but I think I made a start. Anyway, I did what I could. It was a beginning.
>
> Thank you again for the generous loan. Consider this your

promissory note, and call upon me someday to repay it. I
remain your grateful neighbor,

Claudia

I rolled the letter and tied it with a ribbon, then saw that
Congrio was watching me with his head quizzically cocked.
"She was quite impressed with you," I said, at which Congrio
let out a pent-up breath and smiled sweetly.

"A good woman," he said. "A demanding mistress, but she
genuinely appreciates a man's skills."

"You obeyed my orders regarding your own discretion?"

"We were discreet, Master. I regret that I can't say the
same for other men's slaves."

"What do you mean?"

"The visiting Claudii brought along their own slaves, and
the most natural place for slaves to congregate is the kitchen.
I did my best to shoo them out whenever the place became
too crowded, but there was always a throng, and the orgy of
gossip never stopped. I took no part in it, of course, but above
the clanging of pots and pans I kept my ears open, as you
instructed."

"What did you hear?"

"Most of it was of no interest at all—which slaves had
risen or fallen in their master's favor . . . fabricated stories
about amorous adventures when journeying with their masters
to Rome . . . obscene tales about illicit unions between field
slaves and serving girls behind the wine press . . . rude comments about one another's anatomy—just the sort of trivial
filth that you'd expect, and with which I would never consider
polluting my master's ears."

"Was there anything at all of interest?"

"Perhaps. There were some rude insults aimed in my own
general direction. Slaves often take on the colors of their masters, as you no doubt have noticed, and when there is hostility
between masters it may be echoed between their slaves. Quite
a few of the slaves, knowing I served Lucius Claudius long
and faithfully, took crude jabs at me; these took the nature of
bemoaning what they called my sad decline in the world,
having now to serve a master—pardon me, Master, these are
their exact words and it pains me to repeat them—having now

to serve a master 'so far below' the last. I answered them with stony silence, of course, which they merely seemed to find amusing. The point is that such phrases could hardly have originated from the lips of slaves; rather, slaves pick up such phrases from their masters."

"I see. Did you hear anything so direct from the lips of the Claudii themselves?"

"No, Master, not I. As it turned out, I was confined almost exclusively to the kitchen, with hardly a moment to catch a breath of air. Claudia's head cook fell ill—"

"So she mentions in her letter."

"As you might imagine, I was quite busy the whole time. I hardly saw any of her guests, only their slaves invading my—that is to say Claudia's—kitchen."

"And you two?" I asked, nodding to his assistants. They drew themselves up nervously, looking at each other.

"Well?"

"We helped Congrio in the kitchen much of the time," said one of them. "It's as he says; there were rude jibes from some of the visiting slaves, veiled insults regarding our new master—which is to say yourself, Master. But we didn't spend all our time in the kitchen. We were also called upon to serve during the family council and the dinner that followed. Your name was mentioned . . ."

"Yes?"

They displayed acute discomfort. One of them had a rather bad complexion, with pimples scattered over his cheeks. I was surprised Claudia had chosen him to serve, since most Romans prefer to look on something pleasant while they dine. I put this down to her general eccentricity; Claudia seemed always determined to go her own way.

"You," I said to the boy with the pimples. "Speak up! Nothing you say will surprise me."

He cleared his throat. "They don't like you, Master."

"I know that. What I want to know is what they might be planning to do about it."

"Well, there was nothing specific. Name-calling mostly."

"Such as?"

He made a face, as if I had waved something foul-smelling

under his nose and demanded he taste it. " 'Stupid young fart from the city'?" he finally said, wincing.

"Who called me that?"

"That was Publius Claudius, I think, the old man who lives across the stream. Actually, he did state a specific intention, sort of. He said you ought to be dunked upside down in the stream and made to catch fish with your teeth." He winced again.

"That's pretty harmless," I said. "What else?"

His companion chewed his lower lip, then timidly raised his hand for permission to speak. " 'Stupid nobody with no ancestors, who should be put in a cage and carted back to Rome,' " he offered. "That was Manius Claudius, the man who lives up north beyond the wall."

"I see. Still, nothing more than idle grumbling."

The young man with the pimples cleared his throat.

"Yes?" I prompted.

"The youngest one, the one named Gnaeus—"

The Claudian whose own rocky, mountainous property would not support a farm and who, by all expectations, should have inherited Lucius's farm, I thought. "Go on."

"He said that the family should hire some assassins in the city to come up on some dark night and leave a bit of blood on the ground."

This was more serious, though it still might be only more idle talk. "Did he say anything more specific?"

"No, those were his words, exactly: 'Leave a bit of blood on the ground.' "

"And he said this where you could hear?"

"I don't think he knew what household I came from. I don't think any of them knew, except Claudia. They really didn't seem to notice us at all. Also, there was a lot of wine drunk that night, and Gnaeus drank his share."

"But you should probably know, Master," said the other slave, "that Claudia spoke up in your defense. She answered each of these insults and threats, and told the others that there was no point in nursing their animosity because everything had been settled in court."

"And how did her cousins respond?"

"Not very warmly, but she did shut them up. Her manner can be rather . . ."

"Brusque," concluded Congrio. "And remember, it was in her home that the family conclave was being held; she is very much the mistress under her own roof. I think that Claudia suffers no challenges to her authority on her own property, even from her blood relations."

I smiled and nodded. "A woman to be reckoned with. A woman who demands respect. Do her own slaves respect her?"

"Of course." Congrio shrugged. "Although . . ."

"Yes? Speak up."

He wrinkled his plump brow. "I'm not sure that they feel much affection for her, as some slaves do for their masters. She is quite demanding, as I have learned for myself. Nothing must go to waste! Every part of every beast must be rendered for whatever it's worth; every seed must be picked up off the floor. Some of the older slaves swear that they owe their bent backs to her and not to old age."

"The very fact that she owns slaves old enough to have stooped backs speaks of a compassionate nature," I said, thinking of all the farms where slaves are treated worse than beasts of burden. A slave's hide, unlike that of a cow, has no value after death, and thus many masters see no reason not to cover it with scars; and the flesh of slaves, unlike the flesh of beasts, cannot be eaten, and so these same masters see no need to feed them more than the bare minimum. Wise old Cato would certainly have had no wizened slaves about his farm; his advice is to cull out the sick and weak and to stop feeding a slave once he grows too old to do his full share.

Done with the slaves, I dismissed them, but as Congrio was stepping through the door (he had to turn a bit sideways, I noticed, to maneuver his bulk through the passageway), I called him back.

"Yes, Master?"

"This family conclave of the Claudii was mostly about the upcoming elections, I understand."

"I think so, Master, though I imagine they also discussed matters of more immediate concern to the family."

"Such as their unwanted neighbor and what to do about

him," I said glumly. "Did you overhear any rumors of how the Claudii plan to vote? In the consular election, I mean."

"Oh, in that they were unanimous. They will back Silanus, though they appear to have no great respect for him. 'Anyone but Catilina,' was the phrase I heard again and again. Even the slaves had picked it up."

"I see. 'Anyone but Catilina.' You may go now, Congrio. Bethesda will wish to advise you about this evening's meal." After he left the room, I sat for a long while with my fingertips pressed together, staring at the wall, lost in thought.

SIX

FOR the next few days I put aside thoughts of politics and Rome and the great world beyond the farm. I even managed to banish the troublesome Claudii from my mind. No more messengers arrived from the city; no more insults were hurled across the stream that bordered my estate. The city folk were busy with electioneering, and my neighbors were no doubt occupied, as I was, with the haymaking. The sun shone bright and warm, the slaves seemed content at their labors, the beasts dozed in their pens. Meto and Diana seemed to have made peace with each other, at least for the time being, and Bethesda, her maternal nature aroused by the budding spring, took them to gather wildflowers on the hillside. In my idle moments I played at designing the water mill that had been the dream of Lucius Claudius.

The nights were warm but pleasant. I went to bed early, and Bethesda and I made love three nights in a row. (The chance appearance of a handsome young visitor like Marcus Caelius in my household seemed often to have this stimulating effect, but I did not question or object.) I slept well and deeply. It seemed to me that a great peace had descended on my own little plot of land in Etruria, no matter what wickedness was brewing in the world beyond. Thus do the gods sometimes deceive us with a respite before the storm.

The bad news began at mid-month, on the Ides of Junius. Early that morning a slave came running to my library, saying that Aratus wished to see me in the fields. From the boy's uneasy countenance I saw trouble looming.

I followed him to a place at the northern edge of the farm, near the wall that separated my land from that of Manius Claudius. Since this field of grass was farthest from the house and the barns, the slaves had mowed it last. The grass was all cut, but only a few bundles had been gathered. The slaves stood idly about and became nervous at my arrival. Aratus stepped toward me, looking glum.

"I wanted you to see for yourself, Master," he said, "so that there would be no misunderstanding later."

"See what?"

He indicated a bundle of dried grass. His jaw was clenched, and I saw a twitch at the corner of his mouth.

"I see nothing wrong," I said, "except that this bale of hay has been cut open, and these men are standing around when they should be bundling the rest."

"If you will look closer, Master," said Aratus, bending toward the open bale and indicating that I should do likewise.

I squatted down and peered at the mowed grass. My vision at a near distance is not what it once was. At first I did not see the gray powder, like a fine soot, that spotted the hay. Then, having perceived it, I saw mottled patches everywhere within the bale.

"What is this, Aratus?"

"It's a blight called hay ash, Master. It appears every seven years or so; at least, that's my experience. It never manifests itself until after the grass is mowed, and sometimes not until much later, when a bale is cut open in the winter and you find out that the hay within is black and rotted."

"What does this mean?"

"The blight makes the hay inedible. The beasts will not touch it, and if they do, it will only make them sick."

"How extensive is the damage?"

"At the very least, all the grass within this field is almost undoubtedly ruined."

"Even if there is no blight on the blades?" I looked around at the mowed grass and saw no sign of the sooty spots.

"The blight will appear in a day or two. That's why it's often not seen until winter. The hay is already bundled when the blight appears. It works its way from the inside out."

"Insidious," I said. "The enemy within. What of the other fields? What of the hay already baled and stored?"

Aratus looked grim. "I sent one of the slaves to cut open one of the first bales, from the field up by the house." He handed me a blade of hay covered with the same gray soot.

I gritted my teeth. "In other words, Aratus, you're telling me that *all* the hay is ruined. The whole crop that was meant to sustain us through the winter! And I suppose this has nothing to do with the fact that you waited so long to cut the grass?"

"The two things are unrelated, Master—"

"Then if the grass had been mowed earlier, as I wanted, this blight would still have found its way into the hay?"

"The blight was there before the mowing, unseen. The time of mowing and the appearance of the blight have no connection—"

"I'm not sure I believe you, Aratus."

He said nothing, but only stared into the middle distance and clenched his jaw.

"Can any of the hay be saved?" I asked.

"Perhaps. We can try to set apart the good and burn the bad, though the blight may keep appearing no matter what we do."

"Then do what you can! I leave it to you, Aratus, since you seem to think you understand the situation. I leave it to you!" I turned around and left him standing there among the other slaves while I stalked across the shorn fields, trying not to calculate the waste of time and labor that had given me fields upon fields of hay that was good for nothing but kindling.

That afternoon great plumes of smoke rose into the still air from the bonfires which Aratus organized in the fields. I went myself to make sure that only the visibly blighted hay was being destroyed and found bales that appeared to be untouched mixed among the kindling. When I pointed this out to Aratus, he admitted the error, but said that saving any of the hay was only a postponement. I found this a poor excuse for destroying hay that might, for all I knew, be perfectly good. I had only Aratus's word and his judgment that the good hay would yet be blighted. What if he was mistaken, or even lying to me? A fine thing that would be, to be deceived into destroying a whole crop of good hay on the advice of a slave in whom I was beginning to lose all trust.

Plumes of smoke continued to rise into the air the next morning, when Aratus separated more bales of blighted hay and made them into bonfires. Not surprisingly, a messenger arrived from Claudia. The slave was shown into my library, bearing a basket of fresh figs in his arms.

"A gift from my mistress," he explained. "She is proud of her figs and wishes to share them with you." He smiled, but I saw him glance sidelong out the window at the pillars of smoke.

"Give her my thanks." I called to one of the house slaves to fetch Congrio, who seemed a bit startled at being summoned so early in the day. He gave Claudia's messenger an odd look, which made me think something untoward must have transpired between them during his stay at her house; slaves are always fighting with one another. "Congrio," I said, "see the fine figs Claudia has sent to me? What might we send her in return?"

Congrio seemed to be at a loss, but at last suggested a basket of eggs. "The hens have produced an exceptional batch of late," he assured me. "Yolks like butter and whites that stir up like cream. Fresh eggs are always a treasure, Master."

"Very well. Take this man to the kitchens and supply him." As they were leaving the room, I called for the slave to come back. "And in case your mistress should ask," I said in a confidential tone, "the plumes of smoke she sees rising above the ridge come from a blighted crop of hay. Hay ash, my steward calls it. She may tell this to the other Claudii if they come asking her, as I doubt that they will send messengers onto my property to inquire for themselves."

He nodded in the same confidential manner and withdrew with Congrio. Supplying him with eggs should not have taken long, but even so it was at least an hour later when I happened to be strolling around the house and saw him stepping outside through the kitchen door, holding a basket full of eggs and whispering something to Congrio over his shoulder. When he turned toward me, I saw the reason for his tardy departure, for he reached up with one hand to wipe a bit of custard from his lips. Who could resist tarrying for a while to sample a bit of Congrio's cooking? The slave saw me and gave a guilty start, then recovered himself and departed with a crooked smile.

The next day I had more evidence of Aratus's incompetence. Near the end of the day, when I escaped to the ridge to brood in solitude over the loss of the hay, I saw a wagon drawn by two horses turn off the Cassian Way. The heavily loaded vehicle lumbered along the road, sending up a small cloud of dust, and finally stopped alongside the house, near the kitchens. Congrio emerged from within and began to oversee the unloading of the wagon.

And where was Aratus? It was his job to oversee such work. I made my way down the hillside and came upon Congrio huffing and puffing as he helped his assistants unload heavy bags of millet and wooden crates stacked with clay cooking pots. The afternoon had cooled a bit, but Congrio was drenched with sweat.

"Congrio! You should be inside, tending to the kitchens. This is work for Aratus."

He shrugged and made a face. "I only wish that were so, Master." He spoke with an anxious stutter, and I could see that he was as upset as I was. "I have asked Aratus over and over to order certain provisions for me from Rome—you simply cannot get such clay pots anywhere else this side of Cumae. He kept promising he would do so, but then he always put it off, until finally I ordered the things myself. There was adequate silver in the kitchen accounts. Please don't be angry with me, Master, but I thought it best if I took the initiative and avoided confronting him in your presence."

"Even so, it's Aratus who should oversee the unloading. Look at you, as red as a clay pot and sweating like a horse after a race. Really, Congrio, this kind of exertion is too much for you. You should be inside."

"And let Aratus drop a crate and ruin my pots from spite?

Please, Master, I can oversee the work myself. I prefer it that way. The sweat is only the price I pay for carrying a bit of extra girth; I feel quite fine."

I considered for a moment, then relented with a nod.

"Thank you, Master," he said, relieved. "It's really for the best. Bring Aratus into this, and I'll never hear the end of it. He gets in my way enough as it is."

"And in my way as well," I muttered under my breath.

First had come the respite and then the storm, or so I thought, believing that the burning of the hay was disaster enough for one season.

The next morning I rose early, in a good mood despite my troubles. I grabbed a handful of bread and my wax tablet and stylus, and headed for the site of my imaginary water mill. I sketched for a while, but as the day became warmer I grew drowsy. I lay back amid the high grass on the sloping bank. The water rushed and gurgled. Birds twittered overhead. Dappled sunlight played across my closed eyelids, and the same play of cool shadow and warm light delicately caressed my hands and face. Despite the bothers of running a farm, despite having to deal with squabbling slaves, despite the ill will of the Claudii, life was quite good, very good. What had I to complain of, really? Other men had lived much harder lives than I had, and had nothing to show for it. Others had more to show, but to what ends had they gone to acquire it? I was an honest man at peace with the gods, I told myself, and as much at peace with other men as a free man could expect to be in such times.

The late-morning warmth was delicious. I felt utterly relaxed, as if my body glowed contentment from within. My thoughts drifted to Bethesda. Three nights of lovemaking in a row! We had not had such an appetite for each other in years. Perhaps it was another benefit of country living. In my new surroundings I had certainly never been tempted to stray from her. There was not even a pretty slave girl on the farm— Bethesda had quietly seen to that—and my neighbors offered no distractions in that vein. What sort of erotic life did Claudia lead, I idly wondered, and then killed the thought stillborn, as I did not really care to know. Ah, Bethesda . . .

I recalled a particular instant of our lovemaking, a specific sensation, and smiled, doting on the memory. What had set off the sparks between us? Ah, yes, the visit from young Marcus Caelius with his stylish beard and his elegant tongue. I found myself contemplating his face, and found the image not unpleasant. He was quite handsome, after all, if in a wily sort of way. Too wily for such a young man. Catilina liked to surround himself with good-looking young men, as everyone knew; a lascivious mind might well imagine just how young Caelius had managed to insinuate himself so firmly into Catilina's confidence. What would happen if I allowed Catilina himself to visit the farm, as Caelius desired? What sort of effect would that have on Bethesda? Catilina was well into his forties, barely younger than I, but he was famous for having the energy of a man half his age. And for all the insults that had been hurled at him, no one had ever called him ugly. In his own way he was as good-looking as Marcus Caelius, or had been once, for I had not seen him close at hand in many years. Beauty is beauty no matter what the gender. Beauty brings universal pleasure to the eye. . . .

These thoughts unfurled and my imagination drifted into a world of pure flesh, as I find often happens just before sleep. All the words poured from my head like water through open fingers. I lay upon the grass, content to be an animal warmed by the sun, my head full of animal thoughts.

And then I heard my daughter calling me.

I sat up—with a start, because there was no playfulness in her voice, but instead an unfamiliar urgency.

She called to me again, from quite near, and then she appeared over the verge of the hill and came running down to me, her tiny sandals slipping on the lush grass. I blinked and shook my head, not quite fully awake.

"Diana, what is it?"

She slid onto her bottom beside me, gasping for breath. "Papa, you must come!"

"What is it? What's wrong?"

"A man, Papa!"

"A man? Where?"

"He's in the stable."

"Oh, not another visitor!" I groaned.

"No, not a visitor," she said, sucking in a deep breath and then frowning thoughtfully. Later I would wonder how she stayed so calm, so serious. Why did she run to me and not to her mother? How did she keep from screaming after what she had seen? It was my blood in her, I decided, the blood of the ever-curious, ever-deliberating, dispassionate Finder.

"Well, then, who is this man?"

"I don't know, Papa!"

"A stranger?"

She shrugged elaborately and stuck out her arms. "I'm not sure."

"What do you mean? Either you know the man or you don't."

"But, Papa. I can't tell whether I know him or not!"

"And why not?" I said, exasperated.

"Because, Papa, the poor man has no head!"

SEVEN

THE body lay upon its back in an empty horse stall. How it had arrived there—dropped, dragged, or rolled—could not be told, because the straw all around it had been deliberately disturbed and then patted down; this I could tell from the fact that bits of straw had been littered onto the body itself, indicating that the disturbance of the straw had occurred after the arrival of the corpse. Nor were there any footprints or other signs to indicate how the body had come to be in the stable. For all I could tell, it might have grown out of the earth like a mushroom.

It had, as Diana had observed, no head, but all its limbs and digits were intact, as were its private parts. This I could tell at a glance, for the body was naked.

I looked down at Diana, who stared at the corpse with her mouth slightly open. I think she might have seen a dead body before, perhaps in a funeral procession in Rome, but she had never seen a headless one. I put my hand on her head and gently turned her around to face me. I squatted down and held her by her shoulders. She trembled slightly.

"How did you come to find him, Diana?" I said, keeping my voice low and even.

"I was hiding from Meto. Only Meto wouldn't play with me, so I took one of his silly little soldiers and went to hide it."

"Little soldiers?"

She turned and ran to a corner of the stall. She reached down for something in the straw, darted a wary glance at the corpse, then hurried back. She held out her hand, which cradled a little bronze figure of a Carthaginian warrior with a bow and arrow. It was from the board game called Elephants and Archers. After he was elected consul, Cicero had handed out specially minted sets of the game to dozens of guests at one of his celebrations. I had passed the gift along to Meto, who treasured it.

"I might have taken one of the little elephants, but I knew that would make him even angrier," she said, as if the distinction were important for her defense.

I took the bronze archer from Diana and nervously fingered it. "You came to the stable alone, then?"

"Yes, Papa."

The stablehands, I recalled, were up at the northern end of the farm helping Aratus repair a broken section of the wall. Aratus had asked me the night before for specific permission to take them away from their usual tasks. They had fed and watered the horses at daybreak and then gone off to work before the day became too hot. If they had seen the body, they certainly would have informed me. The body had appeared after daybreak, then—but that seemed impossible. Who could have smuggled a body into the stable in daylight? Perhaps, lying low as it did amid the straw in an empty stall, it had simply been overlooked.

But I was getting ahead of myself. I didn't even know who the man was, or had been, or how he had died.

"Whom else did you tell, Diana?"

"I ran straight to you, Papa."

"Good. Here, let's step away, back toward the door."

"Shouldn't we cover him up?" said Diana, looking over her shoulder.

At that moment Meto came running through the open doorway. "There you are!" he said. "Where did you hide it, you little harpy?"

Diana suddenly burst into tears and hid her face in her hands. I squatted down and put my arm around her. Meto looked abashed. I handed him the little bronze soldier.

"She took it," he said haltingly. "I didn't start it. Just because I have better things to do than play hide-and-seek with her all morning, that's no excuse for her to take my things."

"Diana," I said, holding her by the shoulders and speaking softly, "I have a job for you to do. It's very simple, but it's important. I want you to go and fetch your mother. Don't say a word about why, especially if there are any of her slaves about. Just say that I want her to come here to the stable right away, alone. Can you do that for me?"

The crying stopped as abruptly as it had begun. "I think so."

"Good. Now run along. Be quick!"

Meto looked at me in consternation. "But I didn't do anything! All right, I called her a harpy—but can I help it if she's such a crybaby? She took my game piece, and she knows that's wrong."

"Meto, be quiet. Something terrible has occurred."

He drew an exasperated breath, thinking I was about to lecture him; then he saw how serious I looked and wrinkled his brow.

"Meto, you've seen dead men before. You're about to see another." I led him to the empty stall.

Be careful in choosing your own vulgar exclamations, for your children will say them back to you. "Numa's balls!" he whispered hoarsely, his voice abruptly breaking.

"Not old King Numa, I think. Better to call him Nemo— *Nobody*—though a body is not what he's missing. But Nemo it will be, until we find a better name for him."

"But what is he doing here? Where did he come from? Is he one of the slaves?"

"Not one of our slaves, of that I'm pretty certain. Look at his build and coloration, Meto. You know the slaves as well as I do. Could this body belong to any of them?"

He bit his lower lip. "I see what you mean, Papa. This man was tall and rather heavy about the middle, and hairy."

I nodded. "See the hair on the back of his hands, how thick it is? Of our slaves, only Remus has hands like that, and Remus is a much smaller man. A younger man as well; see the gray hairs mixed in with the black, especially on Nemo's chest?"

"But then how did he get here? And who did this to him?"

"Who killed him, you mean? Or who cut off his head?"

"It's the same thing, isn't it?"

"Not necessarily. We can't be sure that he died from having his head cut off."

"Papa, I should think that *anyone* would die if you cut off his head!"

"Are you baiting your father, Meto, or merely being obtuse?" I sighed. "I see no wounds to the front of his body, do you? Here, do you think you can help me roll him over?"

"Of course," he said, but I saw him swallow hard as he stooped to take hold of one of the legs while I reached under the corpse's shoulders. He gave a shudder as his hands touched the clammy flesh. So did I.

I grunted and stepped back, brushing straw from my hands. "No apparent wounds to the back, either. And yet it isn't easy to murder a man by cutting off his head—think about it. You have to have some way to hold him still. Perhaps they cut his throat, or strangled him first. That would be hard to tell, since it won't be easy to find any bruises on his neck amid the gore."

While I knelt to have a closer look, Meto stepped discreetly back and covered his mouth with one hand. He had turned considerably paler, though he was still several shades darker than the corpse, which was as white as a fish's belly.

"He wasn't killed this morning, that's for sure," I said.

"How can you tell?"

"The body is cold and stiff, and all its color is gone. It takes time for that to happen. Physicians say that the lungs are like bellows, heating the blood. Even after they stop working, the body stays warm for quite some time, like a coal slowly losing its heat. Also, look at the wound itself. See how

the blood is clotted and the wound gone dry. The fresher the
wound, the more it would seep. This cut must be at least a
day old to have dried so completely. See, there's not even
any blood on the straw below. And yet he can't have been
dead for too long, because even in this heat the body has not
begun to smell too strongly. Here, Meto, step closer. Observe
the wound with me."

He obeyed, but with considerable hesitation. "What else
can we observe from the wound itself?" I said.

He shrugged and made a face.

"Observe how cleanly the cutting was done. A very sharp,
very broad blade, I should think, and accomplished with what
appears to have been a single blow, the way that chickens are
decapitated on a chopping block. There are no signs of hack-
ing or sawing. Indeed, I can even see traces of the blade's
particular grain, the way one can see the serrations of a knife
after it has sliced through a roast. The subsequent outpouring
of blood should have obscured all such details, don't you
think? I wonder, could the cutting have been done *after* the
blood had already dried within the body? If so, the decapitation had nothing to do with the cause of death. Now why
would anyone decapitate a dead body and then hide it in plain
sight in my stable?"

I felt a flash of anger, a fury at being violated, but I swallowed hard and suppressed it. So long as I could simply play
an old familiar role—examining a corpse for clues, dispas-
sionately studying a situation—I knew I could keep a level
head. I felt incredibly attentive and alert, and everything
around me had taken on a preternatural clarity—the smell of
straw and horse dung, the heat of the day, the swirling motes
of dust captured in bars of sunlight. Yet at the same time a
part of me had gone numb.

I stepped back. "What else can we tell about him? You
say he looks rather heavy about the middle, Meto, but to me
he also looks rather gaunt in the chest and limbs and buttocks,
like a heavy man who has suddenly lost weight. He looks
unwell."

"Papa—the man is dead!" Meto rolled his eyes.

I sighed and found myself missing my elder son, who
would already have grasped all that I had observed and been

far ahead of me. But then, Eco had begun his life as a child of the streets and had learned to use his wits of necessity long before I adopted him. Meto had been born a slave in a rich man's villa and had always been rewarded more for cleverness than cunning. I only hoped he would grow into a decent farmer, for a Finder he would never be.

Still, I persevered. "What can we tell of his place in the world, Meto? Slave or free?"

Meto studied the body from head to foot. "He's not wearing an iron ring," he offered.

"Indeed he is not. But that really tells us nothing. A citizen's iron ring is easily removed, and the opposite—to slip such a ring onto a slave's finger—would have been just as easy. Nemo might be a patrician for all we know, whose gold ring has been pilfered. However, sometimes an iron ring does leave a stain or a band of paler flesh on its wearer's finger. I see none, do you?"

Meto shook his head.

"Still, inconclusive. Certainly he wasn't the field slave of some cruel master—there are no shackle marks on his wrists or ankles, no scars on his back from being whipped, no brand marks on his flesh. All in all he looks well taken care of, and not used to hard labor. See, there are no heavy calluses on his hands or feet, and his fingernails and toenails are well groomed. Nor did he spend much time outside—his skin is not much darkened by the sun. If only we had his head, we could tell much more. . . ."

There was a sudden rustling behind us. I gave a start, but it was only Diana running toward us through the straw. A moment later Bethesda appeared in the doorway. Bright sunlight silhouetted the stray tendrils of her coiffed hair and the long, loose stola belted beneath her breasts and again at her waist. She paused in the doorway and then walked resolutely forward like a woman expecting the worst. When she saw the body her nostrils dilated, her eyes grew wide, and she pressed her lips together until all the color was gone from them. She clutched at her stola and stamped her foot. Bethesda's manner is often imperious or brusque, but I have seldom seen her truly angry. It was a sight to make even the staunchest Roman turn to jelly.

"You see!" she cried. "Even here! You said that life would
be different in the country. No more mobs, no more murders,
no more lying awake at night wondering if my children were
safe! Ha! All lies!" She spat upon the corpse, then turned and
swept out of the stable, hitching up her stola to protect it from
the dung.

Meto staggered back, agog. Diana began to cry. In the
sunlit doorway, motes of dust swirled in Bethesda's wake. I
then turned my gaze to the corpse, clenched my fists, and
muttered a curse against the gods. Meto must have overheard,
for when I looked up, he had turned as pale as the headless
body at my feet.

Later, I would tell myself that I should have kept the discovery of the body from Bethesda. Life would have been simpler
that way. But that was never an option, of course; Diana
would have told her sooner or later, and why not? After such
a shock the child needed to be reassured and comforted by
her mother. Diana could not be expected to keep such a momentous and terrible discovery to herself.

It did seem best, if at all possible, to keep the slaves from
knowing. Such an incident would inflame their superstitious
natures and undermine my own authority, making them un-
wieldy at best and at worst unreliable or even dangerous. Cato
would probably have gotten rid of the whole lot after such a
shock to the household, selling those he could and setting any
others free to starve along the roadside. For me, such drastic
measures seemed both impractical and cruel, and besides, the
slaves might know things I did not. If any of them had betrayed me, they still might have seen more than they knew. I
might ultimately need their knowledge and their help. Something terrible had been unleashed, and I could see neither
where it came from nor where it might lead.

I had to confide in someone, and I chose Aratus. He was,
after all, my steward. I swallowed my mistrust, telling myself
that I had probably been unfair to him all along. Besides, if
he was somehow complicit in the appearance of Nemo, perhaps I could read it in his eyes. When Meto brought Aratus
to the stable, the shock on Aratus's face looked quite genuine.

Aratus knew nothing, had seen nothing; so he assured me.

He would tell none of the other slaves; so he vowed. I told him to take a few slaves from their work on the north wall and to dig a hole for the body amid the brambles in the secluded southwest corner of the farm, where the stream cut through the ridge.

"But what reason shall I give them?" he asked.

"Think up a reason!" I told him. "Or give them no reason at all. You're the foreman, aren't you? I leave it to you to handle the slaves. But not one of them is to know of this, do you understand? And if any of them seems to have any knowledge of it, report to me at once!"

That afternoon, after the trench was ready, I instructed Aratus to set the slaves to some task at the far corner of the farm. Meto, Aratus, and I wrapped the corpse in a sheet and tied it to a cart, then pushed the cart over the rocky soil to the place where the hole had been dug. It did not take us long to cover the body with the moist soil, and then to scatter rocks and uprooted brambles over the torn earth. It would have been unseemly to consign even a naked, anonymous, and headless corpse to the earth without some monument, and it would have been unwise to bury any man without properly propitiating his shade, lest we invite his lemur to haunt the farm forever. So I made sure that black beans were buried with the corpse, and as head of the household I threw a handful of the same beans over my shoulder onto the grave when we were done.

Many days later, I returned to the place and drove a slender stele made of marble into the gravesite, which was almost hidden by thorns. On the stele, reading downward, were inscribed these letters:

N
E
M
O

The artisan in the village had complained that it was an odd request, engraving a stele for Nobody, but he had accepted my silver readily enough.

* * *

The feverish spell of lovemaking between Bethesda and my-self was definitely over, as I discovered that night. She turned her shoulder to me when I came to bed, and when I tried to talk to her about the body in the stable, she pulled a pillow over her head.

I complained that the circumstance was not of my devis-ing; that I knew no more about the body and how it came to be there than she did; that I would do all I could to protect her and the children. She made no answer. Eventually I heard her snoring. Insulted and angry, I left the room.

I paced for a long time in the formal courtyard, circling the pond over and over. I paced for so long that I was able to watch the moon shadow of the roof slide slowly across the paving stones. Half the world was black shadow and the other half a soft, hazy silver, and I strode back and forth between the two.

At last I left the courtyard. I looked in on Meto and Diana in their little rooms and found each of them sleeping soundly and apparently without dreams.

I followed the short hallway to my library. I lit a lamp and hung it above my writing table. I spread a piece of parchment before me and pulled the inkstand nearer. I dipped a reed into the ink and began to write. Aratus did most of my letter writ-ing; my hand was clumsy and I made a number of spots on the parchment before I got the reed to flow properly. I wrote:

To my beloved son Eco at his house in Rome, greetings from his beloved father at the farm in Etruria.

Life here in the countryside continues to be full of sur-prises. It is not nearly as dull as you might imagine. I know you love the excitement of Rome, but I think you would be surprised at how much goes on here.

Keep in mind that we celebrate Meto's sixteenth birthday next month, when he will put on his manly toga. The house in Rome will need to be at its best to receive a number of distinguished (and some not-so-distinguished) visitors. The distinguished visitors will need to be impressed by the fam-ily's best ornaments and plate; the not-so-distinguished ones will need to be kept from stealing them. I trust your new wife will be up to the task of organizing and overseeing such an event. Bethesda will probably take over matters anyway.

By the way, I have a small favor to ask. Do this discreetly, please. There is a young man named Marcus Caelius, a protégé of Cicero and of Crassus. Send him a message for me. Say: "The body without a head." I realize this makes no sense; it is in the way of a private joke. He will understand.

I think of you often. You are missed by everyone. I know you are busy in the city. I hope you are exercising all reasonable caution and keeping yourself safe from harm, as is your loving father.

I sat for a while to let the ink dry, then rolled up the parchment and slipped it into a cylindrical case, tied it and sealed it and pressed my ring into the soft wax. In the morning I would dispatch a slave to take it to Rome.

I stepped into the herb garden. No bees hovered there, having all retired to their hives for the night, but a pair of great luminous moths flitted among the vines. The hour was very late, but I did not feel sleepy. Instead I felt as I had earlier that day in the stable—preternaturally alert, seeing and hearing everything around me with an uncanny clarity. The full moonlight was so bright that I could see everything almost as if by daylight, as if the sun had simply turned to blue fire instead of yellow. All was normal, and yet not normal at all. As earlier in the day, I felt the same strange numbness in the midst of acute perception.

I passed through the gate and walked toward the hillside until I found myself at the southwest corner of the estate, not because that was where we had buried the stranger, but because it was the most secluded place on the farm.

I had tried to flee from Rome, but Rome was too great. Within this world, there is no escape from her. Rome is like a net, and men are fish caught in her sweep. Even if a man could make himself so small as to pass through the net, he would only find himself the prey of larger men; and even if he could be so clever and so fast as to escape those other men, he would still find himself at the mercy of Fortune, which is the sea in which we swim, and of the Fates, which are the crags upon which we are pounded. There is no escape.

And so I sat on a rock and gathered up the hem of my
tunic and rolled it into a ball, then pressed it to my mouth
and screamed into it. I screamed as loudly as I could, and no
one heard—not Bethesda softly snoring, nor the slaves, nor
Meto and Diana sound asleep in their beds. All day I had held
that scream inside me. Something unexpected and terrible had
occurred. I had examined the situation, learned what I could
from it, attempted to control it. But from the first moment I
saw the headless corpse, all I had really wanted to do was to
scream—the furious anguished scream of the wolf caught in
a trap, of the eagle thrust into a cage.

PART TWO

CANDIDATUS

EIGHT

FOR the next several days I waited in anticipation of a visitor who did not come.

In the meantime life resumed its normal rhythm. Work on the farm continued as always. Aratus oversaw the field slaves and worked on my accounts, Congrio cooked, the house slaves went about their business.

The days grew longer and hotter, and the nights grew warmer, except in my bed, where things were quite chilly. Bethesda never once queried me about the body in the stable; she had decided long ago, and rightly, since I was then her master, that if my work brought danger into our lives, then dealing with it was my worry, not hers. Her outburst in the stable had been a rare occurrence, and she clearly did not intend to repeat it and would bite her tongue rather than mention it again. Her unspoken attitude announced that she simply saw no point in wasting her breath on interrogating or chastising me; secretly I knew she was deeply worried.

Her manner was cool and distant, like that of soldiers' wives who must live with the terrible prospect of losing their husbands and yet partly blame their husbands for such a possibility in the first place, and thus feel anxiety and anger and helplessness all together. Feigned apathy is a protection, a steeling of the will against the implacable Fates. Bethesda's aloofness I had experienced before and grown used to, but mixed with it was a harsh new strain of suspicion and hard scrutiny, as if I were guilty of a deliberate breach of faith and were directly responsible for subjecting her to the shock of Nemo's arrival.

She was playing a game of patience, I thought, waiting for me to break and tell her all I knew about the corpse and its appearance. I gave in to her more than once, and with an oblique mention of what had happened in the stable let her know I was ready to confide in her, but every time this happened she responded by loudly changing the subject, slamming doors, stalking from the room, and generally making life miserable for everyone in the household. "This wouldn't be happening if I had kept you a slave instead of marrying you," I would grumble halfheartedly under my breath, but of course there was no one to hear me, and I did not quite believe the words myself.

Meto did not seem particularly upset by the body's unexplained appearance. His having grown to manhood in my household in Rome had apparently so inured him to such madness that he could take it for granted. As with Bethesda, it was not his worry; in his offhand, unspoken way he let me know that he fully trusted his father to deal with any such contingency, no matter how menacing or outrageous. His faith in me was touching, and all the more so because it was considerably deeper than my faith in myself.

Diana, on the other hand, grew moody and cross, though I think her unhappiness was more to be attributed to the discord between her parents than to the shock of having found Nemo. Or was I fooling myself, minimizing the awfulness of the shock of witnessing such a grotesque intrusion into her secure little world, because to contemplate such ugliness perpetrated on a child, my child, was enough to send me back to the brambles howling into my tunic? I tried my best to show her as much attention as I could, holding her and combing her hair, giving her treats of curdled cream and honey, but she squirmed in my lap, threw her sweets on the ground, and displayed a querulous dissatisfaction with all the world. I sighed and remembered that she was the daughter of her mother, after all.

Meanwhile, as subtly as I could, I queried the slaves to discover anything they might know about Nemo. I came up with nothing. Aratus, who vowed to keep his mouth shut and his ears open, had no more success. It was as if only we five had ever seen him, and otherwise Nemo had never existed.

The month of Junius waned. The month of Quinctilis approached, and with it high summer. All the world turned hazy with heat. Mount Argentum to the east shimmered like a wavering reflection in a pond. The stream grew smaller in its banks, and its gurgling voice became a low murmur. Even in the shade it was almost too hot to sleep at midday.

A visitor arrived at last.

He did not come through the gate but left the Cassian Way where it veered closest to the ridge at the southeast corner of the farm, and picked his way through the brambles and oak woods. He was not alone, but accompanied by a hulking giant with straw-colored hair who looked almost too big for his horse. Together they approached slowly and cautiously, surreptitiously examining the main house and the adjoining fields from a distance before coming closer.

By chance I happened to see them before they saw me, for I was up on the ridge that afternoon, sitting and gazing down on the farm. The ridgetop sometimes catches a faint breeze even when the air is still down below, and so, with a skin of cooled wine, it can be a comfortable place to pass the waning of a hot, cloudless day.

Claudia had joined me a few moments before, coming up from her side of the hill. She wore a long, loose brown tunic and a farmer's straw hat with a brim almost as wide as she was tall, so that she gave the appearance of a giant mushroom. We sat in the shade and talked idly about animal ailments and temperamental slaves and the weather—not about Nemo or politics or her hostile cousins, for the heat was much too strong for confiding secrets or stirring up controversy. It was Claudia who first saw my visitors.

"Oh, Gordianus, those can't be two of your slaves, can they?"

"Where?"

"Those two men on horseback, down at the foot of the ridge. No, you can't see them now for the treetops—but now, there," she said, pointing with a down-crooked finger.

"What makes you think they're not my men?" I asked, peering down but still unable to see them.

"Because as I was climbing up the other side of the ridge I sat down to rest for a moment and saw them over on the Cassian Way, riding up from the south."

"The same two men? You're sure?"

"Only because one rides a white horse and the other a

black, and the one on the black is positively enormous. I don't think you have any slaves that big on your estate."

I finally saw them, at rest on their horses beneath the olive trees down below. They faced away from us and seemed to be watching the farmhouse.

"Ah, yes," I said uneasily, "visitors from Rome, I suspect." Catilina, I thought, come at last.

"Anyone I know?"

I cleared my throat, trying to think of an answer, and meanwhile peered down at the men on horseback. All I could see were their shoulders and their round-brimmed hats.

Claudia laughed. "Forgive me for being so nosy. Country habits; if I'd been raised in the city I suppose I'd have learned to mind my own business. Or maybe not. Well, I shall leave you to go and greet your visitors." She rose and put on her hat. "Though why they should be approaching your house through the woods like a pair of bandits, instead of using the road, is a puzzlement. You do know who they are, Gordianus?"

"Oh, yes," I assured her, wondering if I did.

I waited for her to leave, then stood and took a sip of wine from the skin. Down below me, the men on horseback did the same, passing a skin between them. They seemed content to sit and watch from their vantage point beneath the shady olive trees, so I sat and watched them in turn. This went on for quite some time, until I began to grow impatient and a little angry. After all, invited or not, they had no business being on my property without my knowledge, and to spy upon my house, whatever their reason or intent, was inexcusable.

I had decided that I had had enough of their impertinence, and was about to go down the hill to confront them, armed with nothing but my dignity as a citizen and a farmholder, when the larger one suddenly turned and looked up at me over his shoulder. I couldn't see his face, because of the shadow cast by his hat, but he must have seen me, for he said something to his companion, who likewise turned his head and looked up at me. The smaller man gestured for the other to stay, then dismounted and began hiking up the hillside.

I should have realized then who it was, for he seemed to

know at once the right way to come, as no stranger could have. There was also something instantly familiar about his gait and the outline of his body, though his face was still hidden by the brim of his hat. But it was not until he gained the ridgetop and was almost upon me that I knew him and said his name with a start.

"Eco!"

"Papa!" He took off his hat and put his arms around me, squeezing the breath out of me.

"I hope you don't squeeze your new bride that hard."

"Of course I do!" He squeezed me harder and then finally released me. "Menenia is a young willow and she bends."

"And I'm an old yew that can crack," I said, arching my back.

He stepped back. "Sorry, Papa. It's just that I'm so glad to see you." His voice still carried that same hoarse, husky quality that had marked it ever since he had regained it nine years before in Baiae, after many years of muteness. To hear him speak is always a miracle to me, and a reminder that the gods can sometimes be generous beyond all expectation.

"But what are you doing here? And why on earth do you look like that?" I asked, for I suddenly realized that his hair and beard were trimmed in exactly the same fashion as Marcus Caelius's—his hair shorn short on the sides but left long and unruly on top, and his beard trimmed and blocked into a thin strap across his jaw and above his lips. The style would look eccentric on anyone, I thought, but was at least flattering to Caelius with his high cheekbones and red lips; it was not at all suitable for Eco.

Eco raised an eyebrow in puzzlement, then touched his chin. "Oh, the look! Do you like it?"

"No."

He laughed. "Menenia likes it."

"The head of his own household should not put on an appearance merely to please his wife," I said, and immediately thought, Numa's balls, you sound just like every old fart of a Roman father who's ever lived. "Never mind," I quickly said, then frowned. "So long as it doesn't mean you've taken up with some sort of strange clique."

"Whatever are you talking about?"

"I mean, so long as the beard and hair aren't part of joining a certain political set. . . ."

He laughed and shook his head. "It's just a fashion, Papa. Anyway, I came as quickly as I could. I was gone from Rome when your letter came, down in Baiae on business for a client—one of the Cornelii; you know how well they pay. I got back only yesterday. When I read your letter, naturally I put things in order as fast as I could—well, after being gone from home so long I couldn't leave Menenia without at least spending the night. I brought Belbo along with me in case there was real trouble. Oh, and I did as you said and dispatched that cryptic message to Marcus Caelius before I left."

"But, Eco, I didn't ask you to come."

"Oh, didn't you, Papa?" He looked at me shrewdly and pulled a rolled scrap of parchment from his belt. 'My beloved son Eco,' 'his loving father.' Really, so much sentiment at the outset alarmed me right away. And then these peculiar references to surprises in the countryside and hints of something exciting taking place—as if you were writing with someone looking over your shoulder and unable to say what you really meant. Then comes the main point of the letter, ostensibly anyway, reminding me of Meto's coming-of-age party—really, as if I were likely to forget that, or as if we hadn't already discussed all the details in the spring! Then, disguised as an almost forgotten afterthought, your request that I pass on a message that can only be some sort of code—private joke, indeed!—followed by a final entreaty to be cautious and stay out of harm's way. Well, you might as well have sat down and written a letter saying, 'Help, Eco, come as quickly as you can!' "

"Let me see that letter," I said, and snatched it from his hands. "Do you always scrutinize your personal correspondence for messages between the lines?"

He shrugged. "Papa, I *am* your son. Aren't you glad I've come? Isn't it what you wanted?"

"Yes. Yes, I'm glad you're here. I do need someone to talk to." I sat down on the stump and picked up the wineskin.

Eco tossed his hat onto the ground and sat beside me. "Interesting," he said, slipping the palm of his hand beneath his buttocks. "This stump is rather warm, despite the fact that it's in the shade. Was someone else sitting here before me?"

I shook my head and sighed. "Oh, for better or worse, you are the Finder's son!"

"No wonder I found you wearing such a long face," said Eco. He sat with his bare feet in the grass, warming his legs in the late afternoon sun. While we talked, the sunlight and shadows had shifted around us. I had told him everything I could think of that had happened in the last month, and several things I had forgotten, thanks to his persistent questioning. Between us on the grass the wineskin lay flattened and empty. At the foot of the hill the horses were tethered to a rock, and Belbo dozed against a tree trunk.

"So you assume that it was Marcus Caelius who put the headless body in the stable, as a message?" Eco said, gazing thoughtfully down at the farmhouse.

"Who else?"

"Perhaps someone on the other side," he suggested.

"Which other side? That's the problem."

"Then you don't believe that Caelius truly represents Cicero?"

"Who knows? When I told him I would require assurances from Cicero himself, he flatly refused, though not without giving me reasons. He wants no link between Cicero and myself."

"We can find a way around that," said Eco. "You needn't do it yourself. I can get a message to Cicero so that no one will know, and convey it here to you."

"And then what? Let us suppose that Cicero assures us that Caelius is indeed his spy in Catilina's camp—even so, can Cicero see into the young man's heart? Caelius claims to be merely *posing* as Catilina's ally while secretly working on Cicero's behalf. But what if his treachery doubles back on itself? What if he truly *is* Catilina's man? Then, if I go along with what he requests, I still have no way of knowing whose interests I'm ultimately being forced to serve. Oh, it's like being thrown into a snake pit—some are more poisonous than others, but all have a bite. What a choice, choosing which snake to let bite you! And just when I thought I had climbed out of the pit for good . . ."

"But the body," Eco said, pressing on. "You're sure it was a message, then, from one side or the other?"

"That much seems clear. Catilina's riddle—a head without a body or a headless body, so Caelius said, and if I would submit to his wishes I was to send a message: 'The body without a head.' I hesitated—and then the very thing appears in my stable! That was only five days after Caelius returned to Rome. Not much time before he began to strongarm me, was it?"

"Unless, as you say, the message came from a different quarter."

"But the message means the same thing, no matter which side sent it. I am to do as I was told, to welcome Catilina into my house. I postponed giving an answer, and in return I was intimidated, my daughter frightened, my household turned upside down."

"You think it was Catilina who did this?"

"I can't believe that Cicero would stoop to such a tactic."

"Caelius might have done it without Cicero's knowledge."

"What does it matter who did it? Someone has gone to considerable lengths to show me that I'm at his mercy."

"So you acquiesced and had me send your reply to Caelius."

"I saw no choice. I sent it through you because I knew I could trust you, and because an indirect approach seemed wise—and yes, perhaps because in my heart I wanted you to come so that I could confide in you. I didn't count on my message to Caelius being delayed on account of your absence from Rome. Strange, that there have been no further repercussions. Barely five days passed after Caelius's visit before the body appeared. Now twice that much time has passed; you sent my message on to Caelius only yesterday, and yet there has been no further incident in the interval."

"The consular election approaches. The politicians and their cohorts are in a mad rush, canvassing the voters. Perhaps they've just forgotten you for the moment."

"If only they'd forget about me for good!"

"Or else . . ."

"Yes, Eco?"

"Perhaps the message—the body—came from another quarter altogether."

I nodded slowly. "Yes, I've considered that. From the Claudii, you mean."

"From what you say, they're already conspiring against you, and they have no scruples. What was it that Gnaeus Claudius said about assassins?"

"Something about hiring men from Rome to come and 'leave a bit of blood on the ground,' or so it was reported to me. But like most hotheaded young men, he's more talk than action, I imagine."

"And if he's not? He sounds like just the sort who'd leave a corpse in the stable to frighten you."

"But why a headless corpse? No, the coincidence would be too great. And if he wanted to murder someone to make his point, why Nemo, whom I can't even identify? Why not one of my slaves, or even me? No, I've considered the possibility that one or more of the Claudii might be behind the incident, but there's simply no evidence."

Eco was thoughtful for a moment. "You questioned your slaves?"

"Indirectly. I don't want them to know about Nemo if I can help it. Disastrous for discipline."

"Why are you so discreet? Most men wouldn't care if the slaves knew. Most men would have every slave on the farm tortured until the truth came out."

"Then perhaps most men could afford to replace a whole farm of slaves; I can't. Besides, terror is not my way to the truth. You know that. I asked what I needed to ask. Not one of them had seen or heard anything that I could connect with the body's appearance."

"How could that be? To put the body in the stable without anyone seeing, one would have to know when and where the slaves would be sleeping or working, and to know that would in itself require some collusion on the part of one of your slaves, or so I should think. Have you been betrayed?"

I shrugged. "I've told you about my quarrels with Aratus."

Eco shook his head. "You've sat through more trials than I have, Papa. Imagine Cicero making shreds of your suspicions of Aratus. They're groundless. You simply don't like him."

"I don't accuse him," I said. "I accuse none of the slaves. Roman slaves do not turn on their masters, not since Spartacus was put down."

We sat in silence for a while and passed the wineskin between us. Eco finally hardened his jaw and pulled his eyebrows together, a gesture which I knew presaged a decision.

"I don't like it, Papa. I think you should leave the farm and come to the city. You're in danger here."

"Ha! Leave the countryside and go to Rome for safety's sake? Would you advise a swimmer to leave the backwater for the rapids?"

"There can be dangerous undercurrents in the backwater."

"And sharp rocks hidden in the rapids. And eddies that suck you down into darkness and whirl you around and around."

"I'm serious, Papa."

I looked down at the farm. The sun was sinking rapidly, casting an orange haze across the fields. The slaves were driving the goats into their pen. Diana and Meto emerged from the deep green shadows of the trees along the stream bank, heading toward the house. "But summer is a busy time on the farm. I have plans to build a water mill—"

"Aratus can run the farm, Papa. Isn't that what he's for? Oh, I know you dislike him, but nothing you've told me has given you any true cause to distrust him. Bring Bethesda and the children to the city. Stay with me."

"In the house on the Esquiline? Hardly big enough for all of us."

"There's plenty of room."

"Not for Bethesda and Menenia to run separate households."

"Papa—"

"No. It's election time, as you just reminded me, and I have no stomach to be in Rome while the candidates and their retinues swarm through the markets, and every ignorant fishmonger spouts his opinion on the state of the Republic. No, thank you. Besides, the month of Quinctilis is far too hot in the city. When you're my age you'll understand—your bones learn to hate the cold and your heart can't tolerate the heat."

"Papa—"

I raised my hand and put on a stern face to silence him, then let my countenance soften and put my hand on his knee. "You're a good son, Eco, to have come all this way out of concern for me. And you are a dutiful son, to offer me lodging in the house I gave you. But I will not go to Rome. Not to worry—it seems inevitable that Rome will come to me."

We made our way down the hillside to rouse Belbo and take the horses to the stable. I felt as if a great weight had been lifted from me. I told myself it was the wine, which makes a lighter load in the belly than in a skin, but in truth the feeling of lightness and relief came from having unburdened myself to the one person who could understand what I felt. Perhaps I should have taken Eco's advice; who can say what other path the Fates might have woven had I chosen to spend that summer and fall in Rome instead of Etruria? But I am not a man prone to mulling over what might or might not have been, especially in what turned out to have been a small choice amid the far greater choices and the graver puzzles that were yet to come.

Eco's arrival was greeted with great happiness in the household; I had not realized how severe had been the tension that followed in Nemo's wake until Eco came to relieve it. Diana sat happily on his lap, and he obliged her by bouncing her up and down. (With a twinge of mixed feelings I realized that at twenty-seven he was quite old enough to have a daughter Diana's age himself, and now, with Menenia, might announce the advent of my first grandchild at any time.) Meto exhibited the mixture of curiosity, deference, and envy of a youth in the presence of a brother more than ten years his senior, especially when one is still a boy and the other is most definitely a man; despite the difference in their ages and their origins they had always gotten along very well. Bethesda complimented Eco's stylish haircut and beard and doted on him shamelessly.

Belbo, who had protected the house on the Esquiline and its occupants for many years, was beginning to look a bit heavy and gray, I thought, though his shoulders were as broad

as ever and his arms still looked like a metalworker's. Much
to his consternation, Diana made a game out of tugging at his
red and gray whiskers until Bethesda threatened to deny her
Congrio's confection of honey and almonds.

Eco wanted to ride back to Rome the next morning, but I
persuaded him to spend the day. I asked him to look over
Aratus's accounts, which he did in a cursory manner and pronounced them to be above reproach. I showed him my plans
for the water mill, which I was determined to start as soon
as possible, and he offered a few minor suggestions to im-
prove it. As we strolled around the farm, I pointed out
changes I had made since his last visit and talked about improvements I was planning for the future.

That night Bethesda herself took charge of the kitchen and
cooked exactly the kind of simple meal that Eco had grown
up on. His tastes had grown more sophisticated since then,
but he seemed truly to enjoy the dishes of lentils and barley,
if only for sentiment's sake. Afterward the slaves pulled the
couches into the atrium, and the family gathered in a circle
to watch the stars come out. Bethesda was persuaded to sing
one of the Egyptian songs from her childhood, and to the
sound of her voice Diana and Meto fell fast asleep. Beneath
the moonless sky, at Bethesda's prompting, Eco talked about
the small details of his home life in the city with his new
bride. I sat in silence, content to listen.

Later, Bethesda roused Meto and sent him off to his room
and picked up Diana to carry her to bed, leaving Eco and me
alone.

"Papa," he said, "when I get back to the city I'll see what
I can find out about Catilina, and Caelius, and what they
might be up to. Discreetly, of course."

"Don't put yourself in danger."

He shrugged, and in the gesture I saw myself. "A curious
man in Rome is always in danger, Papa. You know that."

"Even so—"

"I can't stand by and do nothing while someone weaves a
plot around you and tries to draw you in. These people, to
have left a dead body as a token—clearly they'll stop at nothing."

"Which is exactly why I have no choice but to submit and

go forward. A man surrounded by a ring of fire cannot stand idle and fret or he will surely be consumed. The only way out is to ride straight through the fire and emerge on the other side."

"And then where will you be?"

I took a deep breath and studied the stars above us. I made no answer, and Eco did not press the question.

Thus passed the last day of Junius. Early on the morning of the Kalends of Quinctilis, Eco and Belbo left for Rome. I went with them as far as the Cassian Way and watched after them for a long time, until all I could see were two wavering spots of white and black to mark their horses on the dusty horizon, which already shimmered with heat.

NINE

THE afternoon of Eco's departure I began work on the water mill in earnest. Aratus, who had far more practical knowledge of engineering than I, reviewed my plans and pronounced them feasible; indeed, I secretly congratulated myself that he was more than a little impressed. He called on the slaves who had the most experience with woodworking to begin fashioning the various parts.

Meanwhile Aratus and I did a rough survey of the spot I had chosen, marking the elevations and the width of the stream. I had thought I might need to dam a small section, but I saw a way to divert the flow instead by digging a channel on my side of the bank. There would be no inconvenience to my neighbor Publius, except a muddying of the waters. Still, his washer-women would no doubt complain, and I had no desire to provoke any further altercations among the slaves. Then there was the matter of the litigation between us, involving my disputed rights to use the stream in the first place. That might take months or years to settle, and I had no intention of waiting to begin the mill. Perhaps, I thought, if I offered to allow Publius to use the water mill himself he

would be more amenable to the project; surely he would see
that it was to his benefit as well. I gritted my teeth and made
up my mind to do the reasonable and forthright thing, and go
calling on Publius Claudius.

No road communicated between our properties. To reach
his house by any road I would have to ride out to the Cassian
Way and make a great loop north of Manius Claudius's farm
and then ride south again. Given the chill between us, it
seemed a bit brazen to simply cross the stream and go riding
across his fields to his house, but there was no other practical
route. I decided to take Aratus with me, along with one of
the larger field slaves, just in case there was trouble. To keep
Meto out of harm's way, I dispatched him to take Aratus's
place and oversee some slaves working near the north wall.
He chafed at being left at home, but I could see that being
given some responsibility pleased him.

We set out in the early afternoon. In summer, most farmers
take a long break in the middle of the day to escape the heat,
and I hoped to find Publius at his leisure, his stomach full
from his midday meal, his head a bit fuzzy with wine. I could
approach him with an open hand, neighbor to neighbor. Our
slaves had had their altercations at the stream, but, so far as
Congrio and his assistants had reported, Publius himself had
made no serious threats against me at the family gathering.
Perhaps we could reason with each other and avoid any further unpleasantness.

Thus had the calming effect of Eco's brief visit banished
pessimism and lulled me into a state of goodwill toward my
fellowmen.

We rode across the stream and up the hillside. As we
crossed the fields, the slaves I saw were taking respite from
the heat, resting in the shade of olive trees and fig trees. They
looked at me strangely, but none of them challenged us.

The farm was less well kept than I had thought. From the
vantage point of the ridge it looked idyllic, but distance ob-
scures a barn made of rotting wood or an orchard where trees
have been spotted by blight. The grass was high, long overdue
for mowing. It hissed all around us as our horses stepped
through the growth, setting grasshoppers and chirring cicadas
to flight. Aratus clucked his tongue in disapproval as he sur-

veyed the conditions of the livestock and their pens. "It's one thing to see such filthiness in the city—there you've got a million people all pressed together, and who can help it? But in the country things should be clean and neat. So long as a man owns enough slaves, there's no excuse for such a mess."

Looking around us at the overgrown hedges, the poorly mended fences, the scattered tools and the piles of debris, I had to agree with him. I had thought Publius Claudius was a rich man. How could he allow his property to fall into such disrepair?

We dismounted and tethered our horses. The house was in better shape than the sheds and barns around it, but the tiles on the roof needed repairing. On the way to the door I tripped on a cracked paving stone and almost fell. Aratus caught my arm and helped to right me.

He rapped on the door, at first gently, then harder. Even if the household was napping in the heat of the day, there should be a slave to answer the door. Aratus looked back at me with his lips pursed. I nodded for him to rap more loudly.

From within came the sound of a dog barking, and then a man shouting for the dog to be quiet. I expected the door to open then, but instead there was silence.

Aratus looked back at me, "Well, go ahead," I said. "Knock again."

Aratus knocked. The dog barked again. The man shouted and cursed, at us now instead of the dog. "Go away or you'll get a beating!" he yelled.

"This is ridiculous," I said. Aratus stepped out of my way to let me bang on the door myself. "Your master has visitors at the door!" I said. "Open it now or it's you who'll get the beating!"

The dog barked and barked. The voice beyond the door cursed us and blasphemed half the gods of Olympus. There was a loud whimpering squeal and the barking ceased. At last the door rattled and swung open. I wrinkled my nose at the smell from within—a mixture of dog, stale sweat, and stewed cabbage.

Beyond the little foyer was an atrium bright with sunlight, so that I saw the man in silhouette and for a moment could only dimly make out his features. I noticed his hair first, long and unkempt like a shaggy mane, streaked with gray. He had the posture of an old man, stooped and slump-shouldered, but he looked neither small nor weak. His tunic was rumpled and worn-looking, all awry, as if he had just pulled it on. As I saw him more clearly, I noticed his grizzled jaw, covered with several days' worth of stubble, and his big, fleshy nose. His eyes were bloodshot, and he squinted as if the light caused him pain.

. "Who are you and what do you want?" he growled, his speech slurred by wine.

Numa's balls, I thought, what a slave to answer the door! Clearly, Publius Claudius paid no more attention to the running of his private household than he did to the running of his farm. "My name is Gordianus," I said. "I own the farm that once belonged to Lucius Claudius, across the stream. I've come to speak with your master."

The man laughed. "My master—fah!"

Behind me, Aratus sucked in a breath. "Sheer insolence!" he whispered.

The man laughed again. Behind him there was a flash of movement in the sunlit atrium. A girl, completely naked except for a crumpled garment she carried in her hands, stepped into the light and looked toward the doorway with wide, startled eyes. She was young—so young that I might have taken her for a boy had it not been for the matted tangle of her long black hair.

I pursed my lips. "Obviously, Publius Claudius must be away from the farm for such behavior to take place in his own house," I said dryly.

The man turned and saw the girl, then lunged at her and clapped his hands. "Out of here, Dragonfly! Put on your clothes and get out of my sight or I'll give you a beating. Ha! What manners—showing your naked backside to visitors! Come back here and I'll add some stripes to go with my handprints, you little harpy!"

He turned back to us, wearing a self-satisfied smirk. With a sinking feeling I glanced down at his right hand and saw that he wore a ring on his finger—and not just a common citizen's iron ring, but a patrician's band that gleamed golden in the soft light.

"You must be Publius Claudius," I said dully. My eyes having adjusted to the light, I studied his face and saw that it was true. I had seen him in court at the Forum in Rome, but only at a distance and with his hair neatly clipped and his beard shaved, and he had worn a fine toga. He had looked as staid and sober as a man running for office. In his own home he showed a very different face.

He looked me up and down. "Ah, yes, I remember you. The man who got away with Cousin Lucius's property. You looked all stuffed full of yourself in the court, silly and dull like most city boys. You still look like a city boy."

I drew myself up. It does not do to be insulted in front of one's slaves. "Publius Claudius, I've come as your neighbor, to discuss a small matter involving the stream that marks our common boundary."

"Fah!" He curled his lip. "We'll settle the matter in court. And this time you won't have that windbag Cicero to come to your rescue by wriggling his silver tongue between the judges' buttocks. I understand he's already got his mouth full just to keep them smiling in the Senate."

"You have a foul tongue, Publius Claudius."

"At least I don't put it where Cicero does."

I took a breath. "As you say, Publius, the matter of water rights will be settled in court. Until then I have no intention to stop using the stream—"

"So I've seen. Oh, come, if it's the feuding between the washerwomen that's brought you here, let the matter go! Yes, yes, one of your slaves was struck by a stone. My foreman told me all about it. Well, can she still do her work or not? If she's ruined, I'll give you one of mine in exchange. But I won't go paying damages just because a washerwoman spilled a little blood—it's not as if she were a pleasure slave and the scar would make a difference. What more do you want from me? I gave every one of the slaves involved a sound beating, and gave special punishment to the little witch who threw the stone—she won't soon try that again. I hope you did the same to your slaves—that's my advice, and if you haven't done so, then do it now. It's never too late. They'll have forgotten what they did wrong, but they'll remember the beating if you do it properly. Sometimes a beat-

ing is a good idea, even if they've done nothing wrong. Just
to remind them who's in charge."

"Publius Claudius, the matter I've come to discuss—"

"Oh, Romulus and Remus, it's far too hot to stand here in
the doorway talking. Come on inside. Who's this behind you,
your foreman? Yes, bring him in, too—but leave the big one
outside. You don't need a bodyguard to enter my house. What
sort of man do you think I am? You, slave, close the door
behind you. Ah, good, my couch is still in the shade."

There was a fountain in the courtyard, but no water; the
basin was littered with twigs and straw. Publius fell back onto
his couch. There was only a stool for me to sit on. Aratus,
having closed the door, took a place behind me and stood.

"You'll forgive the lack of soft furnishings and the like,"
said Publius. A hound appeared and slunk whimpering beneath his master's couch. "I've never had a taste for luxury.
Besides, it takes a woman to make a house all soft and comfortable for visitors, and the only wife I ever took died a year
after I married her. She took with her the only heir I ever
made as well, or the baby took her, whichever way that
works. They went down into Hades, hand in hand, I
suppose." He reached under his couch and produced a wineskin. He put it to his mouth and squeezed, but the skin only
sputtered. "Dragonfly," he crooned. "Oh, Dragonfly, bring
Papa some more wine."

"I came here, Publius, because I propose to build a water
mill on the stream. There will be no need to disrupt the flow,
as I plan to divert the channel into a ditch upstream from the
site—"

"A mill? You mean a sort of machine with wheels run by
the water? But what could you do with such a thing?"

"It could have many uses. It could be used to grind meal,
or even stones."

"But you already have slaves to do that, don't you?"

"Yes, but—"

"Dragonfly! Bring me more wine right now or I shall
spank you again, here in front of these strangers!"

After a moment the girl appeared, dressed now in a stained
tunic that left her arms and legs bare, carrying a bloated wineskin. Publius took it from her and slapped her backside. The

girl began to withdraw, but Publius grabbed her buttock with one hand and pulled her back while he held the wineskin in his other and uncorked it with his teeth. While he swilled the wine, he slid his hand up underneath her tunic and fondled her backside. The girl stood passively, her eyes averted, her face red.

I cleared my throat. "It might interest you to know that I got the idea for building the water mill from Claudia. She told me it had always been an ambition of your cousin Lucius to build such a mill. So in a way, you see, I am fulfilling his wishes."

Publius shrugged. "Lucius had a lot of stupid ideas, like leaving his farm to you. Like yourself, he was a city boy. That's where stupid ideas come from, the city. Put enough fools in one place and you have what they call a city, eh? And then the stupid ideas spread from head to head like a pox." He did something with his hand that made the girl give a start and open her mouth. Publius laughed.

I stood up. "I was thinking, if it would be of any interest to you, that I could allow you some access to the mill once it's finished. You might find it useful."

"What would I want it for? I have slaves to grind my meal."

"The water could do the work of the slaves."

"Then what would the slaves do? Idle slaves only end up getting into trouble."

"I'm sure the slaves could find plenty of other work to do around here," I said dryly. I meant to be insulting, but Publius seemed not to notice.

"A mill is a machine," he said. "Machines break and must be repaired. There is only so much water to run such a thing, especially in the dry months. And when a machine is idle, it's of no use to anyone—while a slave can be useful even when she's at rest." Publius did something that made the girl let out a gasp. She began to draw away, then twitched and stood stiffly upright. A vein stood out in Publius's forehead, and he narrowed his eyes. His shoulder and elbow moved in a strange gyration. The girl pouted and bit her lips. Publius put the wineskin to his mouth. He sucked at the spout, spilling wine on his chin.

"I'll go now," I said. Aratus hurried ahead of me to open the door.

"Oh, but I'm a miserable host!" cried Publius, slurring the words. "Here I am making myself at home and I've offered nothing to my guest. Which would you like, Gordianus, the wineskin . . . or the girl?"

"I'll begin construction on the water mill tomorrow," I said, not looking back. "I hope I may expect no interference from you. I'll thank you for your cooperation."

On the path outside, Publius came hurrying after me. He laid his hand on my arm. I jerked it from his grasp. His breath smelled of wine. His hand smelled of the girl.

"Another thing, Gordianus—you have to build a mill from scratch. But a slave—you can make your own slaves! Why, half the slaves on this farm were planted in their mothers' wombs by me. You don't have to buy them, you see, you can make your own—more fun that way, eh? And doesn't cost a copper. You see the big one over there beneath the olive trees, rousing the others from their nap and putting them back to work—one of my bastards. Oh, I've made some big ones, strong boys who can keep the rest in line. I feed them well and let them play with the Dragonfly now and again, to keep them happy. It doesn't matter if the others are miserable or not, so long as you've got the strong ones to keep them in line. Feed the weaker ones just enough to keep them going, but not so much as to make them stronger than they should be—"

I mounted my horse. Aratus and the field slave I had brought did likewise.

"But what's this, Gordianus, you don't care to discuss agrarian philosophy? I thought all you city boys, all you friends of windbags like Cicero, delighted in a good discussion—" He staggered after me, tripping on the paving stones.

"You shouldn't drink so much on such a hot day, Publius Claudius. You'll fall and hurt yourself," I said, gritting my teeth.

"It's the trouble down at the stream that's still bothering you, isn't it? Fah! That was nothing. Women squabbling. If I'd really wanted to make a point, I'd have sent one of my big bastards over to do it. Oh, yes, you're just what my cousins say you are. Another nobody from the city who's risen too far above his station in life. Rome is in a sad state when a nobody like you can get his hands on a patrician's farm and take on airs like a country noble—and a nobody like your friend Cicero can worm his way into the consulship. Your head is all swollen, Gordianus—maybe someone should pop it open for you!" He slapped his fist into his palm with a crack.

I wheeled around. Publius drew back, startled and coughing from the dust stirred up by the horse's stamping hooves. His enforcers in the olive grove pricked up their ears and began walking quickly toward us.

"What's that you said about heads, Publius?" I demanded.

"What?" He looked up at me with a puzzled expression, waving at the dust.

"Do you make a habit of doing damage to other men's heads, Publius Claudius?"

"I don't know what you're talking about. It's a figure of speech—"

"And if you popped a man's swollen head, Publius—what would you do with the body?"

The enforcers arrived and circled their master. His momentary abashment passed and Publius squinted up at me defiantly. "I think you'd better get off my property. If you have no taste for my hospitality, then go! And don't think I'll forget the matter of the water rights. It's my stream, not yours!"

I turned around and called to Aratus and the field slave to follow me. I drove the horse at a trot, then at a full gallop through the high grass, scattering startled cicadas and grasshoppers in my wake. The heat of the fields rushed over my face, and the wind roared in my ears. The pounding of the horse's hooves against the hard earth vibrated through my body. The slaves returning to their labors drew back in alarm. Even when I came to the stream I did not slow the pace, but urged the beast to bound over the water. Once I was on the far bank I pulled on her reins and bent forward to stroke her neck. I rested in the shade, listening to the breath pass through her nostrils, and the pounding of my heart in my ears.

*   *   *

Aratus and the field slave went back to their duties. I lingered
for a while by the stream, letting my horse drink from the
cool water and eat the tender grass. When she was done, I
rode up to the stable. I was about to dismount when a faraway
movement on the highway caught my eye. I shaded my brow
and peered across the fields. Two men were turning off the
Cassian Way onto the road to my house. One rode a black
horse, the other a white.

Eco, returning so soon? That could only mean trouble, I
thought. I hurried down the road to meet him.

As I drew nearer I thought I recognized Eco by his fashionable beard and haircut, but the other rider, on the white
horse, was not nearly large enough to be Belbo. I reined in
my horse and waited for the men to draw closer. They kept
a slow, steady pace, until the one on the black horse broke
into a trot and rode ahead to meet me. He looked absurdly
happy; indeed, it seemed to me that a great smile was approaching me accompanied by a horse and rider.

When he was close enough for me to see him more clearly,
I knew that I must be seeing the first and foremost face to
wear the fashion so popular among the young men at Rome,
for it could not possibly have suited any other face, not even
that of handsome Marcus Caelius, as perfectly as it suited his.
The strap of beard across his jaw was the ideal frame for his
strong chin and perfectly chiseled nose. The cut of his hair,
long on top and sheared above the ears so that flecks of silver
shone among the black, was ideally suited to his straight black
eyebrows and lofty forehead. His eyes were a piercing blue
that seemed to pin me and hold me in place as he drew nearer.

"Beautiful!" he said as he reined in his mount, taking his
eyes from mine to gaze at the fields around him. "Even better
than Marcus Caelius promised. It couldn't be more perfect—
could it, Tongilius?" he said, calling back to his young companion. He breathed deeply, savoring the sweet smells of hay
and wildflowers. "A beautiful piece of earth. One can almost
picture Pan himself flitting across the fields. The kind of farm
every Roman dreams of." With a great smile on his face he
extended his hand. Reluctantly I took it. His grasp was warm

and strong. "You must be a proud and happy man, Gordianus!"

I nodded and sighed. "Oh, yes, Catilina, I am assuredly that."

TEN

WE had met briefly ten years before, but in all the time since the scandal of the Vestal Virgins I had had nothing to do with Catilina and had hardly seen him, even when he was in the Forum campaigning for office—especially then, for the sight of a politician approaching with his retinue was enough to send me running. (A Roman politician will doggedly pursue an honest man into a shop or tavern or even a brothel to beg for his vote; the only hope of escape is to head speedily in the opposite direction.)

Meeting Catilina again immediately brought back memories of our previous encounter, so that I could see him vividly as he had been then—a man in his middle thirties with black hair and a beard (worn in a more conservative fashion back then), possessing such regular features so harmoniously balanced that one would hardly even think to call him handsome. More than handsome, he was quite remarkably attractive, with an appeal that seemed to emanate from within him in some invisible way, outwardly manifested by the playfulness that lit his eyes and the smile that came so readily to his lips.

Time, if not the tide of human affairs, had been kind to Catilina; as men say of wine and women, he had aged well. There were lines at the corners of his eyes and his mouth, but they were such wrinkles as come from smiling too much. There was a hint of weariness in his sparkling eyes and in his smile, but that only infused them with a mellowness that was all the more appealing. He was a hard man not to like at first sight. No wonder he was thought to be so dangerous.

"Gordianus," he said, still clasping my hand. "Years and years. Do you remember?"

"I remember."

"Marcus Caelius said you would. Then it's all right that I should come to visit you here?"

"Yes, of course," I said. If Catilina noticed the beat of hesitation before I answered, he ignored it.

"Marcus Caelius assured me that it would be. I must have a retreat where I can simply disappear from the world from time to time, and Caelius told me he knew just the place. You're very kind to have me."

I suddenly realized that he was still holding my hand in his. There was something so natural and unassuming in his touch that I had not even noticed. I gently pulled back. Catilina released my hand, but held me with his gaze, as if he were not quite ready to let me go.

"This is Tongilius." He gestured to his companion, an athletic-looking young man with wavy brown hair and a strong jaw, clean-shaven to show the dimple in his chin. I wondered if there was some way that Catilina's charm could be learned or acquired by contact, for Tongilius, with his green eyes and subtle smile, seemed to possess it in miniature. He nodded and said in a very deep voice, "I am honored to meet an old acquaintance of Catilina's."

I nodded in return. The three of us sat unmoving on our horses for a long, awkward moment. It was up to me to make some gesture of hospitality, whether feigned or not, but I found myself confused and unwilling to speak. The moment had arrived. The favor that Marcus Caelius had demanded was at hand. I had resisted this eventuality, dreaded it, steeled myself to see it through, and now that the crisis had occurred I felt strangely deflated, almost disappointed. I sensed nothing ominous in Catilina's presence. Indeed, I felt quite at ease with him, and that worried me all the more, for I had to wonder if my wits were growing dull, not to sense danger and deceit when they were surely close at hand.

It was Catilina who finally spoke. "And this one, riding up behind you—could it be your son?"

I looked over my shoulder and saw Meto approaching on horseback, coming from the north wall where Aratus must have just relieved him of overseeing the slaves.

"Yes, this is the younger of my two sons, Meto." Reminded of the children and their vulnerability, I felt a pang of uneasiness that proved my wits were still with me. "Meto, we have visitors. This is Lucius Sergius Catilina. And this is his companion, Tongilius."

Meto drew nearer with a crooked smile on his face, a bit flustered at meeting such a notorious character. Catilina extended his hand, and Meto took it, rather too eagerly, I thought. In a hushed voice Meto said, "Did you *really* sleep with a Vestal Virgin?"

My jaw dropped. "Meto!"

Catilina threw back his head and laughed, so uproariously that my horse snorted in alarm. Tongilius laughed with his mouth shut. Meto turned pink but looked more puzzled than embarrassed. I put my hand to my brow and groaned.

"Well," said Catilina, "now I know what anecdote I shall be telling tonight after supper!" He reached out and tousled Meto's hair, and Meto seemed to enjoy it.

If I had hoped to drive Catilina away with bad cooking, Congrio made it impossible. That night he outdid himself. Bethesda spurred him on to it. She has always judged strangers strictly by their appearance, and she very much liked the looks of Catilina and Tongilius. Consequently, we dined superbly on a pork stew with fava beans accompanied by an apricot fricassee.

After dinner, as on the night before, I had the slaves pull our couches out into the atrium, but Bethesda did not join us. Since I made her my wife, she has been quite conscious of her status as a freedwoman and matron of a citizen's household, but she draws the line at the modern Roman matron's practice of joining in an after-dinner conversation with men outside her family. She withdrew, taking Diana with her. Meto remained. His presence made me uncomfortable, but I saw no easy way to dismiss him. Our guest had promised him a story, after all.

"A very fine meal," said Catilina. "I must thank you again for having me."

"I admit that I was hesitant at first to invite you into my

home, Catilina." I spoke slowly and deliberately. "You are a figure of considerable controversy, and I have reached a point in my life and fortunes when I no longer seek controversy; quite the opposite. But Marcus Caelius put forward the case for extending my hospitality . . . most convincingly."

"Yes, he is a persuasive young man of talent and initiative." There was no hint of irony in Catilina's voice, and the sparkle in his eyes looked no more menacing than the playfulness that was always there.

"He is eloquent, yes, and persistent. Also, he seems to know that a powerful gesture can speak louder than mere words."

Catilina nodded. Again there was no indication that he perceived any double meaning in what I said.

"You're fond of riddles," I said.

Catilina smiled. Tongilius laughed. Between them passed the look of intimates sharing a private joke. "I confess," said Catilina.

"It is his *only* vice," said Tongilius. "Or so he likes to tell people." That was the joke, then—that a man with such a reputation for depravity should admit to nothing more vicious than a weakness for wordplay.

"And you, Gordianus—I take it you're more inclined to solve riddles than to make them up."

"I used to be."

"Well, then, an easy one." He thought for a moment, then said, "An edible legume of no distinguished pedigree, transplanted from rustic soil to a stony place where it thrives against all expectation and casts its tendrils far and wide."

"Too easy," said Meto.

"Is it?" said Catilina. "I just made it up on the spot."

"The bean is a chickpea. The stony place is the Forum in Rome."

"Go on."

"So the answer to the riddle is Marcus Tullius Cicero."

"Because?"

Meto shrugged. "Everyone knows the family name Cicero comes from an ancestor who had a cleft in his nose, like a chickpea, a *cicer* bean. Cicero came from the town of Arpinum—rustic soil—and made his fortune in the Forum, which is all paved with stone. There he thrives, though nobody ever expected that a man who wasn't from a famous family could rise so far."

"Very good!" said Catilina. "And the tendrils?" he asked, looking not at Meto but at me.

"His influence, which reaches far and wide," concluded Meto.

"You're right, it's too easy," conceded Catilina. "I shall have to make it harder the next time I tell it. What do you think, Gordianus?"

"Yes," I said, "much too obvious."

"The riddle or the riddler?" said Tongilius. For a moment I thought he meant the question seriously, and it seemed that all our masks were about to fall. But when he laughed softly and cast a grin at Catilina, and I saw he was merely jibing his mentor for the sake of punning.

"I understand that you and Cicero go back a long time," said Catilina. "Fifteen or twenty years."

"Seventeen. I met him in the last year of Sulla's dictatorship."

"Oh, yes, Caelius reminded me. The trial of Sextus Roscius."

"Were you at the trial?"

"No, but of course one heard a great deal about it at the time. The talk was mostly about Cicero, but I do recall hearing your name mentioned in connection with the affair, after the fact. It turned out to be an important occasion, something of a landmark. I suppose one could say that you and Cicero made one another's reputation."

"You give me far too much credit. You might as well honor Congrio's spoon for making the sauce."

"Surely you're too modest, Gordianus."

"I take neither credit nor blame for Cicero's achievements. Yes, I've worked for Cicero a number of times over the years, just as I've worked for Crassus and Hortensius and many others."

"Then I'm no more correct when I say that Cicero made your reputation?"

"The trial of Sextus Roscius was a watershed for all concerned."

Catalina nodded. He put his cup to his lips and drained it, then held it up to be refilled. I looked about and realized there was no slave to serve us.

"Meto, go and fetch one of the girls from the kitchen," I said.

"No need." Catilina stood up and walked to the table where the clay bottle of wine had been left by Bethesda. I watched a Roman patrician fetch his own wine and felt a quiver of surprise, but Catilina returned to his couch and reclined as if completely unaware that he had done anything remarkable. "Your own vintage?" he said.

"From the time of Lucius Claudius, who owned the farm before me. One of the better years, I think."

"I think you're right. The flavor is dark and rich, yet very smooth. It warms the throat and belly without being harsh. I think I shall have to beg a bottle of you before I leave."

"Will you be staying long?"

"Only a day or two, with your indulgence."

"I should think the consular election would require your presence in Rome."

"The campaign is well in hand," he said. "But please, I've come here to escape from politics for a little while. Let's talk of something else."

Meto cleared his throat.

Tongilius laughed. "I think the young man was promised a story."

"Oh, yes, the tale of the Vestals," said Catilina.

"There's no need to talk of the matter if you'd rather not," I said.

"What, and let others pollute the boy's mind with their own versions of the story? The only way to subvert the slanders of your enemies is to tell stories on yourself before others have the chance. What do you know of the tale already, Meto?"

"He knows nothing," I said. "I only happened to mention it to him in passing."

"And yet he knows that I was accused of sleeping with a Vestal Virgin."

"And that you were acquitted," I said.

"With your help, Gordianus."

"To some degree."

"Your father is a modest man," Catilina said to Meto.

"Modesty is a fine Roman virtue, though I think it is more praised than practiced."

"Rather like virginity among the Vestals?" suggested Tongilius.

"Quiet, Tongilius. Gordianus is not a particularly religious man, if I remember correctly, but there is no call to be impious in his house. Nor is it necessary to besmirch the virtue of the Vestals in the telling of the tale, for all were innocent, even myself. Ah, Meto, it's been quite a while since I met anyone who didn't already know everything about the scandal of the Vestals, or thought he knew. This is a rare opportunity for me to give my own version of the story."

"Just as you did before the court."

"Hush, Tongilius! No, I won't repeat all that I said before the court, because there's no need to divulge every fact in order to tell the truth. The privacy and dignity of the Vestals should be honored. I will tell only what needs to be told."

He cleared his throat and finished his cup of wine. "Very well. The incident occurred ten years ago, just before the outbreak of the Spartacan slave revolt. I happened to have struck up a passing friendship with a certain Vestal named Fabia, having seen her at chariot races and the theater and at dinner parties."

"I thought the Vestals had no contact with men," said Meto.

"Not true, though since the scandal of which I speak their social lives and public appearances have been circumscribed to prevent the recurrence of an embarrassing episode. But back then the Vestals moved with relative freedom through the world, so long as they were chaperoned and comported themselves with dignity. They are vowed to chastity, not isolation.

"One night I received an urgent summons from Fabia, begging me to come to her in the House of the Vestals, saying her honor and her life were at stake. Well, how could I refuse?"

"But it's death to enter the House of the Vestals after dark," said Meto.

"What better excuse to risk death than to answer the desperate summons of a beautiful young virgin? Did I mention before that Fabia was beautiful? Very beautiful—wasn't she, Gordianus?"

"I suppose. I don't recall."

"Ha! Your father is as cagey as he is modest, Meto. I don't believe him. Having seen Fabia's face, he could never forget it. I never have. Tongilius, don't grimace! You have no call to be jealous. My relations with the girl were pure and blameless and above reproach. Ah, I see that Gordianus looks skeptical. He was skeptical then, too, but his doubts did not prevent him from saving both Fabia and myself from a cruel fate. But I'm getting ahead of the story.

"In answer to the summons, I made my way to the House of the Vestals. The doors stood open, as they always do; it is the law, not wooden doors, that keeps men out at night. I had been to Fabia's room before, always chaperoned and in daylight, of course, so I had no trouble finding it. She was quite surprised to see me, for it turned out that she had not sent the message at all! It was a practical joke played on me by some dubious friend, I thought—until Fabia and I were startled out of our wits by a scream."

"A scream?" said Meto.

"From behind a curtain. The scream of a dying man, as it turned out. I pulled aside the curtain to discover him writhing on the floor, his throat cut, and beside him a bloody knife. The whole house was awakened. Before I could flee, the Virgo Maxima herself entered the room. It was a thorny situation."

Tongilius laughed aloud. "Lucius, what a gift you have for understatement!"

Catilina arched an eyebrow. The gesture was typically patrician, but together with his chin-strap beard and unruly curls, it gave his face the shrewd look of a satyr contemplating an unprotected sheep. "The situation wasn't compromising—Fabia and I were both fully dressed—but there remained the fact that I was on forbidden ground, and of course the presence of a corpse in a holy place. Do you know the penalty for such crimes, Meto?"

Meto vigorously shook his head.

"Really, Gordianus, you've neglected the boy's education. Do you not regale him with anecdotes of your past adventures, dwelling on all the juicy details? When a Vestal is convicted of an improper dalliance with a man, Meto, the man is put to death by public scourging. Painful and humiliating, but not the most terrible of fates—death is death, after all. But for the Vestal—oh, for her, the end is far more gruesome."

I glanced at Meto, who gazed raptly at Catilina. Tongilius, who must have heard the tale many times already, found fresh amusement in Meto's wide-eyed fascination.

"Shall I tell you the punishment for a Vestal found guilty of impiety?" said Catilina.

Meto nodded.

"Really, Catilina," I protested, "the boy won't sleep a wink tonight."

"Nonsense! A young man his age craves images of horror and depravity. A fifteen-year-old sleeps best when he's had his head freshly filled with atrocities."

"I'll be sixteen this month," said Meto, wanting to remind us he was almost a man.

"There, you see," said Catilina. "Really, you're too protective, Gordianus. Well, then: first, the Vestal is stripped of her diadem and her linen mantle. Then she is whipped by the Pontifex Maximus, to whom, as head of the state religion, all the Vestals are directly accountable. After being whipped, the condemned Vestal is dressed like a corpse, laid in a closed litter, and carried through the Forum attended by her weeping kinfolk in a hideous parody of her own funeral. She is carried to a place just inside the Colline Gate, where a small vault is prepared underground, containing a couch, a lamp, and a table with a little food. An executioner guides her down the ladder into the cell, but he does not harm her, as her person is still sacred to the goddess Vesta and she cannot be killed outright. The ladder is drawn up, the vault sealed, the ground leveled. No man bears direct responsibility for taking her life, you see; the goddess Vesta claims her."

"You mean she's buried alive?" said Meto.

"Exactly! In theory, if the court has been mistaken and the Vestal is innocent, the goddess Vesta will refuse to take her life, and she'll remain alive in her tomb indefinitely. But since the vault is sealed, the opportunity to redeem herself is merely a technicality. And surely Vesta would eventually take pity on the girl and snuff out her life whether she was innocent or not, rather than let her live through eternity in a cold vault, alone and miserable."

Meto contemplated this idea with awed repulsion.

"Fortunately," said Catilina, "that is *not* what happened to the lovely Fabia. She is very much alive and still a Vestal, though I haven't spoken to her in years. We can thank your father for her salvation. Really, Gordianus, you *never* told this tale to your son? It's not bragging to simply tell the truth. But if Gordianus is too modest, I will tell it for him.

"Where was I? Ah, yes, in the House of the Vestals, in the middle of the night, alone with Fabia and a fresh corpse. The Virgo Maxima, who found us, was already implicated in a scandal herself and desperate to avoid another. She sent for help to Fabia's brother-in-law, a rising young advocate famed for his cleverness—Marcus Tullius Cicero. Yes, the consul himself, though who then could have foreseen his destiny? Cicero in turn sent for Gordianus. And it was Gordianus who discovered the murderer still lurking in the House of the Vestals when no one else could find him. It turned out that the assassin had miscalculated his opportunity to escape and was trapped in the courtyard when the gates were shut. He was hiding—can you believe it?—in the pool among the lily pads, breathing through a hollow reed. It was your father who noticed that the reed had moved from one place to another. Gordianus strode into the pool and pulled the man sputtering from the water. The assassin swung a knife. I leaped upon him. A moment later the man was impaled on his own blade. But before he died he confessed all—namely that my enemy Clodius had put him up to everything: sending the false note, luring me to the House of the Vestals, following me inside, and killing his confederate, so that I would be found not only in a dubious position but with blood on my hands in a sacred place."

"But there was a trial?" said Meto.

"Of sorts. The assassin was dead, so nothing could be proved against Clodius. Even so, with the biggest prude in

Rome to defend her honor—I mean young Marcus Cato, of course—Fabia was found innocent, and so was I. Clodius was so disgraced he fled to Baiae to wait for the scandal to blow over. He didn't have long to wait. That was the year the gladiator Spartacus began the great slave uprising, and the little matter of the Vestals was quickly forgotten in the wake of more momentous events.

"Alas, Meto, I fear I've disappointed you. The scandal was no scandal at all, you see, only a contrivance designed by my enemies to have me dishonored at best and at worst put to death. I cannot claim to be the man who deflowered a Vestal and lived to tell about it, for I never did such a thing. I merely prevailed over a trumped-up charge, thanks to the help of clever lawyers and an even cleverer man who called himself the Finder. Ironic, is it not, Gordianus, that it was Cicero who called on you to unravel the mystery? Or course it was his wife's half-sister Fabia whom he wished to save from ruin, not me. Even so, in those days Cicero and I were not yet enemies."

There followed a long silence. Tongilius was beginning to nod. So was Meto, despite his enthusiasm for the tale.

"Younger men require more sleep than their elders," said Catilina.

"Yes, off to bed with you, Meto."

He made no complaint, but rose and nodded respectfully to our guests before leaving. Tongilius followed him shortly thereafter, retiring to the room he was to share with Catilina.

The two of us sat in silence for a long moment. The night was warm and still. The lamps were beginning to sputter and sink. The sky above us was moonless and pierced by bright stars.

"Well, Gordianus, did I do justice to the tale and to your part in it?"

I paused for a long moment before I spoke. I stared up at the stars, not at Catilina. "I would say that you put the facts plainly enough."

"You sound dissatisfied."

"I suppose I still have my doubts about the matter."

"Doubts? Please, Gordianus, be frank."

"It always seemed odd to me that a man should spend so

much time and effort courting a young woman sworn to chastity, unless he had some ulterior motive."

"Misunderstood again—it is a curse that the gods have put upon me, that the face the world sees is seldom my true face, but often the very opposite. When my motives are purest, other men doubt me, and yet when my intentions slip from the path of virtue I find that other men flock to me with praise."

"And then, how did Clodius know that you would respond to that forged note from Fabia, unless he had evidence that the two of you were more than friends?"

"Another irony—quite often one's enemies are the best and truest judges of one's character. Clodius knew my sentimental heart and adventurous spirit. He devised the most forbidden lure he could imagine and then tempted me with it. Had I truly been Fabia's lover I would have sensed that the note was false."

"And again, I recall that in Cato's speech in Fabia's defense, he dwelt heavily upon the fact that when the Virgo Maxima rushed into the Vestal's room, the two of you were discovered completely dressed—"

"And don't forget that the assassin said likewise before he expired. Before killing his companion so as to leave a corpse, he had instructions from Clodius to wait until Fabia and myself were undressed so that we would be found that way. But as he himself declared, 'they would not take off their clothes!' He said it more than once, do you remember?"

"I do, and it caused me to wonder, for why did Clodius think you would take off your clothes in the first place, and in the second, it occurred to me that for a man and a woman to have intercourse, they need *not* take off their clothes, but merely rearrange them." I looked from the stars to Catilina, but the lamps had burned so low that his eyes were in shadow and I could not read his face. His lips seemed to curve into a smile, but perhaps I only imagined it.

"Really, Gordianus, you are as devious as any advocate. I'm glad it was that idiot Clodius who spoke against me at the trial, and not you, or else my defense would have been utterly demolished." He sighed. "Anyway, all of that is ancient history now, as dead as Spartacus, just a slightly lurid tale to quicken the pulse of a young man like your son."

"Yes, about Meto . . ."

"Do I hear another note of dissatisfaction in your voice, Gordianus?"

"If you are to stay in my house, I would prefer that you respect my authority as head of this household."

"Have I somehow offended you?"

"More than once you cast doubt on my judgment regarding my son, and you did it in front of Meto himself. I realize your manner is ironic, Catilina, but Meto is likely to take your comments seriously. I ask that you refrain from ridiculing me, however good-naturedly. I will not have my authority undermined."

I kept my voice even and tried to speak without undue passion. There followed a long silence. I could see that Catilina's face was turned up to the stars, his jaw clenched. That he failed to reply seemed to indicate that he was angry and was biting his tongue. If I had offended him, I could not regret it.

Then he laughed. It was a low, quiet laugh, gentle and without harshness. The laughter faded and after a moment he spoke. "Gordianus—but no, you will think I am ridiculing you again. Even so, I must say it. How could I undermine your authority with the boy? Any fool could see that he worships you. Such devotion is like a rock, and my teasing is like a pebble cast against it. Even so, I apologize and ask your forgiveness. I am a guest in this house, here upon your sufferance, and I have behaved as if I were in my own home, without regard to your sensibilities. That is rudeness on my part, not to mention a failure of wisdom. I meant no offense. You see, I was serious when I said that men mistake my meaning. If only I could learn to do the opposite of what I intend to do, then everyone would be pleased with me at last."

I stared at him in the darkness, not knowing whether to be charmed or offended, whether to laugh at his wit or fear him. "If I distrust you, Catilina, perhaps it's because you speak in riddles."

"Men offer riddles when they cannot offer solutions."

"You're cynical, Catilina."

He laughed softly, this time with a touch of bitterness.

"Against the insoluble ugliness of life, one man takes refuge in flippant cynicism while another takes refuge in smug certainty. Which man is Cicero and which is me? No, don't answer." He was silent for a moment, then said, "I understand you've had a falling-out with Cicero."

"I've always had my differences with him. I never care to work for him again." It was not exactly a lie.

"You're not the only one who's become disillusioned with our consul. For years Cicero paraded himself as the fiercely independent champion of reform, a battler against the status quo, the outsider from Arpinum. But when it came his time to stand for consul, he found that I had the constituency for reform already in my hand, so he moved without a moment's hesitation into the opposite camp and made himself a puppet for the most reactionary elements in Rome. It was a transformation to make a man's head spin, yet he changed his rhetoric without a stutter or even a pause for breath! Oh, others were surprised, but I saw it coming from the first days of his campaign. A man who will do anything to get himself elected is a man without principles, and Cicero is the worst. All his old supporters with any integrity—like young Marcus Caelius—have abandoned him, just as he abandoned them to go sit in the lap of the oligarchy. The ones who've stayed with Cicero have no more principles than he does. They simply bend toward power as flowers bend toward the light. The last year in Rome has been a farce—"

"I've been away from Rome the whole time."

"But surely you visit the city?"

"Not at all."

"I can't blame you. The place is full of vipers, and worse than that, it's become a city without hope. The oligarchs have won. You can see the resignation on people's faces. A small group of families own and control everything, and they will do anything not to share their wealth. There was some chance for reform with the Rullan legislation, but Cicero of course saw to it that those reforms came to nothing—"

"Please, Catilina! Surely Caelius told you that talk of politics is like a bee sting to me—I swell up and break out in welts if I'm exposed to it."

Though his eyes were in shadow I could see that Catilina

regarded me steadily. "You're a strange man, Gordianus. You invite me, a candidate for consul, into your home, yet you cannot abide to speak of Rome's fate."

"You said yourself that you came here to escape from politics, Catilina."

"So I did. Yet I think that I am not the only one who poses riddles here." He sat unmoving in the darkness, watching me.

Perhaps Catilina trusted me no more than I trusted him, but which of us had the greater cause to be suspicious? I might have asked him outright what he knew of the headless body that had been left in my barn, but if he was responsible he would hardly have admitted it, and if he knew nothing and said as much I wouldn't have believed him. Still, I thought that I might trap him by laying my words in a circle around him and then pulling them tight.

"The riddle you posed earlier was too easy, Catilina. But I find myself still puzzled by one that Marcus Caelius posed when he visited me last month. He said that you invented the riddle, so surely you can tell me the solution."

"What riddle was that?"

"It was posed in this fashion: 'I see two bodies. One is thin and wasted, but has a great head. The other body is big and strong—*but has no head at all*!' "

Catilina did not respond immediately. From the shifting shadows on his brow and around his mouth I thought I saw him frowning. "Caelius told you this riddle?"

"Yes. Contemplating it has caused me considerable distress." I spoke only the truth.

"Strange that Caelius should have repeated it to you."

"Why? Is the riddle a secret?" I thought of clandestine meetings, messages sent in code, oaths sworn and sealed by drinking from a cup of blood.

"Not exactly. But riddles have their proper time and place, and the time to pose that riddle has not yet arrived. Strange . . ." He rose from his couch. "I'm suddenly weary, Gordianus. The journey has caught up with me, and I think I must have eaten too much of Congrio's cooking."

I roused myself, intending to show him the way, but he was already leaving the courtyard. "Don't worry about waking me in the morning," he said over his shoulder. "I'm an early riser. I shall be up even before the slaves."

Only moments after he left, the last of the lamps sputtered and went out. I reclined on my couch in the darkness, wondering why Catilina would not supply the answer to his own riddle.

Later that night I woke up in my bed beside Bethesda. Nature called.

I rose to my feet. I didn't bother to reach for a cloak to cover myself. The night was warm.

I stepped into the hallway and headed for the privy; Lucius Claudius, never one to stint himself of luxury, had blessed the house with indoor plumbing, just like a city house in Rome. The hallway ran alongside one wall of the courtyard. Through one of the little windows I glimpsed a dark shape on one of the couches and gave a start.

It was a body. Of that I was instantly certain, though in the dim starlight I could tell little about it. I stared at the stiff, unmoving shape. I felt a tremor of fear, and then a hot flush of anger that I should feel such fear in my own home.

Then the body stirred. It was a living man.

He turned his head slightly, and in the dim starlight I discerned the profile of Catilina. He lay upon the couch with his hands folded on his stomach, not making a sound. I would have thought he was asleep, except that his eyes were open. He appeared to be lost in thought.

I watched him for a long moment, then silently continued on my way. I stepped into the privy and did my business as quietly as possible. On the way back to my bedroom I stopped and watched him again. He had not moved.

Suddenly he sprang up from the couch. I thought he must have seen or heard me, but he took no notice of me. He began to pace slowly around the small courtyard, circling the pool, his arms crossed and his head bowed. After a while he fell back onto the couch and covered his face with one hand, dropping his other arm limply to the floor. His posture suggested deep exhaustion or despair, but from his lips came neither snoring nor weeping, not even a sigh, only the steady breathing of a wakeful man. Catilina brooded.

I returned to my room and pressed myself beside Bethesda, who stirred but did not wake. I feared that I would brood and fret like Catilina, but Morpheus came quickly and pulled me deep into the black recesses of forgetful sleep.

ELEVEN

I arose the next morning expecting to find Catilina still abed, despite his claim to be up early, but when I looked into the room he shared with Tongilius I saw two vacant couches with their coverlets neatly folded. When had he slept—or had he slept at all?

Perhaps, I thought with a glimmer of hope, he had grown restless and departed altogether. But one of the kitchen slaves informed me that he and Tongilius had eaten an early breakfast of bread and dates and then had gone out, taking their horses from the stable and leaving word that they would return before noon.

Very well, I thought, the less I have to entertain him, and the less he disrupts the routine of the farm, the better. At least he possessed good manners, as a true patrician should. As a house guest, he could have been much worse.

I took Aratus and Meto and went down to the stream to continue our calculations for building the water mill. For a while, engaged in the work, I forgot about Catilina completely, but then I began to have new misgivings. He had gone out with Tongilius, he had said, but to where and for what purpose? As my guest he was free to wander wherever he liked on the farm, but the two of them had taken their horses with them, and the kitchen slave thought she had seen them headed in the direction of the Cassian Way. Catilina had said he would be back by noon, and therefore could not have gone far; what sort of business could he have nearby, and with whom? I did not like the idea of his using my home as a base for whatever dealings he might have in the vicinity. Nothing of the sort had been mentioned by Marcus Caelius, who had promised that Catilina would visit me only to retire from the city or to rest on his way north. I considered confronting Catilina with my displeasure. It seemed a reasonable thing to do, except that I kept remembering Nemo.

I tried to push such thoughts from my mind and to concentrate on the work at hand, but I was distracted and grew more and more irritated. Meto's obvious disinterest did not help. I had hoped that the water mill would spark his enthusiasm, and one of the reasons I wanted to pursue the project was to give him a practical lesson in building, but he had no head for figures or geometry and grew bored and restless at being asked to hold pieces of string and take a few steps in one direction or the other. Later in the morning he asked to be excused to return to the house, saying the heat was making him dizzy, and I let him, though I suspected he was more bored than faint.

I myself was clumsy with the siting instruments and kept giving Aratus the wrong figures to write down, then correcting myself. Each time he erased the wax tablet with the back of his hand, the gesture grew more curt. I was about to reprimand him, but then he shut his eyes and used the other side of his hand, to wipe the sweat from his brow. The sun was directly overhead. Perhaps it was only the heat that was setting our nerves on edge.

"We'll stop now, until it's cooler," I told him. Aratus nodded and hurriedly gathered up the instruments, then departed for the house. Clearly, he was as tired of my manner as I was of his, and glad to have a break from me. I sighed, wondering if any farmer could succeed on such bad terms with his foreman. For an instant I wondered if I should replace Aratus, but the thought was too much to take on. I fetched my battered tin cup and went down to the stream to scoop up a drink of cool water. I drank it down slowly, then scooped up another cup and splashed it on my face. The day was going to be intolerably hot.

I heard a noise, and turned to see Meto stepping from behind an oak tree. From the smile on his face, the respite from geometry had lifted his spirits considerably. Then I saw the man who followed him. I gave a start, thinking another stranger had appeared on the farm. I stared, puzzled, then realized what had changed.

"Your beard, Catilina!"

He reached up and stroked his naked jaw, laughing softly. "Would you share your cup? Just walking here from the stable has given me a thirst."

I handed him the cup. While he knelt beside the flowing water, I sat down on a broad, flat rock in the shade. He drank his fill, then joined me on the rock. Meto slipped off his sandals and went wading in the shallow water to cool his feet.

"Tongilius did it for me this morning," Catilina said, stroking his jaw again. "Not a bad job, considering the poor light."

"He shaved you before you went out?"

He nodded. When had he slept?

"But the look was so distinctive, Catilina." I meant the words to be ironic, considering that I had seen the same beard on every recent visitor from the city.

"The first to adopt a certain fashion should be the first to abandon it," said Catilina glibly.

"The voters will think you are changeable and frivolous."

"The voters who know me will know better. The voters who despise me would like to think I could be changed, and thus should be comforted, or at least disarmed. And I don't worry that anyone in Rome, whether friend or enemy, considers me frivolous." He frowned for a moment, then turned up his chin and squinted at the bright leafy canopy above. "It was this foray into the countryside that did it. Like a plunge into cold water. New surroundings give a man inspiration to put on a new face. I feel ten years younger, and a thousand miles away from Rome. You should try it, Gordianus."

"Moving a thousand miles from Rome?"

"No," he laughed, "shaving your beard." Meto, wading in the stream, was paying no attention to our conversation. Even so, Catilina leaned toward me and lowered his voice. "Women like it when a man first grows a beard, or when he shaves one. It's the change that's exciting, you understand. Imagine Bethesda's reaction if you should suddenly appear in her bed with a naked face. There, you see, you're smiling. You know I'm right."

I did smile, and even laughed a little, for the first time that

day. I was suddenly at ease, as I realized with surprise. The
change in my mood was because of the cool shade and flowing water, the respite from Aratus's scowl and from the sight
of Meto's delight in the stream, I told myself. It had nothing
to do with Catilina's smile.

Meto emerged from the stream and joined us. He stood
first on one leg and then on the other, drying his feet and
slipping on his sandals. With the stream behind him and the
sunlight glinting on the hair that hung over his face, he looked
like one of those statues of unself-conscious youth that the
Greeks so admire. Impossible, I thought, that he was almost
a man. He was still too pretty, too boyish. Having grown up
myself without the benefit of beauty, I was never quite sure
whether his good looks were an advantage or not. Certainly
men, like Pompey, not to mention Catilina, had used their
looks to further their careers; Marcus Caelius was of the same
mold. On the other hand, Cicero was proof that plainness was
no disadvantage. And for a man of no great means or ambition, as for a woman of the same station, beauty could be as
much a disadvantage as a boon, attracting the wrong sorts of
patrons and leading a young man to rely too much on his
charm. I only wished that Meto had a more serious side to
his nature, and a bit more common sense.

Meto finished fastening his sandals and sat down beside
me. His smile was so open and honest that I felt foolish for
worrying over him. The sunlight, where it pierced through the
leafy canopy, was warm on my flesh. A breeze gently
strummed the high grass alongside the stream. The world was
silent except for the splashing of water, the singing of birds,
and the faint, distant bleating of a goat which echoed off the
hillside. Meto was as well equipped to find his way in the
world as I had been, if not more so. What doors could I have
opened with his looks and his charm, and what did it matter
if he had no head for adding figures? I sighed. Was there
nothing so simple that I could not find an excuse to brood
over it?

"Well?" Meto said, looking at me expectantly.

"Well, what?"

Catilina drew back a little, pursing his lips. "I suspect your
son thinks we've been discussing another matter. You see, I

told him at the stable that if you had no objection—"

"The mine, Papa, that abandoned silver mine up on Mount Argentum," said Meto, suddenly excited.

"What are you talking about?" I looked from one to the other.

Catilina cleared his throat. "Yesterday, as we rode up the Cassian Way, I happened to notice the trail on the mountainside to the east. Later I asked your foreman about it. Aratus told me that the mountain belongs to your neighbor and that the trail leads up to an old silver mine. This morning Tongilius and I rode over to have a look. I have a friend in the city, you see, who believes he's found ways to extract ore even from mines that others have deemed exhausted. One is always looking for such opportunities."

"And did you see the place?"

"Only the goatherds' house, which is not far from the road. We spent a pleasant hour talking to the chief goatherd, who appears to be in charge of the place. He was perfectly agreeable about showing us the mine, but he asked us to come back later in the day, after the worst of the heat. Apparently the way is quite arduous. Tongilius and I were talking about it when we returned our horses to the stable, and Meto overheard. He asked to come with us; it wasn't my idea. I told him he would have to ask for your permission."

"May I, Papa?" said Meto.

"Meto, you know how things stand between Gnaeus Claudius and myself. It's out of the question that you should go exploring on his property."

"Ah, yes, Gnaeus Claudius, the owner of the estate," said Catilina. "But there's no problem there, as Gnaeus is away. The goatherd says he's ridden up north to have a look at another property, a place more suitable for farming. It seems he's quite willing to rent or sell his property here, as he believes the mine to be worthless and he has no taste for goatherding. It's a farm he wants, and so the mountain is available. Thus the goatherd is quite happy to show it to me. I'm sure there would be no objection if Meto came along."

"And does the goatherd know who you are?"

Catilina raised an eyebrow. "Not exactly. I introduced Tongilius, and myself I introduced as Lucius Sergius. There are quite a few Lucius Sergii around, after all—"

"Though not many with the cognomen Catilina at the end."

"I daresay not."

"And only one with the name Catilina who also wears a chin-strap beard."

"Not even one of those anymore," said Catilina, stroking his chin. "Very well, Gordianus, I was not completely forthright with the man, but he's only a slave, after all. If I wish to be incognito here in the country, surely that doesn't surprise you. Didn't Marcus Caelius tell you that I would prefer anonymity while I'm here? I should think you'd prefer it that way yourself."

"My neighbors are no partisans of yours, Catilina. Quite the opposite. Indeed, I strongly doubt that Gnaeus Claudius would deal with you if he knew who you are, so you'll only be wasting your time going to have a look at his mine."

"Now, Gordianus, one hardly has to like a man to do business with him; that's what lawyers are for. Besides, it's not I who would make an offer on the property. I have no money at all, only debts. I'm interested in the mine for my friend, and Tongilius would do the dealing. But seriously, Gordianus, we're far ahead of ourselves. The matter at hand is quite simple. I intend to have a look at the old mine, and Meto would dearly like to come with me. He tells me he's never seen a mine. His education is vital to you, I know, and unless one happens to be impossibly rich or else a wretched slave, how many men have the opportunity to walk through such a place? It will be an edifying experience."

I thought it over, glumly. Meto smiled at me expectantly and drew his eyebrows together. Had I spoiled him so shamelessly that he would try to charm his own father to sway his judgment? What sort of Roman father was I? The question stiffened my spine, but only for a moment. I was no more a typical Roman father than my family was a typical Roman family. Convention and piety were clothing for other men but had always fitted me poorly. I sighed and shook my head and was about to relent when the vision of Nemo loomed up before me.

"Out of the question," I said.

"But, Papa—"

"Meto, you know better than to contradict me, especially in front of a guest."

"Your father is right," said Catilina. "His decision is all that counts. The mistake is mine for not thinking the matter through and putting the question properly. What I should have said was this: Would *you* like to accompany me, Gordianus, and to bring your son along with you?"

I opened my mouth at once to answer, but some intuition told me that no matter how strenuously I objected or how many arguments I marshaled, in the end my answer would be the same, and so why waste my breath? I shut my mouth, considered for a very brief moment, and, feeling Meto's eyes on me, said simply, "Why not?"

A man at my time of life understandably grows cautious and staid, I told myself, but even virtues can become vices when too rigidly adhered to. Occasionally a man must do the unexpected, the unforeseen, the uncalled-for. And so I found myself later that afternoon, after the heat had begun to dissipate, riding a little way north on the Cassian Way to the gate that opened onto the property of my neighbor Gnaeus Claudius. The gate was a simple affair, meant only to keep goats from wandering out onto the highway. Tongilius dismounted, threw the bolt, and swung it open.

"You need not even introduce yourself," Catilina said as we rode onto the rough path beyond the gate. "I'll simply say you're with me. The goatherd will be satisfied."

"Perhaps," I said. "Still, it seems less than honest for me to go snooping about on Claudian land without announcing myself."

"They would do the same to you," said Catilina simply. Someone had already done so, I thought, remembering Nemo.

The foothills of Mount Argentum loomed abruptly before us. The way became progressively steeper. The earth became more rocky and the trees more dense until we found ourselves in a forest strewn here and there with boulders. Animals rustled in the underbrush, disturbed by our passing, but we saw no people at all. Around a bend in the road, at the crest of a steep ridge, we arrived at the goatherds' house.

It was a rustic affair, made of hewn stones and a thatched

roof without adornment. The inside was a single room shared,
if my nose was correct, by all the goatherds together, some
ten or more to judge by the blankets piled against the walls
where they slept. They were absent now, except for their
chief, who lay upon a couch with splintered legs and thread-
bare cushions. The couch was of Greek design and workmanship, finely made but too worn to be worth restoring. It
was the kind of expensive object masters are apt to pass on
to a slave when the thing's beauty is used up, but not its
utility. The goatherd seemed quite happy with it. He snored
softly and batted a fly from his nose.

Catilina roused him by gently shaking his shoulder. The
man blinked the sleep from his eyes and sat up. He reached
for a skin of wine, swallowed a mouthful, and cleared his
throat. "So you came back after all, Lucius Sergius," he said.
"Just to see an old hole in the ground. There's not much to
see, as I told you. Still, for three sesterces . . ." He looked up
at Catilina and cocked his head.

"It seems I remember promising you two sesterces," said
Catilina. "But no matter. You'll be paid."

"And who are they?" The goatherd stroked his grizzled
chin and squinted at our silhouettes in the doorway. "Your
friend Tongilius I met this morning, but not this man, nor the
boy beside him."

"Friends of mine," said Catilina. He moved so that a jin-
gling sound was produced by the little bag of coins within
his tunic.

"Oh, friends of yours are friends of mine!" said the goatherd heartily. He raised the wineskin and squeezed a long
draft of wine between his lips, then stood up and wiped his
mouth. "Well, what are we waiting for? Let me fetch my mule
and we'll begin."

The goatherd's name was Forfex, so called, I imagine, for his
proficiency at shearing his flock. His hair and beard were gray
and his skin looked as brown and tough as old leather. Despite
his age he moved with the wiry agility of a slave who has
spent his life on rocky hillsides, learning to be as surefooted
as the goats in his charge. He struck me as a naturally cheerful
fellow, sitting atop his little mule and humming a song. The

coins in his bag and the wine in his belly had put him in an especially good mood.

The way led at first beneath a high canopy of trees that grew alongside a deep, rugged streambed on our left-hand side. The stream was dry, or nearly so; little ponds of stagnant water appeared here and there among the tumbled boulders. We proceeded toward the south and shortly came to a juncture where a little bridge crossed the ravine and led to the main house. Through the trees and rocks I caught glimpses of a rustic two-story structure set against a steep hillside. Chickens and dogs surrounded the place. The hounds, smelling us across the ravine, roused themselves and began to bark. The more energetic ones ran to and fro, throwing up clouds of dust and causing the chickens to flutter and cluck. Forfex shouted at the dogs to be quiet. To my surprise, they obeyed.

We did not take the bridge but rode on, leaving the house behind. The way became steeper and steeper; the forest became more and more dense. At length we came to what appeared to be a dead end. Only when we entered the little clearing was I able to see the narrow passage that led away to the left through a bower of low branches.

"We'll have to dismount here," said Forfex.

"This is the path that leads to the mine?" asked Catilina.

"Yes."

"But how can it be so narrow? Surely at one time there must have been a great traffic of men and beasts upon it."

"At one time, yes, but not for many years," said Forfex. "Once it was practically a road, as broad as two men laid head to head. But when the mine failed there was no more reason to use the path, except for driving goats. Stop using a path and you see what happens—the woods reclaim it. It's still passable, yes, but not on horseback. You'll need to dismount and leave your horses here."

As I was tying the reins to a branch, I noticed another path that opened into the woods. It was even more overgrown, so much so that I might have missed seeing it altogether. I stared into the shadowy undergrowth, trying to make out its course, then realized that Catilina was standing behind me, looking over my shoulder.

"Another path," he said to me in a low voice. "Where do

you suppose it leads?" Then he called Forfex over. "Is this another pathway?"

The old goatherd nodded. "Or used to be. Nobody uses it at all, so far as I know, except perhaps to go looking for a lost kid."

"Where does it lead?"

"Down to the Cassian Way, if I remember correctly. Yes, pretty much straight down the mountain toward the south and west. It used to let out on the highway not far from the gate to Claudia's farm. That way you could send a slave from Claudia's house all the way up to this clearing and on up to the mines without his having to go up north as you did and enter by the main gate. But the path hasn't been cleared in years and years. It may be blocked by fallen branches and stones, for all I know; we get some fierce storms up here on the mountain in the winter, blowing over trees and setting off landslides. It takes many a slave to keep the pathways clear."

"Then one would pass this pathway on the ride up from Rome, before coming to the main entrance?" said Catilina.

"Oh, certainly. I daresay that's another reason it was built, so that slaves bought at market in the city could be driven up to the mine as directly as possible. It's a very steep path, you see, and very rough—I remember taking it once when I was a boy. A road fit only for mine slaves, too steep for horses; no one would take it by choice so long as there was an easier way. But as I say, it's been disused for many years. I doubt you can see much evidence these days of where it used to branch off from the Cassian Way."

Catilina nodded. Forfex turned away, to tend to his mule. Under his breath, I thought I heard Catilina murmur, "Good, very good."

TWELVE ·

WE proceeded on foot. The narrow path was so steep that in places the stones underfoot had been cut into steps. Within the woods the air was still and hot, but the shade at least provided protection from the lowering sun. I found myself breathing hard and struggling to keep up. Meto seemed not to suffer at all from the heat and the steepness; he would run ahead of the party, double back, and run on again. Tongilius likewise showed no discomfort. But they were both young, I told myself, while Catilina was nearly my own age. Yet he seemed not to suffer at all. He picked up a fallen limb to use as a staff, sang a marching song under his breath, and kept up a steady rhythm. Where did he find such energy, especially without a full night's sleep?

While on the main path, we had moved away from the stream on our left, but now we seemed to be converging with it again, for I began to hear the sound of trickling water. To ascend much higher we would have to cross the stream eventually. I wondered what sort of state the bridge would be in. Given the general condition of the path, I feared it might be no more than a rope wound between tree trunks on the opposing banks. The sound of trickling water grew louder and more insistent.

But there was no bridge. Instead, we came to a vertical stairway of sheer rock, some thirty or more steps cut into the solid stone. Meto ascended first, running up the steps with the sure-footedness of a goat. Tongilius followed him, and then Catilina, who planted his staff in the crevices between each step and pulled himself up by it. Our guide, out of breath, allowed me to pass him. By the time I reached the top my heart was pounding and my brow was covered with sweat.

The steps emerged into a clearing above a high waterfall. Here the stream flowed across a wide, flat bed of rock cut with fingerlike rivulets. We hardly got our sandals wet crossing to the other side. While I scooped up a handful of water to cool my face and wet my lips, Meto scurried to the edge of the cliff, where the water gathered against a lip of rock before spilling over. He picked his way among stones covered with treacherous moss and peered over the abyss. He looked so slight standing against the empty sky that I imagined a puff of wind could blow him over the edge. I followed after him and grabbed his tunic.

"But, Papa, look!"

The tops of high trees shivered below us. The slope of the mountain reared on our right, but to the north the view was wide open. I could see the Cassian Way disappearing into the dusty horizon, its paving stones shimmering like a white ribbon. Away to the west the sun was a bloodred globe hovering above the dark hills. High trees obscured the view of my farm, but I could see quite clearly the ridge where I sometimes retreated and talked with Claudia.

"Yes," I said, "a pretty view."

"No, Papa, at the foot of the waterfall!"

The lip of rock made it impossible to look down without leaning over the edge. I stepped cautiously forward and peered downward. Heights have never particularly intimidated me, but the sheer drop made me catch my breath. The waterfall ended some thirty feet below, where the thin trickle spilled into a shallow pond covered with green scum. The pond was ringed by jagged boulders, and the boulders by high trees with thick, bark-covered roots that coiled among the stones and disappeared in the water. But it was not the stones or the trees that caused me to shiver. It was the skeletons.

Some were all in pieces scattered amid the rocks—a splintered rib cage here, a broken skull there, and farther away a leg bone or a bit of spine. Others were very nearly intact and immediately recognizable as the remains of a whole body, as if a man had been wedged amid the rocks and then been blasted by the gods until only his bones remained. Altogether I saw many more scattered bones among the roots and rocks than I could count.

Forfex, having at last made his way up the steps, walked

up to us, huffing and puffing. He peered over and saw what we were looking at.

"Oh, yes," he said. "You'll see plenty more like them before we're done."

"What do you mean?"

"Plenty more bones."

"The bones of men?"

"What else does a mine owner use to work the pits?" He shrugged. "I suppose you might see the remains of a goat here and there, but goats are generally more surefooted—and if one falls and breaks its neck, you go after it and fetch the carcass so you can eat it, don't you? Whereas the body of a dead slave isn't much worth going after, is it? You might break your own neck hopping from rock to rock and end up like one of these," he laughed. He uncorked the wineskin slung across his shoulder, then sucked at the spout.

"You mean all these men fell?"

He shrugged. "Some of them, probably. A man carries a heavy load of silver up out of the mines and down the hill, comes to this place, and then has to cross the water—it's higher than this, most times of the year. Well, you can see how he might stagger a bit and lose his balance. And then of course this stream drains the whole of the slope below the trail up ahead. A man falls down the hillside and breaks his neck, the vultures get to him first, but then the rains come and wash him down. A few years later, after a big storm, you'll see his skull come bobbing along on the water and shooting over the waterfall." He laughed again.

I looked at his seamed, leathery face. At least half the teeth were missing from his grin. It was no mystery that he should laugh at such an image. Forfex was a slave himself, at the mercy of his master and with no means to escape his fate. To such a man, another slave's misfortune is only a measure of his own good fortune.

"And then of course there were those who were pushed," he said.

"Deliberately?"

He mimed a shoving motion, pressing both palms flat against an invisible phantom at the cliff's edge.

"Murdered?" I said.

"Executed. I remember seeing it once when I was a very young boy and happened to come this way with my flock. That was back in the days when young master Gnaeus's grandfather was still alive and running the mine, just before it was finally closed for good. It was a way he had of punishing the troublemakers, you see. Slaves sold for the mines, they're mostly murderers and thieves, aren't they? The scum of the earth with nothing to lose—the mines are their death sentence, everybody knows that. So a master has to wield a heavy hand to keep them in line. Whips and manacles go only so far. You've still got the wild ones who just won't behave, or the lazy ones who won't carry their load. So the old master would make a public punishment of it. The strong-armers would line up the misbehavers on this very spot and push them over the edge while the others watched. Sort of an example, to show the rest that things could be even worse if they didn't do as they were told."

He took another swallow of wine and shook his head. "And then, in his later years, the old master was a little crazy. It runs in the family, you know. The mine was running out of ore, and he kept blaming the slaves for not digging deep enough. What he needed was a wizard to turn worthless rock into silver, and not a bunch of broken-back slaves. But the slaves took the blame, and the punishments happened more and more often until they were a regular event. A lot of slaves were pushed over this cliff in the final years. Then the old master took sick. The mine was finally shut down. Well, thank the gods I was born to be a goatherd and not a miner, eh?"

We stood for a moment, gazing down at the scattered bones. Forfex turned to go, but Meto clutched the sleeve of his tunic.

"But the lemures!" he said.

The old slave gave a shudder and pulled his tunic free. "What of them?"

"The spirits of the dead—with so many bodies left unpurified, neither burned nor buried, surely their lemures have never been put to rest. They must be everywhere around us."

"Of course they are. But they were slaves in life, broken and weak. Why should they be any more powerful in death?"

"But in life they were murderers and—"

"You're a citizen, young fellow, and besides that you're quick and strong. What have you to fear from the tired, broken lemures of dead slaves? Besides, it's still daylight. At night's when they stir, rising like mist from the earth. They come here and play with their old bones, tossing each other's skulls like balls and using their finger bones for dice."

"You've seen them?" said Meto.

"Well, not with my own eyes. One of the other goatherds, the mad one who can't sleep at night, he comes here sometimes and keeps company with the lemures, or says he does. Oh, no, you wouldn't catch me on the mountainside after dark." He squinted toward the lowering sun. "Come, let's hurry and see the mine, since that's what you came for."

Beyond the waterfall the way became even more arduous. The trail broke out of the trees and onto a bare, rocky hillside without shade. As Forfex had said, the slope was spotted here and there with human bones, as if we crossed an ancient battlefield. The narrow path coiled back and forth on itself like a snake. Up and up we went, until each step became a greater struggle than the one before. In the full blaze of noon, such a trip would have been enough to cause a strong man's heart to burst.

We were rewarded with a truly spectacular view, quite dwarfing the view I so treasured from my ridge. Far below I saw my farm laid out like a picture, surrounded by the farms of Claudia and her cousins and other farms, hills, and forests beyond. The ridge that separated my land from Claudia's looked quite small, like a fold in a blanket. The stream that ran between my land and Publius's land was a thin green band with a glint of silver here and there where a glimpse of water broke through the dense trees. The Cassian Way stretched out of sight to the north and south. It occurred to me that so long as we could see all these places, we ourselves could be seen from below by anyone with sharp enough eyes.

We traversed a bare shoulder of the mountain and dipped into a hollow, shaded from the sun at last and no longer visible to anyone in the world below. Ragged trees grew up around us, and fallen stones blocked the trail. The path took us deeper and deeper into the hollow, to the very heart of the mountain. At last we stepped around a boulder and saw the gaping black pit of the mine.

The entrance was smaller than I had expected, hardly taller than a man, and so narrow that no more than two men could pass through at one time. The scaffolding that had once surrounded it was in ruins, the broken timber lying about in pieces. Rusted picks, chisels, and hammers lay abandoned on the ground, along with cast-off manacles. Here and there flowers grew up through the rusted chains.

Beneath us the ground fell steeply away toward the winding stream below. Down the rugged hillside was strewn a great mass of bones, mixed in with the tailings from the mine to form a talus of crushed rock and bone. Even here whole skeletons had been preserved, and skulls stared up from jagged crevices in the stone.

"Have you ever seen a mine in operation?" asked Catilina, so close behind me that I gave a start.

"No."

"I have." His face was somber in the soft light, with no hint of a smile. "You can't really understand the value of a precious metal until you've seen its true worth at the source—the agony and death required to extract it from the earth. Tell me, Gordianus, when does the weight of a hundred men equal less than a pound?"

"Oh, Catilina, not a riddle . . ."

"When they are stripped of their flesh and weighed against a single cup made of pure silver. Imagine all those bones down there gathered up and stacked high upon a great scale. How much silver would it take to strike the balance? A handful, no more than that. Think of it the next time you press a silver cup to your lips."

He turned toward Forfex. "At least it should be cooler inside the mine. Tongilius, you brought the torches? Good. Are you coming with us, Gordianus?"

I had no particular interest in seeing a hole in the ground and would have preferred to sit for a while and catch my breath, but it struck me that an abandoned mine could be a dangerous place, especially for a fifteen-year-old boy. "Yes," I said wearily, "I'm coming."

Just within the entrance we came to a shoulder-high wall

made of stone. "Good for keeping out goats," Forfex explained. And grown men, I thought, though when it came my turn to step into his hands and scurry over the wall, I did so without complaining, following the examples of Catilina and Tongilius. Meto gave Forfex a boost, and then followed last, pulling himself up unassisted.

Only a little light seeped over the wall, just enough to illuminate our immediate surroundings with a vague twilight. Tongilius knelt and kindled one of his torches, then lit the other and handed it to me. The flames lit a low, narrow chamber that sloped steeply downward into darkness. In such a confined space the burning pitch smelled strongly.

Catilina took a torch from Tongilius and led the way. Meto followed, and then Forfex, with myself in the rear. "This is absurd," I whispered, thinking how easily one of us might trip and fall into the void. I imagined Meto breaking his neck, and cursed myself for allowing him to take part in such folly.

"We needn't go far," said Catilina. "I only want to have a look at the general condition of the mine. How far down does it go?"

"Quite a distance," Forfex said. "Consider that there used to be as many as two hundred slaves inside here at one time."

"Two hundred!" Meto said.

"So I was always told. Oh, this was quite an operation in the old days. That's how young Master Gnaeus's ancestors made their fortune, from this silver mine. That's how they came to buy all the land for miles around. Now of course it's split up among the Claudian cousins, but at one time the mountain and all the land you could see from it made up a single great estate, or so they say. Watch your head, young man!"

Meto, straying from Catilina's lead, had nearly collided with a jagged fist of rock suspended from the ceiling. Forfex laughed. "I should have warned you. We call that one the miner's brains, partly because it looks a bit like a brain, all knobby and slick, but more because many a careless miner lost his brains against that stone! Made of something so hard they could never chisel it out, so there it stays, waiting to bash in the skull of any man who walks too close. If you look at it closely you can still see a coating of dried blood on it."

"It's no laughing matter," I said. "Come," I called ahead to Catilina, "you'll agree this is no place to bring a boy. The place is dangerous."

Catilina's laughter echoed from ahead, distorted and hollow as if he were calling from a well. "I'm beginning to wish I'd left you behind, Gordianus! Are you always so fussy and difficult? Have you no sense of adventure?"

I looked over my shoulder and saw that the opening had dwindled to a dismayingly small spot of gray light. The spot suddenly blinked shut. I opened my mouth and almost cried out, thinking that someone had covered it up. But by moving my head I was able to catch glimpses of light, and realized that because of a slight curve in the path the rock called the miner's brains had come between us and the entrance, blocking out the light. After a few more steps I lost sight of the entrance completely.

"How much farther are we going?"

"Oh, I think this may be far enough," said Catilina.

The path abruptly grew level and we found ourselves in what appeared to be a small, oval chamber hewn out of the solid rock. The air was musty but dry, cool but not chilly. The ground was flat underfoot. Low doorways had been carved out of the rock, leading in different directions.

"It's like a little room, underground," said Tongilius.

"Like the entrance to a maze," said Meto, "or the Labyrinth of the Minotaur!"

"This is only one of several such rooms in the mine," explained Forfex. "Without a guide, you'd need a map to find your way, or else be willing to spend a day wandering about. For that you'd need more than a couple of torches."

"Where does this passageway lead?" said Catilina, ducking beneath one of the rocky lintels.

"Careful, there," called Forfex. And under his breath, "Wouldn't you know, of all the passages he'd choose the most dangerous? Careful, please! They warned me from boyhood about going into that one. There's a sheer drop down into a deep pit. It's one of the oldest parts of the mine. You could easily fall!"

From beyond the narrow doorway, lit up with shivering shadows from Catilina's torch, there issued a sharp gasp of alarm. Tongilius hurried after him. "Quick, Gordianus, bring your torch!"

Together we wedged ourselves into the narrow passage. Meto pressed up against my back, peering over my shoulder, and behind me I heard the goatherd clucking his tongue.

"Lucius, what is it?" said Tongilius.

"See for yourself," said Catilina.

Ringing the pit was a ledge barely wide enough to stand on. The five of us pressed close together, shoulder to shoulder, gazing down. Forfex, who all that day had seemed so inured to the sight of human bones, gave a gasp of shock.

Catilina looked at him sidelong. "I thought you knew these mines?"

"Not this chamber. I told you, as a boy I was always warned away from this part of the mine. I always thought it was just a sheer drop into darkness."

"And so it would be, if it weren't for these, filling up the abyss." Catilina held his torch aloft. By its wavering light the skulls of the dead peered up at us, their empty eyes strangely animated by the flickering play of light and shadow.

"So many!" whispered Tongilius.

"I've never seen anything like it," I said.

"Nor have I," said Catilina.

We had seen many bones that day—at the foot of the waterfall, along the hillside, in the talus that spilled from the mine. But those sights were scant preparation for the vast pit heaped up with skeletons that we now saw below us. There were hundreds of them, perhaps many hundreds, for there was no way to tell how deep the pit was. Whatever dwelled in the cave had picked them perfectly clean, for they were as white as if they had been weathered in a streambed. The sheer number of them was staggering and somehow unreal, for without flesh the bones of the dead lose all identity, and one skull becomes like another, so that to see so many in one place numbs the senses. The meaning of such a thing cannot be comprehended at the moment, only in retrospect, for the mind cannot make sense of what overwhelms the eye.

The cave seemed very dark and our lights very small. The

torch in my hand sputtered and popped and let forth a powerful odor of burning pitch. "Where did they come from?" I asked.

"It must be . . ." Forfex frowned and rubbed his jaw. "There were always vague rumors of such a thing, but I never thought it happened here in the mine. I thought if it were true, the skeletons amid the tailings outside accounted for it."

"For what?" said Catilina.

"It was always said that when the mine was shut down, the master sold off the unwanted slaves to other mine owners or to galley owners down in Ostia. No slave is ever expected to leave a mine alive, so where do you sell a used mine slave, eh? But I remember hearing from some of the older goatherds that the old master didn't bother to try to sell the slaves at all, but got rid of them instead, every one. I never knew it happened here in the mine. They must have blocked up this narrow rim on either side of the passage and driven them through the door—"

At that moment something stirred among the bones. There was a rustling and a hollow, clanking noise, followed by an eerie noise almost like a groan. In the uncertain light of our torches the whole mass of bones seemed to heave and shift. A rat, I thought, and a gust of air from some hidden shaft. But Forfex thought otherwise.

"Oh, Pluto!" he shrieked. "The lemures!" He turned around, shoving so carelessly that Meto staggered and might have fallen into the pit had I not seized his arm.

"Lemures!" Forfex shrieked again, his voice echoing from the stone chamber. From the immediate terror in his voice it was impossible to tell whether he meant the things in the pit or whether he had encountered more lemures in the chamber without.

In a rush we retreated from the narrow stone shelf, pressing against one another in the narrow passageway and emerging into the antechamber. Catilina and I held our torches aloft, but the room was deserted. Forfex, never pausing in his flight, was far ahead of us. From the shaft down which we had descended we heard the echoey cry. "Lemures!" together with a hail of loosened gravel. "Lemures!" we heard again, and then a distant, sickening thud, followed by more tumbling gravel and then silence.

We stood stock-still and looked at one another, wondering what had become of Forfex. In the pale torchlight, every face appeared white and bloodless. Tongilius bit his lips. "You don't think it was really . . ."

"The miner's brains!" said Meto.

Catilina smiled faintly and arched an eyebrow. "Without a doubt." He held up his torch and led the ascent toward the exit. I sighed with relief at the first glimpse of daylight. A little farther up we came upon Forfex, not far from the protrusion of rock he had called the miner's brains. He was lying on his back, trying in vain to get up.

Tongilius and Meto lifted him to his feet and helped him stagger up the slope. His hair was matted with blood, and his face was covered with blood and dirt. In the lurid torchlight he looked like some sort of demon, tripping blindly about with his eyes pasted shut and his hands outstretched.

He was completely helpless, dazed and weakened by his injury and trembling from fear or shock. Eventually we managed to hoist him over the wall. Tongilius helped me over the wall, then followed.

It was Tongilius who tended to the goatherd's wound, splashing it with wine from the man's own wineskin, hushing his squeals of pain, and tearing a strip of cloth from the man's tunic to bind his head. The man who had led us up to the mine with such a bluff demeanor had a considerably different appearance descending. We took turns holding him up by his shoulders; he was able to put one foot ahead of the other, but seemed unable to steer himself.

Shadows began to loom. Crickets and cicadas began their twilight chirping. Forfex must have been a little delirious as well as groggy, for he kept starting back from the shadows and whimpering, "Lemures!" Perhaps he saw things that were not there, or perhaps, having had a close scrape with Pluto himself, his senses perceived the haunting spirits that the rest of us could not see. Those nearest to death, they say, have their eyes and ears opened to those already dead.

We came at last to the place where our horses were tied.

We left Forfex's mule behind, deeming it too slow. Instead, Catilina shared his own mount with Forfex, holding him upright in front of him. The man complained loudly of the pain in his head when we approached a gallop, then quieted and only occasionally whimpered the word "lemures!" at some passing pool of shadow or clump of rock.

A yellow light glowed at the open door of the goatherds' house, and from the pens behind it came the bleating of goats gathered for the night. Catilina and Tongilius dismounted and helped Forfex from the horse. A wide-eyed slave stuck his head around the edge of the doorway and peered at us quizzically, but instead of stepping out to greet us or help Forfex, the man quickly withdrew from sight. A moment later the reason for his timidity emerged from the doorway.

I had seen Gnaeus Claudius several times in the Forum during our litigation. He was a hard man not to recognize at once, with his frazzled wreath of red hair and his chinless neck. He was a tall, broad-shouldered fellow, and while he had evidently inherited whatever brawn there was in the family, he lacked all the charms of youth. His face was set in a perpetually sour expression, as if he resented the Fates for cheating him of any appealing qualities and was determined to make the most of his unappealing ones, such as his loud, grating voice.

"Forfex!" he shouted. "Where in Hades have you been?"

The goatherd relieved himself of Tongilius's support and staggered forward to meet his master, his head humbly bowed as if to show the wound he had received in the mine. "Master, I thought you would not be returning until—"

"And who are you?" said Gnaeus, staring hard at Catilina. There was a look in his eyes that indicated he could almost, but not quite, place Catilina's face.

"My name is Lucius Sergius," said Catilina. "I've come up from the city—"

"Sergius, eh?" said Gnaeus sourly. He spat on the ground and nodded grimly, acknowledging the presence of a fellow patrician. "And what have you been up to with my slave, trespassing on my property in my absence?"

"The goatherd was merely showing us the abandoned mine up on the mountainside. You see, I—"

"The mine? Why in Hades have you been snooping around my mine?"

"I thought that the property might possibly be for sale."

"Is that right? And you have a particular interest in silver mines?"

"I have an associate who does."

Gnaeus spat on the ground again. "Well, you had no business trespassing."

"Forfex assured me that in your absence he was authorized to—"

"Forfex is as worthless and smelly as his goats. 'Authorized,' my balls! No one goes snooping around my land when I'm not here. He knows better—don't you, Forfex? Don't flinch when I raise my hand to you! What, is that a jingle I hear?" He gave the old goatherd a hard shove. Forfex staggered back, covering his head with his hands.

"I do hear a jingle!" shouted Gnaeus. He tore at the slave's tunic and found the little bag of coins, looked inside and threw the three sesterces at Catilina's feet. "I'll thank you not to bribe my slaves! They're unruly enough as it is." He slapped Forfex across the face, hard enough to make the old goatherd stagger and fall.

"Gnaeus Claudius!" said Tongilius. "Can't you see the slave is already injured! He's bleeding!"

"And who are you, pretty boy?" said Gnaeus derisively. "Who are all these strangers that you've brought trespassing on my land, Lucius Sergius?" For the first time Gnaeus seemed to look at my face, and at Meto, but there was no hint of recognition. In the gathering gloom he could not see me well enough.

"Gnaeus Claudius," said Catilina, "my interest is completely legitimate. My associate in the city actively seeks out mines of all conditions, and pays well for properties in which he deems it worth his while to invest. I merely wished to have a cursory look at your mine. Had I known that the slave was forbidden to act on your behalf I would never have set foot on your land."

This speech seemed to mollify Gnaeus, who sucked in his cheeks and seemed to chew them. After a moment he said, "And what did you make of the mine, then?"

Catilina smiled. "I am encouraged."

"Yes?"

"I believe my associate may be interested."

"It's been closed for years."

"I know. But my associate owns engineers who can sometimes extract just a bit more from the earth even when a vein
seems exhausted. Any price he might offer would take the
condition of the mine into account. He would send out some
of his slaves to have a closer look before making up his
mind—if, of course, I recommend that it's worth his bother."

"Then you think the land might be worth—"

"Alas, Gnaeus Claudius, night gathers. I've had a long and
weary afternoon. The trip up to the mine is strenuous, as you
must know. I need a meal and my rest. Perhaps we can discuss this another time." Catilina mounted his horse, as did
Tongilius.

"You have a place to stay, then? If not—" said Gnaeus.

"Yes, a fine place, not too far away."

"Perhaps I should ride with you—"

"No need. We know the way. Meantime, I suggest you
have someone tend to the goatherd's head. He had a nasty
accident—not his fault at all. He was only doing his best to
accommodate me. His concern for your interest is commend-
able. It would be a pity to lose such a slave because a wound
he received in his master's service was not properly seen to."

We rode off, leaving Gnaeus to stare after us, a mingled
expression of greed and uncertainty on his face. Just before
we rounded a bend in the way, I looked around and saw him
raise his arm and strike the cowering goatherd square on the
head.

THIRTEEN

"GNAEUS Claudius—what an awful man!" said Catilina.
"Are all your neighbors so awful?"

"So I'm finding out. Though not all of them," I said, thinking of Claudia. "Is the water hot enough for you?"

"Quite."

"And you, Tongilius?"

"It's perfect."

"I can call one of the slaves to put more wood in the furnace . . ."

"Oh, no, any hotter and I should melt," sighed Catilina, letting himself sink into the tub until only his head was above the steaming water.

My old friend Lucius Claudius had outfitted his country house with many citified luxuries, among them baths complete with three rooms, one for the warm plunge, another for the hot plunge, and the third for the cool plunge. Generally, in summer, I found it too hot even at night to want to immerse myself in warm water; I preferred to do my bathing with a sponge and strigil down at the stream. It was Catilina who had suggested that the slaves might stoke the furnace housed between the kitchen and the baths and fill the marble tubs with heated water. My stiff legs and aching feet had agreed, and so, after a light dinner, we retired not to the atrium but to the baths instead. We stripped off our soiled tunics and began in the warm basin, then moved on to the adjoining room and immersed ourselves in the hot basin. Catilina and Tongilius took turns scraping the sweat from each other's backs with an ivory strigil.

Meto had not joined us, though I think he wanted to stay up and listen to the grown-ups' conversation. All his leaping from stone to stone and running ahead and back on the trail at last began to take its toll at dinner, and he was yawning and dozing on his couch even before the final course of diced onions arrived. When the meal was over, Bethesda roused him and sent him to his bed.

It was just as well, for I was not quite sure I wanted Meto displaying himself naked in Catilina's presence. In matters of the flesh, Catilina's appetites were said to be voracious and his self-restraint nonexistent, notwithstanding his version of the Vestal story. His standards, at least, were rigorous, to judge from the sight of Tongilius in the nude. The young man's sleek, well-knit athlete's physique was of the sort to make boys jealous and older men sadly nostalgic, or else lust-ful. As I discovered in the baths, he was one of those hand-

some, charming youths who became more haughty with their
clothes off than on. There was a trace of self-conscious preen-
ing in the way he lifted his well-muscled arms from the water,
raised his chin, stared into the middle distance and pushed
the shimmering hair back from his forehead, like a sculptor
smoothing and molding his own perfection.

Catilina seemed to approve of this gesture, for he watched
it intently. Though their eyes did not meet, they smiled at the
same moment, in such a way that I suspected that a secret
touch had been exchanged beneath the water.

Perhaps it was a signal, for a moment later Tongilius stood
up and stepped out of the basin. He wrapped himself in his
towel and shook the water from his hair.

"You won't be taking the cold plunge?" I asked.

"I prefer to cool off on my sleeping couch. The steam
rising from the flesh as it dries relaxes the muscles as well as
any masseur. It's a delicious way to fall asleep." He smiled
at me and then bent down until his cheek was almost touching
Catilina's. They said a few words to each other in whispers,
and then Tongilius departed.

"Have you known him long?" I said.

"Tongilius? For five years or so. Since he was Meto's age,
I imagine. A charming young man, don't you think?"

I nodded. The only light in the little room came from a
single lamp suspended from the ceiling by a chain. Its glow
was muted by the rising steam so that the room was filled
with a soft orange haze. The quiet gurgling of the pipes and
the gentle splashing of the water against the edge of the tub
were the only sounds. Hot water swirled about my naked flesh
so that I felt swallowed up by comfort. What had Catilina
said, that if the water were any hotter he would melt? I felt
as if I had melted already.

For a long time we lay at our opposite ends of the big
marble tub. Catilina closed his eyes. I gazed at the ephemeral
patterns made by the rising steam, like a series of dissolving
veils suspended in the darkness.

"The odd thing is, the silver mine just might be worth
buying."

"Are you serious?" I said.

"I'm always serious, Gordianus. Of course, all those bones

would have to be cleared out—too discouraging for the new workers. 'It doesn't do to dampen morale, even among mine slaves.' "

"You're quoting someone."

"Yes. My associate in the city, the one who buys abandoned mines and makes a good profit from them."

"Then there really is such a person?"

"Of course. Did you think I was lying to poor old Forfex?"

"Your friend in the city sounds familiar."

"He is hardly obscure."

"Marcus Crassus?"

Catilina opened his eyes to slits and arched an eyebrow. "Why, yes. You've solved a riddle, Gordianus: who is the secret buyer from Rome? But the clues were perhaps too easy. Well-known—otherwise why hide his name?—experienced with mining, always concerned to maximize the productivity of his slaves. Who else but Rome's wealthiest man?"

"The riddle is that you should be associated with such a man closely enough to be scouting out properties for him," I said.

"Where's the puzzle in that?"

"Your politics are known to be quite radical, Catilina. Why should the richest man in the world ally himself with a firebrand who advocates the forcible redistribution of wealth and the wholesale cancellation of debts?"

"I thought you had no desire to discuss politics, Gordianus."

"It's the water, making me lightheaded. I'm not myself. Indulge me."

"As you wish. True, Crassus and I have our differences, but we face a common enemy—the ruling oligarchy in Rome. You know whom I mean—that little circle of incestuous families who clutch the reins of power so jealously, and will stop at nothing to cripple their opposition. You know what they call themselves, don't you? The Best People, the Optimates. They refer to themselves thusly without the least twinge of embarrassment, as if their superiority were so evident that modesty could only be an affectation. Everyone outside their circle they consider to be mere rabble. The state, they argue, must be run by the Optimates alone, without concession to any other party, for what better way to run a state than to place it in the hands of those who are undeniably and in all ways demonstrably the Best People? Oh, their smug self-satisfaction is insufferable! And Cicero has bought into it completely. Cicero, the nobody from Arpinum, without an ancestor to his name. If he only knew what they say about him behind his back . . ."

"We were talking of Crassus, not Cicero."

Catilina sighed and settled himself more comfortably in the water. "Marcus Crassus is too great a force to belong to any party, even the Optimates. Crassus is his own party, and so he finds himself at odds with the Optimates as often as not. You're right, Crassus has no sympathy with my plans to restructure the economy of the state, which must be done if the Republic is to survive. But then, Crassus cares not a whit for the survival of the Republic. He would just as soon see it wither and die, so long as the dictator who inevitably follows is named Marcus Crassus. In the meantime, the two of us quite often have occasion to find ourselves allied against the Optimates. And of course Marcus Crassus and I go back a long way, to the days when we both served under Sulla."

"You mean to say that like Crassus, you also profited from the proscriptions during Sulla's dictatorship, when the property of his enemies was confiscated and put up for auction?"

"Many others did the same. But I never murdered for gain or used the proscriptions to get away with murder—oh, yes, I know the rumors. One has me putting my own brother-in-law on the lists, because my sister couldn't stand him and wanted his head cut off. Others say I killed him myself and then had his name inserted in the lists to legalize the crime. As if I would have wanted to see my own sister dishonored and disinherited!"

His voice took on an angry edge. "And then there's the wretched lie put about by Cicero's brother Quintus last year during the consular campaign, which had me taking part in the murder of the praetor Gratidianus during those years. Poor Gratidianus, chased down by the mob. They broke both his legs, cut off his hands, gouged out his eyes, and then beheaded him. Hideous savagery! I witnessed that atrocity, yes, but I didn't instigate it, as Quintus Cicero claimed, nor did I swagger about Rome carrying Gratidianus's head like a trophy. Even so, only last year some of the Optimates managed to call me to trial for the murder—and I was soundly acquitted, just as I've been acquitted of every single charge they've brought against me over the years."

"Speaking of heads, your own is turning red as a beet, Catilina. I think the water must be too hot."

Catilina, who in his passion had drawn himself up until his chest was above the water, took a deep breath and sank back into the tub. "But we were talking about Crassus. . . ." He smiled, and I marveled at how easily he could let go of his bitter tone and restore his good humor. "Do you know what really cemented our relationship? The scandal of the Vestal Virgins! Fabia and I weren't the only ones brought to trial that spring—Crassus was accused of polluting the Virgo Maxima herself. Do you remember the details? He had been seen in her company so often that that scheming Clodius had no trouble convincing half of Rome to believe the worst. But Crassus's defense was unbeatable: the millionaire was merely pestering the Virgo Maxima over a piece of property that he wanted to buy from her at a bargain—a story so typical of Crassus that no one could disbelieve it! He escaped with his life, and so did I, but both of us took a blow to our reputations—Crassus, because everyone believed he was innocent but greedy, and I, because everyone thought I was guilty but got away with it. After the trial we celebrated together over a few bottles of Falernian wine. Political alliances are not always founded on hard logic, Gordianus. Sometimes they grow out of shared distress." He looked at me steadily, as if to emphasize his words. "But I understand you've had your own dealings with Crassus."

"He called on me to deal with the murder of his cousin down in Baiae," I said. "That was nine years ago. The circumstances were quite remarkable, but I'm not at liberty to discuss the details. Suffice to say that Crassus and I parted on less than friendly terms."*

Catilina smiled. "Actually, Crassus has told me most of the story, or his version of it. He wanted certain slaves found

---

*Arms of Nemesis (St. Martin's Press, 2001)

guilty of the crime, while you would settle for nothing less than the truth, no matter how disappointing to Crassus's schemes or how personally embarrassing. Believe it or not, he secretly admires your integrity, I think, even if he did resent your, shall we say, inflexible nature. I suppose Crassus himself is rather inflexible, which accounts for your mutual antipathy. But your work for him in Baiae had at least one good outcome. I understand that's how you met your son Meto. Oh, please, don't lower your eyes, Gordianus. I think it's a remarkable thing, to free a young slave boy and then adopt him as your son. I realize it's not a fact you care to advertise, for the boy's sake. But I know the story, and with me you can be frank."

"I would rather forget that Marcus Crassus was ever Meto's master. Had Crassus had his way, Meto would be long dead. As it was, Crassus sold him to a farmer in Sicily, just to thwart my having him. That he was eventually found, that I freed him and made him my son, is proof that even the richest man in the world can be cheated of his petty revenge."

Catilina pursed his lips. "Evidently Crassus didn't tell me the whole story."

"Because Crassus doesn't know the whole story. But you won't hear it from me."

"Now it's you who've turned beet-red, Gordianus! Are you ready for the cool plunge?"

Like Catilina in his agitation, I had raised myself halfway out of the water. I sighed and settled back into the soothing warmth.

"You're very protective of the boy, as well you should be," said Catilina. "These are dangerous times, full of peril. I'm a father, too. I worry constantly about the future of my wife and her daughter. Sometimes I think it would be better to follow your example and withdraw from the world entirely, or as much as a man can. To live in simple obscurity, like Cincinnatus. You know the old story—when the Republic was imperiled, the people called on the farmer Cincinnatus, who laid down his plow, assumed the dictatorship, and saved them all."

"And when the peril was over, he laid down his dictatorship and went back to his plow."

"Yes, but the point is that he acted when the occasion called for it. For a man to turn his back on the world entirely is to relinquish his opportunity to shape the world's future. Who can give up that chance, even if his efforts end in failure?"

"Or in utter disaster?"

"No, Gordianus, when I contemplate the world my descendants will live in, I cannot become a hermit, apathetic and ineffectual. And when I think of the shades of my ancestors watching me, I cannot be idle. The founder of my family stood by Aeneas when he first set foot on Italian soil. Perhaps it's my patrician blood that drives me to take the reins—to rip them from the Optimates' hands if I have to!"

He reached out and clutched a fistful of steam, then relaxed his grip and slowly dropped his open hands into the roiling water. The motion took on a vague and unreal aspect in the orange haze, like an actor's gesture seen from afar.

For a while we were both quiet. A slave stepped silently into the room and asked if he should open the valve from the furnace to add fresh hot water. I nodded, and the slave withdrew. A moment later the pipes gurgled and the tub swirled. The mist thickened and the lamp burned lower. In the dense orange haze I could see Catilina's face only as a soft blur.

"Do you want to know a secret, Gordianus?"

Oh, Catilina, I thought, there are many secrets I would like to know, foremost among them the identity of Nemo and how his headless body came to rest in my barn! "Why not?"

"It's a riddle, actually—"

"Telling a secret and posing a riddle are entirely different things, Catilina. I would like to hear a secret. But tonight I would not care to hear a riddle."

"Indulge me. Well, then: how can a man lose his head twice?"

The water swirled. The mist was as thick as a sea fog. "I don't know, Catilina. How can a man lose his head twice?"

"First, over a beautiful woman, and then to the executioner's blade."

"I understand the answer but not the riddle."

"I lost my head over the Vestal Fabia, and then almost lost my head for the crime. Do you see? I think it's a rather good riddle. I was younger then. What a fool I made of myself. . . ."

"What are you saying, Catilina?"

"I'm telling you that what you always suspected was true. There was more between Fabia and myself than a shared appreciation for Arrentine vases."

"And that night in the House of the Vestals—"

"It was the first time. Before that, she always resisted me. But that night she gave in to me. When the man behind the curtain cried out, we were in the middle of making love. Fabia wore her gown, and I wore my tunic, and we stood the whole time. I wanted her to be naked, I wanted to touch her everywhere, I wanted to take her on the couch. But she insisted we keep our clothing on and do it standing up. Even so, it was one of the most exciting and exquisite moments of my life. When the man cried out, I hardly heard him in the heat of my passion. It might have been myself crying out in sheer ecstasy. Fabia panicked, of course. She pushed at me, trying to make me withdraw, but I told her that would be madness. I wasn't quite finished, you see, and if she pushed me out of her I would either leave a pool of evidence on her floor or else carry a telltale bludgeon inside my tunic. We consummated the act and drew apart only moments before the Virgo Maxima entered the room. Fabia's cheeks were as red as apples. Her breasts were heaving, covered with beads of sweat. I was still tingling—"

"Catilina, why are you telling me this?"

"Because you prize the truth, Gordianus; you're one of the few men I know who does. Because you've never been quite certain what really transpired, and now you can be."

"But why tell me now?"

Catilina was quiet for a long moment. In the dim orange mist I tried to make out his expression, but could not tell if he smiled or frowned, or even if his eyes were open. At last he said, "They say you have a gift for listening, Gordianus. Every politician needs a listener. They say you have a way of drawing out the truth, even if one doesn't mean to speak it."

" 'They?' "

"Crassus, actually. In all these years he hasn't forgotten your latenight conversations down in Baiae. He says he can't recall ever speaking so frankly to another man, and a hireling at that. He says you have some uncanny power to draw the truth from men's hearts."

"Only if their hearts are burdened with something that they need to release."

"What sort of burden?" he said.

"It varies from man to man, woman to woman. Some feel compelled to confess fear of failure, others their remorse for wickedness done to the dead. Some confess their shame at submitting to the cruelty of others, some confess their shame for inflicting such cruelty. Some have committed terrible crimes and gone unpunished by man or god, and yet feel they must tell someone. Others have only imagined such crimes, and yet they feel a burden just as heavy as if they had committed them."

"And what of those who failed to commit a crime when they should have?"

"I don't understand."

"What of those who should have taken action, and then quavered and failed to act? Have you ever encountered a man like that, Gordianus, whose confession was that he did *not* commit a crime when he should have?"

"Is this another riddle, Catilina?"

Despite the dimness, I knew he smiled. "Perhaps. But like the riddle that Caelius repeated to you, the time for its telling hasn't yet arrived. Perhaps that time will never come."

"I should think, Catilina, that you already have plenty of crimes to confess without fretting over those you might not be able to get around to."

I thought my bluntness would offend him. Instead he laughed, sharply at first, and then with a low chuckle that blended with the gurgling of the pipes and the hissing of the water. "I fear that the reputation far outstrips the reality, Gordianus. And if you observe the reality, you will see that I have been the victim of my enemies' unrelenting persecution. Yes, three years ago I was brought to trial, accused of practicing extortion against the locals while I was propraetor in Africa. Were the charges brought because of true misdeeds? No, my old enemy Clodius mounted the prosecution on behalf of the Optimates for no other purpose than to wreck my political career. They achieved their object, in the short run; thanks to the way they drew out the proceedings, I was disqualified from running for consul for two years! But ultimately I was acquitted, a fact no one seems to recall. Did you know that before the trial Cicero himself offered to defend me? Yes, the same lying opportunist who now paints me as the most wicked man in Rome. I think this says more about Cicero than it does about myself.

"Last year I was finally able to stand for consul, and there was nothing the Optimates could do to prevent me. To thwart me, they made Cicero their creature and set his venomous tongue against me. I lost. Even so, they feared that I would run again, and win, and so to prevent me they mounted another prosecution against me, this one for murdering Gratidianus back in the days of Sulla! You can be sure that Cicero did not offer to speak for my defense this time! Even so, again I was acquitted, and the Optimates failed in their attempt to keep me out of the race. I was free of the cloud in plenty of time to stand for consul again this year.

"So then, Gordianus, what are these crimes for which I'm so notorious, except so much dust blown into the faces of the voters by my enemies, who would destroy a man's reputation with no more thought than swatting a fly. When a man is brought to trial again and again, it leaves a taint, I know, but to what crime should I confess, except that I'm a fly in the Optimates' ointment?"

I squinted at Catilina and saw only an uncertain head above half-submerged shoulders, an obscure island floating on the mist. "I was thinking of other crimes, Catilina, offenses of a different order altogether."

"You're too wise a man to believe even half of what you hear, Gordianus, especially from the venomous lips of Cicero and his brother Quintus. I don't pretend to be humble or meek, but I'm hardly the monster my enemies portray—what man could be? Oh, I know the rumors and insinuations. Very well, let's begin with the worst: when I sought to take Aurelia Orestilla as my second wife a few years ago, she refused, because she wouldn't marry into a household that already had an heir, and so to please her I murdered my own son. You're a father, Gordianus. Can you imagine the anguish that lie has caused me? Every day that passes, I mourn the death of my son. If he had lived, today he would be a man, at my side in my struggles, a comfort and an inspiration to me. He died from fever, yet my enemies call it poison, and they use the tragedy of his death as a sordid weapon against me.

"They also say I married Aurelia for her money, to get myself out of debt. Ha! That only shows the depth of their ignorance, to so vastly underestimate my debts. They also underestimate the bond between Aurelia and myself, but that is none of their business, and none of yours, either, if I can say so politely.

"And then there are the tales of my sexual exploits, some of them true, some of them totally fantastic—really, the next thing you know, they'll be saying I raped my own mother and thus fathered myself! What does it matter which of these tales are real, anyway? No one cares about such things except dried-up moralists like Cato and Cicero with their black hearts and their black tongues. Honestly, I have never been able to understand why men who have no appetite should feel such spite for men who eat with relish!"

"A pretty phrase, Catilina, but enjoying a hearty dinner is one thing, while taking a girl's virginity and ruining her chances for a good marriage is quite another, as is convincing young men to ruin their credit on your behalf, destroying their own careers in the process."

The lamp had almost burned out. From the dim haze I heard a sigh. "Alas, Gordianus, I can no longer see your face, so I'll give you the benefit of the doubt and assume that you smile as you speak such outrages, knowing them to be nothing more than slanders concocted by my enemies. Oh, yes, I confess that I have a weakness for the young and innocent. What man with a healthy appetite does not appreciate a blushing fruit plucked fresh from the tree? And in a world so corrupted with machinations and lies, what man would not find a special appeal in those of an unworldly character? Where else can sweetness be found in this bitter world except among the young? But I don't force myself on others. I've been accused of murder and theft, but never of rape—even my enemies credit me with being able to attract my partners without coercion. Nor do I merely take and give nothing in return.

They give me their innocence and in return I give them my worldliness, the commodity I possess in greatest abundance; each gives to the other what the other lacks and desires."

"And what did you give to the Vestal Fabia?"

"Adventure! Pleasure, excitement, danger—all the things her drab existence denied her."

"And was that worth the chance of snuffing out her existence altogether? What if the affair had ended with Fabia being buried alive? It could very easily have ended that way."

"Blame Clodius for that, not me."

"You shrug off your responsibility too easily, Catilina."

He was silent for a long moment, then I heard him stir in the water. He stood, causing the water to splash against the lip of the tub and the vapors to whorl and part before him. His skin was reddened from the heat. Beads of moisture clung to the black hair flecked with silver that matted his chest and ran down to his sex, which floated heavily half in and half out of the water. His shoulders and chest were broad, his belly flat. He was an uncommonly virile-looking man. No wonder his lovers appreciated him, I thought; no wonder constipated, thin-limbed, plain-faced men like Cato and Cicero so despised his physical and sexual prowess.

He seemed to read my thoughts. "You're a fit-looking man yourself, Gordianus. The active life of the farm obviously suits you. Men grow soft and fat in the city—it's one thing to grow old and quite another to grow soft, eh? But I think you're a man of strong appetites yourself." He stood gazing down at me with a thin smile, as if he expected something from me. His gaze made me uncomfortable. "Well," he finally said, "I've had enough of this heat! Will you join me in the cool plunge, Gordianus?"

"No, I think I'll stay here a while longer. Perhaps I'll follow Tongilius's example and simply dry myself and go to bed."

Catilina stepped from the tub. He took his towel from the niche in the wall, but did not bother to cover himself. He paused at the door to the cooling room. "Shall I call for a slave to bring another lamp?"

"No," I said. "The darkness suits my mood."

Catilina nodded and shut the door behind him. A moment

later the light dwindled and died. I lay in the darkness, ruminating on Catilina and his crimes.

I must have dozed for just an instant, for suddenly I was awakened by a faint creaking noise, not from the door through which Catilina had just exited but from the door that led back to the warm bath and thence to the rest of the house. It was just such a noise as might be made by someone leaning against the door without meaning to. At the same instant a thin crack of light appeared at the top of the door frame.

Perhaps the door had moved on its own, swollen by the humidity and heat. Still, my heart began to beat more quickly, and the languid drowsiness of the hot bath was instantly dispelled. Perhaps it was Tongilius returning, I told myself—but why should he be skulking? Perhaps it was a slave come to replenish the extinguished lamp—but then why did the slave not enter?

I listened and heard nothing more from beyond the door, but I was convinced that someone stood there, waiting.

I rose from the water as quietly as I could and stepped from the tub. I reached for my towel, but not to cover myself. A simple towel, wound tightly like a rope, has many uses— as a shield against daggers, as a means of binding an enemy, as a weapon good for strangling or breaking necks. I walked on tiptoe to the door. I reached for the wooden handle, hesitated for a heartbeat, then pulled it open.

He tumbled toward me, staggering. I caught him in the twisted cloth, pinned his arms to his sides and spun him around. He tripped and lurched, but didn't struggle. He tilted his face toward mine.

I hissed a curse and released the towel. My captive stepped free and sucked in a quick breath, and then, as if what had just happened had been nothing more than a game, whispered, "So Catilina *did* sleep with the Vestal!"

"Meto!"

"Sorry, Papa, but I couldn't sleep. My feet hurt from climbing the mountain! When I came to the door, I heard the two of you talking. It didn't seem right to step in on you, but I had to listen. You wouldn't have said anything different if you'd known I could hear, would you? And Catilina might not have said so much if I'd been in the room. I was awfully quiet, wasn't I? Did you really not know that I was there until just now? That was a mistake, leaning against the door like that . . ."

"Meto, when will you learn respect?"

Meto put his fingers to his lips and nodded toward the door to the cool plunge. I lowered my voice. "This habit of yours, skulking and spying, where did you possibly learn such—" I sighed. "No, as a matter of fact, I had no idea you were there until the door creaked. Which means that you are young and agile while I am growing old and dull and possibly a little deaf. I wonder, which of us is more in need of a good night's sleep?"

Meto smiled at me, and I couldn't help smiling back. I gripped the back of his neck and gave his head a firm shake, none too gently. It was time for bed, but before we turned to go I looked back at the thin bar of lamplight that shone from beneath the opposite door. A faint splashing came from the pool of cool water in the room beyond. As on the night before, soon everyone in the household would be abed and sleeping except Catilina, who would still be up, defying Morpheus and who knows what other gods to come and take him.

FOURTEEN

MORPHEUS must have come for Catilina at last, and claimed him until well past sunup, for it was not until midmorning that Catilina and Tongilius appeared in the kitchen seeking food. They both looked a bit bleary-eyed from oversleep, but were quite cheerful—indeed, suspiciously self-satisfied, I thought. They muttered little jokes to one another, laughed out loud, and smiled at nothing. Their appetites were enormous, and they devoured everything Congrio set before them.

Once finished with his breakfast, Catilina announced that they would be leaving before noon. He and Tongilius dressed in blue riding tunics, gathered up their things, said farewell to Bethesda, paid their compliments to Congrio on his cooking, and loaded their horses in the stable.

I asked Catilina which way he was headed. To the north, he told me, saying he had more visits to pay in Etruria, campaigning among Sulla's old veterans, whom the dictator had settled on farmland seized from his enemies. I watched them ride off. Despite having dreaded his visit so much, I was not as happy to see him leave as I'd thought I would be.

Curiously, when they reached the Cassian Way, Tongilius and Catilina turned not north but south, toward Rome. I would never have noticed, for I was no longer watching, but Meto was. He came running up to me outside the pigsties and pointed toward the two figures on the distant highway. "What do you make of that, Papa?"

"Odd," I said. "Catilina claimed he was heading north. I wonder—"

"I'll go watch from the ridge," Meto called back over his shoulder as he broke into a run. He was on the ridgetop long before I came up huffing and puffing behind him. He had already found the ideal lookout between two towering oaks, shielded from sight behind a clump of brambles. We could not be seen from the road, but had a clear view of everything that passed on the Cassian Way.

It was not hard to spot Catilina and Tongilius, as they were the only horsemen on the road. They seemed to have come to a halt at a spot not far from the pass between the ridge and the foothills of Mount Argentum. Why they should hesitate was unclear, until I realized that they were waiting for a team of oxen to pass by, heading north. Once over the rise, the oxen must have passed outside of their sight—just as Catilina and Tongilius passed out of the oxherd's view. They looked stealthily about, then dismounted and led their horses into the underbrush on the eastern side of the road.

Their mounts secured somewhere out of sight, the two men reappeared, but only for a moment before they passed beneath the branches of a large tree and out of sight. Then I saw them again, stepping back onto the road, but only for a moment. So it went, with Catilina and Tongilius disappearing and reappearing, going back and forth along the roadside as if searching for something they had lost.

"What are they looking for?" asked Meto.

"The trailhead," I said.

"What trailhead?"

"You must have run on ahead when Forfex explained it to us yesterday. There's another path that leads up to the mine, beginning somewhere along the Cassian Way. It's long been disused and overgrown. Catilina is trying to find the trailhead."

"But why? He's already been to the mine."

I made no answer. From the corner of my eye I saw Meto frowning at me, not because he was perplexed but because he sensed that I was withholding my thoughts from him. Together we watched as Catilina and Tongilius went in and out of the dense underbrush alongside the road. At length a team of slaves appeared from the south, linked by chains from neck to neck and driven along by freedmen wielding whips. Catilina and Tongilius disappeared for as long as it took the slaves to pass, then reappeared again when the way was clear.

Eventually they vanished into the brush and did not reappear for so long that I began to think they had found what they were seeking. Suddenly Meto clutched my sleeve. In the same instant I heard a rustling in the underbrush behind us, followed by a familiar voice.

"Not your usual spot—oh, please, I didn't mean to startle you! Oh, how rude of me, coming up on you like this. Gordianus, forgive me, I shouldn't laugh, but you gave such a start!"

"Claudia," I said.

"Yes, only me. And here's young Meto—so long since I've seen the boy. Oh, but I mustn't call you a boy, not for much longer, must I, young man? You turn sixteen this month, don't you?"

"Yes," said Meto, darting a glance over his shoulder, back down toward the road.

"A beautiful view from this side, isn't it? You really get the whole effect of the mountain, how vast it is, towering above the road like that."

"Yes, quite impressive," I said.

"But it's so uncomfortable here amid the brambles. Come,

there's a spot close by with the very same view where we can all sit together on a log."

I shrugged, trying not to look down at the road. My eyes fell on the basket in Claudia's hand.

"Oh, but you fear you'll be intruding on my lunch! Not at all, Gordianus. I have quite enough bread and cheese and olives for all of us. Come now, I won't have my hospitality refused."

We followed her to a clearing a few feet away. As she had promised, the view was exactly the same, with the difference that we were in plain sight of the road, should anyone happen to look up.

"Now, isn't this better?" said Claudia, settling her plump bottom on the log and laying her basket before her.

"Much," I said. Meto, I noticed, could not seem to keep from darting furtive but very obvious glances at the spot where we had last glimpsed Catilina and Tongilius. A good watcher he might be, but as an actor he was a disaster. "However, Meto really needs to be getting back to the house."

"Oh, Gordianus, you Roman fathers! Always so strict and demanding. My father was just the same, and I was a girl! Here it is, one of the last fine summer days of Meto's boyhood, and you would have him doing chores at midday. In a very short time he'll be a man, and after that, summer days may be just as hot but they will never be as long and lovely and full of flowers and bees as they are for him at this very moment. Please, let Meto join us."

At her insistence, Meto sat at Claudia's left and I at her right. She passed us food and waited for us to begin before taking some for herself. Once he was settled on the log with his mouth full of cheese, I must admit that Meto did a good job at feigning only casual interest in the doings at the foot of the mountain. More traffic passed on the Cassian Way—herds of sheep, slaves bearing bundles of wood on their backs, a long train of wagons ringed by armed men headed south toward Rome.

"Vases from Arretium," declared Claudia.

"How can you tell?" said Meto.

"Because I can see right through the crates packed inside the wagons as if they were invisible!" said Claudia, then laughed when she saw that Meto seemed to be taking her seriously. "I know, Meto, because those wagons have been coming down the Cassian Way since I was a girl, taking Arretine vases to Rome. They're awfully valuable—hence the armed guard, and the slow procession. If it were anything else valuable enough to justify the guards, the wagons would be going twice as fast. Gold and silver don't break, but fine clay vases do."

The progress of the wagons did seem to take forever as they crept along the ribbon of road. There was no sign of Catilina.

Then Meto made an odd noise in his throat, and when I glanced at him, he made an almost imperceptible nod. I followed his gaze to a point on the mountain at least two hundred feet above the road, where a patch of blue the shade of Catilina's tunic flashed in a clearing amid the green canopy. The blue patch moved and was joined by another; I squinted, and the blue patches resolved quite clearly into two men moving about on the mountainside.

Claudia, busy leaning over her basket, did not see.

"Actually, Gordianus, I was hoping to run into you here on the ridge, for otherwise I should have had to come pay a formal visit, and that would have been no fun at all. And I'm glad that you happen to be here as well, Meto, for I think this involves you, too." She sat back and pursed her lips. For a moment I thought she was looking directly across the valley at Catilina and Tongilius, but she was only staring absently into the middle distance, thinking about what she had to say.

"What is it, Claudia?"

"Oh, this is so difficult. . . ."

"Yes?"

"I had a visit this morning from my cousin Gnaeus. He says there were strangers on his mountain yesterday, men from Rome hiking up to visit the old mine."

"Is that a fact?" I looked across the way and saw that Catilina and Tongilius had disappeared amid the foliage again.

"Yes. Some business about one of them wanting to purchase the old mine, or representing someone who might. Nonsense, if you ask me—the mine is worthless now. There's no more silver to be got from it. Anyway, Gnaeus was asking if I happened to have seen anyone traipsing about on the mountain yesterday—you can see quite a bit of the old trail from my house, you know, though it's a long way off. Well, as a matter of fact, no, I hadn't seen a thing, and none of my slaves had noticed anyone on the mountainside either."

Claudia paused to chew an olive. "Gnaeus says he didn't know any of these men, and only one of them bothered to introduce himself—one of the Sergii, up from Rome, as I said. But afterward Gnaeus questioned the goatherd who had shown the men around, an old fool named Forfex, and do you know what the man told him?"

"I can't imagine."

"He said that along with this Sergius there was a younger man who seemed to be his companion, and then there was another middle-aged man and a youth. He didn't know them, but he seemed to recall hearing the man addressed as Gordianus." She looked at me and raised an eyebrow.

I thought for a moment. "Did Gnaeus see these four visitors for himself?"

"Yes. But the light was growing dim. And despite his youth, Gnaeus doesn't have the best eyesight. That's why he seldom catches a boar!"

"Ah. Then you're asking me—"

"No, I'm asking you nothing. I can tell everything from your face. Well, not everything, but enough. If you wish to go snooping about my cousin's property, that is a matter between you and him. And if Gnaeus wishes to confront you about the matter, he can do so himself; I'm not his messenger. However, Gordianus, I would be derelict in my duties as a blood relation of Gnaeus, and as a good neighbor to you, if I merely kept silent. Gnaeus was not happy when Forfex repeated your name, nor was he happy when he came to see me this morning. I doubt that he'll come to see you or even send you a message; he prefers to keep to himself and brood, disappearing into the woods to hunt his boars. But if there is some untoward business going on, I advise you to consider your position very carefully, Gordianus. Be cautious! My kinfolk are not to be trifled with. There is only so much I can do to mollify them. I tell you this as a friend."

She paused for a moment to allow this to sink in, then bent over and reached into her basket. "And now I have a sur-prise—honey cakes! My new cook baked them fresh this morning. Alas, he's no Congrio, but he does have a way with sweets."

Meto managed to tear his eyes from the mountainside; he has always had a taste for honey. He ate the little cake quickly and then licked his fingertips. Claudia offered me a cake, but I declined.

"You don't care for sweets, Gordianus? The new cook will take it very badly if I return with them uneaten."

"A touch of Cicero's complaint," I explained, touching my stomach and frowning.

"Oh, but here I've gone and upset your digestion with all this talk of Gnaeus. How thoughtless of me, to give you bread and cheese and unpleasant news at the same time. Perhaps a honey cake will settle your stomach."

"I think not." It was not only Claudia's news that upset my stomach, but the tension of knowing that she might spot Catilina on the mountainside or emerging onto the road at any moment. The real cure would have been for her to simply go away. But she had more to say.

"So the toga party is this month. What day?"

"Two days before the Ides."

"Ah, just after the elections."

I nodded but said nothing, hoping my silence would keep the conversation away from politics. It was bad enough that I was planning to be in the city immediately after the voting. Whether Catilina won or lost, his supporters or enemies were likely to be out in the streets rioting in protest. And if, as Caelius had hinted, there was actual revolution in the air, then Rome was the last place I wanted to be.

Claudia nodded and smiled. "Ten days from now, and you will be a man, Meto! But I shall save my congratulations until then. I assume you'll be having some little celebration in the city before he takes his walk in the Forum. Would it be too forward of me to beg an invitation?"

"Will you be in the city, Claudia?"

"I'm afraid so," she sighed. "Along with my dear cousins. They're all planning to be in the city to vote this time around.

Afraid Catilina might somehow slip through, you know. The actual voting is all up to the men, of course, and usually I don't go to Rome at all at this time of year, but there's no way out of it. It's that house on the Palatine that Lucius left me—I'm planning to rent it out, and the slave who runs the place tells me it's due for some renovations. Well, I'm not about to let one of Lucius's old slaves make the arrangements and spend my money. I shall oversee everything myself. I'm leaving tomorrow, and I suspect I'll be there most of the month." She raised her eyebrows and looked at me expectantly.

"Then of course you must come to Meto's birthday party," I said.

"Oh, thank you! I should love to see it. Never having had a son, myself, you know . . ." Her voice trailed off. "And I shall bring honey cakes!" she added, brightening. "Meto will like that." She reached out and touched his shoulder. Meto smiled a bit shyly, then a strange expression crossed his face.

He was watching something down below. I followed his gaze and saw Catilina and Tongilius emerging from the woods onto the road.

Claudia seemed to sense that something was amiss, for I saw her glance oddly at Meto and then felt her eyes on me. "Perhaps—" I began. "Perhaps I would enjoy one of those honey cakes, after all."

"Ah, good, let me see, here's a nice one right on top," she said, bending over her basket.

I took the cake from her and looked her in the eyes as I bit into it. She smiled and nodded, then abruptly looked down toward the road.

"Look there," she said. "Who are those men and where did they come from?"

I started to speak and coughed instead, as the cake seemed to turn to dust in my throat. Meto, seeing that I was helpless, took the cue. "What men?" he asked innocently.

"Those two men right down there, on horseback. Wherever did they come from?" Claudia furrowed her plump brow, cocked her head, and pulled at a strand of red hair that had escaped from the bun on her head.

Meto shrugged. "Just two men on horseback."

"But they're heading toward the north. I didn't see them ride up. Look, you can see the whole length of the Cassian Way coming up from the south, halfway to Rome—oh, I exaggerate, but still, we would have seen anyone approaching for miles. And suddenly two horsemen appear from nowhere."

"Not really. I saw them riding up," said Meto matter-of-factly.

"You did?"

"For quite some time. I think it was when you pointed out the wagons with Arretine vases coming over the pass. Yes, I noticed the two horsemen riding up from the south, quite far away. And now look, the wagons have gone about half that distance. That means the horsemen are going twice as fast as the wagons. Is that right, Papa?"

I nodded dumbly, still clearing my throat, and took back my poor opinion of Meto's acting skills.

Claudia remained dubious. "You saw them riding up all this time—passing the wagons and getting closer?"

Meto nodded.

"And you, too, Gordianus?"

I shrugged and nodded. "Two horsemen on the Cassian Way," I said. "Probably coming up from Rome."

Claudia was perturbed. "Why didn't I notice them? Cyclops and Oedipus, my eyes must be getting as weak as Gnaeus's."

"It's not so odd," I reassured her. "You were distracted by our company and simply didn't notice. It's nothing to make a fuss over."

"I don't like horsemen appearing from nowhere," she muttered. "I don't like feeling . . ." Her voice trailed off, then she managed a smile. "But you're right, I'm being silly. Just a silly old woman, set in my ways and upset when I'm taken by surprise, and more upset when I realize I'm not as sharp as I like to think I am. Ah, well, have you had enough of the cakes? Here, I'll wrap them up again; mustn't waste them. The gods despise a wasteful man, my father always used to say. I really must be going. There, thank you, Meto, for helping me gather things up."

She picked up her basket, stood and straightened her back.

"I leave for Rome tomorrow and won't be back for such a long time—you can imagine all the instructions to be left with the slaves, and the confusion in the household with the new cook, not to mention the packing! Oh, I hate the fuss—why Lucius left me a house in the city I can't imagine! But I'm glad I managed to see you here on the ridge, both of you. And I shall see you again on Meto's toga day! The party will be at your house?"

"Yes, Eco's house now. On the Esquiline. It's a little hard to find—"

"Ah, but you and Lucius were such good friends, I'm sure his old slaves in the city will know how to find the place. I shall be there."

"We look forward to having you."

"And, Gordianus—consider seriously what I said, about Gnaeus. You must watch yourself. You have a family to look after." Before she turned away, her face took on a quite stern, almost severe expression.

The moment she disappeared into the brush I licked the honey from my lips and suddenly craved another cake, too late. Meanwhile, Catilina and Tongilius had picked up speed and made rapid progress on the Cassian Way. Meto and I watched them for a while longer, until their blue-cloaked figures began to merge with the northern horizon, obscured by the rippling heat that rose from the sun-baked paving stones.

"Catilina is a fascinating man," said Meto.

"Catilina," I said, "is a blur on the horizon."

FIFTEEN

THE following days passed without incident—or rather, without any unpleasant interludes of the Nemo variety. Of incident there was an abundance, for transporting a family from the farm to the city, even for a brief visit, is a matter of complex logistics and planning. When I consider that great generals like Pompey are able to move their armies successfully over vast arenas on land and sea, complete with tents and cooking utensils and stocks of food and all their daily needs, I am truly awed.

Aratus told me he had always been in charge of helping Lucius pack his things, and since Lucius had gone back and forth from city to countryside quite often and had no doubt traveled in considerable luxury, this claim at first impressed me. Then I realized that Lucius, being so rich, could have afforded to own two or more of everything, and so had little need to carry his necessities on his back like a turtle. Conversely, Bethesda and I had to plan very carefully to bring enough so that Eco would not be burdened by us, and at the same time make sure that the farm was well provisioned in our absence. It was a considerable job.

Nevertheless, I managed to make time to begin construction on the water mill. The time was right for the project, for the weather continued clear and hot, and the flow in the stream diminished appreciably from day to day. This made it easy to remove stones and to fill areas that needed leveling with mortar and brick. I was disturbed to see the water become so slow and shallow, but, fortunately, the farm had a well at the foot of the ridge. The well had been there since before anyone living was born, Aratus told me. It was situated among olive trees and ringed with a low stone wall. The shaft was so deep it barely sent back a faint echo from its watery black depths. The old well had always been reliable, Aratus assured me, even in years of drought.

Meanwhile, between work on the mill and preparations for the trip to Rome, I enjoyed my respite from worrying over unwanted visitors. The election would be held on the fifth day before the Ides; thus the consular contest would be decided even before we set out for Rome. I could arrive in the city without giving the matter another thought; hopefully, I would be able to enjoy Eco's company and Meto's day of manhood without any further worries about matters over which I had no control and in which I had no interest. Catilina would be elected, or he would not, but in either event his brief incursion into my life would be over.

It bothered me that the mystery of Nemo's death and identity and his appearance in my stable had never been ex-

plained, but it would have bothered me more if further threats
had followed, or if Diana and Bethesda were to stay behind
while I went to Rome. But we would all be together in the
city, safe in Eco's house, or as safe as anyone can be in a
place like Rome.

On the day before we were to leave, I took a few moments
from the preparations for the trip and the work on the mill
and stole away by myself to the place were Meto and Aratus
and I had buried Nemo. I stood before the simple stele and
ran my fingers down the vertical letters that spelled the name
of no one. "Who were you?" I said. "How did you die? What
became of your head, and who arranged it so that I would
find you in my barn?" I tried to convince myself that the
whole incident was now over and done with, but at the same
time I felt something else that was harder to dispel than my
vague foreboding: a sense of guilt and failure, of an obligation
denied. Not my obligation to Cicero, which had now been
discharged, but to the shade of Nemo.

I shrugged. To relieve a kink in the muscles of my shoulders, I thought—or was it to demonstrate my indifference to
the restless dead? What did I owe Nemo, after all? If I had
seen his face, would I have even known him? It seemed to
me unlikely. He had been neither client nor friend, so far as
there was any way of knowing. I owed him nothing. I
shrugged—yet I did not turn my back on his gravestone, and
instead found myself staring at it, studying each of the four
letters of the name I had given him, which was not a name
at all but the very opposite.

Other men live with mysteries, never knowing the truth
from day to day; it is a way of surviving in a world in which
the truth is always dangerous to someone. I would live in
ignorance as well, and prosper, and protect my family. I
would do what the mighty demanded of me, and otherwise
mind my business. So I told myself, but with faltering con-
viction. Why had I come to Nemo's burial place at all unless
it was to pay my respects and converse with his shade? I had
made vows to other dead men, to find their killers, to see that
some semblance of justice prevailed. I had done so because
the gods had made we wayward and dissatisfied with ignorance and injustice. But I had never made a vow to Nemo

while he lived, I reasoned, arguing with myself; he was no one, and I owed him nothing.

I turned my back on the stele, but not easily; I could almost feel the hand of Nemo on my shoulder, holding me back, trying to extract from me a promise I would not make. I tore myself away, cursing everyone from Numa to Nemo, and made my way back to the stream.

I yelled at Aratus for no reason that afternoon, and after dinner Bethesda told me that I had been as cross as a child all day. In bed she did her best to raise my spirits, and succeeded at least in raising something else. Within the familiar recesses of her body I found warm solace and left my worries behind. Afterward she grew talkative. Her speech came quickly, all in a rush, which was not at all like her usual languid way of talking, especially after sex. It was the chance to go back to the city, after being away for so long, that excited her so. She catalogued the temples she would visit, the markets where she would shop, the neighbors she would impress with her new status as a country matron.

At last she grew weary. Her voice slowed and deepened, but I could tell, even with my eyes shut, that she smiled as she spoke. Her happiness gave me comfort, and I fell asleep to the soothing music of her voice.

The gods smiled on the day of our journey. The heat relented and occasional breezes wafted across the paving stones of the Cassian Way. A procession of white, puffy clouds paraded across the sky, threatening no rain but providing long passages of soothing shade. The wagon that carried Bethesda and Diana did not break an axle, and the horses on which Meto and I rode made no complaint. I picked out a few of the brawniest and ugliest slaves to accompany us as bodyguards— more for show than for any skill they might have in fighting— and though they knew little about riding horseback, they managed the journey without mishap.

Just north of Rome the Cassian Way branches in two directions. The smaller, southerly branch leads around the Vatican and Janiculum hills to join with the Aurelian Way, which enters the city at its very heart across the ancient bridges that cross into the great cattle markets and thence into the Forum.

Arriving by the Aurelian Way is always impressive—the first glimpse of the glimmering Tiber, dotted with small ships and lined with warehouses and shipyards along its banks; the clattering of hooves on the bridges; the looming skyline of the great city, dominated by the Temple of Jupiter high atop the Capitoline Hill; the slow progress through the markets and the sheer spectacle of the Forum with its magnificent array of temples and courts. It would have been a fitting way to enter the city for the purpose of celebrating Meto's coming of age as a Roman citizen, but simple pragmatism made me decide against it, for the traffic on the Aurelian Way going into the city on a late afternoon can be as slow as a dead man's pulse, and with a wagon in our retinue I dreaded being trapped on one of the bridges or amid the market stalls.

Instead we took the main, easterly branch of the Cassian Way, which joins with the Flaminian Way at the Tiber some distance north of the outskirts of Rome, and crosses the river over the Milvian Bridge. The entry into Rome by this route is less spectacular, for the countryside recedes and the city insinuates itself in stages, so that the traveler finds himself first on the outer edges and then in the very midst of the great city before he knows it. One passes the marching grounds and open spaces of the Field of Mars on the right, and then the great voting stalls (empty and probably littered with debris after the election the day before, I thought), and then passes through the Flaminian Gate and into the city proper. Our route would stay well north of the Forum and take us to Eco's house on the Esquiline Hill with hardly a glimpse of a priest or a politician, and with far less traffic than if we chose the Aurelian Way.

And yet, as we approached the juncture of the Cassian and Flaminian ways, the traffic became very heavy, and seemed to come to a virtual halt before the Milvian Bridge. The vehicles and riders were of all sorts—old men in oxcarts, groups of young men on horseback, farmers driving cattle to market. It struck me as the sort of crowd that typically thronged the city on an election day, when people gather from all over Italy to cast their votes, except that the traffic was flowing heavily in both directions, and the election was already over. Or so I had every reason to believe.

As we made our way toward the bridge, the noise of the crowd beat on my ears—people shouting, whips cracking, wheels creaking, asses braying. The traffic pressed in on both sides of us, so that we moved ahead with no choice in the matter, like leaves on a sluggish stream. Fortunately the flow carried us into a more vigorous channel while others became trapped in sluggish eddies all about us, and we managed to keep our retinue together in spite of the din and confusion. I looked over my shoulder and saw that Bethesda had lost her composure and was shouting something in Egyptian at a passing farmer who had somehow offended her. I heard a shout in front of me and turned to see that my horse had almost stepped on a child who had fallen from a passing wagon. A slave leaped from the wagon to retrieve the child, while his master in the cart began to shout and gesticulate wildly, whether at the slave or the child or me I couldn't tell. I was jostled on either side by two men on horseback who somehow found openings and raced ahead of me. We were only halfway across the bridge, and I already felt an impulse to turn around and go back to the countryside.

Back in the city! I thought with a groan, but said nothing, thinking there was no point in spoiling the occasion of Meto's return to Rome. He probably could not have heard me above the noise, anyway, and in fact he seemed quite impervious to the distress and discomfort all around him. The expression on his face as we entered the thickest of the crush on the Milvian Bridge was of unbridled delight, as if he actually enjoyed the jostling and the racket and the odors of so many men and beasts jammed together. I glanced back at the wagon and saw that Bethesda too was smiling, as if exercising her lungs on a complete stranger had given a lift to her spirits. She was holding Diana on her lap and the two of them clapped their hands, laughed, and pointed at a flock of bleating goats that scurried past us.

At last the ordeal was over and we reached the far bank of the Tiber. The traffic thinned a bit but continued to be heavy in both directions. At a high place in the road I peered ahead, down the straight course of the Flaminian Way. All along the road, in open spots as far as the Field of Mars, wagons had been pulled to the side of the road and their occupants appeared to have settled for a stay overnight. It was such a scene as one sees in wartime, when great masses of people take to the road unsuitably prepared, and yet there was no sense of panic in the air. Clearly, the strange state of confusion had something to do with the election, but what?

I looked around and saw a friendly-faced farmer on horseback. His copper-colored hair and round face reminded me of my old friend Lucius Claudius, though Lucius would never have been seen in a tunic with so many patches. The man also had Lucius's red cheeks and nose and his unconcerned air, but these may have been attributable to the vanished contents of the deflated wineskin that hung from his shoulder. I hailed him and drew up alongside him.

"Citizen, what do you make of all this?" I said.

"Of what?"

"The crowd. The wagons alongside the road."

He shrugged and burped. "They have to sleep somewhere. I went all the way back home to Veii myself, and now I'm back. There wasn't room for me and the rest of my family at my cousin's house in Rome. I could hardly camp by the road like these others, not by myself."

"I don't understand. People are leaving Rome and then coming back?"

He looked at me a bit suspiciously. "What, you mean you're just now arriving? But you *are* a citizen." He looked to the iron ring on my finger for confirmation.

"Does this have something to do with the consular election?"

"What, you don't know? You haven't heard?" He gave me that look of smug satisfaction that citizens who vote reserve for those who do not. "The election was canceled!"

"Canceled?"

He nodded gravely. "By the mighty-mouthed Cicero himself. He got the Senate together and talked them into calling it off. Filthy Optimates!"

"But why? What was the reason?"

"The reason, or more properly the pretext, was that Catilina is hatching some terrible plot to kill off the Senate, as if most of them didn't deserve to have their throats cut, and so it's not safe to hold an election. It all happened days ago—

what, do you live in a cave? Messengers were sent out all over Italy telling people not to come to Rome, because the election was postponed. Well, a lot of people didn't believe it—thought it was just a trick to keep us away from the polls. Sounds just like the sort of thing the Optimates would pull, doesn't it? So we showed up anyway. Seeing such a crowd, the senators were ready to go ahead and hold the voting. But the day before, thunderbolts were seen on the horizon, out of a clear blue sky, and that night there was a small earthquake. The next morning the auspices were read and the augurs declared all the omens to be terrible. The voting stalls were all shut down. The election? Indefinitely postponed, they kept telling us. What in Hades does that mean? Then the rumors started flying thick and fast, saying the election will be in two days, or three, or ten. You see people leaving Rome and coming back and passing themselves going both ways. The last I heard is that the election will probably be the day after tomorrow."

"What!"

"Yes, the same day as the election for praetors. That's why I'm heading back today. I figure that instead of two days from now, they'll try to have it tomorrow, you see, so they can fool me into showing up a day late! But I won't be fooled by those dirty Optimates. I'll be at the Field of Mars outside the voting stalls bright and early tomorrow morning, ready to be counted with the rest of my tribe, and if need be, I'll be there again the next day and the next. For Catilina!" he abruptly shouted, raising his fist.

Around us, among the small circle who could hear the man's voice above the din, a number of fists went up in the air and I heard the name "Catilina!" shouted again and again, until several voices took it up as a sort of chant.

The man smiled at the demonstration of support he had set off, then turned back to me. "Of course, not everybody can stay in Rome indefinitely," he said, his smile fading. "That's why you see all these people going in the opposite direction. Common citizens have to get back to their farms, don't they? They have to worry about making a living and looking after their families. Not like Optimates, who can travel about at whim and never miss an election." He looked me up and down suspiciously. "I don't suppose you're one of the 'Best People'?"

"I don't have to justify myself to you, citizen," I snapped, and then realized I was not angry at the man, but at what he had told me. So it now appeared that the one thing I had most scrupulously avoided would take place, and I would be in Rome for the consular election! The gods were having a joke at my expense, I thought. No wonder we had suffered no mishaps on the journey—the gods insisted I get to Rome so that I could suffer through the election! I started to laugh. I stopped myself, then realized that it felt good to laugh, and so I let the laughter out. The stranger started to laugh, too, interrupted by a loud burp.

He raised his fist again. "To Catilina!"

My laughter stopped. "To the day when this madness is finally over," I said under my breath.

"What's that?" the man said, leaning toward me. I merely shook my head, slowed my horse, and waved as he moved on ahead of me.

We made slow but steady progress into the city. Great clouds of smoke and dust rose from the Field of Mars, where thousands of voters from outside Rome had pitched their camps; on a normal day one would have seen chariot racers practicing or soldiers staging mock battles. The Villa Publica, the open space where voters gathered, and the adjoining voting stalls, built like a maze of sheep runs, were closed off and empty. Traffic slowed again at the Flaminian Gate, but once through its portals we were at last within the old walls of the city, in Rome itself.

The sun was lowering in the west, casting a red haze over the rooftops, but Rome was still very much awake, especially on the bustling Subura Way. The notorious street took us into the beating heart of the city, not to the place where its temples and palaces are proudly gathered, but into the district of butcher shops and brothels and gambling dens. The smells of the city assaulted my nostrils—horse dung and furnace smoke, raw fish and perfume, a whiff of urine from a public privy mingling with the aroma of freshly baked bread. In a single block I saw more faces than I had seen all year in the countryside. I saw bodies that were old, fat, young, supple, clothed in costly tunics and gowns, or in rags, or almost naked. Women leaned out of the upper-story windows of cheap tenements and gossiped with one another across the street. Little boys played trigon in an open square, standing in a triangle and tossing their leather ball back and forth. An Ethiop in a red gown, her skin the color of lustrous ebony, gathered water at the public fountain.

The fountain caught my eye. It was the chief ornament of the neighborhood it served, with a trough below for horses and a spout above for people. The spout was made of marble, carved in the likeness of a kneeling dryad pouring water from an urn. The fountain had been there since I was a boy. More times than I could possibly count I had put my lips below the spout to get a cool drink of water, had filled my wineskin from it, had watered my horses from the trough. Nothing on earth could be more mundane, yet the fountain, and not just the fountain but everything around me, seemed at once familiar and strange. I had left Rome for good, I thought, and now I was back, and there was no denying that no matter how far afield I strayed or how long I stayed away, it would always be home.

I looked back at the cart. Diana was exhausted. She lay curled up against her mother, fast asleep despite the bumpy ride. Bethesda held one of her small hands and stroked her hair. She felt my gaze, looked up and smiled back at me. I knew in that moment that we shared the same sensation of homecoming, but she was less afraid to feel it, and less afraid to show it. The city was our city, no matter how much I might deny it or how deeply I might bury myself in the countryside. I breathed in deeply and smelled the Subura; I opened my eyes wide and tried to see everything before me at once. I turned and saw that Meto was looking at me oddly, the way I must so often look at him when I see him staring at the world around him in wide-eyed amazement. There is no place in the world like Rome.

We arrived at my old house on the Esquiline Hill dirty, hungry, and exhausted. The fading daylight had turned from red to hazy blue. The lamps in the house had already been lit.

We were later than I had expected to be, but Eco, knowing the chaotic state of the roads into the city, told me he was surprised to see us so soon.

"You must have come by the Flaminian Way," he said, clapping his hands to summon slaves to help with the unpacking. I nodded. "A good thing," he said. "The bridges down by the Aurelian Way are said to be a complete nightmare. They say there are wagons with skeletons at the reins."

"With skeleton oxen to pull them?"

Eco laughed and nodded. "That's the joke they're telling down in the Subura."

"So very typical of the Subura," I said dryly. The macabre sense of humor was familiar yet strange, like the city itself, like the house in which I found myself. My house it had been for many years, and before that my father's. Here was the atrium and the garden where I had played host to so many callers over the years, and where I had first met my dear old friend, Lucius Claudius, when he came to consult me after seeing a dead man walking about in the Subura.

"The garden looks very well kept," I said, with a slight catch in my throat.

"Yes, Menenia oversees the gardening herself. She's fond of growing things."

"The walls have a new coat of wash. I see you replaced those loose tiles along the roof and straightened the hinges on the front door. Even the fountain seems to be working."

Eco smiled and shrugged. "I wanted everything to be just right for Meto's special day. Ah, here's Menenia now."

My daughter-in-law approached with lowered eyes, greeting me with all the deference due a Roman patriarch. She had been quite a catch for Eco, considering his humble origins and the antiquity of her family name. He had picked a dark-haired beauty with olive skin, like Bethesda, which I think pleased his adoptive mother, whether she showed it or not.

The open sky above the garden quickly darkened to a deep blue pierced by stars that twinkled like bits of frost. Tables and couches were brought into the open air, and the slaves served a hearty meal fit for weary travelers, though we were almost too tired to eat it. Before the sky had turned from deep blue to black, everyone was abed except Eco and me.

Once we were alone he asked me a few questions about
Nemo and about Catilina's visit. I answered him wearily, and
once he learned that the situation seemed to have come to a
harmless if not very satisfactory conclusion, he did not press
me with questions. He did inform me that the latest word on
the elections was that they would be held on the day after the
morrow—in other words, on the day after Meto's toga ceremony, while we would still be in Rome.

"Ah, well," I sighed, "it can't be helped. Rome on an election day! We shall certainly get a full taste of the big city."

He showed me to my old room, where Bethesda was already asleep, and which he and Menenia had vacated for our
visit. Meto and Diana were sleeping in the room next door.
Where Eco himself was going to sleep and how he had jug-
gled his household slaves to make room for mine I was much
too tired to try to figure out. I lay down beside Bethesda, who
sighed in her sleep and shifted her hips to accommodate me,
and I fell asleep as my head touched the pillow and my lips
pressed against her scented hair.

A strange sobbing woke me.

I woke in slow, fitful stages, as men of my age do when
drawn from the black sleep of utter weariness. For a moment
I didn't know where I was—a strange thing to experience in
a house where I had lived most of my life. The furniture had
been moved about, that was the problem, and the bed was
different.

The sobbing that woke me came from the room next door.

I thought of Diana. The image of her finding the beheaded
corpse of Nemo sprang into my mind, and I was awake all
at once, conscious but still disoriented. My heart raced, but
my limbs lagged behind. I stood up, banged my elbow against
the wall, and cursed King Numa.

But it was not Diana who sobbed—the noise was not high-
pitched or childlike enough. Nor was it exactly sobbing, but
a kind of rhythmic, choking cry that came through clenched
teeth and tightly pressed lips, the sort of frightened whimper
made by someone in a nightmare.

I walked into the hallway. The sound ceased for a moment,
then I heard it again through the thin curtain draped across

the doorway to the room shared by Meto and Diana. A lamp
set into the wall still burned with a low flame—placed there
by thoughtful Eco, I was sure; he knew his father would have
to rise in the night and pass water and might trip or bump
his knee. I took the lamp, pulled aside the curtain, and stepped
into the tiny room.

Diana was sitting up in her little sleeping couch, her back
against the wall, blinking the sleep from her eyes as if she
had just woken up. She pulled the thick coverlet up to her
neck and looked at Meto with grave concern. "Papa, what's
wrong with him?"

I look down at Meto, who rocked back and forth on his
bed. His coverlet was all twisted and tangled; his hands had
become trapped in the cloth. His forehead was beaded with
sweat, and his jaw was tightly clenched. Behind his shut lids
his eyes seemed to twitch and dart about. He began to whimper again.

Once before I had seen him this way, not long after I had
taken him into my household and before I had manumitted
him and made him my son.

"Papa?" said Diana again, her voice very small. "Is
Meto—"

"He's all right," I said softly. "He's only dreaming. It must
be a very bad dream, but that's all it is. You mustn't worry.
Here, I'll take care of him. Why don't you go sleep with your
mother tonight?"

The suggestion pleased her immensely. She gathered up
her coverlet, draping it around her like a grown woman's
stola, and hopped out of her bed. She stopped so that I could
give her a kiss and then hurried to the door.

"You're sure he's all right, Papa?"

"Yes," I said, and Diana, her expression still grave but not
frightened, hurried off to join her mother.

I stood over Meto, watching his tormented face by the
lamplight, uncertain whether I should wake him. Suddenly he
gave a start and opened his eyes.

He sucked in a ragged breath. He reached to cover his face,
but his hands were caught in the twisted cloth. For a moment
he panicked, whimpering as if he still dreamed and jerking
wildly at the coverlet so that he only became more entangled.

I put down the lamp and gripped his arms to stop his thrashing. After a moment he relaxed, and together we extricated his hands.

He reached up to his face, then pulled his hands away, blinking in confusion at the sweat that glittered on his fingertips.

"You were having a nightmare," I said softly.

"I was in Sicily," he said in a hoarse whisper.

"I thought so. You had a dream like that once before, long ago."

"Did I? But I never think about Sicily. I hardly even remember the time I spent there. Why should I dream about it, especially now?" He sat up and blinked at the sweat that trickled into his eyes.

"I don't know. Here, use the coverlet to dry your forehead."

"Look, the whole pillow is wet! I'm so thirsty. . . ."

I looked about and glimpsed the dull gleam of a copper ewer and a cup on a small table by the door. I poured a cup of water and put it in Meto's hand. He drank it down in a single draft.

"Oh, Papa, it was horrible. Each of my hands was bound up in rags, just as the farmer used to do when he made me stand in the orchard to scare away the crows. He bundled my hands so I couldn't pick the fruit. The day was hot as an oven. The earth was so parched and broken that it was like a field of bricks—I kept stumbling and falling and skinning my knees. My lips were blistered from the sun. Sweat ran into my eyes, and I couldn't wipe it away. I was so thirsty, but I couldn't leave the field to get water or the farmer would beat me. I ran to the well anyway, but I couldn't pull up the bucket. I kept dropping it because my hands were all bound up and clumsy. And then the crows came—thousands of them. They swept over the orchard like horrible, shrill locusts until every tree was stripped bare. I knew the master would beat me. He would beat me until I died."

Meto shuddered. He stared raptly at the dancing flame of the lamp. "And then I was no longer in the field. I was back in Baiae. Not in the villa but in the arena that Crassus built especially to put his slaves to death. It was like being in a well, hemmed in by high walls all around with the sun beating on us. The sand was slick with blood. The mob leaned over the rail and jeered down at us. Their faces were hideous, all twisted with hate—and then the crows again! Thousands of crows, so many that the sky was black with them. They swarmed over everything. They beat their wings in my face and pecked at my eyes, and I tried to scare them away but I couldn't even lift my hands—oh, Papa!"

I poured more water. Meto put the cup to his lips and drank greedily.

"It was only a dream, Meto."

"But so real—"

"You're in Rome, not Sicily, not Baiae. You're in our house, surrounded by your family—"

"Oh, Papa, do I really have a family?"

"Of course you do!"

"No. *This* is the dream. This is what can't be real. I was born a slave, and that never changes."

"That's a lie, Meto. You are my son, just as surely as if you had my blood in your veins. You're free, just as free as if you had been born a Roman. Tomorrow you become a man, and after tomorrow you must never look back. Do you understand me?"

"But in my dream, Crassus, and the farmer in Sicily—"

"Those men owned you once, but that was long ago. They have no power over you now, and never will again."

Meto stared blankly at the wall and bit his lip. A tear spilled down his cheek. A good, stern Roman father would have slapped the tear away, shaken him until his teeth rattled, and then made him go stand in the courtyard and keep watch all night, to face up to his fears and beat them down, and the more miserable the lesson the better. But I have never claimed to be a good father by Roman standards. I embraced him for a long moment, pressing him hard against me until I felt him shudder and relax. I squeezed him tightly, knowing it was the last time I could ever hug him like a boy.

I offered to leave him the lamp, but he said he did not need it. I stepped into the hallway and let the curtain drop, then walked restlessly about the courtyard. It was not long

until I heard the quiet sound of his snoring—the dream as
much as the long day had worn him out.

Diana was with Bethesda, and the bed was not large
enough for all three of us, so I returned to the garden and
reclined on one of the dining couches. I watched the con-
stellations swirl slowly, slowly across the sky, until my lids
grew too heavy to stay open and Morpheus caught me in his
gentle snare.

SIXTEEN

THE day of Meto's majority dawned bright and clear. In the
garden I was up at daybreak, with the first blush of sunlight
on my face and all around me the sounds of the early-rising
slaves going about their chores.

It had been more than ten years since we had celebrated
Eco's toga day. That had been the year before the trials of
the Vestals and the outbreak of Spartacus's slave revolt. My
purse had been leaner then, and the provisions had been quite
humble. Eco's toga day had been a respectable affair, but not
the sort of thing to make the neighbors gossip with envy.
Perhaps it was for this reason that Eco seemed determined to
make sure that his younger brother enjoyed a sixteenth birthday that he would not soon forget.

It was unthinkable that the event should take place anywhere but Rome, and since Eco's house was the logical place,
he had offered early in the year to organize the details. That
role in itself would have been a sufficient gift for Eco to give
his brother, I thought. Eco had worked out the expenses and
had asked me for a sum which I thought generous but reasonable. I discovered only later that he had more than
matched the sum himself.

The day began with the erection of a yellow canopy over
the garden. Slaves trotted about on the roofs of the porticos, .
hoisting the edges of the canopy and pulling the corners tight
to fit them onto hooks. Below, more slaves began assembling

tables and covering them with cloths and setting dining couches all about. Many of the couches were quite exquisite, with finely carved legs and plush pillows of many colors; the best of the couches (as well as the best of the serving slaves) Eco had borrowed from some of his well-heeled clients. From the kitchen came the clanging of pots and the bustling sounds of slaves hard at work.

Our morning meal, however, consisted humbly enough of fresh figs and bread. I watched Meto as he hungrily bit into his handful of bread, and saw no evidence of the doubt and dismay that had visited him the night before. He seemed rested, quietly excited, and only a little nervous. Good, I thought; let nothing spoil this day.

After eating, the family departed for the baths. Two women slaves came along to attend to Bethesda and Menenia. The slave whose duties included grooming and barbering Eco would also be joining us. On this day Meto would receive his first shave.

We did not travel on foot, for Eco had rented a team of three litters and litter bearers for the day. They were waiting for us at the foot of the little trail leading down from the house to the Subura Way. Diana squealed with delight when she saw the broad-shouldered slaves and the long, elegant litters. Bethesda tried to hide her surprise behind a cosmopolitan moue. Menenia smiled knowingly. Meto blushed and looked almost embarrassed at being offered such a luxury.

"Eco," I said under my breath, "this must have cost—"

"Papa, it's only for one day! Besides, it's a special rate. I arranged it over a month ago. At the time the owner thought, of course, that on this date the elections would just be over and the out-of-towners would have already gone back to the countryside, leaving no one to hire his litters. I got them for next to nothing."

"Still—"

"Climb in! Here, you can share this one with Diana. I'll ride with Meto, and the women can ride together. The slaves will follow behind on foot."

And so I took a ride through the streets of Rome with Diana on my lap. I would be a liar if I said that it was anything less than an absolute delight. Even at that early hour

traffic was beginning to thicken, but what did it matter that
we had to pause at every street corner, when everything we
passed held such fascination for Diana? The smell of baking
bread delighted her as much as the scents that wafted from
the perfume seller's shop; she clapped her hands and laughed
at a group of bleary-eyed rustics emerging from a brothel,
finding them quite as absurd and amusing as a team of half-
naked acrobats who had decided to practice their handstands
and cartwheels in a little square off the Subura Way. She
bestowed a smile and a friendly wave on two gray-haired
slave women who smiled but did not wave back, too burdened
with their morning shopping, and then she did the same to a
pair of gaunt, unshaven brutes whom I knew to be paid assassins; the two looked rather chagrined and waved weakly
back. All things were equal in Diana's eyes; everyone and
everything was equally fascinating. That, I thought, is what
it means to be a child and why we long for childhood in our
dreams; later on we are forced to choose and discriminate at
every turn. Being a man and a citizen and a grown-up meant,
for example, having to choose at times between the likes of
Catilina and Cicero—and what fun was that, compared to
Diana's simple delight in looking and laughing and accepting
without question each moment of being alive?

After a while we veered off the Subura Way and took a
series of smaller streets that skirted the foot of the Oppian
Hill and eventually intersected with the Sacred Way. Here we
turned right and shortly came to a halt just outside the Forum,
at the steps leading up to the Senian Baths.

Inside the main entrance, beneath a shaded portico, the
men and women parted ways. Diana was peeved at the sep-
aration and pouted, then was quickly distracted when Menenia leaned down and said that they would take turns
brushing one another's hair. Diana abandoned me at once,
and I watched her skip away toward the women's baths,
flanked by Menenia and Bethesda holding her hands, and the
two slave women following behind with their burden of unguents and brushes and combs.

"She has quite a way with children," I said, looking after
Menenia and her long black hair.

"Yes," said Eco, nodding and smiling.

"I don't suppose—"

"Not yet, Papa."

He led us into the recently rebuilt and enlarged men's baths. The size was impressive, sprawling, almost Egyptian in scale. Even so, Eco complained about the crush. "Normally you'd have room to swing your elbows," he sighed, "but with so many men in the city for the election—well, you see how full it is."

We made our way to the central courtyard, where two naked wrestlers were grappling on the lawn. Their companions stood by, either cheering them on or stretching their own muscles. Beneath the shaded portico a group of Stoics, fully dressed, sat in a circle. As we passed them, I overheard two of them arguing the merits of Cicero's rhetorical style versus that of Hortensius, but it seemed to me that most of the philosophers were more interested in watching the naked young athletes.

Within the walls I was struck at once by the smell of the place (water on stone, bodies filthy and bodies clean) and the vague booming echoes that bounced from the domes in the ceiling (men laughing, boys whispering, water sloshing and dripping and splashing, the rhythmic slapping of wet feet against paving stones). We stripped out of our tunics and piled them onto the waiting, outstretched arms of Meto's barber. The slave folded them neatly and stored them in a niche in the wall, then returned with towels and strigils for our use.

We bathed first in the warm pool, which was gently scented with hyacinth, then in the hot pool, which made Meto yelp and lift his bottom from the water—and inspired the men already immersed to their necks to croak with laughter that echoed about the high-ceilinged room. Meto took no offense and merely laughed with them, suppressing another yelp as he lowered himself delicately but resolutely into the steaming, swirling water.

Scraped clean by the strigils, our faces flushed and our beards softened by the hot water, we removed ourselves from the pool and took turns submitting ourselves to the barber's blade. Meto went first, for this was his special day and the first time a razor would touch his face. The slave got into the spirit of things and made quite a production out of what could have been accomplished with three or four simple passes of the blade. There was, to be sure, a fair amount of downy growth on Meto's cheeks, almost invisible except when seen at certain angles in the light, while on his upper lip and his chin there was hardly any hair at all. Nevertheless, the barber approached the job as if he were faced with a grizzled veteran who had not shaved in months. He whetted the long, slender blade against a leather strop, rapidly passing it back and forth until Meto, watching the glittering metal, became fascinated. The barber applied a hot, steaming towel to Meto's face and cooed to him like a charioteer calming a steed. He circled about him and delicately applied the edge of the blade to Meto's cheeks, jaw, neck, and chin, and, saving the most vulnerable and difficult spot for last, to his upper lip. Meto flinched more than once—being shaved is, after all, the most intimate duty a man can entrust to a slave, and real trust is built only with time. But the man did a splendid job. When it was over there was not a single drop of blood to be seen anywhere, neither on the towel nor the blade nor on Meto's freshly shaved face. Meto seemed almost disappointed not to have been wounded, but he was fascinated by the novel sensation of touching his own denuded flesh.

The barber then produced his scissors—a very fine pair which Lucius Claudius had given to me as a gift and which I had passed on to Eco when I left for the countryside. The barber laid a rough cloth over Meto's shoulders and set about shearing him until he looked quite respectable and remarkably grown-up, with his ears and the back of his neck showing. The barber then treated his hair with a scented oil and was done with him.

I allowed the man to trim my hair and beard a bit, but refused to let him touch me with his razor. Then it was Eco's turn.

"This is your chance," I said, "to get rid of that absurd haircut and that eccentric beard."

Eco laughed. "Absurd and eccentric? Papa, look around you."

I did—and saw more than a few young men of Eco's age affecting the same style that he had adopted along with Marcus Caelius—their hair shorn short on the sides but left long

on top, their beards trimmed and blocked into a thin strap
across the jaw.

"You know where the fashion originated?"

"Yes, with Catilina. Or so you told me, and I've heard
others say the same. Catilina and his circle set all the trends."

"Well, did you know that Catilina has abandoned that particular fashion?"

"Really?"

"It happened under my very roof. One night he had the
thin beard, and the next morning—" I drew my finger across
my jaw. "All gone."

"Clean shaven?"

"As smooth as Meto's cheeks. Isn't that so, Meto?"

Meto, still stroking his face to experience the novelty of
it, nodded in confirmation.

"You see," I said, "it's Meto who has the fashionable look
now. Perhaps you should do the same."

"But everyone else is still wearing a chin-strap beard. . . ."

"For a while." I shrugged.

Eco reached out and the barber handed him a mirror. He
studied his face and ran his forefinger and thumb over the
thin black line of his beard. "Do you really think I should get
rid of it?"

"Catilina did," I said, and shrugged as if I really had no
opinion at all.

"Menenia never really cared for the beard anyway," Eco said
afterward, stroking his jaw and studying himself in the polished copper mirror held up by his barber. He tapped at his
chin and winced a bit; where the hair grew thickest the barber
had resorted to tweezers to pluck him smooth. Eco had borne
the ordeal without flinching. The barber, I suspect, had rather
enjoyed it. By inflicting such tiny discomforts, slaves are occasionally able to vent their frustration against their masters.

"I thought you said Menenia liked the beard," I said, to
needle Eco a bit.

"She'll like me even more without it, I'm sure."

And she did. To judge from the look in her eyes and in
Eco's when we rejoined the women in the vestibule, one
might have thought they had been parted for months, not mo-

ments. But such is the first blush of passion. As for Meto,
Bethesda touched his cheek and sighed, as if she could really
tell a difference where the razor had passed. Diana, with the
brutal frankness of a child, insisted that she could see no
change at all. Menenia again took charge of the situation by
proposing that Diana ride home in the litter with her, a suggestion to which Diana assented at once. Menenia had put up
her long hair in a coil held together with combs inlaid with
bits of shell, in very much the same fashion as Bethesda's—
though Menenia's combs, I noticed, were not quite so ornate.
I admired her tactfulness more and more.

Clean and refreshed, we arrived back at the house on the
Esquiline to find that preparations were almost complete. A
sundial down on the Subura Way had shown the time to be
almost noon; the first guests would arrive soon. It was time
for Meto to put on his toga.

The donning of the toga is no simple matter, even for
advocates and politicians like Cicero, who wear them almost
every day. What seems so simple in its unfolded state—a very
wide piece of thin white wool, cut into a roughly oblong
shape—becomes devilishly intractable and takes on a life of
its own when one attempts to make it into a respectable-
looking toga. That, at least, is my experience. Somehow the
thing must be made to cross the chest, drape over the shoulder, and lie across one arm. The precise placement of the
numerous folds and the way they hang are of supreme importance, or else a man ends up looking as if he simply left
the house wearing a common bed sheet—an absurd appearance sure to elicit the scorn of his neighbors.

Fortunately, as for everything else of importance, Romans
have slaves to take care of the problem of donning the toga.
(Indeed, there was a joke common when I was a young man
in Alexandria that the reason the Romans were bent on conquering the world was to supply themselves with slaves to
help them dress.) The same slave who groomed and barbered
Eco also served as his dresser. Here, as with the tweezers,
was an opportunity for a slave to take petty revenge on his
master, arranging for him to leave the house with the hem of
his toga dragging or some fold tenuously placed so that it
would later lose its shape. But Eco's dresser was quite com-

petent, and more than a little patient as he helped the three of us into our togas, beginning with his master, then myself, and finally Meto.

Eco had purchased Meto's toga from a fine shop at the foot of the Palatine. It took two attempts to get him into it, and quite a bit of fussing with the folds, but at last Meto stood before us perfectly draped in his first manly toga.

"How do I look?" he said.

"Splendid!" said Eco.

"Papa?"

I hesitated to speak, because I felt a catch in my throat. "You look—" I began to say, then had to clear my throat. How fine he looked! He had been a beautiful boy; he would be a handsome man, and in that moment one could see both together, past and future at once. His hair looked very black and his skin very smooth against the white wool; the color made him appear to be wrapped in purity. At the same time the authority and anonymity of the toga itself lent him an air of dignity and manliness beyond his years. I had told him last night that he could put his years of slavery behind him forever, that he need never worry about his unseemly origins again. Now I believed it myself.

"I am proud, Meto. Very proud."

He walked toward me and would have hugged me, I think, but the drapes of cloth over his left arm constrained him. He looked confounded for a moment, then laughed and turned around, realizing that moving comfortably in a toga was a skill he would have to master. "How on earth do I go to the privy with all this on?" he asked, grinning.

"I shall show you that when the need arises," I said, and sighed in mock weariness. "Ah, the duties of fatherhood!"

SEVENTEEN

OUT in the garden, the guests had begun to arrive. The sun was well up, and the filtered yellow light through the gauzy canopy cast a warm glow over the courtyard and into the hallways and rooms around it. Dishes with all sorts of delicacies had been placed on the tables, and the couches were disposed in informal arrangements, so that the guests could feed themselves and gather as they wished, rather than reclining and being served a succession of courses. This seemed rather chaotic and perhaps even a bit ungracious to me, but Eco assured me it was the new fashion.

"And like your beard, I suspect it shall come and go," I said under my breath.

As always with such gatherings, at first there seemed to be only a handful of guests, and then suddenly the garden was full of them, the men in their togas, the women in multicolored stolas. The soft murmur of their conversation filled the air. Their various perfumes and unguents mingled with the floral scents of the garden and the delectable odors of the roasted fig-peckers and stuffed pigeons that kept arriving on trays from the kitchen.

I made my way through the throng, stopping to speak with neighbors and clients I had not seen in years, and at last found Eco and pulled him aside. "Did you invite all these people?" I whispered.

"Of course. They're all friends or acquaintances. Most of them have known Meto since he was a little boy."

"But you can't be intending for all of them to walk through the Forum with us, and then come back here for dinner!"

"Of course not. This is only the general reception. People are invited to come and enjoy themselves, to get reacquainted with the family, to see Meto in his toga, to leave when they wish—"

"To eat you out of house and home! Look, over there!" A

man with a gray beard who looked vaguely familiar—the association was not pleasant, and I seemed to recall that we had been on opposite sides of some litigation—was hovering stealthily over a little serving table, dropping stuffed grape leaves into some sort of pouch inside his toga.

Eco laughed. "Isn't that old Festus? You remember, he came over once saying he wanted to consult you about a lawsuit pending against him, and we never saw that little Alexandrian vase again."

"No." I frowned, shaking my head. "That is not Festus."

Eco cocked his head. "Ah, I have it. Rutilius—his own brother brought suit against him, accusing him of thieving from him. The scoundrel never denied it; instead, he wanted us to dig up something horrible and scandalous about his brother, so as to even the score."

I shook my head. "No, it's not Rutilius, either, but probably someone just as awful. Surely you wouldn't have invited either of those two to Meto's party! Oh, the indignities I've had to put up with over the years to keep our bellies full! I'm just glad I'm away from it all now. And I'm glad you're young and hard-shelled enough to see your own way through the snares and traps of this city."

"You trained me well, Papa."

"I wish I had trained Meto half so well."

"Meto is different from me," he said. "And different from you."

"I worry about him sometimes, about his future. He's still such a boy—"

"Papa, you must stop saying that. Meto is a man now, not a boy."

"Still—oh, now this is too much! Look, now that wretched man has begun pilfering the honeyed dates! There won't be any for the other guests. You see, you've invited far too many people—neither of us can even remember who that man is, though we're both sure we don't like him. This is why it's a mistake to have people serve themselves. If we were all seated with slaves doing the serving—"

"I suppose I should do something," said Eco. "I'll go ask the fellow if he's murdered any wives or poisoned any business partners lately."

With that he ambled toward the old graybeard, who gave
a start and jumped back from the table when Eco touched his
shoulder. Eco smiled and said something and led him away
from the food. The jump must have dislodged the man's hidden cache, for a string of stuffed grape leaves and honeyed
dates began to drop from his toga, leaving a trail behind him
on the floor.

A hand touched my shoulder. I turned and saw a shock of
red hair, a spangling of freckles across a handsome nose, and
a pair of bright brown eyes looking into my own. The next
moment I was locked in a mutual embrace, then held at arm's
length while Marcus Valerius Messalla Rufus looked me up
and down.

"Gordianus! The country life most certainly agrees with
you—you look very fit indeed!"

"And the life of the city must agree with you, Rufus, for
you never seem to age at all from year to year."

"I am thirty-three this year, Gordianus."

"No! Why, when we met—"

"I was about the same age that your son Meto is now.
Time flies, Gordianus, and the world changes."

"Though never enough for my taste."

We had first met years ago in the house of Caecilia Me-
tella, when Rufus was assisting Cicero in his defense of Sextus Roscius. He had been only sixteen then, a patrician of
ancient lineage, politically precocious and secretly infatuated
with his mentor, Cicero. Not surprisingly, the infatuation had
come to nothing, but Rufus's more practical ambitions had
led to a successful career. He had been one of the youngest
men ever elected to the college of augurs, and as such was
frequently called upon to read the auspices and pronounce the
will of the gods. No public or private transaction of importance takes place in Rome, no army engages in battle, no
marriage is consecrated without consulting an augur. I myself
have never had much faith in reading messages into the flights
of birds and divining the will of Jupiter from a flash of lightning across the sky. Many (or most) augurs are mere political
hacks and charlatans, who use their power to suspend public
meetings and block the passage of legislation, but Rufus had
always seemed quite sincere in his belief in the science of

augury. He, too, had been involved in the scandal of the Vestal Virgins, for it was Rufus, as a religious colleague, whom the Virgo Maxima had first summoned for help when Catalina was discovered in the House of the Vestals. Rufus had called on Cicero, and Cicero had called on me. As I have remarked before, Rome sometimes seems a very small town indeed.

"I'm glad you've come, Rufus. There are very few faces from the Forum that I miss seeing from day to day, and yours is one of them. I mean it," I said, and I did, for Rufus had always been a young man of unusual integrity, soft-spoken but passionate in his beliefs and driven by an intensity that was not immediately apparent from his good-natured manner. His natural sense of justice and moral equanimity often seemed out of place among the self-serving oratory and ceaseless back-stabbing of the Forum. "But what's this?" I said. "You're wearing a candidate's toga."

Rufus pretended to dust himself, for the natural woolen color of his toga had been rubbed with chalk to make it a harsh white, as is the practice of men running for office. "That's because I'm running for praetor this year."

"Then I hope you win. Rome needs good men to run the city and give out justice."

"We shall see. The voting will take place tomorrow, just after the balloting for the consular election. Normally the election for praetors and the election for consuls take place on different days, of course, but with the postponement of the consular election—well, it will be an insanely busy day. Caesar, too, is running for a praetorship, as is Cicero's brother, Quintus."

"I suppose you're still allied with Cicero," I said, then saw from his face that I was mistaken.

"Cicero . . ." Rufus shrugged. "Well, you know the circus act he performed last summer in order to win the consulship. Blowing smoke from his mouth and jumping through hoops—though it came as no surprise to see him resorting to the most outlandish tricks to get himself elected. Over the years he's reversed his positions on virtually every issue, yet his rhetoric stays the same—as if rhetoric gave a man consistency, rather than principles. I find myself uncomfortable in his presence these days. I read the auspices on the day he took office—

not officially, but for my own satisfaction—and they por-
tended a year full of deceit and treachery, perhaps even disaster. Ah, Gordianus, I saw the look that just crossed your
face: you have no faith in the auguries. Neither does Cicero,
who thinks they're merely tools that men like himself can use
to manipulate the masses. And manipulate he does, shamelessly. Hypocritically turning his back on the children of
Sulla's victims who seek redress, railing against the Rullan
land reform, the way he handles that riot over special seating
for equestrians in the theater, and now this postponement of
the elections—you haven't been in the city long, have you?"

"I arrived only last night."

"Utter chaos. Voters arriving after hours or days of hard
traveling only to find that the election day has been indefinitely postponed—imagine! Angry farmers from up in Etruria
camping out on the Field of Mars, lighting camp fires that
could burn down the city—and when the praetors ride out to
warn them, the farmers pull out the rusty old swords they
used to carry for Sulla! It's enough to make me want to drop
out of the praetors' race. And all because of this preposterous
notion of Cicero's that Catilina is set to slaughter half the
Senate if he doesn't win the consulship. And now, as if to
prove he has no sense of shame or decorum left at all, Cicero
insists on going about the Forum wearing that absurd breastplate—"

"What's this?"

"Please, I can't even bear to think about it. You'll probably
see for yourself down in the Forum. Oh, Cicero! These days,
I'm aligned with Gaius Julius Caesar." I nodded at the name
of the young patrician who earlier in the year, against all
expectations, had won the election to take the place of the
deceased Pontifex Maximus, head of the state religion. In recent years Caesar had emerged as a standard-bearer for the
party of discontent and reform. His lavish expenditures on
public games and banquets had won the hearts of the masses
(and driven him deeply into debt, it was rumored, despite his
family's great wealth). He was said to be witty, charming,
devious, scornful of the Optimates, and possessed of that
single-minded nature which in men of politics can lead to
greatness, or disaster, or both. There were those who feared—

or hoped—that Caesar would become another Catilina, if indeed Catilina's credibility and hopes for the consulship were about to reach their end.

"Cicero has disappointed us all," sighed Rufus, "whereas Caesar . . ." His brown eyes sparkled. He smiled—a bit coyly, I thought. "The more I deal with Gaius Julius, the more impressed I become. As Pontifex Maximus, he has been an inspiration to me; he respects the religion of our ancestors in a way that a New Man like Cicero never could. His grasp of the world infinitely surpasses that of Cicero—in no small part because Caesar is not just an orator but a man of action who has known true battle and desperate danger—you must know that tale of his being kidnapped by pirates when he was young. He treated them with nothing but scorn, arranged for his own ransom, and later saw that they were all captured and crucified. Cicero would have merely bored them to death with his rhetoric. Caesar has taken up the cause of those who are still suffering from the dictatorship of Sulla, the children of those whom Sulla dispossessed and who now want to regain their birthrights. While Cicero, who always makes such a story of how he stood up to Sulla in the case of Sextus Roscius, won't lift a finger to help Sulla's victims—their claims are perfectly justified, he says, but this is not the proper time to disturb the government with their demands. It never is the proper time, of course! Not when the Optimates who control the state have their property and privileges nicely in place and want nothing to be disturbed. Cicero, who so bravely stood up against the dictator when he was young, does the bidding of the dictator's old friends without the least whimper of protest.

"And while Cicero pretends to be a man of vision, it's Caesar who sees the future. The empire must judiciously enfranchise those it conquers, not just exploit them. Stability may be built on blood and battle, but compassion must accompany victory. Caesar and I have pooled our resources to campaign for our praetorships together, but I feel rather presumptuous putting myself forward as if I were the equal of such a fine candidate. He's brilliant. There is no other word. When he speaks . . ." Rufus's voice trailed off, and he stared into the middle distance.

If Rufus is possessed of a fault, it is that he tends to fall blindly in love with those he respects and admires. So it had been with Cicero, but from the inflection Rufus now gave to the name he had once cherished, it was clear that love, respect, and admiration had all vanished together. Now he was clearly smitten with Caesar, and from what one heard about Caesar, beginning with his long-ago affair with the king of Bithynia, Rufus had a much better chance of finding reciprocation with the new object of his hero worship than he had from the old one—if indeed, to judge from the smitten look on his face, he had not found that reciprocation already.

"Ah, but you were remarking on my candidate's toga," said Rufus. "Actually, I was about to change out of it—"

"Please, you needn't stop campaigning just because you've entered our house," I said, teasing him. "I'd as soon ask a bird to take off its wings as request a politician to lay aside his candidacy."

He looked at me blankly. "But I shall have to put on my augur's robes before we commence the promenade, of course."

"But then—do you mean to say that you'll be reading the auspices for Meto?"

"Of course. That's why I'm here, in my capacity as an augur. Not that I wouldn't have come simply as a friend. But didn't Eco tell you?"

"No. I thought he'd simply find a private augur, the type that handles marriage ceremonies. I had no idea—and for you to take time out from your campaign on the day before the election—"

"What better advertisement at the last moment than for me to be seen somberly performing my duties as augur for the whole Forum to witness? I shall certainly look more respectable than all those candidates bullying and begging the mob for votes." He smiled shrewdly.

"Rufus!" I laughed. "You're a new stripe of politician, I think. Idealism as pragmatism; attention to duty and virtue rather than violence and outright bribery as the means to win an election. A quaint idea, but it just might work."

"Gordianus, you're hopelessly cynical."

"And you, Rufus, are still admirably full of hope and virtue."

He smiled. "But now I really must change into my augur's robes. Oh, and I may have a surprise for you and for Meto later in the day. But we'll talk about it then." I summoned one of Eco's slaves to show Rufus to a private room; his own small retinue of slaves, carrying his robes and augur's wand, followed behind.

I looked about, momentarily at sea amid the bobbing heads. Then, nearby and above the murmur of the crowd, I heard a familiar woman's voice speaking a familiar name: "Ah, then you must have known my late cousin, Lucius Claudius. Yes, a jolly man with hair as red as that of the handsome young man who just paraded through the room, but with a figure more like mine, I'm sorry to say. Yes, well, I inherited Lucius's house up on the Palatine, a huge, sprawling, wonderful old place, but far too big and fancy for my humble needs, though I'm told I can get a good income from it *if* I can find a renter who's rich enough to afford it, and *if* I'll do a bit of investing to pretty the place up, though my cousins think I should keep the house empty as a place for all of us to stay here in the city, but that means keeping at least a partial staff of full-time slaves in the place even when it's unoccupied, and I don't hear any of my cousins volunteering to feed them . . . Oh, but look, here he is, our host and my own dear neighbor. Gordianus, all happiness and pride to you on your dear son's birthday!"

"Claudia," I said, taking her proffered hand and kissing her rouged cheek. I would hardly have recognized her had I not heard her voice, for instead of the common, rather mannish country dress she wore on her farm, she was draped in an exquisite purple stola, the dark draperies of which elegantly accommodated the generous contours of her body. Her wispy hair had been rinsed with henna to give it a darker shade and arranged atop her head in a pillar so high that it must have grazed the door frame when she entered. Nor did she seem her usual relaxed self, but was exuberant to the point of bubbling over. She had been talking to a city neighbor of ours, a mousy little woman who had taken a friendly interest in Meto and Diana over the years and who had met Lucius

Claudius a few times when he had come to visit. The little
woman seemed completely overawed by Claudia's presence,
and looked more relieved than offended when Claudia
abruptly turned to me and thus gave her a chance to quietly
escape.

"Gordianus, I never expected such splendid trappings. The
food is superb—but not Congrio's cooking, I think. Your son
Eco's cook, or some slave he's brought in especially for the
occasion, am I right? Yes, I can usually tell one cook's touch
from another; my palate is quite sensitive that way. And Meto
looks so handsome in his toga! Though I notice that he does
seem to have a bit of trouble keeping it properly draped over
his left arm—there, you see how it's slipped down and he
keeps tugging it up with his right hand and shrugging his left
shoulder. But he'll get the hang of it, I'm sure. Oh, thank you
for letting me come, though I can hardly claim to be family
or even an old friend. Perhaps you can think of me as representing dear old Lucius, who wouldn't have missed this
event for anything."

"Lucius and I sat together and sipped wine many times in
this very garden," I said.

"Charming, charming," said Claudia absently. "Of course
I shouldn't be here at all. I'm leaving Rome for the farm this
afternoon, and given the congestion on the roads—"

"Leaving Rome? I thought you planned to spend the whole
month of Quinctilis here in the city, refurbishing Lucius's
town house."

"Ah, that's just it. I find myself more confused than ever
over what I want to do with the property. I'm at such an
impasse that I think the only thing to do is go straight back
to the farm and collect my wits before trying to come to a
decision. Yes, I know, I'll miss the excitement of the election
tomorrow, but thank Jupiter for that! I'm a woman and the
family doesn't need me for voting, anyway. Besides, I've had
more than enough of the city already. The idea of spending
a whole month here—well, you can see how deranged it
makes me. I feel like a complete impostor all made up like
this: I'd feel much more comfortable in an old sack, and I
get so rattled I can't stop talking . . ."

She suddenly laughed and took a deep breath. "Well,

you're seeing proof of that! And quite frankly, I've had more than enough of my cousin Manius and his shrill wife. They're the ones who have the property north of you but spend most of their time here in Rome. They insist on dropping by to see me every day and inviting me to their house every night, and I've had enough. Their cook is a disaster, to begin with, and their politics are too conservative even for me. You can imagine all the ranting and raving in such a household, what with the elections going on."

Claudia lowered her voice and brought her face close to mine. "But my stay with Manius has borne at least some good fruit, dear Gordianus, and it has to do with you. In fact, that's why I stayed in Rome until now, and today came here first instead of heading straight home to Etruria. Gordianus, promise that you won't be angry, but I took the liberty of bringing cousin Manius with me today. Presumptuous of me, I know, but the opportunity seemed just right and I said to myself, 'Do it!' So I did. And I think it will all be for the best. There he is—Manius! Yes, cousin, come and meet our host."

She was calling to someone over my shoulder. When I turned around, whom should I see but the graybeard who had been pilfering stuffed grape leaves and honeyed dates! No wonder my imperfect recollection of him had made me uneasy; he had been present in the court when Cicero had defended my inheritance from Lucius Claudius, though he was so nondescript that his face had made little impression on me. I remembered him now, and I also remembered the comments about me that Congrio's assistant had overheard him make at Claudia's family gathering: "Stupid nobody with no ancestors, who should be put in a cage and carted back to Rome!" What was such a man doing in our house on Meto's toga day? Claudia was mad to have brought him with her. Had I been a superstitious sort like Rufus, I would have found his presence an ill omen indeed.

Claudia seemed to read my thoughts. As Manius approached, she gripped my elbow and spoke in my ear. "Now, Gordianus, it serves no one's interests to have bad blood between our families. Manius resented your good fortune and has spoken ill of you in the past, as have all my cousins, but he and I have had many a conversation on the subject during my stay in Rome and I think I've convinced him to make peace. That's why he's here. You will be hospitable, won't you?"

I was given little choice, for the next moment the man was standing before me, with a sour expression on his face and his eyes averted. "So you're Gordianus," he said, finally looking up. "My cousin Claudia seems to think we should be *friends*." He made the word drip with sarcasm.

"Now, Manius," cautioned Claudia, smiling apprehensively.

I took a deep breath. "*Friend* is an exalted word, Manius Claudius, not to be bestowed lightly. I was a friend of your late cousin Lucius, and of that I'm very proud. By his will, you and I are now neighbors, if not friends; yet it seems to me that neighbors can at least strive for harmony and the common good. And since we are neighbors—"

"Only through a legal accident and a lapse in my late cousin Lucius's good judgment, not to say good taste," said Manius sourly.

I bit my tongue for several heartbeats. "Claudia, I thought you said—"

"Yes, I did, Gordianus, and I don't understand," said Claudia through gritted teeth. "Manius, before we left the house this morning I thought it was agreed—"

"All that I agreed to, Claudia, was that I would come to this house, behave in a civil manner, and see for myself whether or not I found the family of Gordianus to be respectable, charming and, to use your words, 'entirely the sort of people one would desire for neighbors.' Well, I have come, Claudia. I have behaved with the same decorum as if I were in my own home. And I have failed to be charmed. Indeed, quite the opposite; my very worst suspicions of these people have been confirmed."

"Oh, dear," said Claudia quietly, putting her fingers to her lips.

"I have been conversing with some of the other guests," Manius went on. "There are far too many people here of the radical, populist, rabble-rousing sort. But then, there are too many people of that sort everywhere in Rome, for my taste. I won't deny that there are a handful of respectable people here, even some fellow patricians, though what they should be doing in such a house and at such a gathering escapes me. The standards of those with whom one does and does not mix have fallen considerably since I was young. Collapsed altogether, I should say."

"Manius, stop!" gasped Claudia.

But Manius did not stop. "As I was saying, I have conversed with others here, and discovered just what sort of family inhabits this house and now resides on Lucius's farm. Last year I took no particular interest in investigating the nature of our opposition when Lucius's estate was being settled. I didn't care what sort of person this Gordianus was, only that he be stopped from absconding with a share of the family's inheritance. I did know that he was a plebeian with no ancestors to speak of, and engaged in some sort of shady enterprise or other, but I had no idea what sort of family he had spawned. A most irregular family indeed! Of his own parentage, no one seems to know a thing, which says a great deal in itself. His wife is not Roman at all, but half Egyptian and half Jew, and was once upon a time his slave and concubine! Their elder son, the one who now lives in this house, was born Roman, apparently, but not to Gordianus and his slave woman; this Eco—such a preposterous and uncouth name!—was an abandoned beggar boy adopted off the streets. As for the lad whose birthday and coming of age is being celebrated today, it appears he was born a slave down in Baiae, probably of Greek origin. A slave! And now look at him, standing over there in his toga. In the days of our grandparents, the great days of the Republic, such a desecration would have been utterly unthinkable. No wonder the boy can't seem to make the toga sit correctly on his shoulders!"

I listened to this tirade at first speechless, then with burning ears, then with my fists tightly clenched to keep them from flying through the air. At some point Claudia, her gaze nervously flitting from Manius to me, timidly laid her hand on my elbow. Her gentle restraint was unnecessary, for I had no intention of resorting to violence in my own home and spoiling the harmony of Meto's celebration. Instead I kept my hands at my sides and let the fury boil inside me while Manius continued.

"Last and least there is a daughter, I understand, born free and apparently of both parents. A Roman girl, legally, and no doubt she will someday marry into a Roman house—bringing the Egyptian and Jewish blood of her slave-born mother with her. Is it any wonder the Republic is collapsing into chaos at such a swift rate? Who stands up for the Roman family and the values it once aspired to? Even a fine Claudian like our cousin Lucius was apparently taken in—to use your word, Claudia, 'charmed'—by all this barnyard decadence, but then, Lucius was always eccentric. I suppose that's your excuse as well, Claudia—eccentricity. If you find such an association congenial, then you're welcome to it, but please keep it to yourself. I came here today as an act of goodwill, and as a favor to you, Claudia, but I see now that I was gravely mistaken. I allowed soft words from a woman to weaken my resolve and taint my judgment. My time here has been completely wasted."

An instant later he would have turned on his heel and departed in smug triumph, leaving me gasping with anger and facing no choice but to swallow my fury or run after him and make a spectacle of myself before our guests. But sometimes, in such moments, Nemesis takes a hand and makes fools of those who deserve it.

"Oh, your visit hasn't been a complete waste, surely," I said, not even knowing yet what I meant. The menace in my voice must have alerted Manius, for he stepped back, but not quickly enough. From the corner of his eye he must have glimpsed the upward flicking movement of my hand; he raised his arms to deflect a blow that never landed, for I made no attempt to strike his face or his vulnerable middle. Instead, without conscious intention, I aimed for that place where earlier I had seen his hand disappear into his toga while he pilfered delicacies from the tables. I slapped at a hard, bulging spot hidden within the hanging folds. Manius grunted in alarm. Claudia's hands went to her mouth and she uttered a little shriek, just loud enough to turn the heads of a small circle around us. An instant later, the little cloth bag that had been hidden beneath Manius's toga, tied to his waist, fell at his feet and burst open at the seams. Honeyed dates, stuffed grape leaves, roasted nuts, and sesame cakes spilled onto the ground as if from a cornucopia.

Claudia, who before had shrieked with alarm, now shrieked with laughter, as did not a few of the women gathered around, and there was plentiful laughter in the lower registers as well. Manius Claudius turned so red that I thought he might burst open like the sack at his feet, and his whole body seemed to twitch, as if he desperately wanted to bolt from the garden but was rooted to the spot. He fixed me with a smoldering stare and at last managed to raise his arm and make an inchoate gesture in the air, accompanied by a sputtering, incoherent curse. He spun around and might have exited with some of his dignity intact had not his stamping foot landed on a honeyed date. The slippery misstep sent him sprawling quite as effectively as if I had planted the kick I longed to deliver on his backside. He did not fall—not quite—but his awkward, bumbling withdrawal left him without a foot to stand on, metaphorically at least. He did not grace us with another look at his face, but I could see that his ears were bright scarlet. I could easily imagine streams of smoke pouring from his nostrils.

I began to laugh, so hard that when Eco and Meto rushed to my side, thinking I was choking, it was impossible for me to explain what had transpired. I laughed so hard I wept, and all the bitterness and anger that Manius had stirred up inside me became as sweet as honey.

When at last I managed to catch my breath and wipe the tears from my eyes, I saw that Claudia had vanished, with less fanfare than her cousin but probably with no less embarrassment. Poor Claudia, I thought, you meant well, but all your efforts to make peace between our families have come to naught.

EIGHTEEN

I was not allowed either to brood or gloat over the incident with Manius Claudius, for the party continued and the demands on the paterfamilias went on. I greeted, charmed, said farewells. Eventually, after a few embarrassing lapses, I insisted that Eco stay close by my side, as if I were a politician in the Forum and he were my nomenclator, whispering in my ear the names I couldn't quite remember. The number of people one has met after living continuously for more than twenty years in a city like Rome is staggering. A profession such as mine had brought me into intimate contact with an ever-expanding circle of well-connected clients, and Eco had carried on my work. The remarkable thing was how respectable we seemed to have become. I could remember a time when orators and advocates would never deign to enter my house or invite me into theirs; they dealt with me through their slaves instead. But perseverance and prosperity lend credibility, and over the years I suppose any line of endeavor can become respectable so long as it succeeds and survives, and especially if it brings profit to the right class of people.

My feet began to ache from so much standing. I ate far too much for the middle of a hot summer day, and I drank too much wine (because my throat was dry from so much talking—at least that was my excuse). And yet, altogether, I was elated. I felt light as a feather. I was at the party, and yet I also observed the party, detached and amused, like a visitor from Olympus. It was the wine, I told myself, or the succession of flattering accolades bestowed on myself and on Meto, or the lingering glow of Manius Claudius's humiliation—it was these things, I told myself, that accounted for my mood, which became happier and happier as the day progressed. It had nothing to do with the simple fact of being back in Rome, of feeling myself at the very center of the greatest concentration of humanity in the world, of sensing all around me the power and passion of those who live, love, connive, suffer, triumph, and die every day in such a mad place. I no longer loved Rome, I told myself; we had been lovers once, but that was over now, once and for all. I might return to her from time to time, but merely as a visitor, free of the torrid, squalid, jubilant memory of our tumultuous marriage. I loved Rome no longer, I told myself, and almost believed it.

No moment of all the moments in that day was more purely joyous than the one in which a certain booming laugh struck my ears and stirred my memory to instant recognition. I looked up from whatever superficial conversation I was engaged in and searched for the source of the laughter, but in the crowd I could not discern the face I looked for. Then I heard the same laugh close at hand and turned to see Meto being squeezed in the bearish grip of a broadly smiling, stoutly muscled man with a thick beard all black and white like variegated marble. Behind the bearish man stood another figure in a toga, a strikingly handsome younger man with an enigmatic smile on his lips, like a Greek statue in Roman dress.

At last the man released Meto, who caught his breath and dazedly tried to straighten the folds of his toga. Meto felt my gaze and returned it with a strange expression on his face. "Papa," he called, with an odd quaver in his voice, "look who's here!"

"As usual, I heard you before I saw you!" I said, laughing and striding toward the newcomer. I braced myself for the ironlike hug of my old friend Marcus Mummius.

It was Mummius who had defied the will of Marcus Crassus, sought out Meto in Sicily and saved him from a life of slavery chasing after crows in a dusty field. Mummius had delivered Meto to this house on the very day that Diana was born. In my heart he would always have a special place.

Meto had not been the only one of Crassus's slaves whom Mummius had made a special endeavor to save. Behind him now stood Apollonius, whom Crassus had sold to a cruel Egyptian master. Mummius had sailed across the inland sea to rescue the slave, had brought him back to Rome and had ultimately set him free. Apollonius remained in Mummius's household as his freedman and constant companion. How

Crassus had despised the passion that had driven his lieutenant to care so deeply for the fate of a mere slave! That discord
had been the wedge that drove Crassus and Mummius further
and further apart until Mummius at last switched his allegiance to Pompey—which was just as well, for only in the
service of Pompey, scourge of the sea pirates and conqueror
of the East, could a military man like Mummius exercise his
true genius.

"Marcus!" I cried. "And Apollonius! How good to see you
both, especially on this of all days. But what a surprise! I
should have thought you were still in the East with Pompey."

"What, with no more fighting to be done?" said Mummius.
"Mithridates is finished, the lesser kingdoms have been
brought under Roman control—there's nothing left to do but
make political settlements. Playing Jupiter, I call it, moving
petty princes about like knucklebones on a playing board.
Pompey loves that sort of work, but you know I haven't the
patience for it. It's taking an army into battle that I'm good
at, though I think I must be getting too old and slow to be a
soldier much longer, unless that's how I want to die. Here,
just look at this!"

Without hesitation he hoisted up his purple-bordered senator's toga to show his burly thighs. Since the wearing of a
toga entails the absence of any sort of underclothes that might
constrict the private parts—a man could hardly tend to the
call of nature with his left arm draped, all the folds of a toga
to contend with, and a loincloth as well—Mummius was dangerously near to exposing himself. As I recalled, there was
quite a bit of him to be exposed. I looked about a little nervously and gestured with my hands as if I were putting out
a fire, but one might as well try to stop a bear from scratching
its stomach as try to stop Marcus Mummius from showing
off a war wound. Fortunately the only woman who happened
to be passing by was Bethesda, heading toward the kitchen
with an officious air. At the spectacle of Mummius showing
off his burly legs, she paused, cocked her head, and cast a
cool, calculating stare as if she were passing judgment on a
purchase at the butcher's market.

"Here, see this one!" Mummius pointed to a long, thin scar
that ran from the pale flesh of his upper thigh down to the

region of his knee, where the skin was tanned as dark as an Egyptian's. Amid the furlike covering of hair, the pink, denuded strip of flesh stood out vividly. Mummius flexed the muscles beneath and made the long scar writhe like a snake. He seemed to find this uproariously amusing, to judge by his raucous laughter. I glanced over his shoulder at Apollonius, who rolled his eyes but smiled indulgently. No doubt he had witnessed the scene many times before.

"Battle of the Abas River!" Mummius declared, dropping the hem of his toga. "And I was a fool to let it happen. I was on horseback and the Albanian was on foot, wearing nothing but a bearskin and rushing at me with his sword drawn, screaming at the top of his lungs. I saw him coming—had plenty of time to knock him flat with the blunt end of my spear, or else impale him on the point, or draw my sword and parry his blows, or simply give my horse a good kick to get out of his way. The problem was, I had *too* much time to think—couldn't settle on one choice or the other. Should have been pure reflex, but on that day I found out that my reflexes are as dead as Carthage. Found out the hard way. Oh, the burning when that blade broke the flesh and then tore straight down! I was the one screaming then."

"What did you do?" said Meto, who had always loved soldiers' tales.

"Where before I had done nothing, now I did everything at once! Banged the fellow's helmet with the blunt end of my spear, whipped it around and stabbed him in the chest with the point, unsheathed my sword with my other hand and slashed his throat, then gave my horse a hard kick and headed straight into the enemy ranks! It all happened in the blink of an eye."

"You went toward the enemy, not away? Even wounded as you were?" said Meto.

"I had no choice. Something I've learned in battles before—if you take a bad wound, the worst thing to do is stop. That's the one thing you mustn't do, because then the pain'll come crashing down on you all at once and that's the end of you. I've seen many a man die from a wound that shouldn't have killed him, just because he stopped what he was doing and gave in to the thing. No, you open your mouth in a

scream to let the Furies come inside you, and you plunge into
the thick of it. That way you never even feel the wound at
all, and you don't bleed to death either, because all the blood
rushes into your head and your sword arm, instead of pouring
out of the cut."

Meto stared at him, awed.

"You know, they say there were Amazons fighting with
the Albanians in that battle, though I didn't see any, and there
were no women found among the dead. I'm not sure I'd care
to go up against a woman in combat . . . But here I am talking
about myself, as usual, when this day belongs to young Meto!
What a sight you make in your manly toga! Why, I remember
when you were a small thing, running about the villa at Baiae,
carrying messages and pestering the other—the others . . ."

The last word came out oddly. "Other slaves," he had
meant to say.

I saw again the strange look that had crossed Meto's face
on Mummius's arrival. So long as Mummius carried on in
his usual bluff manner, boasting of his battles, Meto could
simply listen in fascination, but as soon as the conversation
turned to the past, Mummius became a palpable reminder of
the very circumstances from which he had rescued Meto long
ago. Meto's cheeks turned red, but not as red as those of
Mummius, who realized that he had trod upon uncertain
ground. He attempted a hasty retreat, but found himself mired.

"I mean to say—do you remember what Gordianus said
of you then—that you were the eyes and ears of the household? You slipped about hardly noticed, seeing and hearing
all. An arm of Nemesis, he called you afterward, for the part
you played in saving all the other—the others . . ." Once
again, like the general who finds himself lost in a fog and
unwittingly circles back into the same ambush from which he
had fled, Mummius stumbled over the forbidden word. I
groaned.

"The other slaves," Meto said, very quietly.

"What?" stammered Mummius, who could hardly have
failed to hear.

"The other slaves, you meant to say," said Meto. "You
were speaking of my part in saving the other slaves—meaning the others who were slaves, like myself, of Crassus."

Mummius twisted his mouth into various shapes. Was he ever this tongue-tied when addressing his troops? "Well—yes, I suppose that's what I'm trying to say." Or trying not to say, I thought.

Meto lowered his eyes. "It's all right, Marcus Mummius. There's no point in obscuring the truth; so my father has taught me. If we hide what is true, then we see only what is false." He raised his eyes, and his gaze was steady and strong. "We have all been many things on the way to becoming what we are. This toga does not hide what I was; that is not its purpose. It clothes what I am. I am the son of Gordianus. Today I become a man and a full citizen of Rome."

Mummius drew back and raised his eyebrows. Then his face burst into a smile. "Splendid!" he cried out. "What a splendid way you have with words! You shall do us all proud in years to come, I know it!"

The tension was broken. There were smiles all around. Eco gripped Meto's shoulder and squeezed it. My sons have never been very physically demonstrative with each other, and this spontaneous gesture of affection gratified and surprised me.

"You must be very proud," said a voice close to my ear.

I turned to see the handsome face of a young man with a bland smile and a mischievous glint in his dark eyes, framed by a chin-strap beard and a fashionable haircut. The face was out of place and its owner most certainly uninvited; for a brief instant I was disoriented, hardly believing he was there.

"Marcus Caelius! What are you doing here?" I glanced over my shoulder. Meto and Eco were talking together in low voices. Mummius and Apollonius had turned to pay their respects to Bethesda. I seized Caelius's elbow and took him aside.

He raised one eyebrow. "If I were of a sensitive nature I might think you were unhappy to see me."

"Spare your wit for the Forum, Caelius."

"Really, Gordianus, do you think I would waste my wit on politicians? I find that poets and prostitutes appreciate it far more."

"I don't think you were invited here today," I said, trying to keep my voice steady.

"No, but Cicero was. Your elder son Eco made sure that

the consul received an invitation months in advance. But Cicero cannot come today. Too busy taking advantage of his last chance to harangue the voters down in the Forum before tomorrow's election. And of course he could hardly be seen attending this party, given the fictitious state of discord between the two of you. I've been doing my best to sow those rumors of grave unhappiness between Cicero and Gordianus—all to convince Catilina that he can trust you, of course."

"That's all over now, Caelius. Or will be with tomorrow's election."

"All over, Gordianus? I think not. Just beginning, I imagine. Anyway, Cicero sends his regrets, knowing that you'll understand why he can't come himself. Officially, of course, to anyone who should happen to ask, I'm here on behalf of Catilina, to extend his respects on the occasion of your son's coming of age."

"How many masters do you have, Marcus Caelius?" I used the word "master" deliberately to insult him, but Caelius was unfazed.

"Catilina knows that I'm loyal only to him. So does Cicero. But with Cicero it happens to be true."

"I wonder."

His face changed. The crooked smile, like that of a schoolboy with a secret, faded from his lips, and the mischievous glint in his eyes vanished. He lowered his voice. "Forgive me, Gordianus. We're all wrought up after the last few days here in Rome, especially those of us closest to Cicero. Imagine what it's like for me shuttling back and forth between him and Catilina, pretending to serve them both. I tend to behave facetiously when the strain becomes too great."

"Marcus Caelius, why are you here?" I asked wearily.

"For the reasons I've just stated. To convey regards from Catilina, who believes I represent him when in fact I do not, and to give to you Cicero's apologies for his absence, since the pretense of your estrangement from Cicero must be maintained."

"Maintained? But why? I've done as you and Cicero demanded; I opened my doors to Catilina, though for what purpose I still don't know. Tomorrow the voters will decide Catilina's future, and then I'm finished with all of you, for good. Whether Catilina wins or loses, I'll have done as you asked. My debt to Cicero is discharged, and that's the end of it."

"Not quite," said Caelius.

"What do you mean?"

"I mean that things are not as simple as that, Gordianus. I mean that tomorrow's election—if indeed Cicero doesn't manage this afternoon to convince the Senate to postpone it again—is only the opening gambit in the contest to come."

"What contest? Are you saying that Cicero still expects me to carry on this charade of being friendly with Catilina?"

"Your cooperation is more important now than ever before."

"Marcus Caelius, you're beginning to make me angry."

"Forgive me, Gordianus. I'll depart."

"Caelius—"

"Yes?"

"Caelius, what do you know of the body that was left in my barn?"

"A body?" said Caelius, without expression.

"Right after your visit to my farm, right after you posed a riddle about bodies without heads, and heads without bodies. Catilina's riddle, you called it. And then the body appeared on my property. The body without its head."

Caelius wrinkled his brow. Was his consternation real or feigned? Under my scrutiny the light seemed to fade from his eyes so that they became entirely opaque, and I could no more discern the truth in them than I could by looking into the painted eyes of a statue. "I know nothing about a body," he said.

"Would Cicero say the same if I asked him? Would Catilina?"

"Believe me, Cicero would know no more than I do. As for Catilina . . ."

"Yes?"

He shook his head. "I see no reason why you should suspect Catilina of such an atrocity."

"When I hesitated to respond to your demand that I play host to Catilina, the body appeared, headless, as in the riddle—as if to persuade me."

"Gordianus, I know nothing about this, I swear to Hercules. It makes no sense. . . ."

The harder I looked into his eyes, the more impossible he became to fathom. Was he lying? And if so, on whose behalf?

"But if you wish to hear Catilina's riddle complete . . ."

"Yes?"

"Wait until Catilina's rebuttal to Cicero in the Senate this afternoon. What Catilina has to say will be on everyone's lips. Everyone in Rome will know the riddle then."

"Tell it to me now, Marcus Caelius—"

At that moment a hush fell over the garden, and heads turned toward the hallway that led to the private chambers, from which Rufus had emerged in augur's dress. He was resplendent in his trabea, a woolen robe ornamented with a purple border and saffron-colored stripes. In his right hand he carried a long, slender wand made of ivory and decorated with carvings of ravens, crows, owls, eagles, vultures, and chickens, as well as foxes, wolves, horses, and dogs—all the various birds and quadrupeds from whose actions the augurs interpret the will of the gods.

Rufus spoke, his voice full of authority. "The time has come for Meto to set foot in the Forum wearing his manly toga, and to ascend with me to the Temple of Jupiter for the reading of the auspices."

I looked around and saw that Marcus Caelius was gone.

NINETEEN

WITH many wishes of goodwill, the guests dispersed. The kitchen slaves, brooded over by Bethesda and Menenia, began to clear the tables and return the uneaten food to earthen jars. Eco summoned the rest of the household slaves and looked them over to be sure they were clean and presentable. A Roman commands no respect in the Forum unless he has a retinue—the longer the retinue, the greater the respect—and as Cicero says, a slave takes up as much space as a citizen. Our retinue would be small, but with Rufus at its head it would be distinguished. Mummius, too, declared that he and Apollonius would walk with us. Making up the balance were a few other citizens and freedmen, men who owed favors to Eco or had long been bonded to our family by ties of mutual obligation.

We departed down the narrow pathway to the Subura, where our hired litters waited. Diana was left at home (and hardly protested, thanks to some soothing from Menenia), so I shared my litter with Bethesda. Eco rode with Menenia, and Meto, in the foremost litter, with Rufus. I felt some chagrin at having no place to offer Marcus Mummius, but he forestalled my apologies by declaring he would never accept a ride on the back of slaves so long as he still had two good legs to walk on. There followed the predictable boasting about great distances traversed while on campaign; Mummius claimed to have once covered sixty miles in a single day on a rocky mountain road, wearing battle armor.

We settled ourselves in the litters and were lifted above the crowd. The carriers bore us into the Subura Way with our retinue following behind.

Bethesda was silent for a while, watching the people on the street and scrutinizing the vendors and their wares. She missed the bustle of the city, I thought. "It went very well," she finally said.

"Yes."

"The food was excellent."

"Quite. Even by our usual standards, and Congrio spoils us."

"The yellow canopy was a good idea."

"Yes, the sun is strong today."

"And the litters are rather fun."

"A treat," I agreed. For such a light conversation, Bethesda's voice was oddly flat, and her face was pensive as she watched the people of the Subura go by. "I saw that our neighbor Claudia made an appearance."

"Didn't she speak to you?"

"No."

"Well, she left abruptly. She made the mistake of bringing along her cousin Manius. He was rather abusive and made a bit of a scene, but it ended badly for him. Did you see it?"

"No, I must have been busy in the kitchen. But I heard about it later. Eco says the man made a fool of himself. Was he really slipping food into his toga?"

"I'm afraid so."

"How absurd! He must be as rich as Crassus."

"You exaggerate, I'm sure, but I doubt that Manius ever goes hungry. These country Claudii are an odd lot. They appear to have an exceedingly grasping and stubborn nature." Even Claudia, I thought, was distinguished by her miserly hatred of waste.

"And there was someone else who came to the party . . ."

"Yes?" I said.

"That young man who visited us some while ago. The one who prevailed upon you to play host to Catilina. The handsome one."

"Marcus Caelius."

"Yes. I had no chance to speak to him, either."

I tried not to smile. "Now, Bethesda, I understand your regret at missing a second opportunity to charm such a good-looking young man—"

She turned her face from the street. Her expression stopped me cold.

"Husband, do you really think I would brood this way over a lost chance to flirt? What was Marcus Caelius doing in our house today?" Her face was drawn, like a garment worn too tightly, and her eyes had a haunted look that turned my heart to water. She was not angry, but frightened.

"Bethesda!" I reached out to put my arm around her, but she shrugged off my embrace.

"Don't coddle me like a slave. Tell me why that man came to Meto's party. What did he want from you?"

"Very well. He came, he said, to deliver apologies from Cicero for not coming in person."

"Did he ask more favors of you?" When I hesitated to answer, Bethesda's eyes flashed. "I knew it! What will he have us doing this time? Does this involve Catilina again?"

"Bethesda, I told Caelius in no uncertain terms that my obligation was already discharged."

"And did that satisfy him?"

Again I hesitated, and the spark in her eyes ignited. "I knew it! More trouble!"

"Not necessarily, Bethesda."

"How can you say that! Do you know how I've worried since Diana found that horrible body in the stable? I will not have such things going on around us!"

"Then we should probably do whatever Caelius demands."

"No!"

"Yes! Satisfy him—and whomever he really represents, whether it's Cicero or Catilina or—" For the first time it occurred to me that Caelius might actually be representing some other party.

"You must not deal with him," Bethesda insisted.

"He asks very little."

"So far! But it will come to something horrible. When we left the city, you said you would leave such things behind."

"I did leave them, Bethesda. They followed me."

"But this is different. This is not your way, to do things without knowing why. You've always been an open and honest man, even when you worked in secret."

"That doesn't quite make sense, Bethesda."

"You know what I mean!"

I sighed. "Yes, I do. The duplicity that Caelius forces on me doesn't sit well with me, either. In truth, I dread it." Without intention, as naturally as a child, I reached for her hand and twined my fingers with hers. "I'm frightened, too, Bethesda. Frightened and dismayed and a little disgusted—and proud and elated and sentimental, because this is Meto's toga day! If only our lives could be one thing at a time, instead of this mad jumble."

It was my turn to become pensive and watch the street pass by. "Bethesda, when I was young and beginning to make my way in the world pursuing the work that my father did, there was one thing he made me promise that I would never do—use my skills to capture runaway slaves. It was an easy promise for me to make, and I've never broken it, for I have no appetite for such work. Over the years I added another promise to myself—that I would not become a spy for the state, or ever become a dictator's secret policeman if the Republic should fall prey to another Sulla, Jupiter forbid.

"There are times when I have done things of which I'm not particularly proud, and times when distinguishing right from wrong has confounded me—thus did the gods make this world, of multiple uncertainties and questions without answers. But I've always been able to sleep at night and to look at myself in a mirror without shame. Now I find myself compelled to be a spy, or at least to consort with spies, and I'm not even certain for whom I'm working. Am I the agent of Cicero and the Optimates, which is to say the state? Or am I the unwitting tool of Catilina, who would surely make himself a dictator if he could, for how else can he bring about the changes he promises his disinherited and disenfranchised followers? In the end, I tell myself, I don't care so long as my family is left in peace—and my own cynicism distresses me! Am I wise, or merely apathetic—or a coward?"

Bethesda looked at me steadily and squeezed my hand. "You are not a coward."

"Ah, but I don't hear you reassuring me that I'm wise!"

She cooled a bit and slid her hand from mine. She rested her chin on her knuckles and gazed out at the street. She spoke in a tone that was at once detached and determined and that allowed no contradiction. "In your own heart you know what I know: that something terrible looms over us. I'm a woman, what can I do? Meto is barely a man. Eco, too, is very young and has his own life here in the city. It is up to you, husband. All up to you."

I blinked and sighed, and wondered: was this woman ever really my slave?

The litters deposited us at the eastern end of the Forum, not far from the Senian Baths. By custom, the women stayed behind to await our return. Meto set foot upon the Sacred Way wearing a happy smile along with his toga. Whatever he had been talking about with Rufus, it must have been on happier topics than my conversation with Bethesda.

Led by Rufus in his augur's vestments, our little party made its way through the very heart of Rome. Amid the throngs of vendors, voters, politicians, and vagrants, we passed the House of the Pontifex Maximus, where young Caesar now held office, and the adjoining House of the Vestal

Virgins, the scene of Catilina's indiscretion ten years before. We passed the Temple of Vesta, where the sacred fire burns eternally in the hearth of the goddess, and the Temple of Castor and Pollux, where the scales and measures of the state are kept. We passed the tribunal of the commissioners, where justice had been served in the case of Asuvius and the forged will—my first adventure with Lucius Claudius. We came to the Rostra, the orator's platform decorated with the beaks of ships captured in war, from which politicians harangue the masses, and advocates argue their cases before the courts of law. Here young Cicero had pleaded the case that established his career, defending Sextus Roscius from the charge of parricide; I served as his investigator. At that time, a great equestrian statue of the dictator Sulla dominated the square, but no longer; the Senate had ordered it removed only a few years ago. Behind the Rostra stood the Senate House, where today Cicero, as consul of Rome, would be arguing for another postponement of the consular election, and Catilina would be defending himself from charges of disrupting the state.

The square was thronged with people. A politician was speaking from the Rostra to an audience of voters—one of the Optimates' candidates for consul, to judge from his rhetoric, though I couldn't tell whether it was Murena or Silanus—but there were plenty of other speakers all around to vie for the voters' ears. Wherever a flight of steps or a wall allowed a man to stand and be seen above the crowd, there appeared to be a politician addressing anyone within hearing. In places the discourse seemed to be more a debate than an address, with members of the crowd shouting questions or accusations at the speaker or even booing him from his platform. Within the crowd, insults were hurled, men were spat upon, and scuffles erupted here and there. Rome on the eve of an election!

Obviously, the larger a speaker's retinue, the greater his security and the more effective his rhetoric, and so each politician was surrounded by as many of his supporters as he could muster, not to mention freedmen, slaves, and bodyguards. The square had the appearance of warring factions intermingling for no discernible reason, except to cheer for their own favorite and jeer at the others. The threat of violence hung heavy in the air; I thought of a seething pot on the verge of boiling.

With Rufus at its head, our retinue commanded respect. His saffron-striped trabea was immediately recognizable; men parted and made way for the augur. Many in the crowd knew him by name, and hailed him cheerfully; his youth and charm, unusual for an augur, no doubt contributed to his popularity. Mummius, too, cut a familiar and popular figure with the crowd; people still remembered his role in putting down the Spartacan slave revolt, and his more recent service with Pompey earned him even more respect.

Meto was not ignored. The purpose of our retinue was evident at a glance to many in the crowd—an augur, father, son, and followers headed for the Capitoline—and there were spontaneous outbursts of applause for the young man taking his first walk as an adult through the Forum. Meto, smiling happily, eyes wide, seemed dazzled. I was not even sure if he realized that the bursts of applause were for him.

The press of bodies was so dense that several times we had to stop and wait for an opening before proceeding. All around, from one end of the Forum to the other, I caught snatches of heated conversations. Near the Temple of Castor and Pollux two men were discussing an incident in the theater. The mention of Cicero caught my ear.

"—and the speech he made afterward was the best he's ever made!" said the first man.

"Absurd!" countered the second. "It was the low point of his career. Cicero should have resigned in disgrace! Defending such an unfair and un-Roman practice! Once upon a time the theater was the one place where Romans were truly equal. When I was a boy, the rich and poor all sat shoulder to shoulder. We booed the villains and laughed at the clowns and lusted after the young lovers as a single body."

"Everyone equal in the theater? The first four rows have always been for senators."

"Because being in the Senate is a mark of achievement and distinguished ancestry. But why should there be special seats for certain people just because they have money? They're common folk, the same as I am. We should all sit together, like family, instead of splitting ourselves up between rich and poor. What, do I smell too strong from honest sweat for a perfumed merchant to sit next to me? Otho's law is a scandal, it's bad for Rome, and for Cicero to defend it—"

"Otho's law makes perfect sense, as you would know if you had really listened to Cicero's speech."

"I'd rather listen to an actor reciting Plautus—and from the best seats in the theater, if I make the effort to show up early enough to get them, rather than being shooed away because I don't happen to be of the rich equestrian class, like Cicero's family! Why should I have to sit behind some fat-headed equestrian who blocks my view?"

"Obviously you'd rather spit venom than deal in cogent argument."

"Very well, dismiss me because I never had schooling in rhetoric! Perhaps a fist in your nose would be more convincing?"

Fortunately, an opening in the throng allowed us to pass at that moment. I leaned toward Rufus. "What is all this scandal about an incident in the theater? You mentioned it before."

"You haven't heard about it?"

"No."

He rolled his eyes. "It's been the talk of the city for months. It never stops! The easiest way to pick an argument in Rome! You know how it goes sometimes—a simple little incident suddenly attracts everyone's attention, ignites a controversy and becomes the rallying point for issues far greater than anything inherent in the incident itself. Well, a few years ago Lucius Roscius Otho was tribune and passed a bill reserving fourteen rows of seats in the theater for the wealthy equestrians."

"Yes, I remember."

"It seemed a liberal measure at the time, at least within the Senate. There have always been at least four rows reserved for senators; therefore, Otho argued, why not reserve some rows for equestrians? The moneyed set who can't get into the Senate were very pleased, and they've been financing Otho's political career ever since. This year he's serving a term as praetor, and as such he's made sure that his seating law has been scrupulously enforced at all the public festivals. Well, it was in the month of Aprilis, at the very start of the theater season during the Megalesian Games, at a performance of 'The Girl from Andros,' when Otho himself appeared in the audience. A bunch of young rowdies at the back of the theater began to boo and hiss, saying they wanted better seats, and why couldn't they sit in some empty seats up in the equestrian rows? They shouted epithets at Otho. In response a contingent in the equestrian section began to applaud Otho. This was taken as an insult by the rowdies, who saw the equestrians' applause as a way of thanking Otho for not forcing them to sit with such trash. More hissing, more cheering, and soon there were threats and spitballs being hurled. The crowd was on the verge of a riot.

"Almost immediately, word of the incident got to Cicero in his house on the Palatine—Cicero's eyes and ears are everywhere, and nothing important happens in the city that he doesn't know about at once. A short while later the consul himself appeared at the theater, with an armed bodyguard. He summoned everyone in the place to the Temple of Bellona and delivered a splendid speech that ended with the whole crowd cheering Otho and returning to their seats to watch the play without further interruption."

"What did Cicero say?"

"I wasn't there to hear it myself, but I'm sure that Cicero's secretary Tiro transcribed a copy, if you care to read it. Cicero cannot open his mouth without Tiro's scribbling every utterance, as if his master were an oracle. You know that Cicero can be quite convincing when he defends privilege and order. I believe he dwelled upon Otho's honorable service to the state, and scolded those who would be so crude as to hiss and boo an upstanding Roman magistrate. Then he defended extending privileges to the equestrians; not hard for him to do— he comes from the equestrian class himself, of course," said Rufus, with a patrician's disdainful lift of the eyebrow. "It's my theory that the more hot-blooded members of the crowd simply got bored and ran off to expend their energies elsewhere, while the more sedate audience members sheepishly returned to enjoy the comedy. Cicero counted the affair as a personal triumph."

"From the argument we just overheard, there must be those who disagree."

"The controversy rages on and on. It's always little things that prick at people. Catilina has picked it up as a campaign issue, naturally. Catilina is always ready to be the champion of the discontented."

A little later I overheard another argument, this one between an orator on a makeshift wooden pedestal and a citizen who refused to let him deliver his speech, engaging him in a heated debate instead.

"The Rullan land reform would have changed everything for the better!" insisted the orator.

"Nonsense!" shouted the citizen. "It was one of the most poorly thought-out pieces of legislation every proposed, and Cicero was right to speak out against it."

"Cicero is nothing more than a mouthpiece for the Optimates."

"And why not? It's up to the Best People to speak out against these mad schemes put forward by Caesar simply to curry favor with the mob—and to get his hands on Egypt, into the deal."

"It was Rullus who proposed the law, not Caesar."

"Rullus opens his mouth and Caesar's words come out."

"Very well, then, we agree that the argument was not Rullus against Cicero, but Caesar against the Optimates," said the orator.

"Exactly!"

"And you must also agree that if the Rullan bill had become law, there could have been redistribution of land to the people who need it without recourse to violence or unfair confiscation."

"Absurd! It would never have worked. Who in Rome wants to head out for the countryside and become a farmer, anyway, when here in the city there's the circus and the festivals and the free grain dole?"

"It's attitudes like that that are ruining the Republic."

"It's Romans who are ruining the Republic, because they've grown soft and lazy. That's why we need the Optimates to keep their hands on the tiller."

"Their hands in the till, you mean. Better to have the hands of the common man on a plow."

"Ridiculous—look at the mess up in Etruria with Sulla's veterans. Not one in ten of them turned out to be a decent farmer. Now they're all bankrupt and looking to that demagogue Catilina to bail them out, with fire and sword if he has to."

"So you don't want land reform, you don't like Catilina—"

"I despise him! He and his circle of pampered, well-born, irresponsible dilettantes. They've had their chance to lead decent lives and they've wasted themselves instead—going hopelessly into debt to more responsible and upright citizens. This whole radical scheme of his to forgive debts is no favor to the masses—it's a way to get himself and his friends off the hook, and to plunder the property of those who deserve to keep what they and their ancestors have accumulated. If schemers like Catilina end up powerless and impoverished, it's no more than they deserve. And if the voters of Rome have no more sense than to go along with their crazy ideas—"

"All right, all right, far be it from me to stand up for Catilina. But you seem to have just as low an opinion of Caesar—"

"Who is just as much in debt! No wonder they both suck up to the famous millionaire. Catilina and Caesar are like twin babies hanging off Crassus's teats. Ha! Like Romulus and Remus suckling the she-wolf!" The speaker made obscene popping noises with his lips. This last elicited equal parts of laughter and hissing from the crowd, who were either amused or offended by such blasphemy.

"Very well, citizen, you insult Catilina, you insult Caesar and Crassus—I suppose you cling to Pompey."

"I have no use for Pompey either. They're all wild horses trying to break from the chariot. They're in a race with each other, and they care nothing at all for the common good."

"And Cicero does?" sneered the orator.

"Yes, Cicero does. Catilina, Caesar, Crassus, Pompey—every one of them would make himself dictator if he could, and cut off the heads of the rest. You can't say that about a man like Cicero. He's spoken against tyranny since the dictatorship of Sulla, when it took a brave man to do so. A mouthpiece, you call him—very well, that's what a consul should be, speaking out for those in the Senate whose families made the Republic what it is and have been running it ever since the kings were thrown down. We don't need rule by the mob, or rule by dictators, but the steady, slow, sure rule of those who know best."

This last set off a round of jeering from some newcomers who had just arrived in the crowd, and the debate degenerated into a shouting match. Fortunately, the agitation in the crowd provided an opening, and we were able to press on. A moment later Meto drew beside me with an earnest look on his face.

"Papa, I couldn't follow their argument at all!"

"I could, but only barely. Land reform! The populists all promise it, but they can't make it come true. The Optimates turn it into a dirty word."

"What was the Rullan bill they were talking about?"

"Something that was proposed earlier this year. I remember our neighbor Claudia railing against it. I really don't know the details," I admitted.

Rufus turned toward us. "One of Caesar's ideas, in conjunction with Crassus, and typically brilliant. The problem: how to find land for those who need it here in Italy. The solution: sell public lands we've conquered in distant countries and set aside those proceeds to buy land in Italy on which to settle the poor in agricultural colonies. Not a wholesale confiscation and redistribution of land from rich to poor, as Catilina proposes, but the expenditure of public funds to effect a fair reapportionment."

"Why did the man bring up Egypt?" said Meto.

"The foreign lands to be sold include those in Egypt, which the late Alexander II bequeathed to Rome. The Rullan law proposed setting up a special commission of ten men who would oversee the project, including its administration in Egypt—"

"And Caesar would have been one of the commissioners," said Mummius dryly, joining the discussion. "He'd have picked Egypt like a fig from a tree."

"If you like," Rufus conceded. "Crassus would have been on the commission as well, since his support was vital. With

Egypt under their sway, they'd have had a bastion against
Pompey's power in the East, you see. You'd have thought
the Optimates would like that, since they fear Pompey, too.
But as long as Pompey is away from Rome and campaigning
in the East, the Optimates fear Caesar and Crassus more."

"Not to mention Catilina and the mob," I said.

"Yes, but Catilina intentionally distanced himself from the
Rullan bill. Too mild for him; to have been seen as a force
behind it would have compromised his radical reputation. Nor
would his support have been an asset to the bill; his enthusiasm would have further alarmed the Optimates, who were
already suspicious of the idea."

"Even so, I imagine Catilina would have accepted an ap-
pointment as one of the new land commissioners, along with
Caesar and Crassus."

Rufus smiled wryly. "Your grasp of politics is more subtle
than you let on, Gordianus."

"But the bill was defeated," said Meto.

"Yes. The Optimates saw it as merely a tool for Caesar
and Crassus, and yes, perhaps Catilina, to increase their
power, and any talk of land reform immediately sets them on
edge. They always pretend to support the idea in the abstract,
but no concrete proposal ever satisfies them. Cicero became
their spokesman, as he has been since they rallied to support
him for the consulship. But he didn't limit himself to debating
the matter in the Senate. He came here, to the Forum, and
brought the issue directly to the people."

"But it's the sort of bill the people like, isn't it? That's
why they call Caesar a populist, isn't it?" asked Meto. "Why
would Cicero debate against the bill before the very people
it's meant to help?"

"Because Cicero could talk a condemned man into chopping off his own head," said Rufus. "He knows how to make
a speech; he knows what arguments will impress the mob.
First, he said that the law was directed against Pompey, even
though Pompey was specifically excluded from the investi-
gations that were to be made into the acquisitions of other
generals abroad. The people don't like it when they hear that
something will hurt Pompey. Pompey is the darling of the
mob; successful generals always are. To denigrate Pompey is

to denigrate the people of Rome, to call Pompey into question is to insult Rome's favorite son, et cetera, et cetera. Then Cicero took aim at the commission itself, saying it would become a little court of ten despots. They would embezzle the funds they raised, robbing the Roman people of their own wealth; they would punish their enemies by forcing them to sell their lands, which would be almost as wicked as the proscriptions and confiscations that Sulla carried out; they would forcibly move the contented urban poor onto barren tracts of land where they would starve. Well, you know how persuasive Cicero can be, especially when it comes to convincing people to work against their own interests. I do believe he could convince a beggar that a rock is better than a coin because it weighs more, and an empty stomach is better than a full one because it causes no indigestion."

"But Rullus must have defended the law," said Meto.

"Yes, and Rullus was pounded into dust—rhetorically speaking. Caesar and Crassus each wet a finger, held it in the wind, and decided to keep quiet, though in debate either one is a match for Cicero, at least to my ear. The time was simply not right, and the law was dropped. Soon people got distracted by other matters, like the incident in the theater, and Catilina's new campaign for consul."

"You say the time was not right for such reform," I said. "In Rome, and with the Optimates in control of the Senate, when is it ever the right time for change?"

"*Nunquam,*" said Rufus, smiling ruefully: *never.*

Our destination was the summit of the Capitoline Hill, where Rufus would perform his augury. We at last managed to cross the densely crowded area in front of the Rostra and came to the wide, paved path that ascends in winding stages to the summit of the Capitoline. Here we had to pause again, for a large group of men was descending the path, so many in number that they blocked any opportunity to ascend. As the group drew nearer, Rufus's face brightened. His eyes were better than mine, for he had already made out the faces of the two men who walked side by side at the head of their respective retinues. One was dressed in a senatorial toga, white bordered with purple; the other wore a toga with the much broader purple border of the Pontifex Maximus.

They smiled in return when they recognized Rufus, and nodded to Marcus Mummius. For the moment Meto and myself and the rest were invisible to them. Those who wear purple acknowledge one another first; others come later.

"Rufus!" said the Pontifex Maximus.

"Caesar!" said Rufus, bowing his head. He made the same gesture of obeisance to the white-bearded augur who stood beside the Pontifex Maximus, dressed like Rufus in a trabea with saffron stripes. Within their college a younger augur always defers to an elder.

I took a close look at the face of our Pontifex Maximus. Not yet forty, Gaius Julius Caesar had already established himself as a force to be reckoned with in the Republic. His patrician heritage was impeccable; his family ties to the dictator Sulla's old enemy Marius, once a death sentence, had become a part of his credentials as a leader of the populist movement. If Cicero was the master of rhetoric, able to get what he wanted by the sheer force of argument, Caesar was said to be the master of pure politics, a genius at comprehending the multitudinous and often obscure strands of the ages-old web that bound together the state and the priesthoods. He understood the most arcane and cumbersome rules of procedure within the Senate, and could invoke them at the most unexpected moments to the consternation of his enemies; he knew the intricate workings of the ever-growing bureaucracy that carried out (or as often confounded) the will of the Senate and the people; as Pontifex Maximus he oversaw the maze of religious offices and brotherhoods that interpreted omens and sacred texts and thus exercised power over the Senate, the army, and commerce by allowing or not allowing these institutions to function on a given day.

Caesar was not a handsome man, but in no sense was he plain. His narrow face was striking, but beauty did not figure into it. It was the vitality of his eyes that impressed, along with the patrician austerity of his high cheekbones and forehead, and the drawn tension of his thin lips, which seemed perpetually to smile at some ironic jest. His erect carriage and steady gait marked him as a man in absolute control of his every movement, fully conscious of his own fluid grace and

quietly pleased with the image he presented to the world. I
have met only a handful of men (and some women) with such
a way about them, and they have all been either wealthy,
eminently well-educated patricians, or else slaves who possess the natural charm of the unlearned along with the remarkable beauty that sweeps every other consideration before
it. We mortals in the middle can never hope to possess the
perfect grace of these god-blessed others higher and lower
than ourselves. It comes from power, I suppose, political or
sexual—not simply possessing it, but instinctively knowing
how to use it, and having the capacity to enjoy using it. Catilina had a measure of that grace, but in him it was mixed
with something else, an imperfection of some sort that made
him all the more fascinating. In Caesar, that grace was un-
diluted. He seemed to me to be power personified, and thus
he projected (like the beautiful) the illusion of being inde-
structible and immortal. Rend his mortal vessel with wounds,
cut him open to show the blood and bones within, slice his
head from his shoulders—still, it seemed, his lips would wear
that same effortless smile.

Somehow I had glimpsed his companion from the corner
of my eye, or perhaps had recognized his gait from a distance,
for I knew that the man was Marcus Licinius Crassus before
I reluctantly set my eyes on him. There were few men whom
I less desired to meet by chance on this of all days. As Rufus
turned to greet him, Crassus's restless gaze fell on me. He
knew me in an instant, though it had been almost nine years
since the affair at Baiae. Things there had not gone as he had
wished, thanks to me, and Crassus was a man accustomed to
having his own way in everything to do with lesser men; from
the glint in his eye I saw that the memory still rankled. Catilina had indicated that Crassus respected me in a begrudging
way, but if so, he was good at concealing it. His eyes had a
cold gleam without a trace of humor.

He had grown noticeably older since I had last seen him
so close—older and richer and more powerful, his ambitions
held in check only by the conflicting ambitions of men as
shrewd and ruthless as himself. His hair was half-gray and
his face was too stern to be handsome. His countenance displayed a perpetual discontent; he was a man who could never

succeed enough for his own satisfaction. "Crassus, Crassus, rich as Croesus," went the popular ditty, comparing him to the miser of legend, but to me he was Sisyphus, forever rolling the boulder uphill, watching it tumble down and beginning again, achieving wealth and influence far beyond the measure of other men but never achieving enough to earn his rest. He had been vying for power with Pompey for years; with Caesar he seemed to be on excellent terms, at the moment at least.

"We've just come down from the Arx," said Caesar, meaning the northern summit of the Capitoline Hill. Like the acropolis in Athens, the Arx was the high place chosen by Rome's founders on which to build their citadel and their most sacred temples. From the Arx a man can see all Rome below, and can in turn be seen unobstructed by the gods. "We've been taking the auspices for today's convocation of the Senate. A pity that you weren't available to perform the augury, Rufus."

"Today I perform a private augury," said Rufus, indicating those of us behind him with the slightest tilt of his head. "I take it that the auspices for the Senate were favorable, as you wished?"

"They were indeed," said Caesar. The ironic smile seemed to say that the auspices could hardly have been otherwise. "A hawk flew up from the west, and then dipped toward the north. The augur Festus assures us this presages a good day for the Senate to convene."

"For myself," said Crassus dryly, "I thought it more significant that a crow flew over the Senate House, cackling and complaining but going in circles, as if he were not going to have his way no matter how much he squawked. That crow reminded me of someone—could it be Cicero? But then I'm not privy to the secret knowledge of the augurs and am hardly qualified to make an interpretation." His smile did little to soften his sarcasm.

Rufus ignored this veiled insult to his profession. "Will things go well in the debate today?" he asked Caesar.

"Oh, yes," Caesar said with a sigh. "Cicero hasn't the votes to censure Catilina, and he certainly hasn't the support he needs to postpone the elections again. It's not what happens today, but what the voters will do tomorrow that's worrisome. We shall see. But what's this you're up to, a young man's coming of age?" He smiled and nodded amiably in our direction, but did not press for an introduction. "Speaking of Cicero, if you're on your way up to the Arx, you'll pass both of our esteemed consuls on their way down." He glanced over his shoulder. "Cicero should be right behind us; he was eager enough to have the auspices done with so that he could convene the Senate. The debate will begin at any moment. You will miss the opening arguments, Rufus, and you as well, Marcus Mummius."

"We'll come later," said Rufus.

"It's likely to be brief. Cicero is just doing it for show; he'll want to get it over with and make use of what's left of the day to harangue the crowd in the Forum—his last chance to sway the voters against Catilina. You should use the day to do some final campaigning yourself, Rufus. I intend to. I'm counting on you to serve with me as praetor next year."

"Don't worry, after I've performed my augury I shall change into my candidate's toga at once!" Rufus laughed.

Caesar and Crassus began to move on. Our little party stepped aside to make way for their retinues. Crassus had not said a word to his estranged confederate Mummius, and apparently did not intend to. But he did look steadily at me as he stepped past, then paused as his eyes fell on Meto.

"Don't I know you, young man?" he said.

I looked at Meto and felt a pang of dread, remembering his nightmare. An uncertain emotion lit his eyes, but his face remained impassive. "You knew me once, citizen," he said. His voice was quiet but steady.

"Did I?" said Crassus, cocking his head and drawing up his shoulders. "Yes, so I did, however scarcely. So you are a freedman now, Meto?"

"Yes."

"The adopted son of Gordianus?"

I moved my lips to answer, but Meto answered first. "I am."

"How interesting. Yes, only recently a friend of mine happened to inform me of your circumstances." Did he mean Catilina? Or could it have been his once-protégé, Marcus Cae-

lius? Whichever, I did not like the idea of my family being
discussed behind my back. "Odd, how this detail of your
manumission and adoption had somehow escaped my attention all these years."

"It hardly seems a matter worthy of concern to a man as
eminent as yourself, citizen," said Meto, returning Crassus's
scrutiny with an unwavering gaze. I looked at Meto, slightly
awed. Not only had he said exactly what I would have said,
but he had said it just as I would have tried to, with the very
same, deliberately straightforward inflection, neither contemptuous nor servile. Sometimes we open our mouths and hear
our parents speak; sometimes our children open their mouths
and our own voices come out.

"The last I knew of you, Meto, you were in Sicily, where
I had *arranged* for you to be," said Crassus, delicately avoiding the crass vocabulary of commerce and ownership. "Just
as I had arranged for that one to be off to Egypt," he added,
indicating Apollonius and casting a sharp glance at Mummius. "What part did Marcus Mummius play in frustrating
those delicate arrangements, I wonder? Never mind. Now I
meet you in a toga, Meto, on your way up to the Arx to
celebrate your citizenship." His lips compressed into the thin-
nest of smiles. He narrowed his eyes and shifted them between me and Meto. "The goddess Fortune has smiled on
you, Meto. May she smile on you always," he said in a hollow
voice, and turned away, summoning his retinue after him.

Perhaps he meant it, for above and beyond the triumph of
the individual will, a Roman respects and bows to the incom-
prehensible caprices of Fortune, and to a man like Crassus
the salvation of a boy like Meto, in the face of all Crassus's
efforts to the contrary, might very well seem a supernatural
occurrence, evidence of the intervention of the gods and thus
an occasion for respect and the humble expression of goodwill. Who knows, after all, when the goddess Fortune might
turn her back even on the richest man in Rome?

The lengthy retinues passed. We pressed onward and upward, only to encounter another retinue. Coming down from
the citadel, following Crassus and Caesar, was Cicero himself,
together with his fellow consul, the notorious nonentity Gaius
Antonius. At the party, Rufus had said something in passing

about Cicero wearing armor—"that absurd breastplate," he had called it, and had then passed on to another subject without explaining. Now I saw what he had meant, for covering Cicero's chest and reflecting the harsh gleam of the afternoon sun was a burnished breastplate such as a general might wear in combat. Cicero's consular toga was loosened at the neck and throat so that the boldly shaped pectorals of the hammered and filigreed metal were fully displayed. Around him hovered a bodyguard of armed men, surly-looking fellows who walked with their hands on the hilts of their sheathed daggers. It struck me that such a display was less worthy of a consul of the Republic than of a suspicious autocrat—even the dictator Sulla had gone about the Forum unarmed and unguarded, trusting the gods to protect him.

Before I could ask Rufus to explain the breastplate and the heavy bodyguard, Cicero was upon us. In the middle of conversing with Antonius he caught sight of Rufus. His expression passed through rapid changes. He looked at first genuinely pleased, then grave and doubtful, then almost playfully shrewd—the face of a mentor who has lost the allegiance of a once-devoted pupil but does not despair of regaining it. "Dear Rufus!" he said, smiling broadly.

"Cicero," said Rufus in return, without emotion.

"And Marcus Mummius, back from serving Pompey in the East. And . . . Gordianus," said Cicero, finally seeing me. His voice went flat for a moment, then took on a politician's affable familiarity. "Ah, yes, you've come to take the auspices for young Meto's coming of age. We're all getting older, aren't we, Gordianus?"

Some more than others, I thought, though the years had actually done much to soften Cicero's unlovely features. The thin, sharp nose was now rather fleshy; the slender neck with its prominent knob was now padded with rings of fat; the pointed chin had become lost in jowls. The man whose delicate constitution would hardly allow him to eat in the heat of the day had nevertheless managed to grow portly. Cicero had never been handsome, but he had managed to acquire a look of prosperity and self-assurance. His voice, once grating and unpleasant, had been trained and transformed over the years into a melodious instrument. "How I regret that I was unable to attend your party," he said. "The demands of being consul are unending—you understand, I'm sure. But I did send Marcus Caelius to offer my apologies. He did deliver his message, did he not?" The look in his eyes gave a deeper meaning to the question.

"Caelius came," I said. "But his message was misdirected. He left dissatisfied."

"Oh?" Cicero sounded unconcerned, but his eyes flashed. "Well, my fellow consul and I must hurry on—we have pressing business in the Senate. Good luck in your campaign, Rufus! Good fortune to you, Meto!"

As they passed, I said in a low voice to Rufus, "Well, augur, what did you make of that flicker of lightning—the one in Cicero's eyes?"

"Is there trouble between you?"

"There's likely to be. But what is this business of his wearing a breastplate? And going about with such a formidable bodyguard?"

"He looks absurd!" bellowed Mummius. "Like a mockery of a military man. Does he dare to mock Pompey?"

"Hardly," said Rufus. "He began to wear it the day he postponed the elections, saying that Catilina was plotting to murder him in the confusion of voting day—'To save his own life, the consul of the Roman Republic must resort to wearing armor and surrounding himself with armed men,' et cetera. It's a tactic to get the crowd's attention and alarm the voters; it's political theater, spectacle, nothing more. After what Cicero and his brother did to Catilina's good name in the consular campaign last year, no one would be surprised if Catilina wanted to murder him. Who knows, perhaps there *is* a plot to assassinate Cicero; but for Cicero it's just more grist for the mill of his shrill rhetoric."

"Politics!" Mummius barked. "I had enough of it the year I served as praetor. Give me orders to follow and men to order, and I'm happy."

"Well," I said, huffing and puffing from the exertion of the steep ascent, "for the moment, at least, let us put all such unworthy matters behind us." Quite literally behind us, and beneath us as well, I thought, turning my head to glance down at the teeming Forum far below. "We have arrived at the summit. There is nothing but blue sky between us and the eyes of Jupiter. Here in this place, my son becomes a man."

TWENTY

ON battlefields and in the countryside, where there is no permanent place for performing auguries, a sacred tent must be pitched before the augur may begin his work. High up on the Arx in Rome, above a steep semicircular cliff with an expansive view of the whole northern horizon, there is a paved place open to the sky called the Auguraculum, especially consecrated for the taking of the auspices. The only structure is a permanently pitched tent maintained by the college of augurs. Like the special robes they wear, it has a purple border and is shot with stripes of saffron. It is a small tent, so small that one would have to stoop to step inside, though so far as I know no one ever goes inside.

Why a tent? I do not know, especially since the taking of the auspices by definition must be performed outdoors with a view of the sky. Perhaps it is the ancient linkage of the augurs with military campaigns, where their approval of the omens must still be sought before a general can engage his troops in battle. Perhaps it is because the augurs study not only the flights of birds and peregrinations of quadrupeds, but also the occurrence of lightning bolts, the study of which dates back to the Etruscans and beyond; where there is lightning, after all, there is likely to be rain, and thus the need for a tent.

However it may be, we found ourselves gathered on the Arx before the sacred tent. Rufus took up his ivory wand and with it marked out a section of the heavens from which he would take the auspices, like an invisible window frame set into the sky. Through it I could see most of the Field of Mars, a wide bend of the Tiber, and a great swath of land beyond.

The augurs divide birds into two classes, those whose cry signifies the divine will, including the raven, the crow, the owl, and the woodpecker, and those whose flight may be read for the same significations, including the vulture, the hawk, and the eagle, Jupiter's favorite bird. On military expeditions, where an omen may be needed on short notice and wild fowl may be scarce, chickens are taken along in special cages. To determine the will of the gods, the doors of the coop are thrown open and a handful of grain is thrown on the ground. A strong show of appetite on the part of the hens is deemed a good sign, especially if they drop little bits of food from their beaks onto the ground. A reluctance to leave the cage or a show of finickiness is a bad sign. As for the reading of lightning, it has always been my understanding that lightning on the left is good, but on the right is bad. Or is it the other way around?

There are those, like Cicero, who believe that augury is utter nonsense, and will say so in private letters and conversations. There are those politicians like Caesar who see augury as a useful tool, and have no more or less contempt for it than they do for any other device of power, such as elections, taxation, or courts of law. And there are those like Rufus who sincerely believe in the manifestation of divine will in various phenomena and in their own ability to perceive and interpret those manifestations.

For myself, standing in the hot sun and wishing I had thought to bring my broad-brimmed hat, I began to wish that the ceremonial tent behind us contained a chicken coop so that we could get on with the divination. All the birds of Rome appeared to be napping, and there was not a thundercloud in sight.

An augury takes as long as an augury takes. The divine will is not at the beck and call of even the youngest and most charming of the augurs. The gods have other things to do than to make a raven cackle or send a vulture soaring on the hot wind. Patience is the first duty of the pious.

Even so, I found my thoughts wandering. My eyes strayed from the designated section of the heavens to the eastern escarpment of the Arx, over which, if I stood on my toes, I could glimpse the Forum below. It was still full of people, but a stillness and a hush had fallen on the crowd. Within the Senate House the senators were debating, and the men of Rome awaited word of their leaders' decision. Cicero was probably speaking even now. Caesar and Crassus might join in the argument, if it suited their ends to do so, as might Cato, with his heavy moralizing, and the troublemaker Clodius, and the year's forgotten consul, the nonentity Antonius. Catilina would be there as well, to defend himself, to strike back at Cicero, to demand that the election proceed. Was it really possible that he could be elected consul? And if so, could he force the Senate to implement his radical programs? Would Caesar and Crassus support him—to a point? Would the state come to a standstill? Be torn apart? Descend again into bloody civil war? And who then would pick up the pieces—Crassus, Caesar, Pompey . . . Catilina?

"There!" cried a hushed voice behind me. It was Eco, who had spotted something with wings in the sky. I shook my head, drowsy from the heat and trying to remember where my thoughts had wandered. I blinked and stared at the dark spot that hovered above the city. Unfortunately, it flew about in a low spiral and then descended, never having entered the designated section of the sky. Not an omen, after all. Around me I heard a collective sigh of disappointment. Rufus stood near the precipice, his back to us, so that I could not see his face. But his shoulders remained erect, his chin upraised and confident. He had faith in his science, and patience with the gods.

I should not have eaten so much at Meto's party, I thought. Cicero was correct: a man should eat only the lightest of meals at midday. But then, Cicero had always had a complaining belly. I felt no discomfort, only a heavy fullness, and a great sleepiness from the heat and from the tiring ascent to the Arx. I could barely keep my eyes open. . . .

The last time Rome had been plunged into civil war the result had been disastrous. Sulla had triumphed, and with him the most reactionary elements in the state. Laws giving power to the populace had been repealed. The constitution had been reformed to give the wealthy greater influence over popular elections and law courts, and within the upper classes Sulla had done his best to exterminate the opposition. A generation later the state was in greater chaos than ever. Many of Sulla's reforms had been repealed and populist forces were on the move again, but Sulla's legacy lived on in the deprivation of the children of his victims and in the wholesale failure of his agrarian policy—the veterans he had intended to become farmers had ruined their land and were now rallying in desperation behind Catilina. Discontent was everywhere, except among that tiny handful who always had and always would possess more wealth and power than they could ever hope to use in a lifetime. Their comfortable state had been given to them by the gods, they believed; perhaps Cicero had been given to them as well, a sweet voice that could sing the turbulent masses to sleep. . . .

Worst of all had been the heads, I thought. The heads of Sulla's enemies, spitted on poles and lined up in the Forum for all to see. Bounty hunters cut off the heads and brought them to Sulla for a reward. For the bodies they had no use. What had become of all the bodies, the bodies without heads? Suddenly, as clearly as on the day Diana found it, I saw the body of Nemo beneath me on the straw, with the blood all clotted about the stump of his neck. The shock of it was so great that I gasped and my shoulders convulsed.

"Yes! At last!" whispered Eco in my ear, his hand on the back of my neck. "There, flying up swiftly from the river."

I blinked, confused and dazed by the brightness. White stones blazed at my feet and the sun seemed to have filled up the sky. In the midst of so much light a tiny black form took shape, flying from left to right and growing larger until it resolved itself into a body with long, outstretched wings.

"A hawk," whispered Eco.

"No," said Mummius, "an eagle!"

The bird circled once over the Field of Mars and then grew larger and larger as it approached. Its speed was stunning; no horse could have galloped so fast across the sky. A moment later it landed so close to Rufus that he could have bent down to touch it if he dared. We stood transfixed and silent. We stared at the eagle, and the eagle stared back. I had never seen one so close. Then, as suddenly as it had landed, it spread its

giant wings and ascended over our heads, straight up into the
sun.

I lowered my eyes, blinking and half-blind. Rufus turned
toward us with a look of awe on his face.

"The omen," I said. "Was it good?"

"Good?" He frowned at me quizzically, then broke into a
smile. "It could not possibly have been better!"

Had the city not already been consumed with the immediate
controversies swirling around Catilina and the elections, perhaps the prodigious omen that landed at Rufus's feet would
have excited great comment. Had it occurred on a lazy summer day when nothing else of importance was happening in
the Forum, the gossip would have spread through the squares
and taverns—Jupiter's bird, and eagle, alighting at the Auguraculum for a boy's simple passage to manhood, and the
boy who had once been a slave, at that! The superstitious
would have found it either inspiring or fearsome, a sign of
the gods' displeasure or their benediction. But in the general
chaos of that day, the incident went unremarked except
among those who were there.

On the path back down to the Forum, Marcus Mummius
was greatly excited. "An eagle, a military bird! It portends a
great career in the army!" I noticed Meto smiling at such talk,
and I wished that Mummius would be silent.

I turned to Rufus, who had changed from his augur's trabea back into his candidate's toga. "Is that what it means,
Rufus?"

"Not necessarily." Meto overheard and his smile faded, for
which I was glad. I wanted no thoughts of military glory
going through his head. I had not rescued the boy from slavery to see him spill his blood for some ambitious general.

Rufus slowed his pace and let the others go ahead of us.
He touched my arm to signal that I should stay back with
him. His expression was uneasy. His initial ebullience at the
eagle's landing had vanished, replaced by uncertainty. "It's a
powerful portent, Gordianus. Never has such a thing happened to me, and not to any other augur so far as I know."

"But it's a good portent?" I said hopefully. "You seemed
to think so at the time it happened."

"Yes, but what I felt was a kind of religious awe. That can blind a man, even an augur. All omens are awesome, because they come from the gods, but what they mean for mortal men does not always bring us happiness."

"Rufus, what are you saying?"

"I almost wish the auspices had been less prodigious. A simple sighting of a vulture, a crow flying in an upward spiral—"

"But an eagle sent from Jupiter, surely that's good—"

"Such a powerful omen, appearing at such a modest occasion—it worries me. It seems out of place, out of balance. We live in a time when small men are drawn into great events—sometimes elevated to greatness themselves by those events, but more often crushed by them. Meto is so simple and good-natured, what can it mean that such a potent auspice should attend his coming of age? It worries me."

"Oh, Rufus—" I almost forgot myself and would have scoffed in his face, but my respect for him was too great. Still, I felt myself in sympathy with disbelievers like Cicero, who in private shake their heads at the hand-wringing of the pious. Or was I only putting a good face on my own anxiety? "Perhaps the omen was misdirected. Perhaps it has something to do with Catilina or Cicero. Perhaps it was meant for the consuls and arrived an hour too late! The gods do make mistakes from time to time—all the poets say so."

"You won't hear a priest or an augur say so," said Rufus, unamused.

We proceeded down the path. The noise from the Forum rose to greet us. Ahead of us, Mummius had one arm around Meto's shoulders and was enthusiastically gesturing with the other. "When Romans go into battle with flags waving, you'll always see an eagle atop the standards. Pompey wears a golden breastplate with an eagle embossed across the pectorals, its wings spread open—like a great bird come to snatch Mithridates' kingdom from him! Oh, and I remember, before the battle of the Colline Gate, back when I was a young lieutenant for Crassus and we fought for Sulla, the augurs saw three eagles circling over Rome. . . ." Meto seemed completely captivated by such talk.

I was somewhat relieved, then, when we came to the foot

of the Capitoline and Mummius took his leave of us, saying he wanted to catch the last of the debate in the Senate House. He did not tarry over farewells, but gave Meto and Eco each a crushing hug and departed at a quick marching pace, with Apollonius following him.

It seemed a good time for the whole retinue to disperse; I thanked the friends and well-wishers who had accompanied us and released them to go on about any business they might have in the Forum. It would be enough, I thought, for Meto to be accompanied by his father and brother as we crossed the Forum on our way back to the women.

But Rufus had another plan. "Remember, earlier I said I might have a surprise for Meto." He seemed to have put aside his misgivings and smiled slyly, or as slyly as his nature allowed. "I am going to take you into the Senate House with me!"

"What?" My heart sank.

"To hear the senators debate?" said Meto, who seemed almost as interested in this news as he had been in Mummius's military talk.

"The idea came to me as soon as Eco asked me to preside as augur for you. Of course, in the normal course of things the Senate might not be convening at all on this day, but as it turns out, the occasion could hardly be better. The chamber will be full and you may see quite a spectacle. We *are* running late, but still . . ."

"But, Rufus, only sons and grandsons of senators themselves are allowed to attend."

"Not so. There are plenty of secretaries scurrying about."

"But surely the likes of the Gordiani will not be allowed into the Senate House," I said.

"Accompanied by me, you will." He seemed completely certain. Patricians can be very sure of themselves, usually with good reason.

"Oh, Rufus, it is an honor, of course, but I think that we must decline," I said.

Meto looked at me as if I had carelessly thrown one of his birthday presents into the Tiber. "But, Papa, why not?"

"Yes, Papa, why not?" said Eco.

"Because—well, surely, Meto, you would feel self-conscious in such a place."

Meto wrinkled his brow. Rufus answered for him. "We shall hang back in the shadows. No one will even notice us."

"But, Rufus, we shall only be in your way. We've already kept you from your business as a senator by accepting your services as augur."

"And you're keeping me from my business now, by arguing to no purpose. Come, Gordianus, this is the day, the very hour in which Meto has become a full citizen of Rome. What better way to celebrate than to take him into the very heart of the Republic? How could you deny your son such an invaluable lesson in citizenship? I confess, I remained a little uncertain about doing this myself, up until the arrival of the eagle at the Auguraculum. Now I am convinced that it must be the right thing to do. Come, then, let's hurry, before the senators conclude their business and rush back into the Forum to beg for votes!"

He turned and pressed into the crowd. Meto looked at me with a mixture of boyish entreaty and manly impatience. Eco stared at me sympathetically, for he knew me well enough to know how deeply revolted I was by the idea of immersing myself and my family in a sea of politicians, and at the same time he knew that I had no reasonable excuse to refuse Rufus's generous and thoughtful offer, or to deny Meto the opportunity to see such a thing with his own eyes. I suppose I might have left my sons with Rufus and gone skulking back to the women—but then I would not have heard Catilina pose his riddle.

A broad flight of steps leads up to the porch of the Senate House, where great columns flank the doorway. Loitering on the steps were various retainers of the senators within; among them I recognized some of the burly bodyguards who had accompanied Cicero in his retinue. Other guards, attached to the Senate House itself, flanked the tall doors,·which by law remained open so as not to hide the proceedings within from the eyes of the gods. Again it struck me as unlikely that we would be allowed into such a place, even accompanied by

Rufus, but that was because I thought the Senate House had
only one entrance. Rufus knew better.

Next to the Senate House and attached to it is another, less
impressive building which houses various offices of the state.
I had never been inside, and in fact had hardly ever noticed
it. The wooden doors of the entrance stood open on such a
hot day and there was no one to stop us from entering.

Within, a broad hallway ran the length of the building with
rows of small rooms on either side. The rooms were full of
scrolls stacked in cases against the walls and piled on tables.
A few sleepy clerks moved lethargically among the documents, like shepherds tending a docile flock. They took no
notice of us.

At the center of the building a flight of steps ascended to
a second story and then to a third. Rufus led us through a
succession of small, plain rooms. I began to hear echoey
voices speaking in loud, oratorical tones, interrupted occasionally by an indistinct roar that might have been jeering or
laughter. The sounds grew louder as we passed from room to
room, until we came to an iron door that stood half-open.
Rufus put a finger to his lips, though none of us had said a
word since we began to follow him; then he slipped through
the doorway. With one hand he gestured for us to follow.

The Senate House is not an old building, having been rebuilt and refurbished by Sulla during his dictatorship. The
materials within reflect the despot's impeccable taste—the
decorative walls of colored marble, the beautifully carved columns, the ornately coffered ceiling. A vestibule separates the
meeting room from the main entrance. The great chamber is
rectangular, illuminated at night or in stormy weather by great
lamps that hang from the ceiling, and on a bright, sunlit afternoon such as this by tall, unshuttered windows placed high
up in the walls and covered by bronze lattices. Against the
longer walls and in a semicircle against the short wall opposite the vestibule are three tiers of seats, so that the rows
of carved wooden chairs follow the shape of the letter *U*. We
had entered near the left-hand prong of the *U*, between the
vestibule on our left and the tiers of seats on our right. In this
inconspicuous place stood some ten or more clerks who kept
attentive eyes upon the senators in case they should be sum-

moned to fetch some document or carry a message. A few of
the clerks noticed our arrival and gave us a suspicious glance,
but when they saw that we were with Rufus they paid us no
more attention. They seemed too engrossed by what was happening on the floor of the Senate.

Cicero stood at the very center of the room, surrounded
by the seated senators like a gladiator in the circus. If Meto
needed instruction by example on how to comport himself in
a toga, he could have learned much that day from Cicero,
who seemed to be able to speak with his entire body, subtly
turning and twisting his neck, gesticulating with one arm and
clutching the other to his midriff as if it held a shield. He had
come a long way from the impassioned but rather stiff orator
I had met many years ago. One hardly even had to hear him
to feel the force of his eloquence.

He was not delivering a set speech at the moment, but
seemed instead to be engaged in a spontaneous debate with
one of the senators in the tiers. From where we stood I had
to crane my neck to catch a glimpse of the man, but when I
heard his voice, I had no need to see him: it was Catilina.

Sulla, when he rebuilt the Senate House, had used not only
his impeccable eye but his ear as well. The great lover of
music and the theater had learned a thing or two from those
famous Greek theaters where an actor's whisper can be
clearly heard from the farthest seat. Every word that Cicero
and Catilina exchanged pealed as clear as if we had stood
between them.

"Catilina, Catilina!" Cicero cried in a mock-wounded tone.
"I ask not that the elections be postponed to jeopardize your
chances of being elected, if that is the will of the people. I
would do nothing to jeopardize the will of the Roman people!
But so long as I have been entrusted with the guidance of the
state, I will do everything possible to see that the state and
the people are preserved from harm. That goes as well for the
members of this august body! As it stands now, if the voting
is held tomorrow, we are likely to have not an election but a
bloodbath!"

At this there was another mild uproar. Thanks to the
room's extraordinary acoustics, I could hear quite distinctly

the mingled shouts of scoffing and agreement within the general roar.

"Cicero is obsessed with the idea that blood will be spilled on election day," shouted Catilina, "only because he fears it will be his own."

"And do you deny that I have every reason to fear?" said Cicero. Did I see his eyebrows go up, or was it the posturing of his whole body that expressed such eloquent irony? "I have asked you already about the reports that have come to us that you are conspiring against the person of the consul—"

"And I have roundly denied them, and I ask you again: what reports, and from what sources?"

"You are the one who is here to answer questions, Catilina!"

"I am not on trial!"

"You mean to say that you have not been formally charged with a crime, but only because you have not yet had the opportunity to commit it."

This brought on another uproar.

Above the din, Cicero shouted: "And that is only because of the vigilance of your intended victim!" He crossed his arms and drew back his shoulders, wrapping himself in his toga as if to wrap himself in virtue, then seized the folds of cloth about his neck and drew them down to expose the glittering breastplate.

This provoked an even more raucous uproar. A group of the senators surrounding Catilina, presumably his allies, rose to their feet, some laughing, some shaking their fists and jeering. Instead of retreating, Cicero actually stepped toward them, baring more of his breastplate. Such brazenness only provoked an even louder uproar.

"This is worse than the mob in the Forum," I whispered to Rufus.

"I've never seen it quite so chaotic," he murmured. "Even in the most passionate debates there's always a modicum of order and mutual respect, some humor to leaven the animosities, but today the whole chamber seems on the verge of a riot."

Above the continued shouting of Catilina's supporters Cicero managed to make his voice heard. The power of his lungs was astounding. "Do you deny that you have conspired to assassinate members of this august body?"

"Where is your evidence?" Catilina shouted back, barely audible above the roar of his own supporters.

"Do you deny that you have plotted to murder the duly elected consul of the Republic, and to do it on the next consular election day?"

"Again, where is your evidence?"

"Do you, Lucius Sergius Catilina, deny that your ultimate goal is to dismantle the state as we know it, and to do so by whatever means are necessary, no matter how violent or illegal?"

Catilina responded, but his voice was drowned out by his own supporters, giving Cicero, with his trumpetlike voice, the advantage. At last Catilina managed to quiet his own adherents, who returned to their seats. Catilina remained standing. "With all due respect, the esteemed consul's accusations are deranged! He frets over the safety of the Republic like a mother afraid to let her child leave the house. Is the Republic so delicate that an honest election might kill it? Is he himself so vital to the state, is his insight so unique, that we would become blind men without him? Ah, yes, Cicero sees things that other men do not—but I ask you, is that good or bad?" This provoked some scattered laughter, and with it a marked lessening of tension. "Contrary to what this New Man may think, the history of this Republic did not begin and will not end with his consulship." At this there was more laughter and even some cheering.

Catilina smiled bitterly. "It is not I who seek to thwart the will of the people, Cicero, but you!" At this there were catcalls and booing from the opposite side of the chamber. "Yes, for who else but Cicero is determined to keep postponing the election? And why? Because he fears for his own life? This is absurd! If a man had cause to kill our esteemed consul, why wait until election day?"

"To spread chaos," Cicero answered. "To frighten decent voters from the polls so that your own adherents can steal the election."

"Absurd, I say! The true theft is occurring beneath our noses, and at the consul's behest, for by making the date of the election uncertain you disenfranchise those who must travel here to vote and cannot take up lodgings indefinitely in the city. The election has already been postponed once. Do not postpone it any further!"

"The election was postponed because of the auspices," said Cicero. "The earth quaked, thunderbolts creased the sky—" At this there were scattered moans and jeers, presumably from skeptics, followed by a second wave of jeering from the pious who hissed at the doubters.

"Typically, Cicero, you change the subject, hoping to divert our attention from the real issue! The first postponement is over and done with. The auspices now are favorable. You have no religious reason to deny the election any longer." At this, even some of the senators who had so far been silent murmured agreement and nodded gravely.

"Come, Cicero, you have debated long enough," cried one of the older senators. This cry was taken up by many others. Cicero stepped back and surveyed the tiers, as if assessing his strength. He appeared dissatisfied, but as the calls grew louder for the debate to end, he stepped back and gestured to his fellow consul, Gaius Antonius, who commenced the reading of a proposal to postpone again the consular election and to censure Catilina for "disrupting the state." Those in favor were instructed to take seats on the left-hand side of the room; those against were to gather on the opposite side, where Catilina and his supporters already sat.

At this point Rufus left us to join his fellow senators in opposition to the proposal. I noticed that Marcus Mummius was of the same faction, as were Caesar and Crassus and their adherents. When all were settled, even without a strict counting it was clear that Cicero had been thwarted and the election would proceed. Gaius Antonius announced the result and summarily dismissed the assembly.

A murmur of conversation filled the chamber, above which could be heard Cicero's trumpeting voice: "On the morrow we shall see who spoke wisdom. I foresee dangerous times for this Republic!"

"What eyes you have, Cicero, to see so much more than the rest of us!" called Catilina.

Many of the milling senators stopped their conversations

to listen. They might not have had enough of their two colleagues' debate, but I had. I gestured to Meto and Eco that it
was time to go, before we were caught loitering in the chamber without Rufus to vouch for us. We slipped through the
half-open door by which we had entered. Catilina's voice
echoed behind us. "And do you know what I see, Cicero? Do
you know what my eyes perceive when I study this Republic?
I see two bodies—"

I stopped, suddenly alert, and turned back to listen. Meto
was puzzled, but I saw in Eco's eyes that he, too, had heard.

Catilina's voice was echoey and distorted, like a voice
from a dream. "I see two bodies, one thin and wasted, but
with a swollen head, the other headless, but big and strong.
The invalid with a head leads the big headless one about like
an animal on a chain. Ask yourself, what is there so dreadful
about it, if I myself become the head of the body which needs
one? The story would be quite different then!"

Told in context, the meaning of the riddle was clear. I
sucked in my breath at Catilina's audacity. Having had his
way on proceeding with the election, now he dared to mock
not only Cicero but the Senate itself, and in its very house.
For what could the withered body with a swollen head represent but the Senate? And what was the strong, headless
body but the leaderless masses, of whom Catilina proposed
to become the head, and whose discontent he would harness
toward his own ends?

Eco also understood. "The man must be mad," he said.

"Or very sure of his success," I said.

"Or both," said Meto gravely.

TWENTY-ONE

AFTER the Senate dispersed, the space in front of the Senate
House became almost impassable as the various senators' retinues regrouped around their leaders. I had no desire to press
into the throng to make our way through the Forum. Instead

we retreated into the maze of narrow, winding side streets just north of the Forum until we emerged at the place where we had left the women.

No excuses for the length of our absence were needed, for Bethesda herself had just returned from shopping at the various markets all around the Forum. For Diana she had purchased a clay doll with eyes of green glass, for Menenia a blue and yellow scarf, and for herself a small ivory comb. I groaned inwardly at these small extravagances, thinking of all the hay that had been lost to rust and wondering how I would manage the finances of the farm through the winter. But how could I deny Bethesda the pleasure of an afternoon of shopping when she had been away from such opportunities for so long?

The litters carried us back to the house on the Esquiline, where Eco dismissed the bearers. Our dinner that night was eaten in formal courses, on couches gathered in the dining room beside the garden. Only the family was there. The women wore their stolas, and we men kept on our togas. Meto was given the place of honor. He had never reclined upon a couch and eaten a meal in formal dress, but he managed with hardly any awkwardness and did not spill a drop of wine on his toga.

The conversation was chiefly of family matters—Menenia's and Eco's refurbishment of the house, how things were faring on the farm, Eco's relations with his in-laws. There was some discussion of the augury that afternoon, which we all agreed was uncommonly auspicious—all except Bethesda, who has always professed to find Roman religion simplistic compared to her own Egyptian sensibilities. Graciously, she did not criticize the ceremony; her only comment on the appearance of the eagle at the Auguraculum was to ask if it had any human features. Menenia, equally gracious, hid her smile behind a papyrus fan.

There was no talk of Cicero or Catilina, no mention of elections or of bodies without heads. For this I was glad.

After the rest of the household went to bed, I was wakeful and restless and went to the garden instead. The yellow canopy had been removed and the garden was filled with bright moonlight. I listened to the soft splashing of the fountain and studied the broken moon and wavering stars reflected in the black water. The moonlight turned the hard paving stones to shimmering silver and seemed to cover the flowers with a soft coating of gray ash.

How many nights had I found peace and escape from the cares of the city in this garden? In a way I felt as far from the turmoil of the Forum in this place as I did at the farm in Etruria; in some ways I felt even safer and more removed. I sat on a stone bench beside the fountain and leaned against a pillar. I gazed up at the moon and the dome of stars all around it.

I heard the sound of bare feet from the portico, so familiar that I did not have to look. "Meto," I said quietly.

"Papa." He stepped into the garden. His toga had been put away, and he wore only a loincloth about his hips. He stepped nearer and I indicated that he should sit beside me, but instead he sat on a bench a few feet away, facing me.

"Can't you sleep, Meto? Or is it too hot?"

"No, it's not the heat." The angle of the moonlight obscured his face, casting his eyes in shadow, glancing off his nose and making his cheeks and lips look as if they were carved from marble.

"The excitement of the day, then," I suggested.

He was silent for a long moment. "Papa, I'm a man now."

"I know, Meto."

"I'm not a boy any longer."

"Yes, Meto, I know."

"Then why do you still treat me like a boy?"

"Because—what do you mean?"

"You hide things from me. You talk behind my back. You tell Eco everything; you share everything with him."

"Because Eco is . . ."

"Because Eco is a man, and I am a boy."

"No, Meto, it's not that."

"Because Eco was born free and I wasn't."

"Not that, either," I said, wearily shaking my head.

"But I *am* a man, Papa. The law says so, and so do the gods. Why don't you believe it?"

I looked at his smooth, unblemished cheeks, the color of

white roses in the moonlight, which the barber had shaved for the first time that day. I looked at his slender arms and narrow chest, as smooth and hairless as a girl's. But his arms were not really as slender as I had thought; in a year's time the work of the farm had put some muscle into them. Nor was his chest any longer the flat, narrow chest of a child; it had begun to broaden and take shape. The moonlight clearly etched the square prominence of his pectorals and the ridges of his belly. His legs were still long for his body, but they were not spindly; his calves and thighs were hard with muscle.

When had this happened? It was as if I gazed at a stranger beneath the moonlight, or as if the moon itself had transformed him in that moment before my eyes.

"You treat me like a child, Papa. You know this is true. This whole matter of not wanting me to go inside the Senate House—"

"That had nothing to do with you, Meto. It was my own aversion."

"But what about the body we found in the stables? You treated me the same way you treated Diana."

"I did not. I sent her away, but to you I showed what one could learn from observing the corpse—although, as I remember, you were almost too squeamish to look."

"But I did look! And I'm not talking about letting me study the body with you. I'm talking about afterward, when you began to brood over it. You never confided in me. You sent for Eco to come all the way from Rome so that you could share your thoughts with him."

"I didn't send for Eco."

"That's not what he says."

"Oh, I see, the two of you have been talking behind my back."

"Confiding in each other, Papa, as brothers should. And as I wish you would confide in me. Because I am a man now. Because you need me, to help protect you and Mother and Diana—"

"Protect *me*?" The image of the little boy I met in Baiae protecting me from some hulking assassin was so absurd that I shook my head. It was my duty to protect *him*, as I always had. Of course, he was not really so little anymore. But I was still stronger than he was, at least I thought so, though he might be faster, and his stamina might be greater than mine.

"Your body has changed, Meto, that's true, but in other ways—"

"In other ways I'm still a child. I know that's what you think, but where is your evidence?" These words rang strangely in my ears. Where had he picked them up? "It's just not true, Papa. You don't know what sort of things I think about when I'm alone. I worry, too, about the body we found, and Catilina coming to our house, and the terrible things happening in Rome. I saw Marcus Caelius talking to you at the party today. I saw the look on your face. What were you talking about? What did he want? Why don't you tell me, so that I can help? You'll tell Eco, won't you?"

"Oh, Meto, how can I ask for your help when I don't know myself what needs to be done?"

"But that's just it, Papa. Perhaps *I* might think of something."

He lifted his face into the moonlight and in that moment he no longer looked transformed at all. He was a mere child again, gangly and awkward, earnest and innocent and eager to please. I could barely resist an urge to reach out and tousle his hair. How could I treat him as something he was not?

"Papa, I ask for your respect. Whatever danger faces us, I want to know about it. I want to do my part. I want to be included. I have the right to expect that, now that I'm a man. Can't you understand?"

"Yes, Meto, I understand."

"And you'll treat me differently in the future?"

I took a deep breath. "I shall try."

"Good. Then we can begin by going to see the election tomorrow."

"Oh, Meto," I groaned.

"But, Papa, how can I learn if I can't see with my own eyes? That's why today was so extraordinary. Going into the Senate House, hearing him speak—I shall never forget it!"

"Hearing Cicero?"

"No, Catilina! It meant even more to me than the ceremony

at the Auguraculum. I must see what happens tomorrow." He
lowered his eyes. "I could go alone—"

"Never! Gangs, knives, riots—"

"Then we shall go together?"

I wrinkled my brow. "I shall sleep on it."

"Papa . . ."

"Oh, very well." I sighed. "If you must see Rome at her
worst . . ."

"Thank you, Papa!" He gripped my hands in his and then
departed for bed. A few moments later I did the same, since
I would not be sleeping late after all.

When I was a boy, the northwestern portion of the city outside
the Servian Wall, called the Field of Mars, was still largely
undeveloped. Chariot racers trained their horses and military
units practiced their drills on the unobstructed plain, with so
much room that they did not even have to breathe one another's clouds of dust. At the far end of the Field, above a
sweeping bend in the River Tiber, are the medicinal hot
springs at Tarentum, where my father liked to go to ease his
joints; I remember walking to the springs through wooded
areas where goats chewed the grass alongside the road, with
hardly a house in sight, as if one were in the country. Perhaps
my boyish eyes exaggerated these pastoral expanses.

Of course, the southern portion of the Field of Mars nearest
the Servian Wall has long been built up. The morning shadows of the Capitoline Hill have for many years fallen across
warehouses and wharves on the Tiber, the teeming vegetable
markets of the Forum Holitorium, crowded tenements, and
the cluster of shops and baths around the Circus Flaminius,
still the most conspicuous structure anywhere outside the Servian Wall. Even so, in my lifetime I have seen the entire Field
of Mars become much more developed—more warehouses
have gone up on the river, new and taller tenements have
been squeezed between the old ones, the few remaining
groves have been cleared and built over, new roads have been
laid out. The chariot racers and drilling soldiers have been
pressed closer together, so that their clouds of dust mingle in
the air. The road to Tarentum is no longer like a brief respite
in the countryside, but is surrounded by city all the way.

There are even rumors that Pompey, having secured a large tract of public land in the heart of the Field of Mars, is planning to build a great theater of stucco and marble. This has excited great controversy, for if built, the structure will be the first permanent theater in Rome, a city where makeshift stages erected for festivals have always been deemed more proper than the templelike theaters of the decadent, drama-worshiping Greeks.

Because it lies outside the city walls, and because of its flat expanse (as compared to the city's seven hills and the valleys between them), the Field of Mars has from very early days been the gathering place for assemblies too large (and often too unruly) to be accommodated in the Forum. From the time of the founding of the Republic, Romans have gathered there to do their voting.

So it was, very early the next morning, that Meto and I set out for the Field of Mars. I decided to take Belbo with us; if Cicero was right in his prediction of violence, I wanted a bodyguard. We ate a hurried but extravagant breakfast of left-overs from the party and took a bundle of food and a skin of watered wine with us. The sky was pale with dawn as we made our way through the Subura toward the Fontinal Gate. There were already groups of men in the street, all heading in the same direction. We were just passing through the gate when I heard the trumpets being blown to call the people to assemble.

Just off the Flaminian Way, between the built-up, southern area of the Field of Mars and the more open spaces to the north, is the Villa Publica. The walled enclosure is very old, as are the buildings within. Besides housing the offices of the census takers, who keep the registries of voters, the Villa Publica serves the city of Rome as a vestibule or foyer serves a house; foreign ambassadors are lodged there, as are Roman generals who must reside outside the city before making their triumphal entries. It is also the place where candidates withdraw to await the election results.

Adjoining the Villa Publica is another walled enclosure called, without ostentation, the Sheep Pen. On election day ropes are stretched across its length to split the space into aisles. To cast their ballots the voters are guided through the

Pen like sheep through a run. It does not require a great wit to extrapolate the metaphors.

Under the rising sun citizens thronged to the open fields around the Villa Publica. Roman voters are split into various classes according to their wealth, and within those classes are assigned to voting units, or centuries. Organizers within each century were working doggedly to gather their members together; many of the centuries obviously had predetermined meeting places, but in such a vast crowd there was still considerable confusion. Compounding this was the weather. It had not rained for several days, and there was a great deal of dust in the air. The morning was already warm and likely to get much warmer. The atmosphere was not unlike that of a great feedlot on a hot summer day.

It did not take long for me to see signs of outright bribery. I recognized a number of disreputable types in the crowd and I watched them move among the century leaders, smiling and clasping hands and brazenly handing out small, lumpy sacks that could only have been filled with coins. A few of these agents I recognized as henchmen of Crassus, and at least one of them I had noticed in Caesar's retinue the day before, but there were many more whose allegiance I did not know.

There were a few scattered instances of violence, but no general disruptions. We saw a country farmer and his sons beaten and run off by a gang of youths. We watched two redfaced, gray-haired Optimates engaged in a blustering fistfight with each other (one supported Murena, the other Silanus—who but an Optimate could tell the difference?); their attendant slaves stood back helplessly and looked on, variously appalled, alarmed, and amused. We came upon the aftermath of a duel with knives that ended with both parties being carried off, bleeding and moaning, by their friends. All in all, it was a more peaceful crowd than I had expected. Of course, these were only the violent episodes that we happened to witness; within the great milling throng there must have been many more.

A tumult of shouting moved toward us through the crowd, and I turned to see that Cicero and his fellow consul Gaius Antonius were arriving. Cicero was surrounded by his armed bodyguard and wore his toga open to show the breastplate across his chest, a last reminder to the voters of the presumed treachery of Catilina. They disappeared within the gates of the Villa Publica and eventually reappeared at the podium built into the wall. Antonius announced that the auspices had been duly observed by the augurs in the Villa Publica and had been declared acceptable. Without an earthquake and with a blue sky above, it could hardly have been otherwise, I thought, especially since the Senate had made its desires in the matter very clear on the previous day. The election could proceed.

Shortly thereafter the candidates arrived. Each was attended by a long retinue of supporters who pushed and shoved their way through the crowd. Each made an appearance on the podium before disappearing into the Villa Publica. There were mingled hisses and cheers for Murena and Silanus, the Optimate favorites, who appeared one after the other. As the candidates left the podium, the gray-haired fist-fighters, who had called a truce while their favorites were on stage, fell to cursing and striking each other again.

A number of other candidates paraded across the podium, none of them eliciting more than a smattering of applause or angry catcalls. Then Catilina arrived.

We heard his approach long before we saw him. It began with a roar of sound that seemed to come all the way from the Fontinal Gate and grew louder and louder as it approached the Villa Publica. The sound was like a wall, palpable and impenetrable, as if one might be crushed beneath it. What it was made of was hard to tell at first—the aggregate of booing, hissing, cheering, applauding, jeering, cursing was blended into a single roar. Nor was the physical reaction of the crowd easy to determine. When the retinue passed by, men opened their mouths to shout, but were they cursing or cheering? They thrust their arms into the air, but did a clenched fist signal hatred or support? Through the throng I glimpsed Catilina himself, and from the smile on his face one might have thought that every voice was cheering and every upraised fist was his to command.

When he stood upon the podium, the uproar was deafening. The crowd began to chant his name: "Catilina! Catilina!" Around me young men jumped up and down, waving their arms. It seemed to me that the whole crowd adored him, and that all their jeering and cursing must have been not for Catilina, but for his enemies. Cicero, meanwhile, withdrew to the farthest corner of the podium and turned his face away.

Catilina withdrew into the Villa Publica with his rivals, and the voting commenced. The wealthier classes, which vote first, had already gathered outside the Sheep Pen. At the entrance each voter was given a wooden tablet and a stylus with which to write the name of his candidate; the styluses and tablets were gathered up at the end of each roped aisle and the tablets deposited in an urn for counting after the entire century had voted; the overall choice of each century counted for a single vote. In all, there are just under two hundred centuries, of which the two very wealthiest classes claim over a hundred. The lower classes have many more individual voters, but control far fewer centuries. The very poorest class, who might arguably make up a majority of Romans, have only five centuries among them. Often, by the time their turn to vote arrives, the outcome has already been decided and they are not allowed to vote at all; not surprisingly, they come to the elections more to view the spectacle than to vote, if they come at all.

We had found a shady spot and were sitting against the west wall of the Villa Publica, where I was explaining these matters to Meto, when Belbo, scratching his straw-colored hair, asked, "And what class do you belong to, Master?"

I looked askance at his bovine face, but Meto pressed the question. "Yes, Papa, what class? You've never told me."

"Because I haven't bothered to vote for a very long time."

"But you must know."

"Actually, yes. We changed classes this year, thanks to my inheritance from Lucius Claudius. Where before we were members of the Fifth Class—which is to say just above the poor—we are now members of the Third Class, just below the rich, along with most other families who own a single farm and a dwelling in the city."

"And which century do we vote with?"

"*If* we voted, we would gather with those of the Second Century of the Third Class."

"And I would be able to vote as well?"

I made a face. "You *would* if—"

"I want to see it."

"To see what?"

"The Second Century of the Third Class. The other voters of our century."

"But why?"

"Papa . . ." He had only to speak with a certain inflection to remind me of our conversation of the night before.

"Very well. But there's no hurry. It's not quite noon, and the first two classes can't have completed their voting yet. And after them, the equestrians, who have their own special class of eighteen centuries, will vote, and *then* the Third Class. We'll have some wine and a bite to eat, and then we shall go find our fellow voters. The crowd will have shrunk by then; people will start to leave from the heat and the dust and the boredom."

Which was not true, for when we rejoined the crowd, it seemed, if anything, to have grown. Nor was there a feeling of boredom in the air, but rather a charge of excitement, like the rush of wind before a thunderstorm. Men moved about restlessly, with the hush of anticipation in their voices.

At length the Third Class was called upon to vote. A large group of men, better dressed than most but not with the polished look of patricians or the ostentation of equestrian landowners or merchants, gathered outside the Sheep Pen. The First Century filed into the first aisle, the Second Century into the second aisle, and so on.

"There," said Meto, "that would be our century, wouldn't it?"

"Yes—"

"Come, Papa, I want to see!"

We moved into the milling throng that was slowly being funneled into the Sheep Pen. "But, Meto, there's nothing to see—"

"No slaves here, only citizens!" said an election official posted outside the enclosure. He was looking at Belbo, who nodded and backed away.

"But there's no need," I protested. "He can stay with us. We're only—"

"For Catilina!" a voice whispered in my ear. At the same

time a newly minted coin was pressed into my palm.

I looked around and saw the face of one of the crowd workers I had recognized before, one of Crassus's henchmen. He recognized me as well.

"The Finder! I thought you'd left Rome for good."

"I have."

"And I thought you never voted."

"I don't."

"Well, then!" He snatched the coin out of my palm.

Without meaning to, I found that I was shuffling forward with everyone else, hemmed in by the crowd and heading for the second aisle of the Sheep Pen. Meto was ahead of me. He was looking down at a shiny coin held between his fore-finger and thumb.

"Meto, we need to—"

"But, Papa, we're almost there."

And so we were. Before I knew it, we were at the entrance to the voting aisle, and a bored-looking census officer holding a scroll was scrutinizing Meto. "Family name?" he demanded wearily.

"Gordianus," said Meto.

"Gordianus, Gordianus—yes, here it is. Not many of you. And which one are you—you hardly look old enough to vote."

"I'm sixteen," protested Meto, "as of yesterday."

"Oh, yes, so you are," said the official, squinting at the list. "Here, take your tablet and stylus. And you're Gordianus, the pater?" he asked, looking up at me.

"Yes, but—"

"Here, your tablet and stylus. Next!"

And so, like a sheep, I found myself being driven to the voting urn. Ahead of me Meto scribbled on his tablet. We shuffled forward. Another officer at the end of the line col-lected our styluses and watched us cast our ballots into the urn. As I did so, the officer gave me an odd look.

We stepped out of the Sheep Pen, where Belbo was wait-ing for us. I breathed a sigh of relief, then heard a shout behind me. "You, citizen! With the beard!" I turned around. "Yes, you!"

The officer had plucked my tablet from the urn and was

holding it up. "You've made a mistake, citizen!" he laughed. "There's no 'Nemo' in the race for consul."

I shrugged. "Even so, that's whom I'm voting for."

Meto would not say for whom he had voted, protesting that his ballot was secret, but it was obvious from the despondent look on his face when it was announced that our century had gone for Silanus. And so he received his first bitter disappointment as a voter.

The disappointment was even more bitter for many in the crowd assembled before the Villa Publica when later that afternoon it was announced that the centuries of the Fifth Class and the free poor would not be needed to determine the outcome. Silanus and Murena had won. The Optimates had maintained their control of the consulships. For the second time in two years, Catilina had been repudiated at the polls. All around us I heard muttered curses and even cries of despair amid the general applause, and I felt a sudden tension in the air.

Silanus and Murena appeared on the podium, along with Cicero and Antonius. Following tradition, the consuls-elect would say a few brief words to the assembled citizenry, but when Murena stepped forward to speak he was drowned out by a sudden uproar. Catilina had emerged from the gates of the Villa Publica.

From the reaction of those around him, Catilina might have been the winner of the election, not a two-time loser. His partisans rushed to him, cheering, tearful, many of them reaching out to touch him, chanting his name in unison: "Catilina! Catilina!" His own expression was stoic as he strode forward with his jaw set and his eyes straight ahead. From the podium, Cicero gazed down with a tight smile on his lips.

Once Catilina had passed, Murena and Silanus were finally able to speak. Their comments were predictably banal and were greeted by tepid applause. Afterward Cicero announced that the voting for the praetors would begin immediately. I might have actually cared enough to stay and vote for my friend Rufus, but Meto suddenly lost heart and decided he had learned enough about politics for one day. We left the

crowd and made our way back through the deserted streets
of the Subura.

Back at Eco's house, Bethesda noticed that Meto seemed
unusually withdrawn and pensive. She attributed this to the
natural depression that comes the day after a big event such
as a toga party, but I knew that Meto's disappointment sprang
from something deeper than that.

TWENTY-TWO

WE dined informally that evening, with everyone raiding the
kitchen for leftovers from the day before. The heat of the day
cast the whole household into a mood of easy lassitude. The
slaves went sluggishly about their errands, and even Bethesda
was too hot to reprimand them. The sun itself seemed lazy,
and took an unusually long time to set beyond the horizon.
The sky deepened to a rich, dark blue. Meto withdrew to his
room to be alone. Diana snuggled against her mother and
dozed on our sleeping couch. Eco and Menenia retired to
another room at the back of the house to do whatever it is
that young newlyweds do to amuse themselves on long, sultry
summer evenings. I was left alone again in the garden, which
suited my mood.

The first handful of stars were beginning to sparkle in the
heavens when Belbo announced that there was a caller outside
the front door.

"For Eco?" I asked, thinking he would hardly care to be
disturbed at the moment.

"No, he's come to see you, Master. But I don't like the
looks of it."

"Why is that, Belbo?"

"Too many bodyguards, for one thing-one for every finger
at least—and they're all carrying big daggers in their hands,
not even sheathed."

My heartbeat sped up a bit. What in Jupiter's name had I
done now? Why could I not be left in peace?

"Who is this visitor, Belbo?"

"I'm not sure. He doesn't give a name, and he stands back among his bodyguards so that I can't see him properly. His toga has purple on it, though."

"Yes?" I pursed my lips, puzzled.

"And he's armed himself. Or at least he's wearing armor. I can see what looks like a breastplate underneath his toga—"

"I see. Yes, Belbo, I suppose I had better see this visitor. But ask him to leave his bodyguards outside. He has nothing to fear in this house."

Belbo withdrew. A few moments later I was joined in the garden by Marcus Tullius Cicero.

"Gordianus!" he said, giving me a warm, lingering look as if I were a long-lost friend, or perhaps an undecided voter. "Such a long time since I've seen you!"

"Not so very long. You saw me yesterday on the path to the Arx."

"I wouldn't count that, would you, given the circumstances? If I was brusque or distant yesterday—well, you understand. I was unable to acknowledge you as I should and will acknowledge you when all this is over."

" 'All this'?"

"You know what I mean."

"Do I?"

"Gordianus!" he said in a sweetly chiding tone. "Difficult as always."

"What is it you want, Cicero?"

"And so very curt!"

"I'm not an orator, like you. I have to say what I mean."

"Oh, Gordianus! You must still be very weary after the hard journey down from your beautiful farm. You must feel out of sorts here, away from the fields and the lowing oxen. I know how the rigors of the Forum wear on a man—believe me, I know!—not to mention the ordeal of election day. But this election went rather well, don't you think?"

"For those who won."

"Today Rome won. If things had gone otherwise, we'd have all been the losers, yourself included."

"There were plenty of citizens outside the Villa Publica who seemed to think otherwise."

"Yes, there are riots going on even now in scattered parts of the city; you're wise to have retired early and shuttered your windows. Catilina's supporters crave any excuse to turn to violence and looting."

"Perhaps they're overcome with hopelessness and frustration."

"Surely you don't sympathize with that rabble, Gordianus! A clever man like you, and now a man of property, as well? I'm very proud of that, you know, helping you inherit what was rightfully yours. The gods and Lucius Claudius decreed that you should move up in this world, and I was happy to do my part. Most men get what they deserve in this world, in the long run."

"Do they?"

"Take my brother Quintus, for example. Elected praetor this afternoon, following in my footsteps!"

"How did Rufus fare?"

"He won a praetorship as well, and good for him!" Cicero's smile did not seem entirely insincere. He could afford to be generous.

"And Gaius Julius Caesar?"

Cicero did not smile. "He, too, won a praetorship. But then, no one can say he didn't earn it, one way or another, though he may be a long time paying off the debt. But you were there, weren't you? I thought I glimpsed you in the crowd."

"We left early. My son Meto wanted to see the voting. After a while he had seen enough."

"Ah, the duties of fatherhood. My own son is only two, but already quite an orator! His lungs are stronger than mine!"

"I doubt that, Cicero. But tell me, why are you here? Don't misunderstand, it's not that I'm unhappy to be paid a visit by the consul of Rome, or that I object to having his bodyguard camped outside my door—I'm deeply honored, of course. But you say there are mobs in the street. Surely the danger—"

"I care nothing about danger. You should know that already, Gordianus. Didn't I defy Sulla himself at the very outset of my career? You were there, you saw how I stood up to his tyranny. Do you think I would allow a disorganized rabble to prevent me from going about my duties as consul? Never!"

"Yet there must be something you fear, to make you wear such heavy armor, to surround yourself with so many bodyguards everywhere you go."

"Armor frees a man from fear. As for my bodyguards, they are all fine young men of the equestrian class. They follow me because they love me, as they love Rome. Yes, certainly there is danger. There always is, when a man stands up for what is right—you know that. But a true Roman sets his eyes on his course and is not swayed from it, either by a rabble with sticks and stones or by conspirators with torches and daggers."

"Even so, I thought you had deemed it best that you and I shouldn't see each other openly; so Marcus Caelius indicated. Should I take it that your coming here tonight signals an end to our feigned estrangement?"

"Not . . . exactly," he said.

"But the crisis, if there ever was a crisis, is over."

"Not so long as certain parties still threaten the state—"

"But Catilina is finished. You've bested him again. He won't be able to run for consul a third time—he's too much in debt. His allies will desert him now, and so will his friends with money. Two losses in a row mean no more coins left to press into the sweaty palms of the voters. Catilina is finished."

"You're mistaken, Gordianus. The enemy of Rome is not finished. Not yet." In Cicero's eyes I saw a predatory gleam. "What is more dangerous in the woods than a boar, Gordianus?"

"Please, not a riddle, like Catilina!"

"A *wounded* boar. Today Catilina was wounded, but he's far from finished. His resources are greater than you imagine. His 'allies,' as you call them, are more dangerous than you know. You're right, after today he'll be cut off from the more legitimate sources of finance, but it's steel that he's counting on now, not silver."

"Cicero, you must not ask me for another favor," I said wearily.

"Why not? Do you not love the farm I secured for you?"

"Cicero, gratitude can go only so far."

"I'm not talking about gratitude, Gordianus. I appeal not to your sense of obligation but of self-interest. If Catilina isn't stopped, you're exactly the sort of landowner who stands to suffer most."

"Cicero—" I shook my head and held up my hand.

"And you love your family, don't you? Think of them, and their future."

"That's precisely what I *am* thinking of!" I checked myself and lowered my voice. "I'm tired of putting them in danger. And I'm very tired of being threatened and intimidated."

"The threat comes from Catilina."

"Does it?"

Cicero wrinkled his brow, finally perceiving that while he spoke in vague generalities, I was referring to something quite specific. "What do you mean?"

"I mean the headless body that was left in my stable when I failed to respond to Caelius's demands quickly enough."

"Ah, yes, the headless body. Caelius told me you said something about this to him yesterday, but he didn't know what you were talking about, and neither do I. It must have been something thought up by Catilina—"

"But if Catilina was responsible, and Caelius poses as his agent, then why didn't Caelius know about it?"

"Because, I suppose . . ." Cicero frowned.

"Or could it be that Caelius knows things that he doesn't tell you? In that case, how can you really trust him? And if you can't trust him, then neither can I!"

Cicero thought for a long moment before he answered. "Gordianus, I understand your concern in this matter—"

"Or perhaps it's Catilina who doesn't trust Caelius. Could that be it? Could it be that Caelius's pretense of loyalty has failed to fool Catilina, who knows that Caelius is your spy, not his? That would mean that Catilina knows that I'm your agent, as well. That puts my family in even graver danger."

"Clearly, Gordianus, these are deep waters. But there is no way to stay afloat unless you kick! Do nothing and you'll sink—we'll all sink! The state is a life raft. I am steering that raft. The rudder has been entrusted to me. Catilina will set fire to it if he isn't stopped, dooming us all. I must do whatever I can to keep it afloat. But I need your help. I am reaching out to pull you aboard, if only you'll give me your hand."

"What a lovely metaphor. Such fluid rhetoric—"

"Gordianus! You try my patience!" I had angered him at last. I could impugn his courage and satirize his pompous demeanor and he remained aloof, but he would not stand for me to belittle the mastery of his tongue. "Whether you like it or not, whether or not you understand its importance, you must continue to do what I ask of you. Catilina is too vicious a threat for me to bow to your apathy."

"Is he so vicious, really? Under my roof I sometimes thought he seemed more sentimental than seditious."

"Gordianus, you cannot be so naive!" Suddenly his smile returned. "Oh, I begin to see the problem. You *like* Catilina! But of course, we have all liked Catilina at one time or another, everyone has, and eventually, inevitably, to their regret. Ask the shade of his murdered brother-in-law, or the shade of his murdered son, or the miserable families of the young men and women he's corrupted. Before he destroys his victims, Catilina must always make sure that they *like* him.

"Oh, Gordianus, I know that you find your old friend Cicero a bit pompous and vain; you always have. You have a sharp, unforgiving eye for anything pretentious—that's one of your gifts—and I confess that in my success I have grown perhaps a bit too overbearing and self-important. You see through the veils of men's vanity. How can you not see through Catilina at once? Could it be that his conceit is so enormous, so monstrous, that you simply can't perceive it, the way that a man who looks at the sea cannot see a drop of water? Has he seduced you, Gordianus?"

"You're talking nonsense, Cicero. But at least your metaphors are consistent—you have me completely at sea."

He paused and looked at me shrewdly. When he lowered his head that way, the thick fold of fat in his neck pressed up against his chin like a pillow, and his eyes seemed to recede into the puffiness of his cheeks. I thought of how he had looked when I first met him—thin, almost frail, with a neck that seemed barely sturdy enough to hold up his broad-browed head. His girth had grown with his ambition.

"Oh, I can imagine how he went to work on you, Gordianus. Catilina can see into other men's hearts. He senses their needs and desires, and he plays on that knowledge like a piper. Tell me if I hit the mark. He sees at once how to flatter you—he compliments your farm and family. He takes note of your unorthodox household, senses you have a soft spot for the disenfranchised and dispossessed, and so he tells you he is a man of the people, too, and wants to shake things up at Rome to give the wretched masses a better chance in life. He rails against the unfairness of the Optimates and their devious ways—never mind that Catilina would be an Optimate himself if he hadn't squandered his reputation along with his fortune and earned the disdain of every decent man in the Senate. Having insinuated himself into your personal life and warmed you with his politics, especially tailored to suit your own, he then confides some personal secret to you and you alone, letting you see that he trusts you implicitly, that you are very special to him."

I thought of Catilina's confession regarding the Vestal Fabia and felt a prickle of discomfort.

"Catilina will tell you whatever you want to hear. Catilina will be your special confidant. Catilina will cast his spell over you with your eyes wide open, if you let him. I admit it: Catilina is charming. For years I thought so myself, until I saw through him.

"While I, alas, am utterly without charm. Don't you think I know this? You have shown your hostility to me very clearly tonight, Gordianus. You find me irritating and overbearing, and you wish I would simply go away. I annoy you. I have no charm, and I never have had; I was born without it and it cannot be counterfeited. That's precisely why I must rely on rhetoric and persuasion—clumsy tools next to the natural charm of a man like Catilina, who is halfway to winning an argument before he says a word, thanks to that handsome face and that endearing, irresistible, infuriating smile of his. Beside him I must seem very crude and shrill. But think, Gordianus! What is the value of charm if it hides the ugly truth? I speak that ugly truth and you wrinkle your nose. Catilina smiles and murmurs pretty lies and you find him intriguing. Gordianus, you know better!"

What can be worse, for a man of my age, than to begin to doubt his own judgment? Had Catilina cast a spell over me, made me dull and dreamy? Or was it Cicero who was practicing his own wicked magic, using what he knew of Catilina and of me to find the exact words that would disconcert me and bend me to his will?

"Do my words make sense to you, Gordianus? Do you hear the urgency in my voice? Will you not continue to render the single favor I ask of you, to play host to Catilina when he desires it? Do this for the good of Rome. Do this for the sake of your children."

When I didn't answer, Cicero sighed and slumped his shoulders. Was he acting, or was he genuinely weary? And why could I not tell for certain—I, who possessed such a sharp, unforgiving eye for pretense?

"Think on it, Gordianus. When you go back to that lovely, peaceful farm, think on it and remember that Rome is still here, in terrible danger. And if Rome burns, never doubt that the conflagration will spread across the countryside." He lowered his face, thickening the fold of fat in his neck. He studied me for a long moment, but I had nothing to say. "I won't see you face to face again, not until the crisis is resolved. Marcus Caelius will be my messenger, as before. It was a risk, coming to see you here tonight, but my watchers tell me that Catilina's eyes are elsewhere this evening, and Caelius told me that you were wavering, and I hoped that I might prevail upon your better judgment if I could speak to you man to man." He turned away. The stiff folds of his toga rustled softly in the still, warm air of the garden. "I'll go now. There are many calls I must pay tonight before I sleep. No one is safe with Catilina's rabble rioting in the streets, but I can't let that deter me. I know *my* duty to Rome; I only wish it were as easy and simple as yours."

With that he departed.

I sat on a bench by the fountain. The sky was dark and the stars were bright overhead. The moon had begun to rise, its silver light glinting across the tiled roof of the portico. "You may come out now, Meto," I said softly.

He stepped from behind the curtain to his room and into the shadows of the portico.

"Did Bethesda hear?" I said.

"No. I could hear her snoring now and then through the

wall." He stepped into the moonlight. He was wearing only his loincloth. It occurred to me that he was of an age to begin wearing more clothing about the house.

"Good. Eco and Menenia seem to be asleep, or else too busy to have paid any attention to voices from the garden. Only you and I know of Cicero's visit."

"How did you know I was listening? I was so careful not to make the curtain move."

"Yes, but the big toe on your left foot showed beneath the curtain's edge. A bit of starlight glinted on your toenail. In the wrong circumstances such carelessness could be fatal."

"Do you think Cicero noticed?" he asked.

I had to laugh. "I don't think so. Otherwise he'd have summoned his bodyguards from outside and you'd have been full of daggers before I could've said a word."

Meto looked alarmed, then skeptical.

"Well, what do you think of our esteemed consul, Meto?"

He hesitated for a moment. "I think Cicero is a windbag."

I smiled. "So do I, but that doesn't mean he's not telling the truth."

"Will you do what he wants, then?" I was so long in answering that Meto asked again. "Will you, Papa?"

"I only wish I knew."

TWENTY-THREE

AFTER the election we spent five more days in Rome. I enjoyed myself more than I thought I would, strolling about the seven hills, seeing old friends, savoring the delicacies of the food vendors in the markets, observing the comings and goings of every sort of man and woman through the streets of the Subura and feeling swallowed up by the never-ending pulse of life in the great city.

Not all was pleasure. One morning, while Bethesda browsed in the shops on the Street of the Silversmiths, I consulted with the advocate who was defending my rights to the

stream against Publius Claudius's challenge. His name was
Volumenus, and his office was on the second floor of a squat,
ugly brick building just a stone's throw from the Forum. The
whole building was populated by lawyers and breathed the
musty smell of old parchment. The walls of Volumenus's
cramped little office were covered with scrolls in pigeonholes.
He was rather like a scroll himself, tall and straight with a
long face and a very dry manner.

No progress had been made toward having the matter of
my water rights heard by the courts, he told me, though he
assured me he was doing all he could on my behalf.

"Why must it take so long?" I complained. "When the
Claudii challenged my inheritance of the farm, that was surely
a more complicated matter, but Cicero managed to have the
case settled in a matter of days, not months or years."

The corner of Volumenus's mouth twitched slightly. "Then
perhaps you would prefer to have Cicero handle all your legal
affairs," he said wryly. "Oh, or is he too busy for that? Really,
I'm doing all I can. Yes, if I happened to be one of the most
powerful politicians in Rome, then I'm sure I could arrange
for the courts to expedite this matter, but I'm only an honest
advocate—"

"I understand."

"No, really, if you think you can get the mighty Cicero to
take over this case, you're more than welcome—"

"That was a special favor. If you tell me that you're doing
all you can—"

"Oh, but Cicero could do more, I'm sure, and better, and
more quickly—"

I eventually managed to smooth his ruffled feathers before
I left. I stepped back onto the street feeling not so much
dissatisfied with his efforts as reminded of just how great a
debt I owed to Cicero. Without his assistance and his powerful connections, the question of my inheritance, if not settled against me outright, could easily have been held up in
the courts for years while I stayed in Rome and watched my
beard turn gray.

On the evening of our seventh day in Rome we packed for
the trip home, and set out early the next morning.

We arrived at the farm late in the afternoon, stiff and dusty. Diana leaped from the wagon at once and ran from pen to pen to give a hug and kiss to her favorite lambs and kids. Meto, his energy pent up all day, hiked at once to the ridgetop. Bethesda set about seeing how much damage the household slaves had done in her absence, and then, having perfunctorily scolded them, went to her jewelry box in our bedroom and deposited her new acquisitions.

I withdrew to my study and consulted with Aratus over what had transpired in my absence, which was little enough. The stream had dwindled even more, which he assured me was normal for the season. "I would hardly bother to mention it," he said, "except that there might be a problem with the well. . . ."

"What sort of problem?" I asked.

"The taste of the water is off. I noticed yesterday. Perhaps a cat managed to squeeze through the iron grate, or perhaps some burrowing animal dug through the wall of the shaft, fell into the water and drowned."

"You mean there's a dead animal in the well?"

"I suspect as much. The taste of the water, as I said—"

"What have you done about it?"

From the way he tilted his head back I could tell I was speaking too harshly. "The first thing to do in such a case is to lift off the grate, lower a bucket or a hook, and try to lift out the carcass. Dead bodies float, after all—"

"Did you do this?"

"I did. But we were unable to lift anything. At one point the hook became trapped. It took two men to pull it free. It may be that some stones have become dislodged. It could even be that a considerable portion of the wall has fallen in. If that is the case, the foul taste could have been introduced when the dislodgment took place—a burrowing animal may have been crushed or drowned, you see. If the damage is extensive—and that any damage at all has occurred is only a supposition—this could be rather serious. Major repairs to the well would prevent it from being used, and with the stream running so low . . ."

"How will we know whether it's damaged or not?"

"Someone will have to go down into the well."

"Why wasn't this done yesterday? Or this morning? Meanwhile, the dead ferret or weasel or whatever just keeps rotting away, poisoning the water."

He folded his hands and lowered his eyes. "Yesterday, by the time our efforts to use the hook had failed, it was too dark to send anyone down into the shaft. This morning there were storm clouds approaching from the west, and it seemed to me that it was more important to bring the bales of hay from the north field into the barn, to prevent them from getting wet."

"There were bales of hay sitting outside? I thought all the hay had been brought in already."

"It had, Master, but a few days ago I ordered the men to take the hay back out into the sun. The bales that were not lost to the blight may yet succumb, but this might be prevented by exposing the hay to the hot sunlight."

I shook my head, dubious of his judgment once again. "And did it rain this morning?"

He twisted his mouth. "No. But the clouds were quite dark and threatening, and we did hear thunder nearby. Even if the slaves had not been occupied with the hay, I would have hesitated to send a man down into the well with a storm threatening, considering the danger. I know how you value your slaves, Master, and I would not squander them."

"Very well," I said glumly. "Is there still time to send someone down into the well before it gets dark?"

"I was about to do that when you arrived, Master."

I went out to the well with Aratus, where a group of slaves was already gathered. They had made a kind of harness out of rope and had tied it to a much longer rope. One of the men would put himself into the harness while the others lowered him down.

Meto joined us, smiling and red-cheeked from his climb up to the ridge and back. When I explained what was happening, he immediately volunteered to go down into the well himself.

"No, Meto."

"But why not, Papa? I'm the perfect size, I'm agile and I'm not heavy."

"Don't be foolish, Meto."

"But, Papa, I think it would be interesting."

"Meto, don't be ridiculous." I lowered my voice. "It's far too dangerous. I wouldn't even consider allowing you to do it. That's—" I caught myself. I had almost said: "That's what the slaves are for," then realized how the words would strike his ears.

Then, in the next instant, I realized how the sentiment struck my own ears. Had I really grown so callous toward the men I owned? I had inherited a farm; along with it, had I also inherited the contemptuous attitudes of slave owners like Publius Claudius or dead Cato? Use a human tool until it breaks, says Cato in his book, and then discard it for a new one. I had always despised men like Crassus, who attached no value at all to the lives of slaves, only to their utility. And yet, I thought, give a man a farm and watch him turn into a little Cato; give him mines and property and sailing ships and he becomes a little Crassus, no doubt. I had turned away from Cicero precisely because it seemed to me that he had become the very thing he had once despised. But perhaps such a course is inevitable in life—wealth necessarily makes a man greedy, success makes him vain, and even the least measure of power makes him careless of others. Could I say I was any different?

These thoughts flashed through my head like a bolt of lightning. "You can't go down into the well, Meto, because I'm going down myself." The words surprised me almost as much as they did Meto.

"Oh, Papa, now who's being foolish?" he protested. "I should go. I'm so much younger and more supple." The slaves, meanwhile, looked at us in frank astonishment.

Aratus laid a hand on each of our shoulders and took us aside. "Master, I would advise you against doing such a thing. Much too dangerous. That's what the slaves are for. If you take on such a task, you'll only confuse them."

"The slaves are here to do as I tell them, or in my absence, as Meto tells them," I corrected him. "And while I'm down in the well, it's Meto who will make sure that you oversee them properly, Aratus."

He grimaced. "Master, if you were to be hurt—may the

gods forbid such a tragedy!—the slaves would be liable for terrible punishments. For their sake, I ask you to let one of them perform this task."

"No, Aratus, I've made up my mind. Don't contradict me again. Now, how does this harness fit?"

Did I hope to prove something by this escapade? If I wanted to demonstrate that I was not like every other slave owner, I could hardly have chosen a less thoughtful way to show it, for the slaves were anxious and miserable. If I needed to prove to myself that I was still young enough to face danger without flinching, I should have looked in a mirror to bring myself back to reality. Perhaps I thought to earn Meto's renewed respect, when in fact I was once again shunting aside his assertion of his own manhood. I acted on a wild impulse, and only later I thought, This seems the sort of mad thing that Catilina might do!

Aratus, looking glummer than I had ever seen him, oversaw the mechanics of the operation, testing the ropes and fitting the harness over my shoulders. Meto, looking disappointed, was left with little to do. The slaves removed the iron grate from the well and then winced as I climbed into the breach. I was handed a torch. The slaves formed a line and took up the rope, then fed it toward me hand over hand. As I descended step by step, the edge of the well rose and the sky shrank to a round hole above me.

It was not as hard as I had thought it would be. I simply walked backward down the side of the well, carefully placing one foot behind the other. The rope stayed taut, steadying my weight. Above me I could see Aratus and Meto peering down at me, both of them frowning and blinking at the bits of ash that rose from my burning torch.

"Master, be careful!" Aratus moaned.

"Yes, Papa, do be careful," echoed Meto.

The hole above grew smaller and smaller, until it was the size of a small plate. "More rope?" called Aratus.

I glanced over my shoulder. I still could not see the water. "Yes, more rope."

I descended step by step and kept peering over my shoulder until at last the circle of water glistened beneath me, flashing like liquid fire where it was lit by the ruddy torchlight and as black as obsidian where it was covered by the shadow of my body. There appeared to be something smooth and pale in the water, like a large stone showing just above the surface. The walls all around were undamaged. The closer I got, the harder it became to twist my neck far enough around to see the water.

I descended until I was just above the surface. "Keep the rope taut!" I called.

"Yes, Master!" cried Aratus, his voice echoing down the shaft. His face was a dark spot amid the small circle of bright light above.

I intended to turn over, taking small steps until I faced the water. I had almost succeeded when my foot encountered a loose stone in the wall. With a splash, my legs swung downward.

The slaves holding the rope were not ready for the sudden tug. The rope went slack for just an instant and I slipped into the water up to my neck. The rope went taut again, pulling my shoulders above the surface. Water splashed my face. I sputtered and coughed.

I had managed to keep the torch above the water. The fiery light caught on the jagged stone walls and the splashing water, creating a jumbled array of light and shadow all around. With my free arm I thrashed about for something to hold on to. There was a large object in the water with me, lodged stiffly between opposite walls of the well. It gave way as I clutched at it, then it began to bob alongside me. It was cold and fleshy to the touch. I shuddered and felt my bile rise.

I cried out—not a scream of terror but a sharp yelping cry such as a dog makes when its tail is stepped on. Echoing up to the mouth of the well, it must have sounded quite hideous. The slaves above heard it and panicked. The rope jerked hard at my shoulders and I began to rise against my will.

I cried out for them to stop, but perhaps the well twisted my words and they thought I was crying for help. I clutched at the thing in the water, repulsed by it but not afraid of it. The weight of it held me down. The slaves pulled harder, sending a hot stab of pain through my back, but I held fast to the thing in the water. I thought I understood what I had seen, but I had to be sure.

The slaves pulled so hard that I began to rise out of the water, bringing the thing with me. I clutched it with both hands, keeping hold of the torch as well so that its flame flickered close to my face. Before the agony in my shoulders compelled me to release the thing, letting the heavy weight slip back into the water, I was sure of what I had seen.

From somewhere above I heard Aratus cry, "Heave!" I surged upward so swiftly that the torch slipped from my hand. It bounced off my foot and twirled flaming into the water, where it expired in an explosion of steam.

Heaving and straining, the slaves lifted me up, like a deus ex machina on a stage. I careened from side to side in the darkness, legs flailing, shoulders banging against the walls. I hardly felt the pain and the jarring in my teeth. My head was too full of the thing I had seen in the water.

It was a body. And it had no head.

PART THREE

CONUNDRUM

TWENTY-FOUR

DARKNESS had fallen by the time the body was removed from the well.

On the first attempt, a slave was lowered into the shaft carrying with him a second rope, which he harnessed around the corpse's shoulders. The shivering slave was pulled up, looking queasy and pale, and then the body. The sight of the naked, bloated, headless corpse emerging from the well was so grotesque that several of the slaves cried out in horror and loosened their grip on the rope. The rope escaped, sliding like prickling fire through the hands of those who tried to hold it, whipping through the air like a mad serpent. From deep inside the well came the sound of a great splash. An instant later the end of the rope followed the body down the shaft, like a snake disappearing into its hole with a contemptuous flick of its tail.

This disaster unnerved the more superstitious of the slaves. I heard voices all around me whisper the word "*lemur.*" Looking about in the uncertain light of dusk, I couldn't tell which of the slaves had said it. They all looked equally frightened. It was as if the word had been whispered by the warm, dry breeze itself.

It was then that I realized that the well had been doubly poisoned. First, by the pollution of the corpse's bloated, decaying flesh. Then again by the very fact of its presence in the well. The slaves would consider the spot unholy now. They would shun the place, avoid any errands that sent them there, avert their eyes when they passed, perhaps refuse even to drink from it again, fearing it as haunted by the dead man's shade.

It was only thanks to Aratus's mastery at dealing with the other slaves that we were able to stage a second attempt, even as the sun was setting. The slave who had descended the well

balked at doing so again. None of the other slaves was willing
to volunteer. Aratus selected one of the men, who quailed at
the task. Aratus threatened him with a beating and even struck
him across the back. The slave acquiesced and allowed himself to be fitted into the harness. What other choice was there?
To go myself was out of the question after the wrenching that
had been done to my back and shoulders, and I refused to let
Meto make the attempt. In the end, I acted as any other slave
owner would have and allowed my foreman to coerce one of
the slaves into doing it against his will. I could almost hear
the shade of the dead Cato mocking me.

This time, the shock of the corpse's appearance was not
so great, and the men managed to keep their grip. Still, the
sight was unnerving—the waxiness of the bloated flesh, the
gaping wound at the neck, the terrible absence where the head
should have been. The body was pulled onto the paving
stones. A pool of water gathered beneath it and trickled in
various directions. The slaves cried out and jumped back
rather than let the water touch their feet.

I looked toward the house and saw Bethesda's silhouette
at one of the windows. I had sent word to her to keep Diana
away, and to keep herself away as well. What was she thinking now, gazing out at the group of frightened slaves gathered
around the well in the gathering gloom? She would know the
truth soon enough. Everyone on the farm would know—there
was no way to keep the catastrophe a secret, as I had with
Nemo.

I called on Aratus to bring more torches so that I could
see the body by a better light. The slaves milled restlessly
about, eager to be gone from the place. I told Aratus to dismiss them for now, but to see that all the slaves were gathered
together outside the stable within an hour. I stooped beside
the body, wincing at the stabbing pain in my shoulders and
at the cuts on my elbows and knees where the rough walls
of the well had scraped the flesh. Meto, holding a torch, knelt
beside me.

"Well, Meto, what can you see?"

He swallowed hard. Even by the ruddy torchlight he
looked pale. "The flesh is so bloated, it's hard to say. I'm not
sure where to begin."

"Make a list in your head. Either-or, as the philosophers say. Man or woman?"

"Man, of course."

"Old or young?"

"About the same as Nemo?" he said uncertainly.

"Why do you say that?"

"The gray hairs among the black ones on his chest. And the way his joints are all knobby. Not a boy, but not an old man either."

"Dark or fair?"

"It's hard to tell much about his skin, the way it's all swollen and discolored, though I would say it looks weathered by the sun. The hair around his sex is dark."

"Slave or free?"

"Slave," he said, without hesitation.

"Because?"

"From where I was standing I saw his back as the slaves pulled him out."

I reached down to turn the body over but the weight was too much for my injured shoulders. Meto put down his torch, knelt beside me, and helped me tip the corpse.

"There," he said, picking up his torch and pointing. By its lurid glow we saw the proof of the man's slavery. His back and shoulders were covered with scars. Some were old, almost faded away, while others were vivid and fresh. He had been regularly beaten while he was alive.

"What caused his death?" I asked.

Meto bowed his head, considering. "Obviously he was killed before he was put in the well, since his head is off. Unless his head is down there, too." He glanced at the well and swallowed hard.

"I think not. I didn't see it, and neither did the slaves who went down after me. But again, as with Nemo, you're assuming he was murdered. We don't know that. There's no visible wound, except where the head's been cut off, and as with Nemo, that probably happened after he was dead. Who's to say how he died?"

"Unless we can find out who he is."

"And where he came from."

"Surely, whoever left Nemo in the barn also left . . ." Meto frowned. "What shall we call this one, Papa?"

I looked down at the wretched, lifeless mass of flesh. "Ignotus," I said: *Unknown*.

A few moments later a slave arrived from the house. "The mistress is eager for you to come," he said, casting furtive glances at the dead corpse. "And Congrio says that your dinner is getting cold."

"Tell your mistress that I have no appetite tonight. And while you're at it, tell Aratus to gather all the slaves outside the stable."

"Even Congrio?"

"Yes, even Congrio."

By the light of Meto's torch we made our way through the gathering darkness to the stable. The slaves began to assemble and whispered among themselves. A moment later Aratus came down from the house, followed by the kitchen slaves and Congrio.

Aratus stepped beside me and spoke in a low voice. "They're all here. Do you want to address them yourself, Master, or shall I?"

"I'll speak to them."

Aratus stepped forward. "Quiet! Something important has happened, and the Master wants to speak to us all together." He stepped away from me but did not join the other slaves, keeping himself apart. Congrio, too, stood off to one side, while his underlings from the kitchen joined the others. Even among slaves there are the high and the low.

I had not addressed the slaves as a group since I had first come to the farm. In the glow of the torches I could see their faces clearly. They looked back at me anxiously. Lucius Claudius had been a lenient master before me. I had been, if anything, more lenient; perhaps too much so, considering that one or more of them must have betrayed me.

"A dead body has been found in the well," I said. This came as a surprise to no one, since word had already spread among them, but still there was a murmur of excitement. "Who among you knows how it got there?"

No one spoke. "Do you mean to tell me that not one of you has any idea how it happened, or when, or who did it?"

They looked at me and at one another evasively, cleared their throats, shook their heads. At last one of them meekly raised his hand and stepped forward. It was the oldest slave on the farm, a graybeard called Clementus.

"Yes, speak up," I said.

"A few nights ago I thought I heard something . . ."

"Yes?"

"A sound coming from the well. I often wake up in the night—I never sleep straight through. I always have to rise in the night to pass water. It's been like that since I was a young man. Others always chide me and say I have a small bladder, but it makes no difference whether it's full when I go to bed or not, and as I've gotten older—"

"Get to the point!" said Aratus. "What did you hear?"

"It was late at night, closer to dawn than sundown.. The moon had already set, and it was very dark. I was sleeping beneath the lean-to behind the barn when I woke. It was a sound that woke me—a splash coming from somewhere. From the direction of the well, I think. A big splash, but not loud, rather muffled, just as if something large had been dropped down the shaft of the well. I roused myself to piss into the pot I use, then went back to sleep."

"What night was this?" I asked.

"Three nights ago, I think. Or maybe four. I'd forgotten all about it. It only came back to me just now, hearing about this body dropped down the well."

"Ridiculous!" snapped Aratus. "He wakes up needing to relieve himself and hears the sound of splashing! He was dreaming."

"It seems to me that you cut him short for no reason, Aratus," I said sharply. "Why shouldn't he have heard the splash, and why not in the middle of the night? After the splash, Clementus, did you see or hear anything else?"

He scratched his beard. "Did I? It seems there was someone walking about in the dark after I relieved myself, but I didn't think anything of it at the time. It was a hot night, the kind that keeps people awake, and I don't suppose I'm the only one with a weak bladder. Why shouldn't one of the slaves be up and walking about in the dark?"

"But did you see this man? Do you remember anything

about him? Did he speak, or hum a tune? Was he dressed in a certain way or have a certain gait?"

Clementus scratched his beard thoughtfully again, but finally shook his head. "No, I don't remember anything like that. I only seem to remember someone walking about out in the open area by the well. Perhaps I only dreamed it, or perhaps that was a different night altogether."

"Useless," muttered Aratus.

"On the contrary, he seems more alert and aware of what's going on than those who should be responsible for the proper running of this farm and the safety of those who live here," I said in a low voice.

No one else came forward. No one but Clementus had seen or heard anything. I might as well have been questioning a congregation of the blind and deaf. I warned them that I would not hesitate to punish any slave who I later discovered had withheld the truth from me; I searched for flashes of guilt in their eyes, but saw only the natural fear of slaves. I assured them that the well would be purified—as head of the household, the ritual duty would fall to me, though I had no idea how to perform it. So far as I knew, Cato did not cover the subject in his book. Nor did I know how the well might be purified in fact as well as in ritual. What sort of pollution had Ignotus left in the water, and how long would the danger last? I had only Aratus to consult, and as always I didn't fully trust him. I could ask Claudia, but I hardly wanted to share the incident with her.

I charged a group of slaves to take the body of Ignotus to a little shed beside the stable, and dismissed the rest. As they dispersed, Aratus drew closer.

"They should be tortured, Master."

"What?"

"They're slaves, Master. You talk to them as if they were soldiers, or free men in a marketplace. Common slaves like these never tell the truth unless it's forced from them. There's no telling what they know, and no way of getting it except by forcing it out of them. You know what the law says: you can't trust the evidence of a slave unless it's obtained under torture."

"By that logic, I should begin the torture with you, Aratus. What do you say to that?"

He blanched, not sure whether I was serious or not. I was not quite sure myself.

It may have been hot outside, but it was chilly in my bedroom that night. Bethesda was quietly furious. She consented to put a soothing balm on my scraped elbows and knees and even massaged my shoulders, but when I spoke to her, she wouldn't answer. In our bed she turned her back on me and finally spoke. "Whatever it is they want from you, give it to them. No more headless bodies, do you understand? Swallow your pride and think of your children. And no more foolishness like climbing down wells!"

I did not sleep well that night. In my dreams headless phantoms arose from the well and went walking about the fields.

In the morning Meto woke me. His tunic was crooked and his hair was still mussed from sleep. He was breathing hard, as if he had been running. "Papa, wake up!"

I shrugged his hand away and looked up at him blearily.

"Papa, I know the truth. I woke up knowing it! I just ran out to have a look at his body to make sure."

"What are you talking about? Ignotus?"

"Not Ignotus, Papa. Not any longer. I know his name, and so do you. Come, I'll show you. I'll prove it to you."

He waited impatiently while I put on my sandals and slipped a tunic over my shoulders. Bethesda pulled the coverlet over her head.

Meto led the way to the shed, running ahead of me in his eagerness, then waiting for me to catch up. Inside, the body of Ignotus had been laid on a low bench. His odor permeated the little room. He would have to be moved before the sun got much higher, or else we would never get rid of his stench.

"There, Papa, do you see?"

"What?"

"There, on the back of his left hand!"

I stooped, groaning at the ache in my muscles. The lifeless hand was bent so that I had to twist my head to see the little

mark on the back. It was roughly triangular in shape and
hardly larger than a coin, of a rich purple color like the dye
of the murex.

"A birthmark," I acknowledged. "Yes, I noticed it last
night. I thought I would allow you to remark on it, but you
never did, and I never got around to mentioning it myself.
Yes, it could be a valuable bit of evidence if we ever have
the chance to identify him."

"But I already have. Didn't you hear me? I know who it
is. When I saw the birthmark last night I knew it reminded
me of something, but I couldn't think of what. You kept asking me those either-or questions and it went out of my head.
But this morning I woke up remembering. Does that ever
happen to you, Papa?"

"I begin every day with great revelations."

"I'm not joking, Papa. So you don't remember where
we've seen that birthmark before? I do!" He seemed very
pleased with himself.

"If I've ever seen that birthmark before, you're right, I
don't remember. But you think you've seen it?" I said skep-
tically.

"Yes, I know I have, and if you had been observant, so
would you. It's Forfex!"

"Forfex?" I muttered, trying to place the name.

"The goatherd over on Mount Argentum. The slave of
Gnaeus Claudius, the one who took us to see the old silver
mine and hurt his head."

"The one who took Catilina, you mean. We only went
along as an afterthought." I stared at the birthmark. "No, I
don't remember seeing this mark on the back of his hand."

"But I do! I noticed it that day. I remember thinking it
looked like a spot of blood, as if he'd pricked himself. When
I saw it yesterday I couldn't place the memory, but this morning I woke up remembering. I thought you surely would have
noticed, too. You notice everything, Papa."

"Forfex!" I remembered the slave's wheedling manner and
the panic that had driven him from the mine, the blood
streaming from his head and his master's displeasure. I shook
my head doubtfully. "Is there anything else to identify him?"
I studied the body. It was roughly of the same age as Forfex,

and roughly the same size, and of the right coloration. The
dead flesh before us was so horribly different from the living
slave who had taken us up the mountain that I could hardly
reconcile the transformation, though the same might be said
of any man and the corpse he becomes.

"And the marks on his back, Papa! Do you remember how
Gnaeus Claudius began to beat him as we were departing?
He's the type of master who would beat his slaves often, don't
you think? So it's no surprise to see all those scars on Forfex's back."

"Yes, I remember the beating. But not the birthmark . . ."

"Well, what does it matter, so long as one of us remembers
it? The important thing is that now we know who he was,
and where his body came from. It's Forfex, and somehow he
came here from Gnaeus Claudius's estate."

"If we could only be sure of that . . ."

"But we can be! How could two different men have exactly the same birthmark? It must be Forfex, don't you see?"
He smiled at me expectantly, then frowned when he saw the
lingering doubt on my face. "You don't believe me, do you,
Papa?"

"No, it's not that . . ."

"You don't trust my memory. You doubt my judgment."

"If you truly remembered the birthmark, why did you not
recall it last night?"

"Because last night was—" He sought for the words and
could not find them. "Because I didn't, that's all! But I do
now."

"Meto, memory changes over time and can't always be
trusted—"

"Oh, Papa, you always have a saying for everything." He
was quite angry. "If it were Eco telling you this instead of
me, you'd believe him in an instant! You wouldn't doubt him
at all."

I took a deep breath. "Perhaps." Because Eco is Eco, and
you are you, I wanted to say.

"You're jealous!" said Meto.

"What?"

"Yes, because you don't remember it yourself. You never
noticed the birthmark at all, you weren't observant enough,

but I was. Or else you noticed and then you forgot, but I
noticed and I remembered! For once my eyes and my memory
are sharper than yours, and you won't admit it!"

This accusation struck me as quite absurd. It only offered
more proof, if any were needed, that Meto was still more a
boy than a man. Even so, I felt a slight prickle of unease.
What can be worse, for a man of my age, than to begin to
doubt his own judgment?

It was possible, of course, that Meto was right—that he
had seen the birthmark on Forfex's hand, had forgotten it until
this morning, and now had proof of the slave's identity. If
that was so, then I would be obliged to demand an explanation from Gnaeus Claudius. But what if Meto was mistaken?
What if he had seized upon a false memory and now clung
to it out of pride? How far could I press my complaint against
Gnaeus based on Meto's memory, which I myself mistrusted?

And if it was Forfex—what then? Had Gnaeus Claudius
been responsible for putting Nemo in my stable, as well? Who
among the slaves had helped him? Was his motive merely to
harass me, to drive me from the farm? What of the link with
Catilina's riddle—could it be mere coincidence? Or was the
more inexplicable coincidence the fact that Catilina and Forfex had known and dealt with each other? Even if the body
belonged to Forfex, the link might run not to his master but
to Catilina—or by extension to Marcus Caelius—or to Cicero . . .

I found my thoughts racing in the same rutted circles they
had worn since we discovered Nemo. Had I always been so
helpless at thinking things through, and was Meto right to
imply that I had become dull and careless? I was not a young
man any longer, and while there are those whose minds grow
sharper with age, there are plenty of people for whom the
opposite is true.

I realized I had been staring intently for several moments
at the purple mark on the corpse's hand. I looked up to see
that Meto was watching me, his arms tightly crossed, his eyes
narrowed, his foot tapping the ground, waiting for me to respond.

"For now," I said quietly, "we shall assume that Ignotus
is Forfex. If Gnaeus Claudius is responsible, we may expect

that he will disclaim responsibility, so first we should attempt to get the truth from his slaves, if we can."

I had not realized how tense Meto had been until he loosened his shoulders and stopped clutching his arms. I thought he might smile at his little triumph, but instead he looked closer to tears. "You'll see, Papa," he said in a very earnest voice. "You'll see that I'm right and I do remember."

"I hope so," I said, but I still doubted.

TWENTY-FIVE

"WE could confront him directly," suggested Meto, as he climbed onto his horse.

"Not before we try to get the truth from his slaves," I said, gripping the reins and calming my mount.

"But how shall we avoid him? There's only the one road that leads from the Cassian Way onto his property. If Gnaeus is there, he may see us ride up, or else one of the slaves may run and inform him. He didn't seem like the sort of master whose slaves would let strangers onto the estate without telling him."

"No? Forfex allowed Catilina and us to climb all over the mountain."

"Yes, and now you see what's happened to Forfex."

If indeed the corpse is Forfex, I thought. We rode away from the stable on the long, straight road to the highway. "As for our approach," I said, "I have an idea. We won't take the main road that leads to the house of the goatherds and Gnaeus's villa."

"What then? The rocky hills alongside the Cassian Way are too steep and rough to take our horses, and hard going on foot."

"But there's another way. Do you remember when we were on the hillside watching Catilina and Tongilius?"

"And Claudia came up and joined us?"

"Yes. Catilina knew from Forfex that another path, long

disused and hidden from sight beneath the trees, cuts from the Cassian Way and winds up the mountainside. He must have found it, for after a bit of searching he disappeared and then reappeared high up on the hill. I think I remember where he disappeared among the rocks and trees. I think we can find the path he took. We can avoid Gnaeus's house altogether and go hunting for a lonely goatherd among the rocks and brambles."

We came to the Cassian Way and turned not left, which would have taken us to the main gate to Gnaeus's land, but right, toward Rome. We passed the ridge on our right, and I felt curiously vulnerable, knowing how visible we were to anyone up on the hill where I so often sat and gazed over the landscape. But no one would be there to see us, of course, except possibly Claudia, and Claudia would know what had transpired quickly enough if I discovered that Gnaeus had put Forfex down my well.

There was no traffic at all on the Cassian Way. At the high point of the saddle where the road passed between the foot of the mountain and the foot of the ridge, I paused and looked around. Before us I saw nothing but the long ribbon of road disappearing toward the south. Behind us there was a smudge on the horizon that might have been a team of slaves or cattle being driven toward Rome, but it was too far away to worry about. We moved on. The ridge fell away on our right, but low hills still hid our view of Claudia's farm. On our left the land rose sharply. High trees and tumbled rocks obscured any view of the steep mountainside looming above.

"Somewhere close . . ." I murmured. We slowed our horses and together gazed into the underbrush. The tangle seemed impenetrable and undisturbed. We rode slowly on until I was certain that we had passed the place where Catilina and Tongilius had disappeared. The low hills on our right had fallen away, and I could see the slaves at work in Claudia's fields.

"We've gone too far," said Meto.

"Yes. We'll double back."

The view on our return was no different from before, and I began to think that we would have to give it up, or else go thrashing through the underbrush as Catilina had. Then I heard the clatter of hooves on paving stones and looked up to see a young deer on the road ahead. A swaying branch showed where it had emerged from the woods at the base of the ridge. It saw us and for a long moment stood as still as a statue, then bounded toward the mountainside. Off the road, its hooves made a crackling noise in the dry grass. It passed between some scattered young trees into a zone of dappled shadow and sunlight, then seemed trapped against a wall of dense brush. Nonetheless it disappeared into a narrow space between a great boulder and the thick trunk of an ancient oak. Had I blinked I would have thought it vanished in a beam of sunlight. It was a sign such as the poets speak of, a portent.

"Where the deer go," I said quietly, "there often is a trail."

We rode to the boulder and dismounted. The passage was just wide enough for us to slip through and to pull our horses after us. A narrow, open space curved around the boulder and opened onto a small clearing behind it, completely hidden from the road. From this spot we were able to see traces of an old path that headed steeply up the hill.

"The boulder must have fallen at some time," I said, "loosened by rains or an earthquake, blocking the end of the path and hiding it completely from the Cassian Way. The path itself is strewn with rocks, suitable for deer perhaps, but not for horses. We shall have to tie the horses here and proceed on foot."

The way was steep and rugged. Disused as a path, it had reverted to a runnel, and over the years the scouring water had left much debris and damage in its wake. In places the way was overgrown so that we had to stoop and bend and push branches out of the way. Here and there, small branches had recently been broken; someone else had been using the trail.

The path was steep at its beginning and then became absurdly steep. The rocks in the runnel were like steps carved for a Titan. Even Meto began to breathe hard and to sweat, though I could tell that he was holding back and could have been far ahead of me had he proceeded at his own pace. As it was, my heart was pounding and my feet had turned to lead by the time we came to the open space where I had first seen the path from its opposite end and Forfex had explained its existence. We were now on the road we had taken before

with Catilina and Tongilius. To our left the narrow road
would lead downward back to Gnaeus's house and the house
of the goatherds. To our right the footpath proceeded up the
mountain, past the waterfall, and up to the mine.

My body protested the folly of taking another step uphill,
but it was there that we would most likely find a wandering
goatherd, preferably alone and off his guard.

It did not take long. As we approached the steep stone
steps that led up to the head of the waterfall, amid the sound
of rushing water I heard the bleating of a kid, and in coun-
terpoint to it the voice of a goatherd calling in gentle tones.
We stepped off the path, toward the sound of falling water.
The splashing of the falls grew louder, but so did the bleating
and the voice of the goatherd.

We stepped through a mass of hanging vines and leaves
and found ourselves at the base of the waterfall, on the bank
of a foaming green pool. The place was deeply shadowed by
high trees and the cliff above. Scattered about in rocky crevices and caught in the tangle of great tree roots were the skulls
and bones that we had previously seen from above. A shiver
passed through me; the place was dank and cool, even on a
hot summer day.

Only a few steps away we saw the goatherd. He was only
a boy, younger than Meto, dressed in a ragged tunic and worn
shoes barely held on his feet by scraps of leather. He had
found the kid he was seeking. The animal was draped over
his shoulders, its legs crossed over his chest and held tight in
his fists. The sound of the waterfall had covered our quiet
footsteps. When he saw us, the young slave gave a start and
drew back, so suddenly that he almost lost his balance. For
a moment he teetered on the edge of a rock and might have
fallen into the pool if Meto had not stepped forward to grab
his elbow.

The young goatherd recovered his balance and jerked free
of Meto's grip. He drew back. The kid struggled and bleated.
The slave tightened his grip on the beast's forelegs until his
knuckles were as white as the animal's fleece. He stared from
Meto's face to mine with fear in his eyes. "Who are you?"
he finally stammered. "Are you alive or dead?"

A curious question, I thought, until I remembered that the

pool with all its bones and skulls was haunted by the lemures
of dead slaves. Forfex himself had told us so. "We are very
much alive," I said, and meant it; surely lemures do not feel
stiffness in their joints and soreness in their legs as living
men do.

The slave looked at us from beneath drawn brows and kept
his distance. "I suppose your hand felt warm enough on my
arm," he said, glancing at Meto. "But what are you doing
here? Friends of the Master?"

"What are *you* doing here?" I countered.

"They made me come, because I'm the youngest. Somebody heard one of the kids bleating down here by the pool,
so they made me come after it. Sure enough, it had one of
its hooves trapped between two rocks down by the water.
Nobody likes to come down here, because of *them*." He
looked about at the scattered bones.

"Who sent you?" I said. "Was it Forfex?"

"Forfex?" He made the name into a stifled gasp.

"Yes, isn't Forfex chief among the goatherds?"

"Not anymore. Not after—" He looked at us with renewed
suspicion. "Does the Master know you're here?"

"Tell us what happened to Forfex," I said, putting as much
authority into my voice as I could. The slaves of Gnaeus
Claudius were of the sort that responded to such a tone of
voice—easily intimidated and unable to press their own questions, even against a trespasser. This said much about their
master and the way he treated them.

"Forfex—the Master didn't mean to do it, not really. He
gets around to beating all of us sooner or later, but he's never
before—at least not with his own hands—or not since I've
been here, and I've been here since I was a boy . . ."

"You're saying that Gnaeus Claudius killed Forfex, aren't
you?" demanded Meto, glancing at me with a hint of a smile
on his lips. He might have cause to feel vindicated, but his
interruption was a mistake. He was neither old nor fearsome
enough to make the young slave quail. The goatherd again
drew back, unsure whether he was more afraid of answering
or of not answering. The kid across his shoulders bleated
pathetically.

"How did your master kill Forfex?" I asked sternly, stepping forward and pinning the goatherd with my gaze. He was only a boy, and a slave, and regularly abused by his master. He had no defense against a direct interrogation, even from a man who had no right to administer it, so long as I held him with my eyes and hardened my voice.

"His head—Forfex had already hurt his head not long ago . . ."

I remembered Forfex's striking his forehead against the rock in the mine—the blood streaming down his face, his visions of lemures, his pitiful moaning as we carried him down the mountainside. "Yes, go on," I said.

"After that he became a bit addled—slower than usual, not always making sense, with an ache in his head that came and went, sometimes so bad he woke up at night bleating like a kid."

Poor Forfex, I thought. If only Catilina had not bribed you into going where your deepest fears warned you not to go.

"The Master isn't very patient. He was always beating Forfex for being stupid, anyway, but after the accident he was often really furious with him. He blamed Forfex for hurting himself, saying that he should never have taken it on himself to show the mine to strangers in the first place—but then, you must be . . ." He peered at us with a dawning awareness in his eyes.

"Never mind, go on!" I snapped.

"A few days ago the Master ordered Forfex to slaughter one of the goats, but Forfex slaughtered the wrong one, or so the Master insisted. The Master flew into such a rage—terrible to see, like lightning when it strikes the mountain. He beat Forfex across the back with his whip so hard he ripped his tunic. There was blood on the whip. Then there was a terrible change in the Master's face. I was standing close enough to see. The sight of it turned me to water. It was as if he had made up his mind that Forfex was ruined and not worth keeping. Like a cracked clay bottle that a man might smash just for the thrill of it. That's what he did to Forfex. He turned the whip about in his hand and began to strike him with the handle—it's made of leather wrapped around iron, with hard iron studs. He began to strike Forfex all about his head. He laughed and said, 'Since it's your head to blame,

I'll take it out on your head!' And all the time Forfex bleated
and moaned and then started making other noises. Oh,
please—"

The memory had turned his face the color of chalk. His
eyes were red and moist. He blinked and staggered uncertainly. The kid across his shoulders bleated at the sudden
jostling and began to kick, so violently that the boy lost his
grip and the animal went flying through the air, landing with
a clatter of hooves on a flat stone. It bounded into the water
and then out again and went running through the underbrush
toward the path, shaking itself and sending beads of water
flying from its snowy fleece.

The young goatherd staggered back against a wall of rock
and slid downward until he sat on a stony bench, holding his
hands to his stomach. "It makes me sick to remember," he
said weakly.

"I'm sure it does," I said earnestly. How much sicker
would it make him to see Forfex now? "When did this happen?"

"Five days ago."

"Are you sure?"

"Yes. It was just after the Ides. The Master was gone for
a few days, down to Rome for the election. He came back as
soon as it was over. They say the voting went as he wanted,
but he was in a terrible mood anyway. Perhaps something
else went wrong for him down in Rome besides the election.
I think he would have found fault with Forfex no matter
what."

"Five days ago," I said, exchanging a glance with Meto.
"And last night Clementus told us he heard the splash from
the well three or four nights before—that would fit exactly.
What was done with Forfex's body?"

"Brought here," said the boy dully. "When it was over,
when Forfex lay upon the floor, not moving, the blood and
gore from his head all—" He broke off and swallowed hard.

"Go on."

"The Master's face changed again. I don't think he quite
knew what he had done until he had done it, if you know
what I mean. His face, the look in his eyes—I've never seen
such a look, except in a slave's eyes. As if he were frightened

of what he had done. They say there's a goddess who punishes men, even free men, if they go too far. There's a Greek
word—" He wrinkled his brow.

"*Hubris,*" I said. "Insolence that borders on madness; arrogance that flouts all sense of decency. Hubris is punished
by the goddess Nemesis, who brings retribution against the
wicked."

"Perhaps in some places," said the boy, "but I don't think
that goddess ever comes to this mountain. Even so, for just
a moment I think the Master knew he had gone too far. He
dropped the whip and trembled. But then he hardened his jaw.
He clenched his fists to stop them from shaking. He looked
around the room, blinking as if it were too dark for him to
see, though the sun was still up. His eyes fell on me, just
because I happened to be closest, I think. 'Clean it up!' he
said, as if it were a mess left on the floor by the goats. 'Clean
it up and take what's left of him to the waterfall. Throw him
off the cliff and let him join the rest of the bones!' "

"And is that what you did?"

"Yes, only we didn't cast him off the cliff. We carried him
down here, to the pond. One of the older slaves said we
should strip his body and clean the blood off him, to make
him fit to enter Hades. The old slave said a few words over
the body, a prayer to some god or other. Even slaves have
gods, you know, though I don't think any of them live on
this mountain, and certainly not your Nemesis. We carried
him across the stream, over to that jumble of boulders there,
and laid him in a narrow place between the stones. We covered him with a few large rocks, and then we left. It was
beginning to grow dark. No one comes here after dark."

"Poor Forfex!" I said. "To be left among the lemures he
dreaded so much. To join their number."

"That's why no one wanted to come here today to search
for the bleating kid. They've always been afraid of the old
spirits that dwell here, and now there's Forfex as well. How
can his lemur rest after such a horrible death? He could never
take revenge on the Master; the Master is too powerful. But
on another slave, alone and helpless . . ." The boy's voice
trailed to a whisper, and he looked across the water at the

tumbled boulders and the deep shadows among them. "It must be here now, watching us."

"I think not, if his lemur follows his mortal remains. Come, show us where you put the body."

The boy blanched.

"Come!" I said. "If I'm right—"

Meto cleared his throat.

"If *my son* is right, the body is long gone. Come, show us!" It was a testament to Gnaeus Claudius's cruelty that the boy could be controlled by a harsh voice alone. A less cowed slave would have required a few blows, or at least the threat of violence, to be prodded to his feet by a man who was not his master and then sent skipping across the stones in the stream to revisit a gravesite he believed to be haunted. The young goatherd obeyed, though he began to tremble violently as we climbed the tumbled rocks.

"Just on the other side of that big stone," he said, his voice quavering. He pointed the way, but would go no farther.

Meto and I climbed past him and stood atop the jagged stones. We looked down into the narrow cleft and saw what there was to see.

"The body is gone," I said.

"Gone?" The young goatherd climbed reluctantly after us. He stared down into the empty cleft with a look of superstitious dread on his face.

"Not the work of gods or lemures," I assured him. "Men put him here, and it must have been men who took him from this place."

"The same man who killed him!" declared Meto.

I turned my face away from the goatherd and frowned at Meto. We had no proof yet of what he said. More than that, it is unfair to a slave to gossip about his master in his hearing, for he may repeat what you say, to his regret.

Meto scowled back at me. He had been right about Forfex, after all, despite my doubts. Just to be certain, he asked the slave, "Was there a marking of some sort on one of Forfex's hands?"

"A marking? You mean the little purple birthmark on the back of his left hand?"

Meto's face was suffused with triumph.

"But where has the body gone?" said the slave.

"You needn't know, at least not now," I said. "You shouldn't know. You've braved enough danger already, simply talking to us and telling us how Forfex met his end. I should reward you, but I have nothing to give you."

"There's nothing you could give me," he said. "The Master lets us keep nothing for ourselves. The man who wanted to see the mine gave Forfex a few coins, but the Master found them and took them all away."

"This man who saw the mine—has he been back since?"

The boy shrugged. "I don't know. I never saw him. I was tending a flock on the far side of the mountain when he came." He narrowed his eyes. "They say there were others with him. Was it you?"

"I've managed so far not to answer any of your questions," I said, smiling. "I don't think I shall start now. The less you know, the better for you. You should forget that we were ever here."

"Like lemures in the mist," he said.

"If you wish."

"There *is* one other question we should ask," said Meto. "When you put Forfex's body in this rocky place, what had become of his head?"

"Beaten to a pulp. I told you that," said the slave, turning pale again.

"Yes, but was it still attached to his body?"

"Of course."

"Not cut away? Being so badly mangled, perhaps—"

"The body was all in one piece!" protested the goatherd, his voice shaking.

"No need to press the matter," I said to Meto, laying my hand on his arm. "Tell us: was there another death among the goatherds, about a month ago?" I asked, thinking of Nemo.

The boy shook his head.

"Among your master's other slaves, then?"

"No. One of the kitchen slaves died of a fever, but that was well over a year ago. There's been only one death since then, and that was Forfex."

We descended the tumbled rocks strewn with bones and crossed the stream. The young goatherd went on his way,

while Meto and I rested for a bit before pressing on. The
shady glen was a beautiful place, even if despoiled and made
fearsome by the presence of so much death and suffering. Not
a bad resting place, I thought, for the lemures of dead slaves,
who must have been far more miserable in life, toiling beneath the hot sun or burrowing into the dank, stony earth.

TWENTY-SIX

"WE should confront him directly," said Meto as we made
our way down the mountain path.

"I agree."

"We know now beyond any doubt that the body in the
well was Forfex. We know that Gnaeus killed Forfex. And
we know that he doesn't like us one bit. He thought he was
going to inherit the farm from Lucius Claudius, didn't he?
Therefore, motive: to spoil the well and try to drive us away."

"There are a few gaps in your logic," I observed wryly,
negotiating a steep step and bending back a whiplike branch.

"Such as?"

"Why was the head of Forfex removed?"

"So that we wouldn't attribute the act to Gnaeus. He knew
that we had met Forfex and might recognize him despite his
injuries, and thus might surmise where he came from. Gnaeus
is the worst kind of coward, skulking about and afraid to own
up to his actions. He cut off the head so we wouldn't know
where the anonymous body came from. He didn't count on
my sharp eyes recognizing the birthmark on the back of Forfex's hand, did he?"

"No, the culprit did not. But why did Gnaeus order the
slaves to dispose of the body at the waterfall if he intended
to use it elsewhere?"

I looked over my shoulder. Meto shrugged. "The idea
didn't occur to him until later. Obviously he didn't kill Forfex
just so he could drop his body down our well; the murder
wasn't premeditated, and neither was the outrage against us.

But once he had the body at hand, it struck him that he could make use of it."

"The young goatherd said nothing of being ordered to retrieve the body."

"The goatherd didn't know anything about Catilina, either. Surely Gnaeus has other slaves more suitable for doing what was done with poor Forfex's corpse."

"And what about Nemo?"

"That must have been Gnaeus's doing as well. He put Nemo in our stable to frighten us, but it didn't frighten us enough. So he tried the same cowardly trick again, only this time he did something truly dangerous, polluting the well. What a despicable man!"

"But where did Nemo come from? The goatherd told us that there have been no other deaths on the mountain."

"Who knows? Perhaps Gnaeus waylaid a wandering freedman, or murdered a visitor from Rome."

"A stranger, you mean. A stranger to us."

"Yes."

"Then why was Nemo's head removed? You postulate that the head of Forfex was removed to conceal his identity. That makes sense. But what of Nemo? Who was he and why was his head cut off?"

Meto was silent. For several moments the only sounds I heard were the crackling of branches, the scraping of our feet on the rough, uneven path, and my own labored breathing. "I don't have an answer for that," Meto finally admitted. "But does it matter about Nemo? We know now where Forfex came from, and that's the key. Gnaeus Claudius is the culprit. He should be whipped. He should be tried for murder, if there were any justice. But there's no law against a man killing his own slave, is there? I suppose the best we can do is take legal action against him for polluting our well."

"Hard to prove, since we have no witnesses."

"But, Papa, the circumstances are obvious!"

"A court will require more than circumstantial evidence."

"Then we'll have to find a witness. He could hardly have done it without the collusion of at least one of our own slaves, could he? Whichever of the slaves it was who turned on us, he must be made to talk!"

"How much force would you have me use against the slaves? I've already questioned them, and you saw the result. There are many masters who would use indiscriminate torture to obtain the truth. Aratus himself suggests I do so."

"I wouldn't have you do that, Papa."

"Torture is inevitable where slaves and the law are concerned. Suppose we do find a witness among our slaves. A Roman court will not accept the testimony of any slave unless it's extracted under torture. Would you have me force such a thing on another man, even of a slave who plotted against us? And what if one of the slaves merely saw the act and is otherwise guiltless? Still, he would have to be tortured in order to bear witness. No wonder the slaves are so reluctant to speak. If they admit to being witnesses, it's like volunteering to be tortured."

"I hadn't thought of that."

"But they have, I assure you. Given your premise, the best witnesses would be the slaves of Gnaeus Claudius himself, such as our young goatherd friend. But there again the law defeats us. No man's slave can testify in court without his permission, and thus no slave can be made to testify against his master."

"What if you could get Cicero to represent us? He's so clever and powerful, perhaps he could find a way—"

"Please, I want no more debts to Cicero. Besides, I don't imagine that our esteemed consul has time to trifle with such a matter now or for a long time to come."

We reached the clearing behind the boulder. We untied our horses and led them through the narrow cleft between the old oak and the rock, onto the grassy, shaded verge. Over on the road a group of slaves trudged wearily past, linked neck to neck by a stout rope and driven along by a team of overseers on horseback. The slaves were either naked or covered with the merest scraps of cloth. For shoes they wore bits of leather tied to their feet. Neither slaves nor drivers took any notice of us. We stood in the shade, waiting for them to pass.

I turned to Meto and said in a whisper, "Your argument against Gnaeus Claudius is clear enough, even if it does have lapses. Even so, my thoughts keep returning to Catilina."

"You misjudge him, Papa!" whispered Meto, with surprising vehemence.

"Consider his connection with Forfex. Consider the coincidence of the headless corpses and his riddle of the headless body. Consider also that Nemo appeared just after Caelius first proposed that I play host to Catilina, as if to intimidate me into agreeing. Now Caelius and Cicero have again insisted that I open my door to Catilina, I have protested, and Forfex appears in our well. Catilina is a desperate man—"

"Why blame Catilina? Or Caelius or Cicero, for that matter? You've been on the wrong scent all along, Papa. You said just now that no court would accept circumstantial evidence as proof, yet you've let coincidence rob you of your better judgment and blind you to the obvious. Gnaeus Claudius is the culprit. He must think he's very clever, laughing at us behind our backs. If we confront him directly, I'll wager that he admits his guilt out of sheer vanity and spite."

"You may be right," I admitted. "We shall give him the chance today."

The last of the roped slaves, a man with skin like leather and hair like matted straw, passed before us, and as he did he tripped on a stone in the road. He fell briefly to his knees, tugging at the rope around his neck and sending a ripple of distress up the line. An overseer quickly doubled back and struck at the man with a whip until he gained his footing and plodded on.

"When will this world ever change?" a voice whispered. It might have been in my own head, but it came from Meto, who gazed after the slaves with a solemn, sad look in his eyes. Without looking at me he mounted his horse. I did likewise, and we rode quickly back to the farm.

I wanted a suitable retinue surrounding me when I set foot again on Gnaeus Claudius's property. I ordered Aratus to come with us, partly because it seemed fitting that my foreman should accompany me and partly because I wanted to watch his reactions while I dealt with Gnaeus; I still did not trust him. I also chose a few of the burliest men, thinking I might need protection.

We set out after midday. I hoped that Gnaeus had eaten a

heavy meal. I've often found it useful to accost a man while he's sleepy and off his guard.

We rode up the Cassian Way and turned onto the road to Gnaeus's house, openly and without stealth. The way grew steep. The foothills became thick with boulders and trees. In the midst of the forest we came to the house of the goatherds, where we had first met Forfex. The road came to the deep streambed and ran alongside it. At length we came to the little bridge, crossed the ravine, and so arrived before the house of Gnaeus Claudius.

The two-storied structure was of rustic design, more Etruscan than Roman. It was a very old house and not well kept up, to judge from the plaster crumbling from the walls and the shutters hanging from broken hinges. It was set against a steep, wooded hillside and surrounded by shadows. The air was dank and musty. Even on a summer's day a gloomy pall hung over the house and the little ramshackle sheds clustered around it.

Chickens and dogs inhabited the dry, dusty courtyard. At our approach the dogs roused themselves and barked, while the chickens cackled and scattered in a panic. The door to the house opened and a voice cried out sharply for the dogs to be silent. The beasts whimpered and ran about in nervous circles, but stopped their barking.

The slave at the door saw our company and backed away. I suspect his master had few enough visitors, especially from a group as formidable as I hoped ours appeared to be. The slave gave us a hard look and shut the door without saying a word.

A few moments later the door opened again. Gnaeus Claudius himself stood staring back at us, looking as ill-humored as when I had last seen him ingratiating himself with Catilina and punishing the hapless Forfex. He was a strikingly ugly young man, with his unkempt mop of red hair and his chinless neck, but his height and brawny frame gave him an imposing presence. At his appearance the dogs began to bark again. Gnaeus growled back at them as if he were a hound himself. In his hand he held a bone on which he had been chewing; bits of flesh clung to his lips. He cast it into their midst, and the beasts fell on it at once and competed for the prize, slavering and sniping and tearing it from one another's mouths in an appalling melee.

"Stupid dogs," muttered Gnaeus. "Still, smarter than most slaves, and they can't talk back." His grating voice was as hard to listen to as his face was to look at. He squinted up at us. Claudia had said that his eyes were weak, but despite the gloomy shadows he seemed to recognize me easily enough. "Back, are you? And this time without your scheming friend from the city. Come to spy on me again, I suppose. What in Hades do you want, Gordianus?"

"I should think you'd know the answer to that question, Gnaeus Claudius," I said.

"Don't try to be clever with me," said Gnaeus. "I don't take to cleverness. Ask my slaves if you don't believe me. No one invited you here, Gordianus. You're trespassing on my property. I'd be perfectly in my right to pull you off that horse and beat you like a slave. State your business or get out. Or do you want a beating? I could give one to the boy, as well."

"Papa!" said Meto under his breath, bristling. I touched his arm to quiet him.

"We've come, Gnaeus Claudius, because someone has committed an atrocity on my farm. An act of desecration. An offense against the law and against the gods."

"If the gods are offended, perhaps it's because a plebeian nobody from Rome has got his hands on a piece of property that's been in my family for generations! Perhaps you should have thought of that before you set your backside down where it doesn't belong."

"Papa, we shouldn't stand for this," said Meto.

"Quiet! Are you admitting your responsibility, Gnaeus Claudius?"

"For what?"

"For the desecration I speak of."

"I don't know what you're talking about. But if some catastrophe has fallen on your head, then it's good news to me. Keep talking. You amuse me, plebeian."

"You don't amuse me, Gnaeus. Neither did the little prank you pulled a few days ago."

"Enough of the riddles! Make your meaning clear or get out!"

"I'm talking about the body you threw into my well."

"What? You've been out in the sun too much without a hat, Gordianus. That's the first rule you should have learned if you want to be a farmer: wear a hat."

"You deny it?"

"What body? What well? Give your father a good hard slap, boy. He's babbling."

Meto seemed barely able to restrain himself. I saw his knuckles whiten as he gripped his rein.

"I'm talking about the body of your slave, Forfex. Do you deny that you killed him five days ago?"

"Why should I deny it? He was my slave for years, and before that he was my father's slave. I had every right to kill him, and may Jupiter strike me down if he didn't deserve it!"

"You're an impious man, Gnaeus Claudius."

"And you're a fool and an upstart, Gordianus, so-called Finder. You managed to find a body in your well, then? Good for you, and good for whoever put it there. But don't lay the blame at my door. I had nothing to do with it."

"The body was that of Forfex."

"Impossible. My slaves disposed of the corpse. I gave the orders myself, and my slaves are not in the habit of disobeying me, you can believe that!"

"Even so, the body ended up in my well."

"Not Forfex."

"Yes, most certainly Forfex."

"Would you even have known Forfex if you'd seen him alive? Oh, but that's right, you were along when Forfex showed your friend the way to the mine, weren't you?"

"Was I?"

"So Forfex said later; he claimed that one of the trespassers was called Gordianus, though I didn't recognize you in the gloom that evening. If I'd known it was you, I'd have had you dragged from your horse and whipped."

"You're very generous with your threats and insults, Gnaeus Claudius. You seem quite proud to confess that you killed a helpless slave. Why are you so timid when it comes to admitting that you had Forfex dropped down my well?"

"Because I did no such thing!" he shouted. The dogs began to bay and howl.

"I say that you did. If it had been anyone else but Forfex—"

"You keep insisting that this body was my slave. Prove it, then. Show him to me."

"And if I do, will you admit to this act?"

"No, but at least I might believe you when you say that it was Forfex you found in your well."

"But how can I do that, when you yourself took steps to see that I couldn't prove the slave's identity by showing his face?"

"What do you mean? I may have crushed his skull, but he could still be recognized. You must have recognized him yourself since you say you knew him by sight."

"I never said that."

"Then how do you know it was Forfex?" he shouted, infuriated.

"I have my ways."

"What do you mean? Have you been trespassing on my land again, talking to my slaves, putting lies in their ears?" He squinted, so fiercely that I could not see his eyes. "How did you know that I killed Forfex? Who told you? Who dared?"

"I also know about the *other* body," I said, partly to change the subject, partly to see his reaction. At the same time I glanced at Aratus, whose face remained impassive. I had not caught a single look exchanged between him and Gnaeus; if they shared some secret, or even knew each other by sight, their eyes and faces did not betray it.

"*What* other body?" cried Gnaeus.

"You proclaim your ignorance too quickly, Gnaeus Claudius—the sure sign of a guilty man. You know what I'm talking about. Furthermore, I have strong proof against you for that offense as well, and you shall regret your impudence."

Gnaeus cocked his head and made a face. He spat on the ground and waved both hands at me. "You're mad, utterly mad. You make no sense at all, and now you've begun to threaten me in front of my own home. Get out, now! Get out or I'll call the dogs on you. They can seize a man by the leg and pull him off his horse in an instant, and tear the throat out of his neck in the blink of an eye. If you don't believe me, just give me an excuse to prove it! And there's no law to keep me from doing it as long as you're on my land, as you well know. Now get out!"

I looked at him steadily for a moment, then reined my horse and turned around. "But Papa—" Meto protested.

"Our business is done, Meto," I said under my breath. "And I think he means his threat about the dogs. Come!"

Reluctantly, and not before he cast a glowering look back at Gnaeus, Meto turned his horse around. Aratus and the other slaves had already done so at my signal. I set the pace, riding at a gallop across the little bridge, down the trail past the goat-herds' house and through the rock-strewn woods. The dappled sunlight felt good on my face, but my spirits did not truly lift until we emerged into the full sunlight again, not far from the Cassian Way.

Meto rode up beside me. "But, Papa, we left before Gnaeus Claudius admitted his guilt!"

"We would be a long time waiting for him to admit something he didn't do."

"I don't understand."

"You saw the man with your own eyes, Meto, and heard him speak with your own ears. Do you believe he knows anything about the body in the well?"

"He admitted to killing Forfex!"

"Without hesitation, which makes his protestations of ignorance all the more convincing. I believe him when he says he knows nothing about the body in the well. He killed Forfex and ordered his slaves to dispose of the body, and that is the last he knew of the matter. You noticed, I suppose, that I never mentioned that the body had no head, though I alluded to it. He showed no comprehension at all, and assumed that we recognized Forfex by his face, not by his birthmark."

"But he could have been lying."

"The man is not much of an actor. He shows everything on the surface. I know his type. He was raised to have all the pomposity and pride of a patrician without any of the polish of his class. He threatens and bullies other men with impunity, because he thinks it's his birthright. Not a devious or even deceitful type; he has no use for lying, because he's never ashamed of anything he does, no matter how outrageous. He says whatever he wants because he always expects to get his way, and he probably does."

"He didn't get his way about keeping you from having the farm."

"True, but if he was serious about attacking us, I think he would do so in a less underhanded manner. And if he was involved in these outrages, I think he would admit his part when we accused him, don't you? He would boast about it. He's a crude man; he has no subtlety at all—you've seen the way he handles his slaves and his dogs. Whoever gave us Nemo and Forfex has a shrewd mind, almost playful, however wicked. That hardly describes Gnaeus Claudius."

"I suppose not. But just before we left, you accused him outright of being responsible for Nemo, too. You said you could tell he was lying. You said you had proof!"

"A final bluff, a last effort to convince myself that he knows nothing at all about either of the bodies appearing on the farm. No, Gnaeus is not our tormentor. He killed Forfex, true, and for that I pray that Nemesis will punish him. Forfex somehow came to be in our well, with his head missing—I give you credit for remembering the birthmark when I did not, and I confess to doubting you wrongly. But between the crude interment of Forfex's body and its decapitation and appearance in the well, someone else had a hand."

"But who, Papa?"

"I don't know. Without some further crisis, we may never know."

I could see by the look on his face that this was not good enough for Meto. Nor was it satisfactory for me, but the years had given me more patience. "I still say we should bring charges against him," said Meto.

"It's not worth bothering Volumenus. You've seen how long it's taking him to get a judgment on our water dispute with Publius Claudius. What is the point of bringing a suit where we have no evidence at all?"

"But we do have evidence!"

"A headless corpse with a birthmark? The testimony of a goatherd who could never be compelled to testify against his

master? The complete denial of the charge by Gnaeus Claudius? The testimony of an old, senile farm slave who thinks
he might have heard a splash and might have glimpsed a
shadow one night when he got up to pass water? No, Meto,
we have no evidence at all. Granted, we might be able to
bribe a jury, which is one way of winning a lawsuit in Rome
when you have no case, but my heart would not be in it. I
don't believe that Gnaeus Claudius was responsible."

"But, Papa, someone must have done it. We have to find
out who!"

"Patience, Meto," I counseled wearily, and wondered if I
should counsel resignation also, knowing all too well that
many mysteries are never resolved. Men go on living anyway,
in ignorance and fear, and though they may call their state of
puzzlement intolerable, they seem able to tolerate it nonetheless, as long as their hearts keep beating.

Aratus gave me counsel on the purification of the well. Hardly
a priest, he seemed nonetheless to take a practical view of the
matter, and he had seen others purify wells polluted by ro-
dents and rabbits, if not dead slaves. He thought it significant
that Forfex had been properly buried, at least for a slave,
before his remains were disturbed. This meant there was a
good chance that Forfex's lemur had been put to rest before
he was disinterred. If so, the lemur might have clung to the
more familiar site of the waterfall on the mountainside, rather
than follow the desecrated and beheaded corpse onto unknown soil. The arguments seemed to ring true with the
slaves, who accordingly relinquished their newfound terror of
the well. Whether Aratus himself believed the arguments he
put forth I did not know, but I was grateful for their pragmatic
effect and for his politic handling of the situation.

There remained the literal pollution of the well, for while
a lemur might or might not have been involved, there was no
doubt that a bloated corpse had been in contact with the water
and had tainted it. A man or beast could grow sick and even
die from drinking such water. Aratus believed that the well
would replenish and purify itself, given time, and meanwhile
recommended that we drop heated stones into the well, to
make the water roil and steam. This seemed to me like cau-

terizing a wound with a hot iron and made no sense in connection with a well, but I reluctantly took his advice. In the
meantime, we had some water that had been stored in urns,
and the stream was not completely dry. Still, there were dry
days ahead.

Much of our hay for the winter had been blighted. We ran
a grave risk of running short of water. I began to realize, with
great uneasiness, that if another such disaster struck, I might
be compelled to sell the farm. For a rich man, a farm in the
country is a diversion, and if it loses money the loss is merely
the cost of the diversion. But for me there was no fortune
back in the city; the farm was the enterprise on which I had
staked my future. Its success was essential; its failure would
ruin me. That summer it seemed to me that the gods themselves were conspiring to rob me of what Lucius Claudius in
his generosity had given me, and Cicero with his cleverness
had secured for me by law.

Each day, Aratus fed a bit of well water to one of the farm
animals, usually a kid. It did not kill them, but it did loosen
their bowels and cause them to vomit. The water remained
undrinkable.

I persevered with the building of the mill on the stream.
Aratus had the slaves tear down a little unused shed to provide building stones and beams. Day by day the vision in my
mind began to take shape. My old friend Lucius would have
been surprised and proud, I thought.

I anticipated a visit from Catilina, or perhaps from Marcus
Caelius, but for the rest of Quinctilis and well into the month
of Sextilis I was undisturbed. In the meantime I posted slaves
to act as watchmen each night, relieving each other in shifts,
like soldiers in a camp. Whether this was the cause or not,
we received no more rude surprises in the form of headless
bodies. There was another unsettling event, however.

It was just after the Ides of Sextilis, almost a month after
our return from Rome. The day had been unusually busy. We
had reached a critical pass in the construction of the mill; the
gears would not mesh, though I had measured and remeasured
the proportions and worked out all the calculations beforehand. Also, a thunderstorm had blown over us during the

night, bringing no rain but scattering broken branches and other debris all over the property; the men had a full day's work cleaning up the mess. As the long summer afternoon dwindled to twilight, I at last had found time to rest for a moment in my study, when Aratus appeared at the door.

"I didn't want to disturb you before, because I thought it might pass, but as he's getting worse, I suppose I should tell you now," he said.

"What are you talking about?"

"Clementus. He's ill—very ill, it appears. His complaints began this morning, but as they seemed to come and go, and as he appeared to be in no great distress, I saw no reason to bother you with it. But he's grown worse through the day. I think he might die."

I followed Aratus to the little lean-to by the stable where Clementus slept at night and as often napped in the daytime. The old slave lay in the straw on his side, clutching his knees to his chest. He moaned quietly. His cheeks were flushed, but his lips were slightly blue. A slave woman hovered over him, dabbing his face from time to time with a damp cloth. At intervals he was seized by a shuddering spasm, drew even more tightly into a ball, and then slowly relaxed with a pathetic whimper.

"What's wrong with him?" I whispered.

"I'm not sure," said Aratus. "He was vomiting earlier. Now he can't seem to swallow, and when he tries to speak his words come out slurred."

"Do any of the others share the same complaints?" I asked, thinking that a plague on the farm would be the final calamity.

"No. It may simply be because he's old." Aratus lowered his voice. "Such storms as we had last night are often harbingers of death to people of his age."

As we watched, Clementus convulsed and stiffened. He opened his eyes and peered up at us with an expression more of puzzlement than pain. He parted his lips and released a long, rasping moan. After a moment the woman attending him reached out and touched his brow with trembling fingers. His eyes remained unnaturally open. The woman drew back her hand and crushed her knuckles to her lips. Clementus was dead.

He was quite old, of course, and the old are apt to die from many causes, and at any time. But I could not help remembering that it had been Clementus who had heard a muffled splash when Forfex was dropped into the well, and afterward had witnessed a vague shadow walking about in the night.

TWENTY-SEVEN

THE water mill would not work.

I told myself ruefully that I was not an engineer—any more than I was a farmer, added another voice in my head—and so should hardly have been surprised when my plans turned out not to be workable. I had kept the design as simple as I could. I had built a little model out of slivers of wood that seemed to work well enough. Aratus himself, never hesitant to inject a negative note, had deemed the idea practical and the construction sound. But when I set the slaves to turning the master wheel (for at midsummer in the month of Sextilis there was not enough force in the stream to turn it), the gears revolved only for a few degrees and then jammed fast. The first time this happened, the slaves kept pushing at the master wheel until two of the wooden axles split asunder with a great noise like a thunderclap. I was more careful the next time, and the next, but the mill simply would not function.

At night I dreamed of it. Sometimes I saw it as it should be, with the stream sliding along its banks, the master wheel spinning, and the crushing blocks gnashing together like teeth, with grain pouring from the outlet in endless abundance. In other, darker dreams I saw it as a sort of monster, living but malicious, spinning out of control, crushing hapless slaves in its gears and pouring blood from its mouth.

Why did I lavish so much energy and imagination on the completion of the mill? I told myself that it was a gift to the shade of my benefactor, Lucius Claudius. It was a sign of my full adjustment to country life, a signal that I had not simply accommodated myself to being a farmer but was mastering

the elements around me. It was a gesture of defiance against
Publius Claudius, who thought he could rob me of my water
rights. It was all these things, true enough (besides being what
it concretely was, or should be, a building of intrinsic value),
but it was also a diversion. The mysteries of Nemo and Forfex
remained unsolved. Rather than allow these failures to prey
on me, I fretted over the continuing failure of the mill instead;
rather than turn my fantasies to the professional satisfaction
I would feel if I could somehow resolve these mysteries once
and for all—an old, familiar satisfaction, as comfortable as a
worn garment—I turned my fantasies to the technical triumph
of a water mill that would actually work. In the same way,
my obsession with the mill allowed me an escape from the
problem of our dwindling water and the looming prospect of
a winter without enough hay.

These crises seem small now when compared to the greater
crisis that was brewing all around us—not only down in
Rome and in Etruria, but all up and down the length of Italy.
I might claim that I had no intimation of the catastrophes to
come, but that would not quite be true. A man who turns his
back on a fire can truthfully say that he cannot see the fire,
but he can feel its heat against his back; he can see the lurid
light that colors the objects around him and his own shadow
cast before him. But if I had an inkling of where the struggle
between Cicero and Catilina would lead, I chose to fret over
my water mill instead.

Toward the end of the month of Sextilis, Diana reached her
seventh birthday. The birthdays of little girls are not much
celebrated among Romans, but this day—the twenty-sixth day
of Sextilis, four days before the Kalends of September—was
doubly special in our household, for it was not only the day
that Bethesda had given birth to Gordiana, but also the day
when Marcus Mummius had delivered Meto to us after res-
cuing him from his bondage in Sicily. We had made the day
a family holiday and always celebrated with a special meal;
several days beforehand Bethesda began overseeing Congrio's preparations in the kitchen. Eco had always been present for the event, and this year would be no exception. As
we had journeyed down to Rome for Meto's toga day, so Eco

and Menenia would come up from the city for the private celebration.

They arrived by wagon on the day before Diana's birthday, with Belbo and five other slaves in attendance. The slaves, I noticed, were among the strongest in Eco's household and were all armed with long daggers tucked into their tunics. I made some joke about his going out with a bodyguard to rival Cicero's, but Eco did not laugh. "Later," he said enigmatically, as if to acknowledge that he owed me an explanation when I had only been jesting.

Bethesda took great pains to make Menenia feel at home, returning the courtesy that her daughter-in-law had shown her in the city; the warmth between them seemed quite genuine. Meto and Diana were delighted to have their older brother on the farm, if only for a brief visit. While all the others were engaged in one another's company, I took the chance to slip away. I found Belbo with the other slaves from Rome relaxing in a patch of shade beside the stable and taking turns in a round of trigon. They stood in a triangle, batting the leather ball back and forth. Belbo, famous for strength rather than agility, was soon out of the game. I called to him to join me. He followed as I strolled around the corner and out of hearing of the others.

"My son surrounds himself with a considerable bodyguard to protect two people with nothing valuable on their persons, on such a short journey and on such a well-traveled road."

Belbo grinned and shook his head. "The old Master misses nothing, as always."

" 'As always'—Belbo, I wish I were half as observant and canny as I once was, or thought I was. Why so many daggers?"

"Times in the city are tense."

"That's awfully vague. What has my son got himself into?"

"Shouldn't that be for him to tell you?"

"If you were new in the household, I'd excuse you from talking to your old master about your new master behind his back, but you know me too well to hide anything from me, Belbo. Is Eco up to something dangerous?"

"Master, you know the life. You remember the danger from day to day."

I stared at him steadily, unimpressed with his evasions. He was as strong as an ox and as loyal as a hound, but he was as bad at keeping secrets as he was at playing trigon. I watched his face blush red to the roots of his straw-colored hair.

"It's the new work he's doing," he confessed.

"For whom?"

"For the young man who was at Meto's party—you saw him, you talked to him. He came back several days later to hire the young Master. The man with the fashionable beard and hair."

"Does that young man have a name?" I asked, knowing it already.

"Marcus Caelius," said Belbo.

"Numa's balls, I knew it! They've cast their web over Eco as well."

Once his meager resistance had been breached, Belbo seemed eager to speak. "It's something to do with a conspiracy—a plot to murder Cicero and bring down the government. The young Master's been going to meetings at night in secret. I don't hear a lot; I stay outside with the other slaves and bodyguards. But there are big people at these meetings, I can tell you that—senators, equestrians, patricians, people I've seen in the Forum for years. Marcus Caelius is often there as well."

While he spoke, I shook my head and clenched my teeth. Eco should have known better, I told myself, than to let himself be drawn into the affairs of Marcus Caelius and his master, whether that master was Cicero or Catilina. To investigate the circumstances of a simple murder or ferret out the truth in a property dispute was one thing; to put on a blindfold and be pushed back and forth in the devious plot and counterplot between Cicero and Catilina was quite another. It was more than the unacceptable degree of danger and uncertainty; I had taught Eco to be a Finder, not a spy. To my mind, there is honor in uncovering the truth and laying it out for all to see in the sunlight, but none at all in covering it from view and whispering in the dark.

It occurred to me that Eco might have been allowed no choice in the matter. The idea of a headless body appearing at the house in Rome caused me to clutch at Belbo's tunic. "Has he been threatened? Intimidated? Have they dared to make him fear for Menenia, or for us, here on the farm?"

Belbo was taken aback at my vehemence. "I think not, Master," he said meekly. "Marcus Caelius came to the house not long after you left Rome. It all seemed cordial enough—the young Master is like you were; he doesn't like to take work from people he doesn't trust, not if he can help it. He seemed quite willing to do what Caelius wanted. If there were threats or the like, I never knew of it."

To hear such a placating tone of voice from such a giant suddenly struck me as absurd; almost as absurd as the sight of my fist, clutching the neck of his tunic and looking like a child's hand against the massive width of his neck. I released him and stepped back.

"See that the others keep their knives about them, even while they're playing trigon," I said. "And have someone keep an eye on the road that leads from the Cassian Way. If Eco believes he needs a bodyguard, I trust his judgment. But he should know, and so should you, that he's no safer here than in the city."

I took a long walk around the farm to gather my thoughts. When I returned to the house, I found the family gathered in the atrium to escape the heat of the afternoon. Bethesda and Menenia reclined on couches facing each other; Diana sat cross-legged on the floor between them, playing with a doll; Meto and Eco sat side by side on a bench beside the pool. Between them was the little board game that Cicero had once given me and that I had passed on to Meto, called Elephants and Archers. They had evidently finished their game, for the bronze pieces had all been pushed to one side of the checkered wooden board. As I approached, I overheard Meto say something about Hannibal.

"What are you two discussing?" I asked, as blandly as I could.

"Hannibal's invasion of Italy," said Meto.

"With elephants," added Eco.

"Actually, the elephants never reached Italy," explained Meto, turning back to Eco. He seemed quite pleased for a chance to play the pedagogue with his older brother. "They died in the snow, crossing the Alps. So did Hannibal's men, by the tens of thousands. Don't you remember, years ago, when I first came to Rome, one of the magistrates put on a spectacle in the Circus Maximus—Hannibal crossing the Alps. They piled up mounds of dirt to make little mountains and ravines. For snow they used thousands of bits of white cloth, and slaves were hidden in little nooks with great fans to make them bluster and swirl. But the elephants were real. They didn't actually kill them; somehow the beasts had been trained to lie on their sides and play dead." His smile faded. "One of the slaves playing a Carthaginian soldier was trapped beneath an elephant and horribly crushed. It was awful, the red blood against the white snow—don't you remember, Eco?"

"Yes, of course."

"Do you remember, Papa?"

"Vaguely."

"Anyway, Eco, the point, as Marcus Mummius says, is that victory in battle hinges not only on superior numbers, bravery, and tactics, but on the elements as well—rain, snow, a muddy field, an unexpected sandstorm. 'Elephants and elements both matter,' he says, and 'Men make war, but gods make weather.' You should talk to Mummius about it sometime. He knows everything there is to know about great generals and famous battles."

I shook my head. "How did you ever end up talking about Hannibal? Oh, I see—Elephants and Archers."

"Actually, Papa," said Eco, "Meto is very keen on military history."

"Is he? Well, if you can leave the battle behind for just a moment, Eco, I'd like to ask your opinion of the water mill."

Eco shrugged and stood. Meto began to stand, but I waved him back. "Stay here. Visit with Menenia; try to keep your sister out of trouble. Surely you've seen enough of the mill by now." Meto started to speak but bit his tongue and lowered his eyes. He sat down on the bench again and began to fiddle with the little bronze warriors.

"He really is fascinated by things military," said Eco as we walked toward the stream. "Where he picked up such an interest I can't imagine. I suppose he's always been fond of Marcus Mummius—"

"More to the point, what have you been up to in Rome lately?"

Eco sighed. "Somehow I didn't think you had come to fetch me just to have a look at your water mill."

"There's not much point. The thing is a failure, like almost everything else on the farm."

"Things are going badly?"

We reached the mill. I found a shady spot and gestured for Eco to sit beside me. Together we stared at the hard, baked mud along the banks and the thin trickle of water over the stones. "I shall tell you my troubles first," I said. "Then you'll tell me yours."

I gave him a full account of all that had happened since we left Rome—the discovery of Forfex's corpse, the pollution of the well, the encounter with Gnaeus Claudius, the death of Clementus.

"Papa, you should have let me know. You should have written."

"And you should have let me know about your dealings with Marcus Caelius." Eco looked at me askance. "I wrangled it out of Belbo," I explained. "It wasn't hard."

"And I confess, I already knew about the body in the well."

"How—"

"Meto told me. Most of the story, anyway."

"Yet you let me tell you the story again, as if you knew nothing!"

"I wanted to hear it from you, from beginning to end. Meto's account was more dramatic, but yours was more coherent. Meto seems quite proud that he was able to identify Forfex by the birthmark on his hand. You glossed over that in your version."

"Did I? Meto remains convinced, I suppose, that Gnaeus Claudius is the culprit."

"He leans toward that opinion."

"Even if Gnaeus Claudius were, I'd be powerless to press

charges against him. But he knows now that we suspect
him—I as much as told him I had proof against him, so if he
is guilty, and if he's capable of being intimidated, notice has
been served. But there's something else I wanted to talk to
you about—"

"Papa, you act as if it were nothing, finding another headless body on the farm! And this time it was an act of malicious destruction, not just intimidation. Really, if the matter
can't be resolved, I think you should bring the family back
to Rome, before something truly terrible happens."

"Eco, we've discussed this before," I said impatiently.
"There's no room for all of us at the house, and besides, I
have no stomach for living in the city. Instead of my leaving
the farm, I'd suggest that you leave Rome and come here.
Better that than putting yourself in the hands of Marcus Caelius. What does it mean that you've allowed him to send you
into secret meetings with Catilina and his circle? Don't you
realize the danger?"

"Papa, I'm working for a Roman consul."

"Slim protection if you're caught in some crime with these
men and slain on the spot, or if they find out you're a spy
and lay an ambush for you. Where will Cicero be then?"

Eco pinched the bridge of his nose. "I know you've come
to have a low opinion of Cicero in recent years, Papa. You
seem to have lost respect for him entirely since he won his
election against Catilina. But you must give him credit for
being true to his friends."

"Don't tell me you're spying on Catilina out of friendship."

"Why, no, Papa, I'm doing it for money. *You* would be
the one who's doing it out of friendship." There was an edge
in his voice I had never heard before—the voice that had
always been beautiful to my ears because for so many years
he was mute. We had never had a true fight before. I suddenly
realized that we were on the verge of having our first. I looked
away and took a deep breath. Eco did the same.

"I suppose it would relieve my anxiety to a degree if you
would explain to me the exact circumstances of your involvement," I finally said. "What is Catilina really up to?"

"What Marcus Caelius says is true: Catilina and his colleagues are conspiring to bring down the state. They had hoped he would win the election, in which case he would commence his revolution from the top, using his consular powers and the powers of his friends in the Senate to bring about their radical reforms by law if they could, and by civil war if they couldn't. That was the route Catilina himself preferred. He seems to have thought he had a genuine chance of being elected. Now that the only course remaining to him is an armed revolt, Catilina hesitates. He finds himself ringed in by doubt and uncertainty."

"I sympathize," I said, under my breath.

"So far, the conspirators have done nothing illegal, or at least nothing that could incriminate them. They put nothing in writing. They meet in secret, sub rosa." Eco smiled. "Catilina is quite literal-minded about it; he actually hangs a rose from the ceiling in any room where his friends conspire, to remind them that the rose means silence and that their words must never reach the world beyond. Still, Cicero knows everything they do."

"Because you spy for him."

"I'm hardly alone. And I'm only a lowly spy, not a member of Catilina's inner circle. I belong to an outer tier of men he thinks he can trust and who, he thinks, may be valuable when the crisis comes. Still, I hear a great deal, and I'm good at sorting the truth from all the fantastic rumors woven through it. These people are full of grand delusions; sometimes I wonder if they pose any danger at all."

"Don't tell Cicero that! It's not what he wants to hear."

Eco sighed. "Papa, you're impossibly cynical."

"No, that describes Cicero. Don't you see that he craves the role this crisis gives him? If there were no conspiracy against the state, I think he'd invent one."

Eco gritted his teeth. We were again on the brink of a rupture. I drew back. "Give me details," I said. "Who are these conspirators? Do I know them? Who else spies for Cicero?"

"Do you really want me to tell you these things? Once spoken, they can't be unspoken. I thought you wanted to wash your hands of Rome."

"Better to know than not know."

"But secrets are dangerous. Whoever possesses them takes on the burden of keeping them. Do you really want that responsibility?"

"I want to know what company my son is keeping. I want to know who threatens my family, and why."

"Then you've given up on hiding your head in the sand?"

I sighed. "The feathers of the ostrich are highly prized, but easy to pluck. Burying his head in a hole gives him no room to maneuver."

"And leaves his long neck exposed to daggers," said Eco.

"A sharp observation."

"A sharper pun." We both winced, then laughed. I reached out and clutched his hand for a moment. "Oh, Eco, you say these conspirators are deluded, but not half so deluded as I've been, imagining I could escape from Rome. No one can! Ask any slave who's fled all the way to the Pillars of Hercules or the Parthian border, only to be trapped and carted back to his master in a cage. We're all slaves of Rome, no matter how we're born, no matter what the law says. Only one thing makes men free: the truth. I've tried to turn my back on the truth, thinking that by ignorance I could escape the Fates. I should have known better. A man can't turn his back on his own nature. I've lived my life searching for justice, knowing how rare it is and how hard it is to find; still, if we can't find justice, sometimes we can at least find the truth and be satisfied with that. Now I've given up on justice altogether, and I even seem to have lost my appetite, not to mention my instinct, for finding the truth, until I despair of ever finding it again; but to give up on that search is to be utterly lost." I sighed and shut my eyes against the brightness of the shimmering leaves above. "Do these ramblings make any sense to you, Eco? Or am I too old, and you too young?"

I opened my eyes to see him smiling sadly at me. "I think you sometimes forget how much alike we are, Papa."

"Perhaps I do, especially when we're apart. When you're with me, I'm a stronger, better man."

"No son could ask for more. I only wish you felt the same . . ." His voice trailed off and he bit his lip, but I knew he was thinking of another who was not with us—of Meto, up in the house with his mother and sister, excluded once again from his father's counsel.

TWENTY-EIGHT

"SO," I said, making myself comfortable on the grass, "tell me all you know of Catilina and his circle."

Eco made a rueful expression.

"I accept the responsibility of knowing," I said.

"It's not only you I'm thinking of but myself. If word ever got back to Catilina that there had been a breach in his secrecy and that I was responsible—"

"You know you can trust me to keep quiet."

He sighed and settled his hands on his knees, locking his elbows. I recognized the posture as if I looked in the mirror. "Very well. To begin with, there are more of them than you might think. Cicero and Caelius always speak as if their enemies were legion, but you know how Cicero tends to exaggerate."

"Cicero exaggerate?" I said, feigning shock.

"Exactly. But in this case, he has good reason to be alarmed."

"What exactly are these conspirators conspiring to do?"

"That remains unclear, probably even among themselves, but some sort of armed insurrection is definitely in their plans, and Cicero's death is their first priority."

"Do you mean to say that all those bodyguards and that absurd breastplate were not just for show? I thought it was merely a vulgar display to frighten the voters."

"I'm not so certain that Catilina wanted Cicero dead before the elections, at least not badly enough to actually plot his assassination. If Catilina had won the consulship, things might have gone very differently. But now the conspirators are all resolved on one point, if on nothing else: that Cicero must be eliminated, partly from revenge, partly as a lesson to others who serve the Optimates, partly as a practical matter."

"Who are these men? Name names."

"There's Catilina himself, of course. Everywhere he goes

nowadays he's attended by a young man named Tongilius."

"I know them both, from the time they spent under my roof. Who else?"

"Chief among them, after Catilina, is Publius Cornelius Lentulus Sura."

"Lentulus? 'Legs' Lentulus? Not that old reprobate!"

"The very one."

"Well, Catilina has chosen a colorful enough character for his chief conspirator. You know the man's history?"

"Everyone does within Catilina's circle. And like you, they smile at the mention of his name."

"He's an old charmer, I won't deny that. I did some work for him myself, six or seven years ago, right after he was expelled from the Senate. Everything about the man cried out 'scoundrel,' but I couldn't help liking him. I suspect his fellow senators liked him, in a begrudging sort of way, even as they were voting to expel him from their ranks. Does anyone call him 'Legs' to his face?"

"Only his fellow patricians," said Eco.

Sura is the nickname, meaning the calf of the leg, that had been earned by Lentulus in the days of Sulla's dictatorship, when Lentulus held the office of quaestor. A rather substantial sum of state money disappeared under Lentulus's administration. The Senate called on him to explain the matter. In response, Lentulus came forth and in an offhand and contemptuous manner stated that he had no account to render (the accounts being empty), but that he would offer them *this*—whereupon he stuck out his leg, as boys do when they play trigon and miss the ball. Lentulus got away with his show of contempt, thanks in no small part to his kinship with Sulla, under whose dictatorship a mere crime of embezzlement was child's play, but the nickname stuck.

At another point in his career Lentulus was brought to trial for some malfeasance or other, and was acquitted with a plurality of two judges voting in his favor. Later he was heard complaining that he had wasted his money by bribing one judge too many. A scoundrel, as I have said, but not without a sense of humor.

The scandals surrounding him did not prevent him from attaining the praetorship and finally the consulship; unfortunately, he was elected to the office at the worst possible time, during the slave revolt led by Spartacus. Virtually everyone in power at the time was discredited by the state's faltering attempts to contain the rebel slaves; an orgy of recriminations and finger-pointing erupted when Spartacus was finally defeated. A year after his consulship, bereft of allies and vulnerable to his political enemies, Lentulus was expelled from the Senate on charges of misconduct. This time he showed his fellow senators not his bony leg but the back of his bowed head as he departed in disgrace.

But Lentulus persevered. At a time in life when most men would have been crushed by such a humiliation and too weary to recover, he reentered the electoral fray, beginning at the bottom like a young man. A year ago he was elected to a praetorship, more than ten years after his first term as a praetor, and thus won readmission to the Senate. Sheer brazenness had fueled his reemergence, but he possessed many other assets—the distinguished patrician name of Cornelius; a populist pedigree handed down by a famous grandfather who died sixty years ago in the anti-Gracchan riots; his marriage to the ambitious Julia, kinswoman of Julius Caesar, with whom he was raising her young son Marcus Antonius; and not least, a seemingly lazy but shrewdly calculated oratorical style which imparted the full charm of his jaundiced sense of humor and his compelling ambition.

"What are the man's motives in conspiring against the state?" I asked. "After all, he's recovered his senatorial rank. He could actually run for consul again."

"With no hope of ever winning. Behind his jaded sense of humor there's a great store of bitterness, and a burning impatience. Here's a man who had to start over at the middle of his life; he's eager for a shortcut to reach his destiny."

"His destiny?"

"There seems to be something new in his character of late: a weakness for fortune-tellers. It seems there are some rather shady soothsayers. They've regaled Lentulus with verses purportedly from the Sibylline books that prophesy that three men of the Cornelius family will rule Rome. We all know of two—Cinna and Sulla. Who could be the third?"

"These soothsayers tell Lentulus outright that he's to be dictator?"

"Nothing as obvious as that. Oh, these fortune-tellers are clever. You know how the Sibylline verses are said to be written in acrostic, with the first letters of each line spelling out hidden words? Well, what do you think the first letters of these particular verses spell?"

I pursed my lips. "Does it begin with an *L*?"

"Exactly: *L-E-N-T-U-L-U-S.* Naturally, they didn't point this out to Lentulus, but left him to notice it for himself. Now he's convinced that he's meant by the gods to rule Rome."

"He's mad," I said. "I see what you mean by delusions. Still, a man like that, having risen so high, fallen so low, and risen again—he must feel that Fortune has some special role in store for him." I stretched my legs on the grass and gazed up at the sun-spangled leaves. "So Lentulus is the 'leg' on which Catilina stands?"

Eco winced. "The chief leg, yes, but as with most bodies there are two. The other is not quite so strong."

" 'Why does Catilina's conspiracy limp?' Please, no more riddles concerning body parts!"

"Even so, the second leg is another senator of the Cornelius clan, Gains Cornelius Cethegus."

"No nickname?"

"Not yet. Perhaps he's too young to have acquired one. If he did, it might be Hotheaded."

"Young, you say, but if he's in the Senate he must be at least thirty-two."

"Barely. Like Catilina and Lentulus, a patrician, with all the trappings. Men are different who are brought up from infancy to think so highly of themselves."

"Yes, they are," I agreed, thinking of Catilina's effortless poise and self-assurance, and thinking also of how an ambitious New Man like Cicero must envy and despise that natural, unaffected assumption of superiority.

"Like Lentulus, Cethegus is of the Cornelius clan, with many powerful connections by blood and ancient obligation. But he lacks Lentulus's long-suffering perseverance; he's young, impetuous, impatient, with a reputation for violence. He's not very effective in the Senate; he's not a very good

orator—he itches for action, and words make him restless.
He's also had a falling-out with his immediate family; he has
an older brother, also in the Senate, with whom he hardly
speaks. They say there was a bitter dispute over inheritance.
Cethegus believes himself to have been slighted, not just by
his family, but by the Fates."

"An ideal candidate for revolution. He sounds sane
enough, if not very charming."

"He casts a spell nonetheless, over those who are susceptible. He appeals to well-born young men like himself who
distrust rhetoric and hate the slow hand of politics, who find
themselves shut out by the Optimates and who lack the money
to launch successful careers but have a craving for power
nonetheless."

I picked up a twig and poked at the ground. "These are
the principal conspirators?"

"Yes. Lentulus because of his perseverance, Cethegus because of his energy and daring."

"These are the legs, you said." I scratched two lines in the
dirt. "And Catilina is the head." I drew a circle. "But between
legs and head there must be a trunk. Not to mention arms,
hands, and feet."

"I thought you'd had enough of physical metaphors."

I shrugged. "And I thought I wanted to know none of this,
but I'm asking you nonetheless."

"Very well. The trunk would be the people of Rome, of
course. If Catilina could persuade them to follow him, if Lentulus and Cethegus could carry the plot forward, then the
body would be powerful indeed. As for the arms and hands,
there are a number of men in regular contact with Catilina
and his friends—senators, equestrians, men who were once
rich and now are not, men who are rich and want to be richer,
as well as common citizens and freedmen. There are some
who seem to be attracted by the simple excitement and danger
of the enterprise, and others who seem to be fascinated by
Catilina himself. I suspect there are even a few high-minded
idealists who think they are about to change the world."

"Eco, you've become as jaded as your father. Perhaps they
are about to change the world, though who can say if for
better or worse. Names, Eco!"

He recited a lengthy list. Some of the names were familiar. Others were not. "But you will know the names of Publius and Servius Sulla," he said.

"The dictator's grandsons?"

"The same."

" 'How are the mighty fallen,' " I said, quoting one of Bethesda's Eastern maxims. "Unless they land on their feet."

"The Sullan connection runs deep. Among Catilina's most fervent adherents are the dictator's old soldiers who were settled in farming colonies up north. Most of them have fallen on hard times; they chafe at the yoke, so to speak, recalling the grand old days campaigning with their master in the East and helping him win the civil war at home. Once all the world was at their feet; now they find themselves knee-deep in mud and manure. They think that Rome owes them better than they received. Now that their current champion, Catilina, has lost his bid to become consul, not once but twice, they may be ready to take up arms for what they want. They're busy rummaging behind plows to find their old armor; they're polishing their breastplates and greaves, sharpening their swords, fixing new points on their spears."

"But can these aging veterans really stage a revolution by arms? I should imagine those old breastplates are getting a bit rusty, not to mention tight across the belly. Sulla may have once commanded the world's best army, but his soldiers must be getting a bit gray and soft."

"Their military leader is an old centurion named Gaius Manlius. He's the one Catilina keeps running to Faesulae to confer with. He's represented the veterans' interests for many years and become their leader. It was Manlius who headed the veterans when they came to Rome on election day to vote for Catilina, and it was Manlius who kept them from resorting to violence when Catilina lost. A bloodbath after the election would have been premature; Manlius kept discipline in the ranks. He has hair the color of snow, but he's said to be in superb health, with shoulders like an ox and arms that can bend a steel bar. He's been drilling the veterans and secretly storing up arms."

"Is Manlius really up to running an army?"

"The conspirators down in Rome think so, though perhaps

it's only another of their delusions born of despair."

"Perhaps they're right. Sulla did have an unbeatable army, once upon a time. They fought for glory and pillage when they were young; now they'd be fighting for their fortunes and their families. Who else supports Catilina?"

"There are the women, of course."

"Women?"

"A certain set in Rome—mostly women of high birth who have an appetite for intrigue. His enemies make out Catilina to be hardly more than a pimp for such women, connecting them with his young friends in return for jewels he can sell, or secrets about their husbands. But I suspect that many of these women—wealthy, educated, exquisitely bored—crave power no less than men and know they will never attain it in any ordinary way. Who knows what sort of promises Catilina makes to them?"

"Politicians without a future, soldiers without an army, women without power," I said. "Who else supports Catilina?"

Eco hesitated. "There are hints and rumors, vague indications that there may be men far more important than Lentulus and Cethegus involved, men considerably more powerful than Catilina himself."

"You mean Crassus?"

"Yes."

"And Caesar?"

"Yes. But as I say, I have no evidence of their direct involvement. Yet among the conspirators it's taken for granted that they'll both support whatever Catilina decides to do."

I shook my head. "Believe me, Crassus is the last man who would benefit from an armed revolution. Caesar might, but only if it served his own specific ends. Still, if they're involved, or even if they only tacitly support Catilina . . ."

"You see how the scale of the thing changes."

"Yes. Like a trick of the eye—a low hill capped with white flowers turns out to be a distant snow-peaked mountain. No wonder Cicero is nervous and covers the city with spies."

"Cicero always knows about everything that happens in the city, and I do mean *everything*—they say the consul is never taken by surprise, whether the crisis is a riot at the theater or a slur against him in the fish market. He has a passion for gathering intelligence."

"Or an obsession. The mark of the New Man—nobles don't need constant surveillance to feel secure about their station. And to think that it started with me, when I investigated the case of Sextus Roscius for a rising young advocate with a peculiar name. I suppose I was the first agent in Cicero's network. And now you," I said sardonically. "Who are the others?"

"Cicero is too clever a spymaster to let his agents know of one another's identity. Because I report to him, Marcus Caelius is the only one I'm sure of—"

"If indeed we can be sure of him."

"I think we can, unless he's even more clever than Catilina and Cicero put together. For that, Caelius would have to be a god come down in human form to play havoc among us mortals."

"At this point even that would hardly surprise me. The whole business stinks. Give me a good, honest murder any day."

"It's the times we live in, Papa."

"Speaking of time, how imminent is this crisis?"

"Hard to say. Like a pot on a flame, it simmers. Catilina is cautious. Cicero bides his time, waiting for his enemies to make some slip that will give him irrefutable evidence against them. In the meantime, Marcus Caelius says you've agreed to do as you did before, letting Catilina stay here if he wishes."

"I never agreed to that."

"You refused Cicero when he came to you in the city?"

"In so many words," I said.

"To Cicero anything but an outright 'no' means 'yes,' and even 'no' means 'maybe.' He must have misunderstood. Caelius seems certain that you agreed to continue as before. Papa, do what Cicero asks of you. Catilina may not return. Or he may, and when he does you need only give him shelter. It's such a simple request. It doesn't even require you to take sides. I've cast my lot with Cicero, Papa, and you should do the same, if only by your passive assistance. In the end it will be for the good of everyone you care about."

"I'm surprised at you, Eco, advising me to put everyone on this farm in danger because it will somehow make them safer in the long run."

"The course of the future is already set. You said it yourself, Papa: you can't completely avoid danger, any more than you can give up your search for the truth."

"What about my search for justice? Where does that stand in the midst of all this confusion? How will I know it, even if I find it?"

To this he had no answer, or at least no opportunity to give one, for at the moment a strangely garbed visitor strode over the crest of the hill behind us. We both looked around and drew back in surprise. "What in the name of Hercules!" I said, while Eco threw back his head and laughed.

Diana marched down the grassy slope with as pompous a gait as Cicero had ever affected, her chin held high. Her haughtiness was compromised by a few awkward missteps; the sandals she wore were much too big for her tiny feet. Wrapped around her and dragging on the grass behind was a thin coverlet from her bed, tucked and folded in imitation of a toga.

"It's my birthday!" she announced. "Now it's my turn to put on a toga and take a walk."

"Your birthday is not until tomorrow," I said. "As for a toga—well, you're nowhere near sixteen. Besides that—"

I was saved from delivering a lesson on the hard facts of male and female by the appearance of Meto above the crest of the hill, who bore down on his sister, glowering. "My sandals, you little harpy!" he snapped. He grabbed her by the shoulders, lifted her out of the sandals, and set her down again. He didn't shove or pinch her, but his grip was not gentle. As her bare feet struck the grass, Diana started to cry.

Meto paid her no attention as he slipped the sandals onto his feet. Then he shot me a dark look, turned around, and disappeared over the crest of the hill.

The makeshift toga came apart and fell to the ground. Diana, dressed in her tunic, clenched her little fists and cried, striking such a shrill pitch that I put my fingers in my ears. Eco scrambled to his feet and ran to comfort her.

Where was justice, indeed?

TWENTY-NINE

IT had perhaps been a mistake to exclude Meto from my conversation with Eco; on the other hand, his childish behavior with Diana seemed to contradict his own insistence that he was as grown-up as his brother. I brooded over this for the rest of the day, while Meto brooded over being slighted. Eco brooded over the appearance of Forfex, and his father's stubbornness; Menenia brooded over her husband's disquiet. Bethesda brooded over the general atmosphere of unhappiness on the farm. Ironically, once she stopped crying, Diana recovered her good humor at once. The general uneasiness seemed to confuse her, but it did not quench her spirits.

Diana's birthday passed without any outward unpleasantness. Congrio once again outdid himself. If our spirits were ill at ease, our bellies had no cause for complaint. Menenia had gone shopping in the markets at Rome, and Diana was showered with little gifts—a blue ribbon for her hair, a wooden comb, a blue and yellow scarf like the one Bethesda had bought for Menenia on Meto's toga day, which Diana had coveted. As if to shut away our anxieties, we concentrated all our attention on Diana, who accepted this outpouring of affection as if it were no less than her due for the accomplishment of turning seven years old.

Eco returned to Rome the next day.

The few remaining days of the month of Sextilis passed quickly. In the blinking of an eye we were well into September. It was a busy time on the farm, with much tending to crops and preparations for the harvest. The long days afforded time to deal with the endless repairs and improvements that had accumulated in the winter and been put off through the busy spring and summer. Every day there was more work than could be accomplished before sundown. No longer did I while away my days on the ridgetop or in my library; instead

I plunged wholeheartedly into the operation of the farm. Rather than feeling burdened by this ongoing labor, I felt liberated by it. Confronted by the mysteries of Nemo and Forfex and unable to resolve them, uneasy over Eco's involvement in the plots and counterplots afoot in Rome and yet unable to affect his fortunes, I found escape in the simple, physical exhaustion of working myself to the limit each day and falling into a dreamless sleep at night. The slaves seemed uncertain of what to think of a master who drove himself so hard; I can scarcely imagine that Lucius Claudius ever did so much as pick a single olive from a tree. By sheer energy I believe I finally began to earn Aratus's grudging respect, and by working beside him day by day, seeing how he handled the daily crises and the slaves in his charge, I finally began to trust both his judgment and his loyalty.

I tried to delegate as much responsibility as I could to Meto, thinking to assuage his complaints of being slighted, but whatever tasks I gave him ended up half-done. He was growing bored with the farm, I feared, or else had decided to shirk any task his father might give him, simply out of spite. The more I tried to include him in the running of the place, the more the rift between us seemed to widen. He became increasingly inscrutable to me.

My relations with Bethesda, however, entered a delightfully mellow phase. She has always loved hot weather, for it reminds her of her youth in Alexandria, and as the long summer wore on into September she became more and more her essential, sensual self. She took to leaving out the pins and combs from her hair and wearing it down, in long tresses that cascaded over her shoulders and down her back. There was more silver amid the black than there had been in past summers, but to me these silver strands were like the rippling face of the moon reflected in black water. My own newfound physicality seemed to please her; she liked the smell of sweat on my body, and the hardness of my arms after a day of strenuous work. Often, when I went to bed thinking I was completely exhausted, she would prove to me that there was indeed a measure of strength left in my body. She would summon it up and take it from me, leaving me limp and covered with a fresh sheen of sweat, drained of all anxiety and empty of every appetite, motionless, thoughtless, utterly at the mercy of Morpheus.

The stream continued to dwindle, and the water from the well remained impure, but Aratus expressed the opinion that we would last until the rains came in the fall; as head of the household I was advised to pray to the gods to avert a dry autumn. As for the shortage of hay, which would loom large in the coming winter, I asked Claudia if I could purchase a quantity from her; unfortunately, she said, she had none to spare. To ask any of the other Claudii for help was, of course, out of the question. Other farmers in the region were not yet ready to sell their own private stocks, uncertain whether they had a surplus or not and preferring to wait until it was truly needed, when they could get a better price for it. I would have to solve the hay shortage when the time came; hopefully I would have the money on hand to buy what I needed, rather than see my livestock perish or face premature slaughter.

Though by comparison with these problems it was a minor complaint, I continued to be thwarted by the water mill. Aratus had no solution. I even invited Meto to help, but perhaps he detected the suppressed skepticism in my voice, for he exhibited an extreme disinterest. The failure of the mill would not have mattered so much if I had not begun the labor in memory of Lucius Claudius. Nor did it help that I had told Publius Claudius across the stream about it and had even invited him to share in its use. I hated to think of the wicked fool laughing smugly at my failure and passing the tale to his cousins Manius and Gnaeus behind my back.

On the morning of the Ides of September, I took a trip into the nearest village. We were constructing a new stone wall along one side of the stable, and I needed to hire a few extra laborers for the day. There was a market in the village where this could be done. I might have sent Aratus alone on the errand, but given the ugly events that had transpired on the farm that summer, I wanted to see for myself where any hired laborers came from and look them over before letting them on my property.

Aratus and I left on horseback early in the morning and returned a few hours later, leading a band of six workers on foot. They were slaves, but not shackled; these were trusted men, lent out by their masters for a fee. I would have preferred to use freedmen, but the man who ran the labor market in the village said that they had grown scarce in recent years. In hard times freedmen tend to give up the one thing they own, selling themselves back into slavery just to keep from starving.

As we turned off the Cassian Way, Aratus rode up beside me. "Visitors, Master," he said.

Sure enough, two strange horses stood tethered outside the stable, a dot of black and a dot of white against the wall. I left the slaves to Aratus and rode ahead. Meto had been in charge of the farm in my absence; I had made a point of conferring the responsibility on him, thinking it might help salve his pride. But when I reached the house he was not in sight, nor did he come when I called. The slave who was on watch—since the finding of Forfex, I had always kept watchers posted—scurried across the pitched roof of the stable and jumped to the ground.

"Where is Meto?"

"Down at the mill, Master."

"The visitors?"

"Also down at the mill."

"Only two?"

He nodded.

I rode at a gallop but slowed as I approached the mill. I dismounted and let the horse wander down to the streambed in search of tender grass and any pools of water that might be found among the dry stones and caked mud. As I approached, I heard a familiar voice from within.

"Then the problem must be *here*. Well, it's obvious these two gears were never meant to mesh—like trying to mate an ass and a goat."

This was followed by good-natured laughter—Meto, laughing with more genuine enthusiasm than I had heard from him in many days, and someone else. I stepped into the doorway and saw Tongilius leaning against one wall with his arms crossed. His tunic was dusty and his hair windswept from riding. Meto stood nearby. They were both looking toward Catilina, who crouched among the great wooden wheels and axles. As I entered they all looked toward me.

"Gordianus!" said Catilina. "What a piece of work you've created! You thought up this design yourself?"

"With some help from Aratus."

"Amazing! You're already known for cleverness; let no man say you lack ambition as well. I thought all the engineers were busy building catapults and siege towers for the legions, or else constructing bridges and aqueducts for the Senate. You have quite a talent. Who taught you?"

"Books and common sense. Having eyes and ears also helps. But not enough, I'm afraid. The mill doesn't work."

"Ah, but it will. There's only one thing stopping it."

"What do you mean?"

"Look here, at this shaft. It's exactly wrong."

"What do you mean?" I found myself irritated at his self-assurance, but at the same time I had a glimmering that he knew what he was talking about.

"It should originate there," he said, pointing, "and be precisely perpendicular to its present arrangement."

"But that would mean moving everything else around, changing the structure completely," I said, hardly believing the solution could be so easy.

"Not at all. The two gears will meet side by side rather than at right angles. As it's now arranged, the mechanism must tear itself apart within a revolution. But with that single change—"

"By Hercules!" I tried not to look a fool, agape at how simple it was. He was absolutely right, without a doubt. "Why could I not see what was before me?"

Catilina shrugged and laid his hand on my shoulder. His hair was windswept like Tongilius's, and his face was ruddy from riding. He looked half his age, happy and sure of himself, not at all like a skulking conspirator. "You created the mill from scratch, and your head is cluttered with all the multitude of choices that went into its design; amid so many others, the single small detail that keeps it from working is invisible to you. I, on the other hand, came upon the design in its elegant entirety, and to me the one thing wrong with its perfection is glaringly obvious. You see, Gordianus, sometimes a fresh perspective can be of immeasurable help to a man. You're not the only one who needs that from time to time." His voice lent a certain gravity to these final words, and he gave me a significant look as he gave my shoulder a squeeze before releasing it.

I contemplated the gears, trying to convince myself to accept the simplicity of Catilina's solution. Was his deduction as unremarkable and logical as his unassuming explanation made it sound, or was he a genius? How could he see in a moment an answer that had been perplexing me for months? I was at the same time irritated, impressed, elated, and still dubious.

"You've been riding," I said absently. "Surely not all the way from Rome this morning?"

"No, from up north," said Tongilius. Catilina had been conferring with his general Manlius and the Sullan veterans up in Faesulae, I thought.

"Your invitation to me still stands, doesn't it?" interjected Catilina with a smile. "Marcus Caelius led me to think so."

I took a quick breath and pretended to examine the gears again so that there would be an excuse for the hollowness in my voice. "Yes. Of course."

"Ah, good. You'd be surprised, or perhaps not, at how many of my friends and colleagues suddenly have no room for me under their roofs after my latest disaster at the polls. But then other friends appear, to make up the balance."

Catilina and Tongilius retired to the house to rest and change their clothes. I was too excited at the prospect of finally completing the mill to join them. Instead of building the new wall at the stable, I set the hired laborers to work realigning the gears. We worked into the night. Bethesda sent Diana to call me to dinner, but I told her to send down some bread and cheese instead.

Eventually the new arrangement of gears was set in place. In the absence of a rushing stream, slaves pushed the paddle wheel. Within the mill the mechanism shuddered and began to turn. The shafts revolved; the teeth fitted and meshed; the grinding wheel turned for one revolution, and another, and another, without mishap.

Small adjustments would be necessary, the housing would

have to be completed, and actual use would no doubt suggest improvements, but for all practical purposes the mill was a success.

This moment filled me with a greater sense of achievement than I could have anticipated. Aratus wore such a smile as I had never seen on his face before. Even Meto dropped his sullen frown and seemed to share in my excitement. Catilina should have been with me. I looked toward the house, at the darkened windows, and wondered again at the simplicity of his genius.

THIRTY

THOUGH the day had been long and hot, the night was pleasant. I was covered with dust, sweat, and grime. It was late, but in the flush of my excitement, sleep seemed far away. While I spent a few final moments doting on the water mill, I sent word to the household slaves to prepare a hot bath. Given the shortage of water, this was a considerable extravagance—for many days we had all made do with sponges and strigils to clean ourselves. But I deserved a reward, I told myself.

Meto declared himself too exhausted to share the bath with me; instead he sponged himself from a bowl of water and went straight to bed. As I opened the door to the baths, a wave of warm steam flowed over my naked body, swallowing me. The lamp burned very low. I could hardly see the tub, but located it by following the sound of its gentle gurgling. I climbed over the edge and lowered myself gingerly into the hot water, hissing as it nipped at my scrotum. I slowly settled into the pool until the water came to my neck. I let out a long breath and felt my muscles turn to mist.

As I stretched out my legs, I touched another limb beneath the water. I gave a start, but only a small one. I was not really surprised to find that Catilina was already in the water.

We sat at opposite sides of the tub, facing each other. Our

calves touched, but I didn't bother to draw away. I was too tired to move, I told myself. Through the veils of mist I saw Catilina smiling. He held up a cup of wine and took a sip.

"You don't mind my being here, I hope? In your bath, I mean."

"I should be a poor host to deny any guest that pleasure." Besides, I thought, Catilina deserved to share in this small gift to myself, since without him I should have had nothing to celebrate or to keep me up so late.

"I heard the slaves pass the order to stoke the furnace and I couldn't resist. I've been riding horseback so much lately that my buttocks have turned to stone." He groaned and flexed beneath the water. The motion caused his leg to rub against mine.

"Where is Tongilius?"

"Already abed and sleeping like a baby. Your mill—it works, now?" he said.

"Yes. Glorious! You should have been there."

"The triumph was yours, Gordianus, not mine. You must be very proud of your accomplishment."

"It was sweet when we set the wheels in motion and the thing began to move, like a creature coming to life. I would have sent for you, but I thought you must already be asleep."

"No fear of that. Lately I've given up sleep altogether. No time for it."

"You're managing to stay busy, then?" I said, then realized the implication—that a man who has just lost a bid for power usually has time to spare.

"Busier than I've ever been in my life. Quite as busy as if I had won the election, I imagine. I doubt there's another man in the Republic who has as hectic a schedule as I do."

"Oh, I can think of one," I said.

"The consul. Yes, but Cicero can afford to close his eyes occasionally. He has so many surrogate eyes—and ears—all over Rome to keep watch for him while he slumbers."

For a long moment I scrutinized Catilina's face through the mist, and decided there was no ulterior meaning in this reference to Cicero's spies. It was doubtless a subject much on Catilina's mind, no matter in whose company he found himself. The circle of those he could trust was growing smaller and smaller.

The water loosened my muscles. I felt my mind relaxing as well. "You came from up north?" I said.

"Faesulae and Arretium."

"Heading down to Rome?"

"Tomorrow."

For a while we were silent. The water cooled a bit. I knocked on the wall. A slave appeared. I told him to add fuel to the fire and to bring us each a fresh cup of watered wine.

"You must be very happy in this place, Gordianus," said Catilina. His tone was desultory, that of a tired man sharing a bath with another at the end of a long day, making minor conversation.

"Happy enough."

"I myself have never attended to the day-to-day running of a farm. I used to own a few outside Rome, but I sold them long ago."

"It's not exactly the bucolic dream that sentimental poets like to imagine."

He laughed softly. "I suppose reality has somewhat rougher edges."

"Yes. There are problems—small ones, big ones, always more than you can shut back into Pandora's box, no matter how hard you work."

"Running a farm is not so different from running a republic, I imagine." There was an edge to his voice, at once wistful and bitter.

"It's all a matter of scale," I said. "Of course, some problems are probably the same for all men—wondering whether one can trust a slave, trying to placate a demanding wife . . . do I see you smile, Catilina? Trying to do the right thing by a son who thinks he is a man but is still only a boy . . ."

"Ah, Meto. You're having trouble with him, then?"

"Ever since he put on his manly toga, we cannot seem to come to an understanding. He puzzles me. To be fair, my own behavior toward him perplexes me. I tell myself that he's at an awkward age, but I wonder if it's not my age that's the problem."

Catilina laughed. "How old are you?"

"Forty-seven."

"I'm forty-five myself. An awkward age, indeed! Who are we, where have we been, to what end are we headed—and is it too late to change the destination? All in all, I think it's harder to be forty-five than sixteen, if only because one sees so much more clearly all the possibilities that are forever out of reach. Old enough to have grown tired of one's own cleverness and skills, old enough for the passions of one's youth to have grown stale. Old enough to have seen beauty wither, while death claims more of one's acquaintances than are still alive. And yet one still goes on living. Certain ambitions and appetites diminish, but others take their place. All the while, the petty business of life continues—eating, drinking, copulation; grappling with the contentious natures of parents, spouses, children. I don't know what your problems with Meto might be, but I think you're very lucky to have him. My own son, being gone—I often wish, especially nowadays . . ." He left this thought unfinished.

For a while we were both quiet. I felt myself melting not only into the heat of the bath but also into a familiar role. Catilina was changed from his previous visit, when he had been in such total, calculating control of all that passed between us. He was a man who needed to speak, and I, as I had been for so many before him, was a listener, the sieve into which he could pour the raw material of whatever burdened him—bitterness, remorse, frustration, fear. There is something in me that draws the truth from other men; this curse, or gift, was passed in the blood from my father, bestowed on us by the gods. Cicero might say that Catilina was using that gift against me, turning me into his confidant for his own ends. A part of me, too, was skeptical.

But there was nothing disingenuous in the sigh that passed from Catilina's lips. "Were you in Rome on election day?" he asked quietly.

"Yes. The whole family was there, for Meto's coming-of-age."

"Ah, yes, I remember Caelius telling me that the boy had just turned sixteen."

"He cast his first ballot."

"For me, I hope."

"Yes, as a matter of fact. Our century went for Silanus, though."

Catilina nodded gravely. He didn't ask for whom I had voted, taking my support for granted, I suppose. What if he had asked me? *For Nemo*, I could have said. *For Nobody. For a headless corpse buried in a hidden grave not far from where we sit.* For a moment I considered confronting him with the riddles of Nemo and Forfex. I tried to imagine where such confrontation might lead. If he was responsible, he would never admit it, no matter how self-revealing his mood. If he knew nothing of the matter and I blamed it on Caelius, a confrontation between them must ensue, and Caelius would be compromised. I could hardly voice my suspicions of Cicero without revealing my own role as Cicero's tool, and by extension endangering Eco.

I had time to tread this barren circle more than once in my thoughts before Catilina spoke again. "Do you ever find yourself plagued with doubts, Gordianus? Ah, I see the look on your face, though just barely. Thank the gods for this steam—the naked face of doubt is hard to look at!" He sipped his wine. "Do you think it's only the closeness of our ages, the coincidence of having been born a few years apart, that gives us this mutual understanding? What else do we have in common? I'm a patrician, you're a plebeian; I love the city, while you've abandoned it for a farm; I believe in exploring every appetite, while you appear to be a man of great restraint. I'm bold and rash in my politics, while I suspect that you would turn your back on politics altogether if you could. But you hate the powers-that-be in Rome as much as I do—so Marcus Caelius tells me—and though you won't do more, I'm thankful at least that you'll grant me refuge when I need it. Caelius also drew my attention to your son Eco. A valuable man, as canny as his father, some say. Caelius and Eco both tell me not to burden you too much with my plans, and so I won't. You do enough to let me sit here on a September night, sharing with me your wine and your bath, listening to a failed candidate ramble on about his misfortunes. Would you call for your slave again? I'd like some more wine."

I realized then that the cup from which he had been drinking when I joined him was not his first; no wonder his tongue was loosened and his guard relaxed. I called for the slave, who brought fresh wine.

"Should I have him heat the water?" I asked.

"It's more than hot enough already, don't you think? I'm fairly cooked." With that, Catilina pulled himself up and sat on the edge of the tub, leaning back against the wall. Steam billowed from his flesh. Rivulets of water reflected the lamp's amber glow and made the hair on his broad chest glisten. "Perhaps it's time to take the cool plunge."

"There is no cool plunge tonight."

"What? A hot bath without a cool one to follow? Rather like lovemaking without the climax."

"Blame the interrupted coitus on a small problem with my well."

Catilina raised an eyebrow. I studied his face for a sign that he understood, but saw none.

"Until the autumn rains come, we're short of water here on the farm. The well was polluted last month."

"Polluted?"

I hesitated, but only for an instant. Since the subject had come up, why not mention Forfex and see how Catilina reacted? "We found a body at the bottom of the well."

"How awful! I suppose you took your foreman to task. What was it, a goat?"

"It wasn't the body of an animal."

He cocked his head, made a strained face and blinked several times. The wine had slowed his wits temporarily, but it also exaggerated his expressions; it was hard to tell whether he was acting or not. "What do you mean?" he said.

"I mean it was a man we found in the well."

"What, one of your slaves took a fall?"

"Not one of mine. A neighbor's slave. You knew the man."

"I doubt it."

"No, he was known to you. I know, because I was there. Forfex."

He knitted his brow. "The name means nothing to me."

"You remember, my neighbor's goatherd up on the mountain. He showed us the abandoned mine."

"Oh, yes! Of course, Forfex. But dead, you say. Fell down your well. Polluted it, you say . . ."

"He wasn't discovered until several days later."

"I shouldn't like to have seen it when you pulled him out." I nodded. "The body was badly bloated and decayed."

"But you were able to recognize him, despite that?"

"Despite what?" I looked at him carefully. Did he already know the body had been missing its head?

"The decay, I mean. I've seen what happens to corpses left to nature, especially in water."

"We were able to figure out his identity, even so."

"What was he doing on your farm, anyway?"

"We're not sure."

"An unpleasant fellow, that neighbor of yours. He should keep his slaves on his own property."

"You might have an easier task convincing Gnaeus Claudius of that if you hadn't gone trespassing on his land yourself."

"That's right, I suppose I did," said Catilina with a laugh so genuine that I could scarcely believe he was hiding anything from me. "And I took you with me, didn't I?" He slid back into the hot water with a hiss and shut his eyes. He was quiet for so long that I almost thought he was asleep. Then, opening his eyes, he announced: "Too hot! But no cool plunge to follow," he mused. "Have you had enough, Gordianus?"

"I think so. Any more and Congrio will be serving me on a platter tomorrow with an apple in my mouth."

"Well, then, let's cool off in the open air," suggested Catilina.

"I thought I'd simply dry myself—"

"Nonsense! It's a beautiful night. On the far side of the horizon where the sun descended, the god of the warm west winds is stirring in his sleep; he dreams of spring; he sighs, and the grasses sway. Let's take a walk and let Zephyrus dry us with his gentle breath." He rose and stepped out of the tub. "Come, join me, Gordianus."

"What, without getting dressed? Without even drying ourselves?"

"Oh, we'll put on our shoes. Here, I've slipped mine on

already. And I'll take these towels, in case we need something to sit on."

I stepped from the tub. With his toe, Catilina pushed my shoes toward my feet. I stepped into them, bent down and drew the straps taut.

"The hallway is dim," he said, opening the door, "but I think I remember the way." He walked toward the atrium. Naked and wet, my skin hot from the bath, I followed.

The moon was bright and full, like a lamp set high above the atrium. Its white light shimmered in the pool and lit the columns along one side, casting stark shadows behind them. Thinking we had reached our destination, I stopped and looked down at my naked reflection foreshortened in the black water. The pool was so still that I could see the stars reflected in it. Reflected, too, was the bemused expression on my face—which abruptly gave a start at the sound of the front door creaking open.

"Catilina!" I said. But he had already slipped outside. All I saw was a naked arm beckoning me.

"Absurd," I muttered to myself, but followed.

Outside, as Catilina had said, a gentle zephyr was stirring across the valley. The wind was warm and dry, like a caress against my naked flesh. Ahead of me I saw Catilina, his glistening body pale and sleek as marble beneath the bright moonlight. Clouds of steam rose from his wet, warm flesh, so that he seemed to walk in a mist, with bits of ragged vapor trailing from his broad shoulders and muscular legs. I looked down and saw that my own body emitted the same warm mist. Nearby the oxen lowed in their pen, and a kid bleated sleepily.

"Catilina, where are we going?" I whispered loudly. He made no answer but walked on, gesturing for me to follow.

What a strange sight we must have made. I heard a noise from the roof of the stable and saw that the slave posted to keep watch for the night was staring down at us with an odd look on his face, uncertain, I suppose, whether we were naked men or spirits wrapped in vapor.

"Master?" he called in a low, uncertain voice. I waved, which seemed to satisfy him, though he kept gazing down at us with the same baffled look.

We walked past the pens, through the vineyards, into the olive orchard. I caught up with Catilina but no longer questioned him. I was too exhilarated by the strangeness of walking naked beneath the moon, by the kiss of the zephyr on my skin, by the dazzling flight of a huge white moth across our path. "This is mad," I said.

"Mad? What could be less mad than for a man to walk naked across the face of the earth? What could be more piously in keeping with the will of the gods who made us after their image than to show ourselves to them thus?" We reached the foot of the ridge. Catilina pressed on, striding carefully but quickly up the steep path. "When I was young, after a hot bath on a mild night, I used to do this in the city."

"In Rome?"

He laughed, remembering. "On the Palatine Hill, outside my house. Sometimes alone, sometimes with another. We would take a long walk around the block, naked and steaming, letting the wind dry us. It's delicious, isn't it? Rome is full of naked statues which offend no one's dignity; why should a naked man? You might think it would have caused a scandal, but it didn't. Would you believe that no one ever complained?"

"Had you not been so good-looking, they might have," I said.

"You compliment me, Gordianus." We had reached the top of the ridge. Catilina dropped the towels and stepped atop one of the tree stumps to take in the view. I looked up at his heaving chest and the muscular arms crossed over it, his flat belly, his sturdy legs and the pendulous sex between.

"You are resplendent in your nakedness, Catilina!" I said, laughing and trying to catch my breath. I gazed at him openly, and not without envy. "Truly, like a statue on a pedestal." I felt a little drunk, not on wine any longer but on moonlight and the peculiar novelty of being naked out of doors. The wind had dried the steam from my body, but I was covered with a fresh sheen of sweat from the exertion of the climb.

"Do you think so? My lovers have said the same thing." He looked down at himself, as if his body were familiar but separate from him, just another of the things he owned, like a finely crafted chair or a beautiful painting. "Impressive for

a man of forty-five, I suppose." He complimented himself
without irony or false modesty, but with the matter-of-
factness of a man who has inhabited a body for a long time
and is neither unduly impressed nor takes it for granted.

Below us the valley slumbered. I saw no lights from the
distant houses of the Claudii, and from my own house only
a single lamp was visible, set outside the front door by one
of the slaves who must have seen us leave the atrium. Yet
how could the world sleep, when the moon was so bright?
The Cassian Way was a ribbon of purest alabaster skirting
the base of the mountain. The roof of the house seemed to
be made of tiles that glowed with a pale blue light. And when
the zephyr sighed through the olive orchard below us, the
rustling leaves shimmered black and silver. An owl hooted
from a nearby tree.

Catilina sighed. "I have never stinted myself of the pleasures that my body could take, nor stinted others of the pleasures it could give. Such a simple principle by which to live,
don't you think? Yet even that has been turned against me
by my enemies, twisted into something ugly and depraved.
You were in the city during the final days of the campaign.
You must have heard how they vilified me. The same as last
year, but worse. Last year Cicero and his scheming brother
Quintus tasted my blood; this year nothing would satisfy them
but to tear out my heart and eat it."

Catilina drew himself up and gazed down at the valley.
When I had said he looked like a statue on a pedestal, I had
meant it half in jest, but half in earnest. In his marmoreal
nakedness, wearing a stern face, he might have been the image of a god. Not the gods of boyhood, Mercury or Apollo;
Vulcan perhaps, or more likely Jupiter, master of order and
shaper of the greater destinies, gazing firmly down from
Olympus.

"If you had a beard, you'd look like Jupiter," I said.

The thought amused him. He thrust his right arm stiffly
before him, palm down, and spread his fingers. "If only I
could cast lightning bolts, like Jupiter." He gazed at the back
of his hand. "Cicero can—did you know that? Lightning bolts
emanate from his fingers. A kind of lightning, anyway. He
points at the mob in the Forum; sparks gather at his fingertips

and flash into blue flame. He shoots shafts of lightning straight into their eyes and ears, blinding them to the truth, turning them deaf to reason." Catilina thrust out his arm again and pointed down with his forefinger, miming the action. "Cicero's forefinger: *the Vestal Virgins must be protected from Catilina!* Crack! The lightning strikes, the voters quiver with superstitious awe and revulsion. His middle finger: *Catilina seduces young men!* The lightning flashes, the voters grimace with distaste—and perhaps a little jealousy? His next finger: *Catilina pimps for rich matrons!* The voters howl in disgust. His little finger: *in the name of serving Sulla, Catilina murdered good citizens and raped their wives and children!* The voters tremble with loathing. And on his other hand— well, with his other hand, he's busy masturbating, isn't he?"

I laughed out loud. Catilina grunted and began to laugh as well, a rich, good-natured laugh, I thought at first, until a taint of bitterness seemed to swallow it up before it had run its course.

"He has destroyed me with lies and distortions, and the mob acclaims him as the First Citizen in the land. Still, I had rather be Catilina than Cicero," he said, studying his hand for a moment and then dropping his arm to his side. "What about you, Gordianus?"

"What, had I rather be myself than Cicero?"

"No! Which would you choose to be: Cicero or Catilina?"

"An odd question."

"An excellent question."

"You're forever playing games, Catilina."

"And you are forever avoiding them. Do you fear the element of chance? Must you always know the outcome ahead of time? Then choose to be Cicero!" He gazed down at me. Pockets of shadow obscured his eyes, but his lips had a quizzical twist. "Do you know what I think? I think it would frighten you to be Catilina." He jumped down from the stump. He picked up a broad towel, spread it on the ground and lay down on it, joining his hands beneath his head and gazing up at the moon.

"Lie down beside me, Gordianus."

I hesitated.

"Come, join me. Gaze up at the face of the moon. You

call your daughter Diana, don't you, after the goddess of the moon? Look up at her face with me."

I lay down beside him, acutely aware again of my nakedness as I was bathed in bright moonlight. "Diana is short for Gordiana," I explained.

"Vaguely impious, even so, to call a child by a goddess's name," said Catilina. "But fitting, I suppose. Diana, patron goddess of the plebeians, who inspired the Sabine women in their revolt. Diana, goddess of fertility and birth, dweller in mountains and woods, lover of all wild things. One tends to forget her in the city, just as one forgets the moon there amid so many lamps. She's stronger here. Her light bathes all the world with its glow. Lie here and worship her with me for a while."

We lay in silence. Except for the occasional rustling of leaves and the hooting of the owl, the world was so quiet that I could hear my own heartbeat and Catalina's breathing beside me. After a while he said, "May I speak with you frankly?"

I smiled. "I doubt that I could stop you."

"We seem to share the same taste in women, Gordianus. Your wife Bethesda is quite spectacular; she reminds me more than a little of my own Aurelia. Their beauty is much alike, as is their haughtiness, their mysteriousness. But it seems that we do not share the same taste in young men."

"Apparently not."

"Yet I can't imagine how anyone could fail to find Tongilius beautiful, even Cicero. His green eyes, the way his hair sweeps back from his forehead—"

"Tongilius *is* beautiful," I acknowledged.

"Yet you do not desire him?"

"That would hardly be proper, would it, since I am your host and Tongilius is your companion?"

"Now who plays games with words, Gordianus? My point is this: if you have an eye for beauty, why do you not act on it? How can you resist?"

I laughed softly. "First of all, Catilina, like many unusually good-looking men and women who encounter constant temptation, you seem to think such opportunities are as rampant for others as for yourself."

"Do you really underestimate yourself so ludicrously, Gordianus? Tongilius, for one, finds you quite attractive. He tells me so."

At this I felt an unexpected and dubious quiver of gratification. "You're joking, Catilina. Tongilius would never have told you such a thing. How could the subject have ever arisen?"

"It seems a quite natural subject to me. Unless they're talking about politics, what else do people talk about, except the relative attractiveness and desirability of other people? Indeed, what else *is* there to talk about?"

"Catilina, you are incorrigible."

"No, insatiable perhaps, but eminently corrigible. I am always ready to learn something new and to be corrected when I'm mistaken. You'd do well to follow my example, Gordianus. In this matter, as in others."

"What matter?"

"The unreasonable restraint you show in your relationships with beautiful young men."

"Catilina, you mustn't try to corrupt me! I'm unworthy of your efforts!"

"Nonsense, I find you entirely worthy."

"I suppose I should be flattered?"

"No, grateful and attentive."

I laughed deep in my throat, surprised at how much I was enjoying this banter between us. It was the spell cast by the full moon, of course, looming huge and white above us, almost close enough to touch. It was my own nakedness, and the moth which had flitted across our path, and Catilina's indisputable charm that made it possible to speak of things that never were or would be.

"Do you know what I think, Gordianus? I think we are opposites in many ways, and yet complementary. Caelius says that you have quite a reputation for extracting the truth from others, that you're something of a legend that way; men naturally want to empty their hearts to you. My gift is the same, yet different. I see into other men's hearts, into the places where they never look, and it's *I* who tell *them* what resides there. Do you know what I see in your heart about this matter?"

"This matter, which fascinates you more than it does me?"

"I think not. I see inside you an extraordinary moral character, a man very much out of step with the world in which he lives. We both know the Roman way of sexuality: power is everything, even more important than pleasure. Indeed, pleasure as an end in itself is something alien to a good Roman—decadent, Eastern, a vice of the Egyptians and the Greeks. Power rules, and power means penetration. Men possess that power; women do not. Men rule Rome and have made it what it is: an empire bent on conquering all the world, penetrating and subduing every other nation and race."

"This seems far from the subject of lust."

"Not at all. In such a world the natural proclivities of love are bent; pleasure bows to power. Everything is reduced to penetrating or being penetrated. How simple-minded, how much more suitable to the mechanics of your water mill than the complexities of the human spirit, but there you have it. Penetrate or be penetrated: women have no option in this matter and are thus permanently reduced to an inferior status. On the other hand, any man who submits to being penetrated by another man relinquishes his power and is thought to be no better than a woman, or at least so goes the consensus, though we all know that behind closed doors men tend to do whatever they wish, compelled more by pleasure than prestige. Thus all the gossip about Caesar in his younger days when he played catamite to King Nicomedes of Bithynia—such un-Roman behavior! But of course Caesar was young and virile, Nicomedes exuded an Eastern sensuality, and who really cares what they did, except a political manipulator of Cicero's stripe, who might be able to make a campaign issue of it—a matter of faulty character and judgment, they call it. Illicit sex brings down the wrath of the gods—just ask Cato—and if a Roman like Caesar allows himself to be plowed in his youth, who knows what famines and military catastrophes might result!

"The Greeks allow for such passions, of course, but only, ostensibly, between the old and the young; it is suitable and proper for a young man to submit to his mentor, given the correct circumstances and decorum. Still, you see, the balance of power depends on the role to be played. Naturally, there must always be exceptions, behind closed doors, that do not fit the model of the masterly mentor and the docile protégé.

"We Romans, alas, do not even have a model to depart from. We scorn the Greeks, ridiculing their obsessions with philosophy and athletics. Lacking their time-honored traditions, in matters of vice we are left to our own devices. Mostly, we take horrendous advantage of our slaves, male and female alike. Such passion has no honor, and is thus unfettered and untempered by any rules of dignity or decorum, much less restrained by law. The excesses of the Romans in exploiting their human tools are literally without limit. Slave girls are commonly raped against their will, slave boys are stripped of all their dignity and exploited just as rapaciously. They are treated with a degree of contempt that most men would not inflict upon a dog; indeed, a well-trained dog costs considerably more than a reasonably pretty boy or girl at the market.

"In such a world passion must invariably mean degradation for someone—or so the consensus decrees. So a man like Gordianus the Finder, this strangely moral being, finds other ways to shape his longings. Sex he must have, of course; in that way he is like every other man. But even so he is unconventional: he devotes himself to a slave woman, dotes on her beauty, indulges her haughtiness, and ultimately makes her his wife, thus elevating her rather than degrading her. His behavior is almost a satire upon the Roman dictum to choose a wife for her status and a whore for her beauty. So far as anyone knows, he is more faithful to his wife than ninety-nine out of a hundred of his countrymen are to theirs. A love match, that rarest of Roman marriages!

"As for the pleasure to be had with young men, he will not approach the matter at all. Or rather, he skirts it. He has too much respect for them, whether citizen or slave, to blithely follow the formula that inevitably elevates one man and degrades the other. He prefers the role of chaste mentor, instead. This behavior is rare but not unheard of; I have seen it before and recognize it in you. Gordianus does not exploit and rape his slaves. Nor does he seek out an uncertain middle ground with a companion of his own station. He teaches; he nurtures and dotes; he elevates. He makes sentimentality a

fetish; his gestures are grandiose. He goes so far as to adopt
a street urchin and a slave boy and to make these young men
his heirs. Such an unconventional family! And while he remains exquisitely sensitive to the beauties of young men, he
sees, but he does not touch. What reticence, more given to
compassion than passion! He is a man out of step with a
world that encourages the strong to devour the weak, that
rewards cruelty and punishes kindness, that measures manhood by a man's will to dominate other men, women, children, and slaves, the more ruthlessly the better. He is a
stranger fellow than ever Catilina was!"

He fell silent. We lay next to each other, equally naked
beneath the bright moon. "And Catilina," I said, my voice
strange in my ears because Catilina's words had made everything seem strange, "how does he fit into such a world?"

"Like Gordianus, Catilina makes his own rules, to suit
himself."

We lay on the hill, musing and amusing ourselves long into
the night.

As sometimes happens when the body has been heated by
a bath, then cools, and then exerts itself again after an already
strenuous day, I fell asleep without meaning to. Fortunately,
the night remained mild and there was no morning chill. I
awoke before cockcrow. The towel had been folded over me
like a coverlet. Catilina was gone.

The moon was long departed. The sky was neither blue
nor black but in between. The lesser stars had vanished. In
the east Lucifer, the morning star, glittered just above the
dark, brooding mass of Mount Argentum.

I stood, covering my nakedness with the towel and slipping
on my sandals, which I had taken off during the night. I
climbed slowly down the slope of the ridge, my back stiff
from having slept on the hard ground.

The watcher atop the stable, yawning from his vigil,
blinked his eyes wide open at the sight of me.

"My guests," I said, "the ones who arrived yesterday—"

"Gone already, Master. Took their horses an hour ago.
Turned toward Rome when they reached the Cassian Way."
He bit his lip. "I was a bit worried about you when he came

down from the hill alone. I went up to check on you, and you seemed all right. Sleeping like a stone. Did I do right not to wake you?"

I nodded dully and went into the house.

Bethesda was asleep, but stirred when I slid my body next to hers. "You smell like wine," she murmured, with an edge to her voice. "Where have you been all night? If this were Rome, I would think you had been with another woman."

"Absurd," I said. "No chance of that happening here."

I closed my eyes and slept till noon.

THIRTY-ONE

THAT night on the ridge with Catilina was one of the last moments of calm before the deluge.

September continued dry and mild. The first days of October turned leaves to gold and quickened the harvests. With the puzzle of the mill solved, I gave myself over to running the farm again, and the work continued at a busy pace. I busied myself with small matters to distract me from the looming crises of hay and water, and from Meto's continuing coolness toward me.

Catilina visited once again in September and three times in October. On each occasion he brought other companions besides Tongilius, but there were never more than five or six. These men were large and armed: bodyguards. Bethesda did not care for the look of them, but they slept in the stable and ate the same fare as the slaves without complaint, and Catilina never stayed for more than a night.

On each succeeding visit Catilina became less communicative and more distant. I sensed in this the reticence of a man increasingly distracted and pressed for time. He would arrive late in the day and leave early in the morning. He did not haunt the atrium or go walking naked under moonlight, but took to his bed soon after dinner and rose at dawn. I was seldom alone with him for even a moment; we shared no more revelations about the anguish of his defeat or the obscure geometries of desire.

He did not even spare the time to revisit the water mill, though I offered to show it to him more than once. I had found it necessary to rebuild some parts of the mechanism to match better with Catilina's solution, and once the general design had been altered, Aratus also suggested a few minor adjustments to the overall scheme. This work was done in desultory fashion, in bits and pieces as the more pressing work of the farm allowed. By late October it was virtually finished, though its true utility could be confirmed and measured only when the stream once again rose high enough to drive the wheel. I looked to the skies every morning and night, hoping for rain.

It was on a day near the end of October that I decided to show Claudia the mill. It was Claudia who had told me of her cousin Lucius's intention to build such a mill; without her, I would never have known. I sent a message that she should meet me on the ridgetop at midday, suggesting we share a simple meal and telling her I had something to show her.

I brought cheese, bread, and apples. Claudia brought honey cakes and wine, and the greatest delicacy of all: a jug of fresh water. I told her that the honey cakes were sweet and the wine delicious, but that it was the fresh water from her well that ravished my palate.

"Has it grown that serious, your shortage?" she said.

"Yes. We're able to collect some water from the trickle in the stream; once the silt settles, it's good enough to drink, but there's hardly enough to quench the thirst of every slave and animal. Then there's a tiny spring that comes out of the ridge. That, too, is low; an urn placed under it is only half full by the end of the day. So to water the stronger animals we still use the well, though it loosens their bowels. Fortunately, there are still a few tall urns of water that were drawn before the well was polluted—I've set them aside as if they were filled with silver. And there's plenty of wine, but sometimes a man must have water to drink."

"I suppose the well water is good enough for washing," said Claudia.

"Aratus advises against it. Still, we use it sparingly with sponges and strigils. The well is low anyway, thanks to the lack of rain. Instead of immersing herself in a hot tub of water, Bethesda dabs herself with scented oils. She's normally as fastidious as a cat; unable to preen, she pouts. I'm afraid we've all become rather tawdry. This tunic I'm wearing could use a good washing."

"Alas, I wish I could spare you more water myself, but my own well is dangerously low, or so my foreman says. Enjoy the water I've brought—drink up, and see if it won't make you drunk," she laughed. "Where is young Meto, by the way?"

"Busy, I suppose. He preferred not to come."

"Oh, but I haven't seen him in so long; hardly at all since his birthday. Well, I won't press you about it," she said, reading the look on my face. "Though I wouldn't be surprised to learn that he's less than happy here. I've told you before that you belong in the city, and the same is even truer for Meto. Not everyone was meant to be a farmer, especially when the city can offer such a full, rich life. Ah, but I said I wouldn't press the matter, and here I am giving unsolicited advice like the bossiest Roman matron who ever lived!"

We ate for a while in silence. It was a magnificent autumn day, the air crisp, the sky cloudless. The landscape below us was arrayed with subtle shades of ocher, gray, and evergreen. Slender plumes of smoke from the farms all around, from bread ovens and burning piles of leaves, rose straight into the air like white pillars. From the valley below, the lowing of the animals and the calling of slaves carried across the crystalline air.

"Was there ever such a day as this in the city?" I said quietly.

"You have a point there," said Claudia, who looked down on the scene with a placid smile. "But your messenger said that you had something to show me."

"So I do, as soon as we've finished eating."

"I'm done," she said, popping her plump fingers into her

mouth to clean the morsels of honey cake. "Though you mustn't leave your apple half-eaten."

"We have more apples than we can eat."

"But it's such a waste!"

I laughed. "I shall feed it to the pigs on our way down."

"Down?"

"To the stream."

"Oh, Gordianus—are you going to show me the water mill?" She wore a strange expression.

"I am."

"I've seen you building it, you know. I can't help but notice it whenever I'm up here on the ridge. The building is quite handsome."

I shrugged. "It was made from bits of other buildings. It's no temple, but I suppose it doesn't pain the eye to look at it."

"It's charming!"

"Perhaps. More important is what's inside. The mechanism actually works."

"Then it's finished?"

"As finished as it can be, without a stream to move it."

We rose from our respective stumps and gathered up the slim remains of our meal. I glanced toward the Cassian Way, as I always did whenever I was leaving the ridgetop. I noticed two horsemen coming up from the south. There was nothing remarkable in that, but even so, I felt a bit uneasy as we stepped down the path, and I kept glancing toward the road even after the brush and trees had blocked it from view.

Claudia was quite impressed; indeed, her enthusiasm was so extreme as to appear a bit forced, especially considering that she seemed to have no understanding of the mechanism at all. She asked the purpose of this gear and that shaft in such a way that it was clear that no explanation would suffice. When I summoned slaves to push the wheel and set the grinding blocks in motion, she gave a start and her smile cracked. "Oh, dear!" she said. "Like horrible, huge, gnashing teeth! Like being in a Titan's jaw!" Deep down she did not like the mill very much, I thought, and she felt uncomfortable being near it. I ascribed this to her class and its deep conservatism, which, distrusts all innovations, whether social or mechanical.

Her cousin Publius had put it quite eloquently when I had told him that the mill could be to his benefit: "What would I want it for? I have slaves to grind my meal!" I had hoped Claudia would be more receptive, but in some ways she was no different from her cousins.

The gears were in full motion when a voice called out, "Magnificent, Papa!"

I turned and saw Eco standing in the doorway, with Belbo behind him—the two riders I had seen on the highway.

I laughed in happy surprise and stepped forward to embrace Eco. Meanwhile the slaves ceased their labor and the gears ground slowly to a halt. Claudia smiled crookedly, then jumped as one of the gears made a loud popping noise.

"It's nothing," I said, but the only way to calm her was to get her out of the mill house. I ushered everyone out the door and onto the rocky stream bank. Eco wanted to see the mechanism demonstrated again, but I nodded discreetly toward Claudia to indicate that we should defer to our guest. "Perhaps later," I said. "Drive the slaves too hard and one of them is likely to injure himself."

"But how did you solve the problems you were having? Don't tell me: inspiration came to you in a dream! Just as it has so many times when you've been faced with a mystery that seemed to have no answer."

"Not this time. As a matter of fact, a mutual acquaintance suggested the solution."

"An acquaintance?"

"An occasional guest." I indicated Claudia with a twitch of my jaw.

"Ah!" Eco understood the need for secrecy and nodded. "That man from the city."

"The very one. But we mustn't ignore today's guest," I said. Eco acknowledged Claudia with a bow of his head.

"Oh, Eco, how lovely to see you," crooned Claudia. Our brief conversation had give her time to recover her composure. "What news from the city?"

"Actually . . ." Eco looked uncertain. I could tell in a glance that news from the city was precisely the reason he had come to visit me, but what he had to say was not for other ears. He blinked and I saw that he had quickly calculated how much he could say without saying too much. "Actually, that's why I'm here. The atmosphere has been tense and unsettled in Rome all summer—as I suppose you must already know."

"Oh, yes, my cousins have been predicting trouble ever since the election," said Claudia.

"Then your cousins could find work as soothsayers," said Eco. It was a facetious comment, but Claudia was not amused. The mill had set her on edge.

"There's talk in the city of armed revolution," he went on. "Cicero has gotten the Senate to vote him emergency powers—what they call the Extreme Decree in Defense of the State."

"Ah, yes, the decree our ancestors created sixty years ago to get rid of that rabble-rouser Gaius Gracchus," said Claudia with a bit of relish.

I nodded gravely. "Gaius Gracchus was killed by a mob in the street while the laws against murder were temporarily suspended. Is that what they're planning for Catilina?"

"Nobody knows," said Eco. "The decree is vague. Essentially it gives the consuls powers over life and death that would otherwise have to be granted by the people's Assembly—power to raise an army and send it to battle, and the right to apply what they call unlimited force against citizens in order to protect the state."

"In other words, the Optimates in the Senate have circumvented any moderating influence that might have been wielded by the people's Assembly," I said.

"And why not?" said Claudia. "When the state's security is threatened, there must be recourse to extreme decrees. It's only a pity that such power should fall to a New Man like Cicero, who hardly deserves the honor and whose family background could scarcely have prepared him for the responsibility."

"However that may be," said Eco, "everyone knows Cicero's fellow consul Antonius is useless. If anything, he's in sympathy with Catilina. Which means everything falls on Cicero's shoulders."

"Or into his lap," I said.

Eco nodded. "At this moment, in theory at least, Cicero

has more power than any man since Sulla was dictator."

"Then Cicero finally has what he wants," I said. "Sole ruler of Rome!"

"Well, if he can rid us of Catilina once and for all, then he deserves the post," said Claudia. "What other news, Eco?"

"Rumors of war. Catilina's general, Manlius, has openly mobilized his troops up in Faesulae. There's also talk of slave revolts, instigated by Catilina, of course. One in Apulia, another in Capua—"

"Capua? Where Spartacus started his uprising!" said Claudia, her eyes widening.

Eco nodded. "All gladiatorial schools throughout Italy have been ordered to lock away their weapons and disperse their gladiators to other farms in chains. That was one of Cicero's first acts under the Extreme Decree."

"To stir up memories of Spartacus!" I said ruefully. It was a clever move, to keep the people frightened and to solidify his support. The terror and chaos of the Spartacan revolt was fresh in everyone's memory. Thus, in a time of declared crisis, who could possibly be against breaking up the gladiator schools—even if they were in no way involved, and the only reason to draw attention to them at all was to stir up panic? At the same time, the association served to identify the impeccably patrician Catilina with a rebellious Thracian slave. I began to see what Catilina meant when he spoke of Cicero and his thunderbolts.

"Meanwhile, charges have been brought against Catilina."

"Again? What sort of charges?" I said.

"Something more serious than bribery or embezzlement. One of the Optimates has indicted him under the Plautian Law against political violence."

"And Catilina's response?"

"Uncharacteristically meek. He's voluntarily placed himself under house arrest at the home of a friend. That means he won't be leaving Rome." Eco looked at me meaningfully.

"Good," I said, automatically, as one shakes one's hands after washing them. The news disturbed me more than I cared to admit, but my own involvement might at last be over.

"Good!" echoed Claudia. "Perhaps the whole matter can be settled without bloodshed. If Catilina can be tried and sent

into exile, maybe his band of rabble will dissolve back into
the mud. Cut off the head and the body withers!"

"Odd," I said. "I was thinking of the same metaphor."

Claudia left us shortly afterward, saying she would have to
share the news with her cousins and learn if they had news
of their own. Once we were alone, at his insistence, I showed
Eco the mechanism of the water mill, but it seemed to me
that the intricacies of what was happening in Rome were far
more complex and, in spite of my aversion, fascinating.

That night, after dinner, we gathered in the atrium. The
night was cool, but the sky was clear. At the turning of the
seasons the fountain had been drained and a brazier put in its
place. We sat in a circle around the fire. Meto joined us. I
had made a point of asking him to stay and listen, but it had
not been appreciated; the look on his face indicated that he
found my efforts to include him merely condescending. Bethesda joined us after putting Diana to bed. The mood of
impending crisis had penetrated even her catlike composure
to pique her curiosity.

"This is the situation," said Eco. "The Senate is raising an
army to send against Manlius up in Faesulae, to join battle in
Etruria or at least to keep Manlius from marching on Rome.
In Rome the garrison has been put on alert, with extra night
watches set all over the city. Catilina is under house arrest,
but his fellow conspirators are all free; Cicero has no evidence
against them. There may or may not be an uprising in the
city. There may or may not be a battle or several battles
between the Senate's forces and those of Manlius. There may
or may not be other uprisings elsewhere in Italy."

"Is the Senate really in danger?" said Meto.

He asked the question of Eco and seemed disappointed
when Eco deferred to me. "Everywhere in Italy there is poverty, indebtedness, and forced enslavement due to bank-
ruptcy," I said. "Our family has been favored by Fortune, not
to mention the will of Lucius Claudius, to rise rather than fall
in the world at such a time, but all around us simple citizens
starve, while proud nobles find themselves dispossessed and
unable to rise again. The few possess great wealth and power,
which they dispense in stingy increments to the many who

struggle to survive. The corruption of those in power is naked for all to see. Men long for change, and know that they will never have it so long as the Optimates maintain their unshakable grip on the Senate. Can Catilina and his allies ignite a general revolution? Obviously the Senate believes it is possible, or else they would never have voted the Extreme Decree to give the consul extraordinary powers." I spread my hands before the flames. "How Cicero must relish the grave honor his colleagues have bestowed upon him! Was their gesture of faith in him spontaneous, I wonder, or did Cicero pull a few strings to manage the vote?"

"Yes, Papa," admitted Eco, flinching at the sarcasm in my voice, "you can be sure that Cicero lobbied hard for the passage of the Extreme Decree. The cooperation of the Senate was helped along by the anonymous letters that Cicero introduced into the debate."

"Letters? You haven't mentioned these before."

"No? I suppose I was watching my tongue around Claudia. On the evening before Cicero requested that the Senate pass the Extreme Decree, he was paid a visit by several distinguished citizens, among them Crassus. They came knocking on his door at midnight, demanding that his slaves rouse Cicero from his bed. It seems that each of these men had received anonymous letters that night, warning of impending bloodshed."

"How did these letters arrive?"

"By a messenger whose face was hidden. He handed the rolled letters to the doorkeepers and departed without a word. The letter to Crassus addressed him by name, but was unsigned. It read: 'In a few days all the rich and powerful men of Rome shall be slaughtered. Flee while you can! This warning is a favor to you, from a friend. Do not ignore it.' "

"And Crassus brought this letter to Cicero?"

"Yes, as did several others who had received them the same night. Well, you can see that such a letter put Crassus in a compromising position. He's under suspicion already for his past associations with Catilina as well as his own shady political dealings. There are those who think he's a part of this conspiracy, perhaps even one of the powers behind it. To avert suspicion, he brought the letter to Cicero at once, dis-

avowing any knowledge of its origin or the impending bloodshed of which it gave warning."

"But these letters were unsigned?"

"Anonymous, yes. Of course everyone assumes they came
from someone close to Catilina."

"Which is exactly what they're meant to assume."

"But who else could have sent them?" said Eco.

"Who, indeed? Who would stand to profit by stirring up
panic among the powerful, while at the same time ascertain-
ing the position of a man like Crassus? And it was largely
due to this incident that Cicero was able to convince the Senate to pass the Extreme Decree?"

"That, along with word that Manlius was about to put his
army into the field."

"Knowledge of which came from—"

"From Cicero and his informers. And of course there were
the rumors of planned slave uprisings—"

"Rumors, you say, not reports?"

Eco looked into the fire for a long moment. "Papa, are you
arguing that Cicero might have sent those anonymous letters
himself? That he's creating a panic on purpose?"

"I make no argument. I merely posit questions and
doubts—like the consul himself."

THIRTY-TWO

OCTOBER ended with gusty winds from the north and a
lowering pearl-gray sky. The Kalends of November dawned
cold and bleak, with streaks of rain that never amounted to a
storm, but seemed to fall from the sky one at a time, like
tears, with all the niggardliness of the gods when they deign
to weep.

So it continued until the eighth day of November. Twilight
dawned and the day never grew brighter. A mass of roiling
black clouds gathered to the north. High winds swept through
the valley. The animals were gathered into the stable. The

Cassian Way was almost deserted, except for a few shivering bands of slaves driven by men on horseback.

Except for a few excursions to look after the beasts and make sure that doors had been secured and loose implements had been put away, everyone stayed indoors. Diana was bored and out of sorts; when the thunder came, it frightened her and made her even more intractable. Her mother was endlessly understanding and comforting—with Diana. With everyone else she was in a foul mood all day.

Meto shut himself away in his narrow little room. I walked in on him unannounced and saw a scroll of Thucydides open on a table and his metal soldiers spread on the floor in battle array. When I smiled and asked what combat he was reenacting, he acted embarrassed and resentful and pushed the soldiers against the wall.

The least good fortune that such a miserable day could bring would be a skyful of rain, I thought. All through the day I stepped from time to time into the little walled garden off my library to watch the sky. Beginning at a point halfway to the peak, Mount Argentum was lost in a hazy black mantle of clouds, lit now and again with glowing bolts of lightning. It must have been raining madly up on the mountain, but down in the valley there were only wind and darkness.

The rain finally began after sundown, if indeed there was a sundown on such a day when the sun had never shown itself. It began with a quiet pelting against the tiled roof, then grew to a steady torrent. We discovered a few new leaks in the roof; with all the relish of a general too long away from battle, Bethesda sent the kitchen slaves to fetch pots and pans to catch the dribbles. Diana abruptly recovered her good spirits; she opened a shuttered window and gazed out at the rain with squealing delight. Even Meto's mood was lightened. He came into my study to return the scroll of Thucydides, and we talked for a while about the Spartans and the Persians. I said a quiet prayer of gratitude to the gods for opening the sky at last.

Having been restless and kept indoors all day, we were wide-awake that night. We had been smelling the scent of Congrio's cooking all day and received the meal with enthusiasm. Afterward I asked Meto to read to us aloud. Herodotus, with his accounts of strange lands and customs, seemed a good choice.

The hour grew later and later, but no one seemed inclined to sleep. The rain poured down.

I had set a watchman that night, as I did every night. Unable to post himself on the roof of the stable, his place was in the loft, where he could keep watch from the little shuttered windows. He, too, was wakeful that night. When the men turned off the Cassian Way and rode toward the farm, he saw them.

Above the din of the rain, no one heard the banging on the door. It was only when the slave began to shout and struggle with the latch, knocking the doors against the bar, that we noticed the commotion. Bethesda was apprehensive at once; a few bad experiences in Rome had made her wary of nocturnal visitors. Her agitation communicated itself to Diana, who squirmed on her lap. Meto set down the scroll and rushed with me to the atrium. We kept beneath the colonnade to avoid the pelting rain. I opened the peephole and looked out.

The slave was pointing wildly toward the highway and shouting. The rain suddenly came down in a rush, and I couldn't make out a single word.

We unbarred the door. The slave rushed in, soaked with rain, his bedraggled hair streaming. "Men!" he said hoarsely. "Coming from the highway! A whole army of them on horseback!"

He exaggerated. Thirty men do not make an army, but they do make an intimidating sight when seen rushing toward you in the darkness, wrapped in black cloaks. The pounding hooves joined the din of the rain and rose above it, like a constant peal of thunder drawing closer. The horsemen were less than a hundred feet away.

"Catilina?" shouted Meto.

"I can't tell," I said.

"Papa, should we bar the doors?"

I nodded and pulled the rain-sodden slave inside. We slammed the door and dropped the bar. Toward what end, I wasn't sure. It was meant to keep out sneak thieves and burglars, not an armed force. Armed men could easily force the doors to the library or the kitchen. But it would buy us time to find out who they were and what they wanted. At the other end of the atrium, beyond the curtain of rain, I saw Bethesda standing erect with Diana in her arms, both of them staring back with huge eyes.

The banging at the door came so swiftly and so loudly that I bolted backward and almost tripped. Meto seized my elbow and steadied me. I pressed my eye to the peephole.

"Catilina?" whispered Meto.

"I don't think so." I could hardly see their faces for the darkness and the shadow of their cowls. The man at the door banged again, not with his fist but with something hard that resonated through the wood—the pommel of a dagger.

"Escaped slaves?" said Meto. I turned my head and saw that he was looking at me with fear in his eyes. I put my hand on his shoulder and drew him closer to me. What had I done, to bring my family to such a place? In the city one might always hope to flee, to raise a call to neighbors, to hide amid the jumble of walls and rooftops. The farmhouse and the fields around it suddenly seemed to me a very naked place, open and indefensible. I had my slaves, but what protection were they against a band of armed horsemen?

The banging resumed. I put my mouth to the peephole. "Who are you? What do you want?"

One of the men who remained on horseback, the leader, I supposed, gestured to the man at the door to stop his banging. "We want the man you're hiding here!" he shouted.

"What man? Whom do you want?" I felt a stab of relief. It was all some bizarre mistake, I thought.

"Catilina!" the man shouted. "Bring him to us!"

"Papa?" Meto looked at me, confused.

I shook my head. "Catilina isn't here," I shouted.

"Catilina *is* here!"

"Papa, what is he talking about?"

"I don't know." I looked at Bethesda, who stood as stiff as a statue while Diana clung to her neck and hid her face. I put my mouth to the peephole. "Who sent you?"

In answer the banging began again. From somewhere outside I heard shouting and screams. I looked through the peephole. Beyond the men on horseback, I saw a confusion of cloaked figures running in and out of the stable.

In the next instant I heard a crashing noise of splintered wood from within the house. I swung around. Bethesda looked toward the hallway to the library and screamed. She clutched Diana more closely to her breast, while Diana struggled in a panic. The men were within the house.

I ran through the atrium, knocking over the brazier. Bethesda clutched at me, and Meto pressed against my back. Aratus appeared from somewhere, his face a mask of confusion and fear. There was another crash from the kitchen, and Congrio came running toward the center of the house, bellowing in fright.

A bolt of lightning splintered just above the house, casting everything into stark light and shadow. The thunderbolt followed without a pause, a booming blast that seemed to shake the floor. It quieted into a crackling rumble that rolled around the house like a giant grinding stone. Above the din of the rain I heard the noise of tables overturned, the clatter of metal pans knocked across the floor, the crash of breaking pottery. From either side of us, men poured into the atrium, bearing long daggers in their fists. We shrank back while they rushed to the front doors, unbolted them, and swung them open.

The leader jumped down from his horse. Mud and water splashed about his feet. He drew his dagger and came toward the house, taking high steps to pull his feet clear of the sucking mud. He was so tall that he had to stoop to enter the doorway.

He walked past the overturned brazier, kicking it out of his way. "Gordianus the Finder?" he said, shouting to make himself heard above the rain and the continual crashing and clatter inside the house. Diana began to wail.

I stood as tall as I could and pulled Bethesda closer. Meto moved from behind me to stand by my side. "I am Gordianus," I said. "Who are you, and what do you want?"

Because of his cowl I could see only the lower half of his face. He grinned broadly. "We want the wily fox we've run to earth. Where is he?"

"If you mean Catilina, he isn't here," said Meto, his voice cracking slightly.

"Don't lie to me, little boy."

"I'm not a boy!"

The man laughed. I recognized the laugh, if not the man; it was the laughter of exhilaration that comes when men give themselves over to pillage and plunder, the cruel, barking laughter that comes at the climax of a chase or in the thick of battle. It turned my heart to ice.

Men continued to swirl around us, their daggers flashing amid the glinting raindrops. A few had pushed back their hoods. They were mostly young and clean-shaven, with glittering eyes and tightly pressed lips. A few faces were vaguely familiar. Where had I seen them before?

Meto pressed his lips to my ear. "Cicero's bodyguards!" he hissed. "That day in the Forum—"

"What are you whispering about?" the man bellowed. "Where have you hidden him?"

"Catilina isn't here," I said.

"Nonsense! We know this place is his refuge. We've followed him all the way from Rome. The fool thought he could slip away unseen! We've come to take him back—one way or another."

"He isn't here. Not in the house, anyway. Perhaps the stable—"

"We've already searched the stable! Now hand him over!"

One of his companions ran up and spoke in his ear.

"Impossible!" he shouted. "They're hiding him somewhere."

"But there were at least ten men in his party," said the other in a strained voice. "They couldn't hide ten men and ten horses in a house like this—"

"Ten men and nine horses," said the leader. "You forget the one we found riderless on the road." He turned toward me. "For hours we've chased him. He had a good lead when we started, but soon we were nipping at his heels. Never mind that the night's as black as pitch and as wet as a lake. Up the road a bit there was a break in the clouds, just one tiny hole, and we caught a glimpse of them under starlight ahead of us, like ants in the pass between the mountain and the ridge. Then the hole in the sky closed and blackness swallowed them. By the time we caught up with them, they'd vanished—except for a lone horse, wandering on the road without a rider. Was it Catilina he threw? Is that why they stopped here, thinking they'd be safe and we would pass them by? Where is he? Hand him over!"

The man was shouting, but the desperation in his voice made me feel safer than when he had laughed. He was no longer a huntsman caught up in the ecstasy of the kill, liable to do anything; he was a bedraggled, drenched pursuer whose game had eluded him. He was furious, but also miserable. Weariness was catching up with him.

It was his weariness I sought to play on, echoing it with my own voice. "Catilina never stopped here tonight. Don't you think I'd tell you if he had? Have I not been as loyal to the consul as you have? If you know my name, and if you also know that Catilina has taken refuge here in the past, then you must also know the part I've played for Cicero. What will he think when he learns of the mess you've made of my home, of the fright you've given my family? Catilina isn't here, I tell you! We haven't seen his face for many days. He's given you the slip. If you hope to catch him, you'd better set out on the Cassian Way at once."

The man stamped his feet and shook—with rage, I thought, then realized he was shivering from the cold. He pushed back his cowl and roughed his sopping hair with his hands. Despite his height, he was quite young.

The tumult in the house had gradually quieted. The party of men began to gather around us in the atrium, waiting for whatever was to come next.

The leader looked at me from under his brows. "Catilina's henchmen tried to murder the consul yesterday morning. They came to Cicero's house at daybreak, pretending to make a social call, thinking they could fool the slaves into letting them inside and then fall on him with daggers. But the consul was warned ahead of time and wouldn't let them in."

If only I could be so lucky at keeping armed men out of my house, I thought, but bit my tongue.

"Today Cicero convened the Senate in the Temple of Jupiter and exposed all the details of Catilina's crimes against the state—such a speech, they say, it threatened to shake the temple apart! Catilina huddled in a corner with his confederates while every senator with a shred of patriotism shunned him. Whenever he tried to speak, they shouted him down. He saw the fate in store for him. Tonight the scared rabbit bounded from his hole."

"You called him a fox before," grumbled Meto, as surly to the stranger as he had ever been to me. I sucked in a breath and held it.

"Did I? Well, no matter. He'll be skinned soon enough, and a rabbit's pelt is as fine as a fox's." He turned to his companion. "You searched all the buildings? Circled the pens?"

The man nodded. "No sign of them, not even fresh hoofprints in the mud."

The man pulled the hood over his head again and gestured for the others to return to their horses. "Quickly!" he said.

He pulled his cloak around him and looked at me gravely. "If Catilina should return, give him no more food and shelter. The time for pretenses is over. Catilina is as good as dead, and so are all his followers. No one could have said it more eloquently than Cicero did today to the Senate, right in front of Catilina: 'The time of punishment is at hand. Alive or dead, we will set them aflame upon the altar of the gods, in retribution without end!' "

"No, no, no!" said Bethesda. "You are not going out, either of you! Are you mad?"

Shortly after the men had left, and once we could see that they had turned onto the Cassian Way heading north, Meto and I began to get ready to go out into the night. We were of one mind and one intent, and had both come to the same conclusion without speaking of it; it felt good to be in accord with my son again. That good feeling went a long way toward mollifying the shock of what had just happened.

Bethesda, however, was not mollified. She stood with her hand on Diana's shoulder, pressing the child against her. "Take off that heavy tunic, husband! Meto, put away that cloak! Where do you think you're going?"

"If Catilina and his party were seen at the pass between the ridge and the mountain—" said Meto, ignoring her.

"Then suddenly vanished—" I said.

"And then one of their horses was found riderless—"

"They must have taken refuge somewhere off the road."

"That open space concealed behind the big rock—would it be large enough to conceal nine horses?" said Meto.

"I think so. We'll know soon enough."

"You cannot invite him to come here!" said Bethesda firmly. "What if his pursuers give up the chase and turn back? If they should return and find him here—you heard what the man said: give him no more food and shelter. Think of your daughter!" She pressed Diana more tightly to her.

"Food!" said Meto. "I almost forgot. What can we take to them?"

"I forbid it!" said Bethesda.

"Wife, think of handsome Catilina and the beautiful Tongilius. Would you have them wither to skin and bones for want of a few bites from Congrio's kitchen?"

Apparently my facetiousness struck the right note. Bethesda wavered and softened. "We have some bread that was baked this morning," she said begrudgingly. "And there are plenty of apples—"

"I'll fetch them," said Meto.

Bethesda pursed her lips. "The men will be cold and wet. A dry blanket or two . . ."

"There are blankets on our bed," I said.

"Not those! We have others that are worn and need mending. Here, I'll get them myself."

And so Bethesda was suborned into helping with our mission.

We avoided the open road that went out to the Cassian Way, and cut across fields and orchards instead. The ground was muddy and grew rocky and uneven along the foot of the ridge. I feared that one of our horses might stumble in the muck and break a leg, but we reached the highway without mishap. The hard, flat paving stones of the Cassian Way, spangled with falling raindrops, clattered beneath the horses' hooves. There is nothing so well made and impervious to the elements as a good Roman road.

We made our way to the trailhead we had found before. I had thought it might be impossible to find it amid the dark, dripping underbrush, but we rode straight to it, so easily that I thought the hand of a god must have guided us. We dismounted and slid between the trunk of the oak and the great boulder, not without difficulty, for a bundle of apples and bread was strapped to Meto's back and a bulky roll of blankets was strapped to mine. We pulled our horses after us. As I had expected, the little clearing beyond, hidden from the highway, was filled with horses tethered to tree trunks, rocks, and branches.

There was a burst of lightning. The bright white glare pierced the naked branches and shone like flames in the horses' eyes. They snorted, jostled one another, stamped their hooves. The thunder pealed above us. The horses threw back their head and whinnied.

I counted them. There were nine.

The floor of the little clearing was stony, and instead of turning to a morass of mud it had become a veritable pond. The horses stood in water above their hooves. My own feet were completely submerged. The reason for so much water was clear enough. The broken path that led up the mountainside had become a runnel. I looked at the rushing water and the mud and rocks on either side of the sluice and shook my head. "Impassable," I said.

"But Catilina and his men must have hiked up it," said Meto.

"We're burdened with these heavy apples and cumbersome blankets—"

Meto adjusted the load strapped to his back and leaped up the steep, watery path, as surefooted as a fawn. "Come on, Papa! It's not as hard as it looks."

"Old bones break more easily than young ones," I grumbled. "And old feet have a harder time finding their balance." But I was talking to myself, for Meto had disappeared ahead of me. I raised my knees and put one foot ahead of the other, trying to negotiate a safe way up the slippery rocks and sliding mud.

What had I been thinking when I set out? The answer was simple: I had not been thinking at all. The excitement of the assault on my house had rattled my mind. The elation of not being murdered in my home had blotted out all memory of the agony of my previous ascent up the old pathway. If it had been difficult before—overgrown, rugged, absurdly steep—it

was made twice as difficult by the rain, and the burdens we
carried doubled the difficulty again. My heard pounded. My
feet turned to lead—not only heavy and unresponsive, but
clumsy, slipping on loosened pebbles and sliding on treacherous mud. I began to realize that the ascent was not only
strenuous but perilous. It was a very real possibility that I
could slip and fall down the runnel out of control for a very
long way. If I broke my back, would Bethesda be scolding
or sympathetic?

The descent would be even more dangerous, I realized,
then pushed the thought from my mind. Meanwhile, Meto
scurried ahead of me, as agile as a goat and as impervious to
the water as a duck.

At last we came to the first opening, where the path joined
with the last of the road from Gnaeus's house, and a footpath
continued up the mountain. The muddy open space was well-
trampled, offering evidence of Catilina's passage.

I shrugged and stretched my shoulders, which ached from
the strain of the blankets and the climb. "The question now,"
I said, "is whether he turned right or left."

Meto was taken aback. "Right, of course, up to the mine."

"Do you think so? A secret connection between Gnaeus
and Catilina might begin to explain a few things. The murder
of Forfex, for example."

"How could there be a link?"

"I don't know, and I'm too cold and wet and tired to think
it through. But what if Catilina eluded his pursuers, not with
the point of reaching the cave, but making his way to
Gnaeus's house unseen?"

Meto shook his head. I thought that he rolled his eyes as
well, but in the darkness I couldn't be sure.

He appeared to be correct, however, and my suspicions
were unfounded, for on the road that led to Gnaeus's house
there were no signs of footsteps in the mud. We turned back
and headed up the path to the mine.

We heard the roar of the waterfall long before we came to
it. A glimpse of the cascade through the trees showed that the
stream was greatly swollen. The stone steps leading upward,
sharp-edged and slick with rain, were like a treacherous test
posed by an ill-humored god. With the blankets strapped to

my back, I had to take each step as slowly and cautiously as an old cripple.

Meto reached the top long before I did. I finally took the last step and came up behind him. When he looked back at me, for the first time that night I saw a flicker of doubt in his eyes.

The prospect was enough to make any man quail. The streambed, which had been almost dry when we had crossed it before, was a rushing torrent of water, thigh-deep. Only a few feet to our left, it reached the falls and poured over the precipice with a hollow roar.

Meto stared at the stream and bit his lip.

I have always had an aversion to water. I am a poor swimmer. Once, down at Cumae, I had a nasty experience trying to negotiate my way into a sea cave. I would prefer a trial by fire to a trial by water any day. But on this night I had no choice.

For once, while Meto hung back, I stepped forward.

"Papa, be careful!"

His advice was well given. The stream pulled at my ankles. The stone bed, carved by rushing water, was smooth and sinuous, marked by deep pockets and abrupt ridges. I moved forward, feeling the way with my feet.

"Here, Meto, take my hand."

He stayed on the bank, looking at me dubiously.

"Here, we'll be stronger if we cross together."

He hesitated. I saw that he was not doubtful of my judgment but of his own courage.

Perhaps we should turn back, I thought, looking into the black, rushing water pocked with raindrops. We had begun the journey on an impulse. A reaction against Cicero's brutish bodyguards had driven us toward Catilina, for no real purpose. We owed him nothing; we were not obliged to bring him blankets and food, certainly not at the peril of our own lives. And yet Meto and I had both, without question, made the decision to set out. I had endured the misery and danger of the ascent, and I was loath to turn back now.

I held out my hand to Meto, half-wishing he would refuse to take it. If he came to harm, I would never be able to bear it. He hesitated a moment longer, then gripped my wrist and stepped into the cold water.

We crossed at a diagonal, cutting against the flow. I felt the way with my feet and warned him of each irregularity. Midway across, the flow suddenly became more powerful, and I staggered a bit. Meto tightened his grip. I stared at the slick, black face of the stream, thinking that my lifelong apprehension about water must have been a message from the Fates. They had seen into the future and knew that my end would come from water, and so they had given me a fear of it as fair warning. My heart beat very fast.

Something struck my leg. I looked down and saw a skull, washed down from the mountainside. It spun about for a moment, trapped in an eddy made by my leg, then was caught by the rushing stream. I watched it bob madly on the water and then go plummeting over the falls.

"Papa!" said Meto anxiously.

My feet had become heavier than ever. I was tired, I told myself, but in fact my feet felt rooted to the spot, as if they had melded with the stone. I swallowed hard and struggled to move my toes. At last my foot lifted and crept along the rock, like a timid fish.

Somehow, at last, we gained the other side. Meto loosened his grip on my wrist, but not before I felt the trembling in his fingers. My hands were shaking, too.

While we were crossing the stream, I had forgotten the rain and the cold, but once we were safe I felt the full measure of my misery. I was weary, wet and shivering. And there was still a long, steep ascent before us. But there was no turning back; I would not cross the stream again until I had to.

We pressed on and came to the switchbacks. Up and up we trudged, doubling back and forth as we gained the ascent. At last we came to the long uphill slope that wended back into a hidden fold in the mountainside. Here the rain diminished to a drizzle, and our footsteps made a grating noise on the loosened pebbles. As we approached the opening to the mine, so hidden in darkness that I could only guess at it, I whispered to Meto to quiet his footsteps.

But the warning was too late.

THIRTY-THREE

IT is a peculiar experience to see a spear come hurtling out of the darkness, heading straight for a spot on the bridge of your nose midway between your eyes. One does not even apprehend the approaching object as a spear—the angle does not permit it, for one sees only a sparkling, whirling point illuminated by a flicker of starlight piercing the shredded clouds. And yet one knows enough to duck—at once!

As I dropped to my knees, I could see that it was indeed a spear—I glimpsed both the sharpened tip and the long shaft behind it. It made a shrill, whistling noise as it passed over my head, followed by a low thud. Something seemed to strike my back with a jarring, shuddering blow; I could make no sense of it. Beside me, Meto shrieked. My heart, completely frozen, suddenly gave a jolt and started beating again. I thought he had been struck, then caught a glimpse of his face and saw his fear was all for me. We dropped to our knees together and scrambled toward the low scrub. The bushes trembled wildly at our assault and pelted us with raindrops.

I tried to change direction and swung around, only to find that I was entangled somehow in the bushes. It made no sense, until I realized the spear had pierced the roll of blankets strapped to my back and was stuck fast, its shaft pointing above my head.

I was as good as wounded, unable to maneuver. Meto lurched beside me, trying awkwardly to get a grip on the spear, still thinking that I was hurt.

"Friends!" I called, hoping the word could travel faster than the next spear.

There was a moment of silence, then a flash of lightning cracked open the sky and struck the mountainside. By the garish glare I saw the spearman, crouching on a shielded crag of rock above the entrance to the mine, his arm poised to hurl a second shaft. Below him, at the mouth of the mine itself, stood Catilina. His arm was raised, his mouth open.

"Stop!" he shouted.

The lightning died and the world turned black. I flinched. The command had come too late, I thought. The spear was already on its way. Not even Catilina, with all his cleverness, could snatch a spear from its flight.

A huge, booming peal of thunder jolted the mountainside, so overwhelming that I could not tell if I was struck by the spear or not. I huddled, hands over my head. A moment later a hand touched my shoulder. I looked up. Distant lightning cast a pale, flickering light across the smiling face of Catilina.

"Gordianus! You look a fright," he said gently. "Come in out of the rain."

On the other side of the wall that had been built to keep out goats and children, the interior of the mine was dark. A small fire had been kindled, but most of its light seemed to be swallowed up by jealous shadows. This was their kingdom, and the light was an intruder.

Catilina crouched and warmed his hands over the flames. "Fortunately, we were able to find some scraps of wood. When we run out, I wouldn't advise pulling down any supports for firewood, though; the roof might fall in on us. The smoke presents no problem—whoever built the mine was smart enough to drill narrow shafts for ventilation. Crassus was a fool to pass up this property. I told him it was well worth the investment. But he said he'd dealt with this branch of the Claudii before and didn't care to deal with them ever again." He stared into the flames. "Well, what more is there to say about Crassus? He has abandoned me now."

"Look, Lucius, they've brought bread," said Tongilius, crouching down beside him. "And apples—we can spit them and roast them over the fire for something hot to eat! And a roll of blankets. The inner ones are almost dry."

The others in Catilina's party hung back in the shadows. Some were men I had seen before, when they had stayed in my stable overnight. Others were strangers. Some appeared to doze, while the open eyes of their companions glinted in the firelight. They looked older than Meto, but considerably younger than Catilina or myself. All were heavily armed.

They took turns keeping watch outside the mine.

"I don't think you're in any danger of being discovered, at least not tonight," I said. "No goatherds are out on a night like this, and the men who pursued you from Rome are gone. After they ransacked my house looking for you, they moved on, heading north."

"Unless they followed you here," said Catilina. There was no accusation or suspicion in his voice, only a pragmatic shrug. "I haven't come this far to be slain in a hole by Cicero's bodyguards, not if I can help it. As long as we're here, we'll keep watch."

Tongilius handed him an apple spitted on a spear. Catilina smiled. "Food! Blankets! Did you bring a tub of hot water with you as well?"

"Would you believe that I forgot?"

"By Hercules, too bad! How delicious it would be on such a night to settle down into a steaming tub with you and while away the hours till dawn."

Meto brightened. "We could go back to the house—"

I stiffened. Catilina noticed and shook his head. "That would be neither practical nor safe, Meto. Too dangerous for you and your family. Too dangerous for me, as well. No, I think I can never go back to your house now, not until this crisis is settled. I wonder how they knew to look for me there? Do you think Marcus Caelius betrayed me?"

He saw the look on my face, then looked at Meto, whose guilty expression was even more pronounced. Catilina pursed his lips and a shadow of doubt crossed his face. "It was Caelius, then. It must have been. But you didn't betray me to the men pursuing me; you guessed that I was here, but you didn't tell. Did you?" He looked uneasily toward the mouth of the mine.

"No, Catilina. We came here in secret."

He sighed and studied the flames that danced beneath his spitted apple. "Forgive me. These last few days have dealt me quite a blow. Men whom I thought my friends have turned their backs on me. Men whom I never thought to fear have wished me dead to my face. Cicero! May his eyes rot!"

"May his tongue turn black!" said Tongilius, with a vehemence I had never seen in him before. He picked up one of the apples and hurled it against a nearby wall, where it exploded against the stone.

"His tongue is already black," said Catilina, "as we know from having heard the offal that flowed from his mouth today."

"Then let it be eaten by worms!" shouted Tongilius, who clenched his fists and began to pace. There was not room enough for his anger; after a moment he went to the wall and pulled himself over with a single bound.

"The rain will cool him off," said Catilina, whose eyes had never left the fire.

"My son Eco was here a few days ago," I said. "He told me that you were under voluntary house arrest, pending charges under the Plautian Law. Why have you left Rome? What has happened?"

Catilina raised his eyes from the fire. By some trick of the flames his face appeared to be both amused and grim. "The world has come apart at its seams and is quickly unraveling."

"Another riddle?"

"No. For you, Gordianus, I shall bite my tongue and speak without devices. Your son Eco told you that I was under house arrest. What else did he tell you?"

"That Cicero persuaded the Senate to pass something called the Extreme Decree in Defense of the State."

"Yes, the same tool their grandfathers used to get rid of Gaius Gracchus. I suppose I should be flattered. Of course, every bit of evidence that Cicero put forward was fabricated."

"How?"

"He told them I planned to massacre half the Senate on the twenty-eighth day of October. For proof he brought forth anonymous letters that had been received by certain parties warning them to flee the city. What sort of proof is that? Do you know who I think wrote those letters? Cicero's oh-so-clever secretary, Tiro, taking dictation from his master. The vile little toad."

"Speak no ill of Tiro to me, Catilina. I have fond memories of him, from the days when he helped me investigate the case of Sextus Roscius."

"That was years ago! Since then he's grown as corrupt as

his master. Slaves follow the course of the man who owns them, you know that."

"Never mind; you say the letters originated with Cicero himself."

"Do you think *I* wrote them? Or some hand-wringer among my supporters, wanting to secretly alert a few friends before I set loose a bloodbath? Nonsense! The whole concoction was devised by Cicero for two purposes: to create hysteria and fear among the senators, who are always ready to believe someone is out to murder them—as they should rightly fear—and to test those who received the anonymous letters. Crassus was among them. I had thought I could count on him—if not on his overt support, then at least on his discretion—but when presented with the opportunity to turn his back on me he took it. To keep himself out of trouble, to separate his fortunes from mine, he went directly to Cicero to report the warning in the letter. Surely he must have known it came from the consul himself! What a farce, the two of them playacting for the benefit of the Senate! How could a man as proud as Crassus allow Cicero to manipulate him in such a manner? Don't worry, he'll take his revenge on the New Man from Arpinum in his own way, sooner or later.

"To keep the senators in a state of hysteria, Cicero made more shocking revelations, all based on his supposedly infallible network of spies and informers. First he claimed that on a particular day—the twenty-seventh day of October—my colleague Manlius would take up arms in Faesulae. What of it? Manlius has been training the Sullan veterans for months, and there's nothing illegal in that. But sure enough, on the very day that Cicero had predicted, one of the senators reads aloud a letter that he's received, saying that Manlius and his soldiers have taken up arms and begun to fight. To fight whom, where? It's all nonsense, but Cicero nods sagely and the senators swallow hard. He predicted it, and it came true. The letter proves it. A *letter*, do you see? Another piece of Tiro's handiwork, taking dictation straight from Cicero's lips.

"And then came Cicero's outrageous accusation that I was planning a surprise attack on the town of Praeneste on the Kalends of November. To fend it off, Cicero called out the garrison of Rome—how convenient that Praeneste is so close to the south. No attack materialized; not surprising, since none was planned, and even if one had been planned, announcing knowledge of a secret attack ahead of time by definition prevents the possibility. Puffing himself up like a frog, the consul declares himself the savior of Praeneste—when the whole affair was a fantasy! What a mighty general, able to foresee and forestall attacks that were never to take place!

"No tactic is too low. He issued orders to break up the gladiator farms across Italy—as if I were the instigator of a slave uprising! He offered huge rewards to anyone who would come forward and betray the so-called conspiracy—for slaves, freedom and a hundred thousand sesterces; for free men, two hundred thousand sesterces and a full pardon! So far, no one has come forward to claim these glittering prizes. Such silence is merely proof of the fear these monsters inspire in their minions, says Cicero—ignoring the obvious point that there is no plot to betray!"

Catilina shook his head. "When one of his lackeys brought charges against me, using the Plautian Law, I thought it best to simply submit, to make a show of cooperation. My enemies have subjected me to so many spurious trials that one more hardly casts fear in my heart. Not that I didn't manage to have a bit of fun at Cicero's expense." Lit by the flames, I thought I saw a mischievous smile on his lips.

"What do you mean?"

"Why, I went straight to Cicero and offered to put myself into his custody! If I must be under house arrest, I said, let it be in the house of the consul himself—where else might I be more closely watched and kept from my nefarious plotting? What a quandary that posed for Cicero! If I was such an immediate menace, it would seem to be his duty to take me into custody; on the other hand, how could he continue to rant about my mad schemes if he had me safely under his own roof? It didn't suit his purpose, so he turned down my offer. Even so, he managed to twist matters to his own advantage. Not being safe in the same city with me, he said, how could he be safe having me in his house? I would murder him and his whole family if I had the chance, with my bare hands if I had to. Others turned down my offer as well, either because they were afraid to associate with me or were afraid for their lives. When I finally put myself into the charge of Marcus Metellus, as impartial a man as I could imagine, Cicero said I was merely taking refuge with one of my supporters. Poor Metellus! Now I've given him the slip, and everyone will think the worst of him."

"Why did you flee the city?" said Meto.

"Because today, before the Senate, Cicero said that he would see me dead—as bluntly as that! I have no reason to doubt him. I fled for my life."

"The men Cicero sent after you tell another story," I said. "They say you sent men to murder Cicero, yesterday morning."

"The men Cicero sent after me will murder *me* if they catch me!"

"But what they say—is it true?" said Meto.

"Another lie!" He heaved a weary sigh. "Cicero claims that two nights ago I slipped out of Metellus's house and attended a secret meeting where I hatched a plan to assassinate him. Supposedly two of my friends—Gaius Cornelius and Lucius Vargunteius—were to show up at his door, pretending to make a morning visit, get inside and stab him. As if either of them would commit such an act, without hope of escape or of being able to show just cause to the Senate! But Cicero is clever; in the middle of the night he sends for certain senators who still doubt his rantings. Come at once to my house, he tells them. What can it be, they wonder, to rouse us from our sleep? When they arrive, lamps are lit everywhere and the house is full of armed guards. You see how he sets the stage for exploiting their credulity by resorting to cheap melodrama? He tells them that an informant has just arrived with terrible information: Catilina and his conspirators have been meeting that very night at a house in the Street of the Scythemakers, plotting his murder. The agents will be Gaius Cornelius and Lucius Vargunteius, known associates of Catilina and notorious troublemakers. Just watch, he says, they will arrive in the morning, bent on bloodshed. You will be my witnesses.

"And lo, the next morning, Cornelius and Vargunteius duly arrive at Cicero's house. They bang on the door; the slaves refuse to admit them. They bang more, demanding to see the consul. The slaves hang from the windows and pour abuse on them; Cornelius and Vargunteius become abusive in turn. Bodyguards appear and show flashes of steel; Cornelius and Vargunteius turn on their heels and flee.

"Cicero's prediction has come true. The witnesses see it all. But what have they seen? Two men, already in a precarious position because of their association with me, who arrived at Cicero's door—not with the intention of killing him, but because they were roused from their beds by a summons from an anonymous caller, who said that if they valued their lives they had better go at once to the consul's house! Yes, it was Cicero who engineered the whole episode! Everything appeared just as Cicero wished, for of course Cornelius and Vargunteius arrived in an agitated state, fearful and not knowing what to expect, and when they encountered abuse they quickly became abusive and threatening in return. They were duped into playing the part of frustrated assassins, and never knew it until Cicero's speech in the Senate today, when he announced his absurd story of having survived a murder plot and gestured to his so-called reputable witnesses, who all nodded their heads in agreement! The man is a monster. The man is a genius," said Catilina bitterly.

"You see, when he first used the trick of saying his life was in jeopardy back in the summer, when he tried to postpone the elections a second time, no one believed him; his exaggerated bodyguard and the breastplate beneath his toga were too absurd. This time he came up with a wilier and more subtle trick. When he told his tale to the Senate today, I could hardly believe my ears. I had no rejoinder. Only afterward did I speak with Cornelius and Vargunteius and see through his deception. There was no plot to murder Cicero. Oh, not that I would mind seeing him dead. Few things would please me more—"

"Nothing would make me happier," said Tongilius, who quietly reappeared in the glow of the fire. His cloak was wet, and beads of water clung to his ruffled hair. "The storm shows no signs of stopping; it's raining harder than ever. The sky is aflame with lightning. Here, your apple is seared enough, Lucius. Time to pull it from the fire. Don't eat it too soon, though, or you'll burn your tongue. Would that I could set

Cicero's tongue aflame!" He looked into the darkness of the tunnel and laughed aloud at the image in his mind. Did the look of cruelty on his face enhance his beauty or mar it? His laughter was brief; he began to pace, unable to keep still.

"Tongilius has his own reasons to be bitter," said Catilina in a low voice. "Cicero hasn't hesitated to bandy his name about, calling him my catamite. Curious, how sexless creatures like Cicero love to exploit the very details of intimacy which they claim to find so repulsive. Everyone knows that Cicero despises his wife, and he married off his poor daughter before she was thirteen! Hardly a lover of women; hardly a lover at all. Yet he holds up Tongilius for ridicule without the least quiver of shame. Shameless, sexless; the cavities in Cicero's character where those qualities should be are filled with arrogance and spite."

"What happened today in the Senate, Catilina?" I said.

"I received word that Cicero planned to deliver a speech against me. I could hardly stay away, could I? I thought I could defend myself and show him up for a fool. That was my hubris, I suppose, thinking myself his match with words; now the gods have punished me for it.

"There was no formal speech. Cicero shouted; I shouted; the senators shouted me down. I found myself abandoned and sitting almost alone, except for a handful of those closest to me. I think you cannot know the shame of that, Gordianus, to be shunned by your colleagues in such a manner. I implored them to remember my name—Lucius Sergius Catilina. A Sergius was there at the side of Aeneas when he fled from burning Troy and made his way to Italy. We have been among the most respected families in Rome since her very beginnings. And who is Cicero? Who ever heard of the Tullius family from Arpinum, a town with one tavern and two pigsties? An interloper, an intruder, hardly better than a foreigner! An immigrant—that's what I called him to his face!"

"Strong words, Catilina."

"Hardly strong enough, considering that he was threatening my life! 'Why is such a man still alive?'—he said those very words to the Senate. He brought up instances in the distant past when the Senate put reformers to death, and mocked those present, saying they lacked the moral fiber to do the same. He noted the laws that prevent a consul or the Senate from executing a citizen, and declared that I stood outside those laws, a rebel and not a citizen any longer. He was inciting them to murder me! Failing that, he would see me exiled, along with all my supporters. Take your vermin and go, he said. Rid Rome of your pestilence and leave us in peace. Over and over, he made it clear that my choice was to flee the city or be murdered.

"Of course he couldn't resist repeating the most vicious and painful lies about me one more time, to my face and before all my colleagues. Again, the sneering allusions to my sexual depravity; again the horrible insinuation that I killed my son. He intended to provoke me, to make me lose my head. I hate to admit that he succeeded. I began by calmly denying every charge he made, and ended by shouting at the top of my lungs—shouting to be heard above the jeering of my colleagues.

"When Cicero insinuated that all his enemies should be herded into a segregated camp, I could stand no more. 'Let every man's political views be written on his brow for all to see!' said Cicero. 'Why?' I said. 'Will it make it easier for you to choose which heads to lop off?'

"At that, the inside of the chamber roared like the ocean in a storm. But Cicero has trained his voice to carry above any noise that man or nature can contrive. 'The time for punishment has come,' he shouted. 'The enemies of Jupiter, in whose temple we convene, will be rounded up and laid to sacrifice on his altar. We shall set them aflame, dead or alive—dead or alive!'

"There was such an uproar I was afraid for my life. I rose from my seat, put on the most brazen face I could manage, and strode toward the doors. 'I am surrounded by foes,' I shouted. 'I am hounded to desperation. But I tell you this: if you raise a fire to consume me, I will put it out—not with water, but with demolition!' "

His voice was shaking with emotion. His eyes glittered. I had never seen him so stripped of his composure. Tongilius knelt beside him and laid a hand on his shoulder. We were silent for a long time. The flame needed to be rekindled, but no one moved.

At last I spoke. "Are you telling me, Catilina, that you are completely innocent of conspiracy? That your secretive comings and goings, your alliance with all the discontents of the city, your military link with Manlius—that these things exist only in Cicero's feverish imaginings? Are you telling me that you have no intention of bringing down the state?"

His eyes reflected the firelight but somehow seemed to sparkle from within. "I claim no false innocence. But I do say that my enemies have manipulated me into a position where no other option is open to me. I have always worked within the political system of the Roman state. I have suffered the indignities of spurious trials, I have made endless compromises with men like Caesar and Crassus; I have submitted myself to electoral campaigns of ferocious ugliness. Twice I have run for consul; twice the Optimates have engineered my defeat. No one can say that I looked to violent action until no legitimate recourse remained. The Republic is a shambles, a tottering pile of bricks about to fall, with the Optimates standing jealously on top. Who will bring it down? Who will pick up the pieces and refashion it to their choosing? Why should it not be me, and why should I not use whatever tools are called for?

"Yes, for some time I have contemplated the possibility of violence, but to say that I have a plot afoot is absurd. I have met in secret with friends; I have consulted with Manlius about the readiness and loyalty of his troops. Call it conspiracy if you want, but so far it has remained a vague expression of a shared will for creating a change, with no consensus about how to do it. Manlius is eager to use his veterans. Lentulus favors inciting slaves to revolt, an insanity I utterly reject. Cethegus, always hotheaded, would resort to burning Rome." He shook his head. "Do you know what my dream is? I think of those ancient revolts of the plebeians, when to claim their rights they banded together and simply walked out of Rome, leaving the patricians to cope for themselves and ultimately to seek compromise. If I could draw all the discontented to me—the poor, the indebted, the powerless—and bring the Optimates to their knees without shedding a drop of blood, I would do it. But that is only a sentimental folly; the Optimates will never give up a shred of their power. The leaders of a peaceful withdrawal would be massacred and their followers enslaved.

"It's Cicero who has forced matters to a crisis. Where there was no evidence of a plot, he invented evidence. Where my colleagues and I have procrastinated, he has forced us to take a stand. He has set the stakes; he must die, or we must die, and there can be no middle ground. He provokes a premature conflict, for his own purposes. He thinks that if he can destroy us now, during his term as consul, he will have achieved true greatness; the people will love him, the Optimates will kiss his feet, he will be the savior of Rome.

"Yet even now I waver. From his speech, from his repeated demands that I go into exile, I wonder if Cicero would be satisfied with that. Would that sate his appetite for exercising power? Would that be a great enough achievement for the New Man from Arpinum, to have saved Rome from a conspiracy that never existed and to have driven a dangerous rebel into exile before he ever had a chance to rebel!"

"Will you go into exile, then?" said Meto, drawing closer to the fire. "Or will you take up arms?"

"Exile . . ." said Catilina, not as an answer but as if he were testing the quality of the word. "Before I left Rome, I dispatched letters to several men of rank—former consuls, patricians, magistrates. I told them that I was leaving for Massilia, on the southern coast of Gaul—not as a guilty man fleeing justice, but as a lover of peace eager to avoid civil strife and no longer able to defend myself against persecution and trumped-up charges. I could go to Massilia—if they allow it, if they don't block the passes to Gaul. To take up arms—I'm not ready, I'm still uncertain. Cicero has pressed the crisis to his own advantage; he has made a fugitive of me against my will. He wants me to take desperate action, and in doing so, stumble."

"And what of your wife?" I said.

He turned his face so that the fire no longer lit it. "Aurelia and her daughter I commended to the care of Quintus Catulus. He is one of the staunchest of the Optimates, but an honest man. She'll be safe with him, whatever happens; he will not harm her, and no one could ever accuse him of colluding with me."

* * *

The storm grew worse. The wind howled outside the mine like a screaming chorus of lemures. Thunderbolts pounded the mountain and made it shudder like the belly of a drum. Water poured down the steep slopes in great sheets, carrying uprooted trees and rocky debris. Bethesda would be mad with worry, I thought, and felt a pang of dread. In such a storm, even the dogged pursuers of Catilina might have turned back. What if they had sought shelter in my home and found me gone? Spinning out the consequences of such thoughts kept me far from sleep.

The hours passed uneasily. Catilina's men took turns trying to sleep, wrapping themselves in the blankets I had brought and pressing against one another for warmth. The watch at the entrance grew lax; not even a Titan would have dared to scale the mountain and attack us on such a night. Catilina sat against a stone wall. Tongilius lay curled on his side, clutching a blanket, his head on Catilina's lap. Catilina's face was in shadow, but I could see that his eyes remained open; now and again they caught the flicker of the flames.

Meto dozed, but at one point he opened his eyes and was wide awake. He stared at something set atop a rock against one of the walls. The cloth in which it was wrapped had come loose, exposing a glint of silver.

"What is that?" he whispered, rising to a crouch and stepping toward it with an odd look on his face.

Catilina slowly turned his head. "The eagle of Marius," he said in a low voice.

I peered at it through the gloom. It was an eagle with its beak held high and its wings spread. But for the glimmer of silver, it might have been a real bird, frozen in glory. Meto reached toward it, almost but not quite touching it with his fingertips.

"Marius carried it in his campaign against Cimbri, when you and I were boys, Gordianus."

"It's absurdly heavy," murmured Tongilius sleepily. "I know; I carried it up the mountain."

Catilina ruffled the youth's hair and then gently stroked it. "If it should come to battle, I intend to carry it atop a pole as my standard. An extraordinary object, is it not?"

"How did you ever come to possess it?"

"That is a long story."

"The storm rages; we have all night."

"Suffice to say that it came to me through Sulla, during the proscriptions. It has a bloody history. Cicero told the Senate that I keep it in my house as some sort of shrine, bowing down to worship it before commencing with my murders. He tarnishes even pure silver with his acid tongue."

"An eagle," said Meto, turning his face toward me so that the firelight reflected from the silver lit his face like a strange mask.

"Yes," I murmured, suddenly sleepy.

"But an *eagle*, Papa—don't you see?"

"Yes, an eagle," I said, closing my eyes.

THIRTY-FOUR

THE storm abruptly lifted to reveal a sky littered with clouds shredded like torn pennants, lit from beneath with a pale orange glow by the first rays of dawn. Catilina's men roused themselves, gathered up their things, and helped one another scale the wall that blocked off the mine. The only evidence left behind of their stay were some bread crumbs and apple cores, scattered pieces of charcoal and the tangy smell of a wood fire.

The path was littered with small rock slides and broken branches, but these were minor impediments. A greater handicap for me was the aching in my legs. After climbing the mountain, my knees had turned to rusty hinges and my shins to splintered wood. When I was a boy, my father told me that it was a joke of the gods that going downhill was more painful than going uphill. I had not understood him then. Now, looking at the younger men around me who had ridden from Rome, gotten a desultory sleep in a dank mine, and were now tramping down the path with smiles on their faces, I understood him only too well. Each step sent a little thunderbolt quivering through my knees.

I dreaded the crossing of the swollen stream. As I had feared, it was more turbulent than before, or at least looked that way in the light of dawn, which picked out every scudding eddy and treacherous hole. But the task was made easy by our numbers. By linking arms, clasping hands to wrists, we formed a chain stronger than the rushing waters. The young men of Catilina's company seemed exhilarated by the plunge into icy water up to their thighs. I bore it as best I could and laughed along with them, if only to still the chattering of my teeth.

At the place where the path diverged, leading one way to Gnaeus's house and the other way down the disused, steep descent to the Cassian Way, I pulled Catilina aside. "Which path do we follow here?" I said.

He raised an eyebrow. "We go down the way we came, of course." His men waited for him at the head of the narrow trail. He waved for them to proceed without him. "Otherwise we should end up stealing on tiptoe by the house of that awful neighbor of yours, with all those howling dogs. Surely you remember—"

"I do. But there are other things I remember as well."

"Gordianus, what are you talking about?"

"You must never come to my house again. Your enemies will watch for you there—"

"I understand."

"My family—I must think of their safety."

"Of course. And I must think of keeping my head on my shoulders!"

"Catilina, no jokes, no riddles!"

He mirrored the distress on my face. "Gordianus—"

"Lucius, are you coming?" Tongilius waited at the trailhead, with Meto beside him.

"Go on without me," said Catilina over his shoulder, in a jovial voice. "The old men must rest their legs for a moment."

Tongilius pursed his lips thoughtfully, then nodded and ducked out of sight. Meto followed, but not before looking me in the eye and hesitating, long enough to be invited to join us. At last he followed Tongilius, scowling. Why did he have to take everything I did as a personal affront?

"Now, Gordianus, what is this all about?"

"Ever since Marcus Caelius first approached me about playing host to you, strange things have been transpiring on my farm. The first was a headless body discovered in the stable." I paused and studied his face. He only stared back at me blankly. "Then came the body in the well—"

"Yes, you told me about that. The poor goatherd who showed us this path. What did you call him?"

"No, what did *you* call him, Catilina?"

"What do you mean?"

"What did you call poor Forfex? Was he your spy, your confederate, your dupe? Why did he die? Why was his head cut off before he was dropped down my well?"

Catilina looked at me gravely. "You do me an injustice to ask me such questions, Gordianus. I have no idea what you're talking about."

I took a breath. "You have no secret relationship with Gnaeus Claudius?"

"Your disagreeable neighbor? I saw the man only once, and that was with you! Afterward I told Crassus about the mine. I advised him to make an offer on this property, but I told you, he wasn't interested in dealing with the Claudii. So I never came back."

"But you're here now, hiding on Gnaeus's property."

"Without his knowledge. Though not for much longer if we linger here; one of his goatherds will come along and raise an alarm. When I first saw the mine, I knew it would make an ideal hiding place, especially if Crassus bought the property. Of course, that was postulated on Crassus's remaining loyal to me." His eyes flashed with bitterness. "Still, the place turned out to be useful, didn't it? As for these strange happenings on your farm, what have they to do with me?"

"They occurred at key moments, when I resisted Caelius's pressure to put you up."

"Pressure? Are you saying that you never wanted to have me?"

I shook my head, not wanting to speak. How could I say that the idea had come from Cicero?

"Gordianus, I never told Caelius to strong-arm you into

having me. Caelius told me you were happy to do so."

"But your riddle in the Senate, about the headless masses and the Senate with its withered body. The coincidence of the headless bodies on my farm . . ."

"Gordianus, are you telling me that all this time, you've hosted me only because Caelius forced you to? Well, there you have your villain. Someone told Cicero's henchmen to go looking for me on your farm last night: Caelius, obviously. He must have been loyal to Cicero all along. By Jupiter, when I think of the confidences I divulged to him . . ." He threw back his head with a pained expression. "Gordianus, have you then no affection for my cause at all? Were you merely doing Caelius's bidding when you let me into your house?"

Now it was my turn to mirror his look of consternation. I might have said yes and not told a lie, but the truth no longer seemed as simple as that.

"Never mind," he said. "The important thing is that you didn't betray me last night, when you had the chance. Unless—" He looked at the trailhead, and his face turned gray.

"Unless Tongilius and the others are descending into an ambush!"

He put his hand on the hilt of his sword. I felt a quiver of panic. He turned to me with murder in his eyes, and for the first time I saw the true depth of his despair. Lucius Sergius Catilina was a patrician, born into privilege and respectability. Trust was his birthright and highest value—trust in the gods, trust in the immutability of his station, trust in the high regard of his fellow citizens; trust, also, in the invincibility of his own innate charm. Now these layers of trust had been stripped away from him one by one; gods and men alike had betrayed him.

I laid my hand on his. I had to grit my teeth with the effort to keep his sword in its scabbard. "No, Catilina, your men are safe. I haven't betrayed you! Think—Meto is with them. I wouldn't send my own son into a trap."

He slowly relaxed. His lips registered a cracked smile. "Do you see what's become of me?" He gazed toward the empty trailhead, as if he could still see the young men who had descended ahead of us. "But they still look to me for strength, as they always have. Come, hurry!"

As I had feared, the way down was more treacherous than the way up. The trail was littered with the debris of twigs and branches, and the rain had turned the rigid earth into a treacherous soup of mud and stones. We descended as much by sliding as by stepping. We tumbled against each other and clutched at each other's arms, using the solidity of our bodies to gain a mutual balance against the unsteady elements. I banged my elbows and scraped my knees; I slipped and fell on my rump so many times it almost stopped hurting. The near-impossibility of the descent eventually took on an air of absurdity. From below us we heard the high-spirited whooping of Catilina's men, a warning of more slipping and sliding ahead. I braced myself for the final stretch, too out of breath to laugh.

At last we came to the stony clearing where the horses waited. The beasts looked ragged and miserable after their long night in the rain, but they nickered and shook themselves at the sight of Catilina's men, as eager to set out as their riders. Everyone was covered with mud, myself most of all.

"I've already had a look at the highway," said Tongilius. "The road is clear."

We led our horses one by one through the narrow passage between the boulder and the oak. To make up for the missing horse, I gave them my own. Meto and I mounted his horse together.

The exhilaration of the descent had restored Catilina's confidence. He clutched his reins and let his mount canter about. She stood upright on her hind legs and whinnied, happy to be out of the mud and muck. When he had calmed her, he came over to us, leaning forward to stroke the beast's neck. "Are you sure you won't come with us, Gordianus? No, I'm only joking! Your place is here. You have a family. You have a future."

He circled, waving for his men to form a bodyguard around him. How strange his company looked, filthy and ragged and yet wearing smiles as if they had just won some glorious battle. "Tongilius, you have the silver eagle? Good. Gordianus, I thank you for what you've done. And for what you might have done against me but did not do, I thank you even more."

He turned and rode away at a swift gallop. Meto and I followed him to the crest of the hill and watched the company for a long time as they grew smaller and smaller, vanishing into the north.

Meto said aloud what I was thinking: "Will we ever see him again, Papa?"

I let my body answer—a twitch of the shoulders to form a noncommittal shrug. Who but the Fates could answer such a question? Even so, I feared that we had seen the last of Catilina.

When we returned to the house, Diana was delighted, thinking we must have been out early playing in the mud. Bethesda was appalled, but also relieved, though she tried not to show it. Exhausted, I let her scrub me with a sponge and then crawled into my bed. At some point she joined me and made love to me with a consuming ferocity she had not shown in a long time.

On that very day—while I dozed, while Catilina and his company raced northward—Cicero made a second speech against Catilina in Rome, not to the Senate but directly to the citizens assembled in the Forum. This I learned the next day from a slave who brought a letter from Eco, which warned me, too late, of Catilina's flight. The speech to the people reiterated much of what Cicero had said to the Senate, but with even greater venom and a crude hyperbole that showed no small contempt for his audience's sophistication. Eco made no comments on the speech—understandably, for what if the letter had fallen into other hands?—but instead quoted it at length. Perhaps he was as appalled as I was and thought that rendering Cicero's words verbatim would convey all that needed to be said, or perhaps he was merely amused at such outrageously inflammatory rhetoric, and transcribed it for my amusement.

In his speech Cicero announced Catilina's flight from Rome and humbly took credit for "removing the dagger from our throat." He then coyly acknowledged that some might fault him for not putting the scoundrel to death instead (though he could not have done so legally; only the courts and the people's Assembly have that right). Catilina's flight was proof of his guilt, and Cicero berated those who had been too stupid to see the truth before. If there were those who portrayed Catilina as a guiltless martyr and Cicero as his vengeful persecutor, then Cicero would bear the burden of such slander for the sake of saving Rome. As for those in league with Catilina who remained at large in the city, that band of perfumed and overdressed "warriors" could hope to have no secrets from him; the consul's eyes and ears followed them everywhere, and he was aware of their innermost thoughts.

As for rumors that Catilina was headed for Massilia and exile rather than for Manlius and his soldiers, Cicero hoped it might be true but doubted it: "By Hercules, even if he were utterly innocent of traitorous designs, Catilina is precisely the sort of person who had rather die an outlaw's death than wither away in exile." Cicero had gauged his opponent shrewdly.

He dwelt on Catilina's sex life repeatedly and at great length, calling him the world's most accomplished seducer of young men, mentioning Tongilius and others by name, and saying that Catilina made some of his conquests by murdering young men's parents at their request and thus sharing their inheritances even while he plundered their orifices. Catilina, Cicero said, was shameless in taking both the dominant and the subservient role. His once-famous attributes of physical endurance and energy had long ago been squandered in mindless orgies.

Catilina's inner circle shared his sexual excesses. Like their mentor they flaunted their skill at playing either role in bed. Pretty boys made for dancing and singing, they had nevertheless learned to flail daggers and sprinkle poisons, and were thus more dangerous than their pouting faces and neatly coiffed beards might suggest. They frittered away their fortunes on gambling, harlots, and expensive wines, and the vomit that came from their mouths was vile talk about murdering loyal citizens and burning the city to the ground merely to cancel their debts. Now that they were fugitives, what would Catilina and his boys do without their debauched socialites and whores to tuck them in at night? Perhaps, Cicero pondered, their notorious practice of dancing naked at parties had only been conditioning for the cold nights to come by the camp fire.

The crowd in the Forum would devour such leering wit. But could even the least discriminating among them swallow the exaggerations that Cicero served up? "What crime or wickedness has Catilina not been guilty of?" he demanded. "In all of Italy there is not one poisoner, gladiator, robber, assassin, parricide, will-forger, cheat, glutton, wastrel, adulterer, prostitute, corrupter of youth or corrupted youth who has not been his intimate. What murder has been done in recent years without him? What nefarious debauchery, except through him?"

The issues could not be clearer, for the two sides were like day and night. On the side of his cause, said Cicero, was everything modest, chaste, honest, patriotic, level-headed, and self-restrained; on the side of Catilina was everything insolent, lecherous, fraudulent, traitorous, hysterical, licentious, and hot-headed. "On one side of this confrontation are justice, moderation, courage, wisdom, and all that is good; on the other side are injustice, luxury, cowardice, recklessness, and everything bad. Prosperity struggles against poverty; right against wrong, sanity against madness, hope for the future against bottomless despair. In such a conflict, even if human efforts may fail, will not the immortal gods themselves ordain that such a league of vices must be overthrown by such a glorious army of virtues?"

What patriot in the Forum could fail to cheer such a sentiment?

Along the way Cicero managed to reiterate the danger of a slave uprising, saying that even if Catilina succeeded in his revolt, he would merely bring chaos, and that would mean a country overrun by escaped slaves and gladiators. He deplored violence, but promised the people that in the dreadful event of war he would strive for the lowest number of casualties. And he piously called on "the immortal gods themselves" to give strength to "this invincible people, this glorious empire, this most beautiful of cities."

Cicero's voice was in fine form and his timing impeccable, Eco said; the speech was well received. Reading these excerpts left me profoundly depressed.

*   *   *

The messenger who had arrived with Eco's letter returned
bearing my reply. I told him that the house guest he had
inquired about had indeed passed by on the Cassian Way, but
had not stopped at my house. Indeed, by mutual agreement,
the man would not be staying with me in the future. I did not
want Eco to worry.

The rains continued. The earth was refreshed and the
stream was recharged. Though our worries over the shortage
of hay were just beginning, our great worry about water was
finally over, and for the first time I saw the water mill move
without human intervention, driven by the power of the rushing current. To see it in motion, the great wheel revolving in
its circle, the gears meshing against one another in harmony,
made me think of my old friend Lucius Claudius, whose demeanor had been likewise harmonious. He would have been
delighted by the mill, and that pleased me. I thought also of
Catilina, whose practical genius had solved the riddle of the
water mill where I had failed. Those thoughts pleased me less,
for I could see no happy outcome for Catilina and his company. I tried not to think of them at all.

That would not be possible for long, I knew. All Italy must
be talking about Catilina, awaiting word of his fate. Some
would listen in hopeful expectation of an uprising against the
Optimates; others would listen with spite in their hearts, pray-
ing for the traitor's demise; and others would simply wait
anxiously, remembering the devastation of the wars, purges,
and uprisings that had wracked Italy in recent years.

I secretly hoped that Catilina would do as he had said, and
flee to Massilia. But this was not the case, or so it seemed
from the letter I received from Eco a few days after the Ides
of October:

Dearest Papa,
     The press of events here prevents me from coming to visit
you, or I surely would. I miss your steady counsel and the
sound of your voice. I miss Bethesda as well, and Diana, and
my brother Meto. Give them my love.
     The news here is that Catilina has definitely taken up arms
with Manlius in Faesulae. He is said to have stopped in Ar-

retium first and to have stirred up trouble there. We hear fresh rumors every day of uprisings to the north and south, near and far. The people of Rome are in a state of great agitation and anxiety. I remember nothing like it since the years of the Spartacan revolt. People talk of nothing else, and every fishmonger and shop owner has an opinion. As the playwright says: "The underworld shivers like a web being plucked at one corner."

The Senate, at Cicero's urging, has declared Catilina and Manlius outlaws and enemies of the people. Any man who takes them under his roof will be considered an enemy of the people as well. I know you understand.

An army is being raised under the command of the consul Antonius. There will almost certainly be war. People speak of Pompey rushing back from his foreign duties to save the day, but people always say that about Pompey in times of domestic crisis, don't they?

Please, Papa, come to Rome and bring the family. Surely the farm is disagreeable at this time of year. Rich men abandon their farms for the city in the winter, so why shouldn't you? If there is a war, it is likely to be waged in Etruria, and I cannot sleep when I think of your vulnerable position. The city would be so much safer for all of you.

If you will not come for a long stay, then please come for a visit very soon, if only so that I may speak to you in terms more frank than a letter permits.

This is the fond desire of your loyal son, Eco.

I read the letter twice. On the first reading I was touched by his concern, smiled to see him quoting Bolitho (a second-rate playwright, but Eco has always loved the stage), and shook my head at his admonishment not to let Catilina under my roof again; why did he worry when I had already let him know that my guest would not be returning? On a second reading I was mainly struck by the unease and unnatural restraint of his tone.

Eco had come to the farm when I needed him, even though I had not directly asked him to. I could hardly do less when he pressed me so passionately to visit him. I consulted with Bethesda. I asked Aratus when I would be least missed (knowing he would be happy to have me gone and out of his way at any time). Between them I decided that the family would take a trip to the city at the beginning of December.

For a man who professed a weary disgust for politics, my timing could not have been more ironic. My summer trip had subjected me to political harangues and led me through the voting stalls against my will. My winter trip would make me a witness to a far grander spectacle, for with less than a month remaining of his year as consul, Cicero was about to experience the crowning moments of his career. Life is like the Cretan Labyrinth, I sometimes think; whenever we bump our noses against a wall, somewhere the Minotaur is laughing.

PART FOUR

NUNQUAM

THIRTY-FIVE

WE departed for Rome before daybreak on the day after the Kalends of December. The wind, bracing but not bitter, was at our backs, and our horses were full of spirit. We made excellent time and arrived at the Milvian Bridge when the sun was strongest.

Traffic was light, especially compared to the jam of horses and wagons we had encountered on our last trip. Even so, a knot of people had gathered at the nearer end of the bridge. I thought at first that tradesmen selling wares had attracted the crowd, but as we drew nearer I saw that the only commodity being traded was conversation, much of it quite animated. The men were of various classes—local farmers and freedmen, as well as a few well-dressed travelers attended by their slaves.

As we drew nearer, I signaled to the slave who drove the cart carrying Bethesda and Diana to stop beside the road. Meto and I dismounted and walked into the crowd. Several men were talking at once, but the voice that carried above the rest belonged to a farmer in a dusty tunic.

"If what you say is true, why didn't they kill them on the spot?" the farmer said.

His remarks were addressed to a merchant, a man of some wealth, to judge from the rings on his fingers and the coterie of slaves around him, all of whom were more finely dressed than the farmer. "I only repeat what I heard before I left the city this morning," the merchant said. "Business takes me north; otherwise I would have stayed to see what transpires this afternoon. It's rumored that Cicero himself may address the people in the Forum—"

"Cicero!" The farmer spat. "Chickpeas turn my stomach sour."

"Better that than a barbarian's knife in the stomach, which

is what these traitors had in mind for you," snapped the merchant.

"Bah, a bunch of lies, as usual," said the farmer.

"Not lies," said another man, who stood just in front of me. "The man from the city knows what he's talking about. I live in that house just over there, on the river. The praetor and his men spent the night under my roof, so I should know. They waited in ambush, then trapped the traitors on the bridge and arrested them—"

"Yes, you told us your story already, Gaius. Certainly, soldiers arrested some men from Rome, but who knows what it really means?" demanded the angry farmer. "Just wait and see, the whole thing is another scheme concocted by Cicero and the Optimates to bring down Catilina." Several others joined him with a chorus of angry shouts.

"And why not?" demanded the merchant. As the crowd grew more animated, his slaves drew around him in a protective ring, like trained mastiffs. "Catilina should already be dead. Cicero's only fault is that he didn't have the fiend strangled while he was still in Rome. Instead, he continues with his plots, and you see where it's led—Romans plotting with barbarians to stage their revolt! It's disgraceful." This set off a round of jeering from the farmer's contingent, and an equally vociferous response from those who agreed with the merchant.

I touched the shoulder of the man called Gaius, who claimed to live nearby. "I've just come from up north," I said. "What's happened?"

He turned around and peered at us with eyes puffy from lack of sleep. His chinless jaw was grizzled and his hair unkempt. "Here," he said, "let's step away from the crowd. I can't hear myself think! I've told the story a hundred times already this morning, but I'll tell it again." He sighed in mock weariness, but I could see he was only too happy to recount his tale to anyone who hadn't yet heard it. The men in the crowd were too busy arguing to listen to him any longer. "Are you headed into the city?"

"Yes."

"They'll all be talking about it there, have no doubt. You can tell them you heard the facts from a true witness." He looked at me gravely to see that I grasped the importance of this.

"Yes, go on."

"Last night, long after I was in bed, they came banging on my door."

"Who?"

"A praetor, he said he was. Imagine that! By the name of Lucius Flaccus. On a mission from the consul himself, he said. Surrounded by a whole company of men all wrapped up in dark cloaks. And all carrying short swords, like the men in the legions do. He told me not to be afraid. Said they'd be spending the night in my house. Asked to put his horses away in my stable, so I sent a slave to show his men. Asked if there was a window where he could keep an eye on the bridge. Asked if I was a patriot, and I told him of course I was. Said if that was true, then he knew he could trust me to keep quiet and out of the way, but gave me a piece of silver anyway. Well, that's customary, isn't it, to pay something when soldiers put themselves up in the house of a citizen?"

"But these men weren't soldiers, were they?" said Meto.

"Well, no, I suppose not. They weren't dressed like soldiers, anyway. But they came from the consul. The Senate passed a decree last month—you must have heard about it— charging the consuls to protect the state by whatever means are necessary. So it's not a big surprise to see armed men being sent around by the consul, is it? Of course, I never thought I'd find myself in the middle of it!" He shook his head, smiling faintly. "Anyway, the praetor stations himself at the window and opens the shutters—well, lean forward a bit and you can see it from here, how that side of my house looks out over the river and the bridge. He sent one of his men to bring him a bit of burning wood from my brazier, then held it up in the window and waved it. And do you see that other house just opposite mine, across the river? From a window in that house someone else waved a bit of flame in answer. So they had men hidden away in houses on both sides of the bridge, don't you see? An ambush for somebody. I could see that myself, even without being told."

He paused and peered at us, making sure we had absorbed the full drama of the situation. "Yes," I said, "go on."

"Well, the night drew on, but I couldn't sleep, of course, and neither could my wife or children. But we couldn't have any light, so we sat in darkness. The praetor never left the window. His men huddled together, wrapped up in their cloaks, talking to each other in low voices. It was sometime between midnight and dawn when we heard the clatter of hooves on the bridge—it was a clear, cold night with hardly a sound besides the water in the river, and the noise on the bridge carried like drumbeats. Quite a few horses, it must have been. The praetor went stiff at the window, watching, and the men sucked in their breaths. I stood across the room, but I could see over the praetor's shoulder. That bit of fire appeared again at the window across the way. 'This is it!' said the praetor, and the men were on their feet in an instant, with their swords already drawn. I just stood back and flattened myself against the wall to keep out of their way as they rushed out the door.

"There was quite a racket on the bridge then, enough to wake the lemures of the drowned—men rushing onto the bridge from both ends and the clatter of horses in the middle, along with shouts and curses, some of it in that awful tongue the Gauls use."

"Gauls?" said Meto.

"Yes, some of the men on the bridge were Gauls, from the tribe of the Allobroges, as the praetor told me afterward. The others were Romans, though they don't deserve the name. Traitors!"

"How do you know this?" I said.

"Because the praetor Lucius Flaccus told me. After the ambush, he was quite proud of himself, flushed with excitement, I guess, after all that waiting, and then—" He clapped his hands. "To have it all over so fast, just as he wanted, I suppose. Not a drop of blood was shed; at least you can't see any on the bridge this morning. The traitors were pulled from their horses, disarmed and bound. Once it was all over, Flaccus thanked me and slapped me on the back and told me I had done my part to save the Republic. Well, I told him I was proud, but I'd be even prouder if I knew what had happened. 'It will be on everyone's tongue soon enough,' he said, 'but why shouldn't you know before the rest? These men we've just arrested are part of a conspiracy to bring down the Republic!'

" 'Catilina's men?' I asked him. Living on the highway as I do, I keep up with what's happening in Rome, so I know the problems that the consul's been having with that scoundrel.

" 'We shall see,' said the praetor. 'The proof of that may be here.' And he held up some documents, all of them tightly rolled and sealed with wax. 'Letters from the traitors to their fellow conspirators; we'll leave them for the consul to open,' he said. 'But there's the worst evidence against them—the Gauls who were traveling with them.' He pointed toward a group of barbarians in leather breeches who were still sitting on their horses.

" 'Enemies?' I said, not understanding why they hadn't been dragged from their horses and bound as well.

" 'No,' said the praetor, 'loyal friends, as it turns out. Those men are official envoys of a tribe called the Allobroges, who live in the province of Gallia Narbonensis, beyond the Alps, under Roman rule. The traitors tried to bring them into their plot. They wanted the Allobroges to make war up in Gaul, to tie up the troops there while the traitors carried out their revolt in Rome. Imagine, turning to foreigners to make war against fellow Romans! Can you think of anything more despicable?' I told him I could not. 'These conspirators are men without honor or loyalty,' he said. 'You'd think the mere fact of being Roman would've stopped them from even contemplating such foul crimes, but men like these have no respect for either their country or the gods. Fortunately, the Allobroges betrayed the plot to their Roman patron, who in turn revealed it to Cicero, whose eyes and ears are everywhere. The traitors, still thinking the Allobroges were on their side, dispatched their messages with the barbarians to carry word to Catilina and on up to Gaul. But this is as far as they got. We'll be taking them back to Rome now. The Senate and the people can decide what to do with these scum.' "

The man paused, both for breath and for dramatic effect. He had delivered his long monologue with considerable skill, no doubt having honed it with each successive repetition. "Well, I haven't slept at all since I was roused from my bed

last night, as you can imagine. Too scared at first, then too
excited after it was all over. Then dawn came, and all the
neighbors wanted to know what the noise was about in the
middle of the night—they thought they were hearing bandits
or runaway gladiators and closed their shutters tight. So I
found myself standing here telling the tale, and every traveler
on the road wants to hear it." He suddenly stretched his jaws
in a great yawn and wiped the sleepiness from his eyes. "Ah,
well, it's not every day that such mighty events take place
right under a man's nose. Like the praetor said, I've done my
part to save the Republic!"

Just then, a clump of horse dung came sailing through the
air and struck the side of the man's head. He gave a yelp and
clutched his ear in confusion.

"Jupiter turn you into a toad!" shouted a shrill voice, which
I recognized as that of the pro-Catilinarian farmer. It was he
who had thrown the dung; his target had been the wealthy
merchant, who was more adept at ducking than I would have
thought.

"How dare you?" shouted the merchant.

"Keep your filthy slaves away from me!" screamed the
farmer, who was suddenly surrounded.

I saw the glint of steel in the crowd and clutched at Meto's
arm, but he was already ahead of me. We mounted our horses
while the driver set the wagon in motion. Midway across the
bridge—in the very place where the praetor Lucius Flaccus
had intercepted the plotters and their unfaithful Gallic allies—
I looked back. The incident had erupted into a small riot.
Missiles of dung were thick in the air, as was the roar of vile
curses. The angry farmer came staggering out of the crowd,
supported by a few allies. He clutched his head with both
hands. Trickles of blood streamed down his forearms. The
proud witness Gaius, meanwhile, had made a strategic retreat
to his house by the river, where he stood watching from the
doorway, yawning with his eyes open wide.

Rome, I thought, is like Bethesda. Just as I have learned to
sense my wife's moods by the most subtle signs—the angle
at which she holds her head, the disarrangement of a comb
and brush on her table, the way she takes a breath—so I have

learned to gauge the mood of the city by small manifestations. Forewarned by the news at the Milvian Bridge, my eyes were keen for signals. Shopkeepers were shooing customers from their counters and closing their doors early. Taverns were filled to overflowing. I saw few women about. Gangs of boys ran through the streets, while men stood on corners in small crowds and debated. Among those who went about their business on horseback or on foot, there appeared to be a strong general drift toward the Forum; some proceeded to the center swiftly and surely, while others seemed drawn inward in a spiral approach, like bits of straw circling an eddy. So strong was this impression that as we made our way up the Subura Way to Eco's house, I felt as if we were swimmers working against a slow but steady current.

Menenia greeted us. As Diana ran to leap into her arms, I asked for Eco, and received the answer I expected. "He went to the Forum, only a little while ago," she said. "They say Cicero will be addressing the people this afternoon. We didn't know how soon to expect you, but Eco said that if you came in time you should go down to the Forum and try to find him."

"I think not—" I began to say, imagining the scene, but Meto interrupted.

"Shall we take the horses or walk, Papa?" he said, looking at me eagerly. "I'm for walking, myself. My backside aches from all that riding! Besides, it's always so hard to find a place to leave the horses, and it's not that far. . . ."

We decided to walk.

The sensation of being caught in a current grew stronger and stronger as we neared the Forum. Just as a stream grows swifter as it narrows, so the traffic of bodies hastened and grew more congested. By the time we came to the Forum itself, the crowd was quite thick. Rumors swirled all around us like darting fish, and from passing tongues I heard the same words over and over: "Traitors . . . Allobroges . . . Cicero . . . Catilina . . ."

It would be impossible to find Eco in such a press of bodies, I thought, but in the next instant Meto waved and called out his name. An arm rose above the crowd nearby, and beneath it I saw Eco's surprised and anxious face.

"Meto! Papa! I didn't know if you'd get here so early. Did you go to the house first? Hurry, I think he's already begun." Indeed, far ahead of us I heard echoes of a distinctly familiar voice.

We headed toward the open space in front of the Temple of Concord. Behind the temple the cliff of the Arx rose steeply. To our right stood the Senate House and the Rostra, from which Cicero had many years ago made his speech in defense of Sextus Roscius. To the left was the foot of the path ascending to the summit of the Capitoline Hill and the Arx. It was to the Temple of Concord that the prisoners had been taken after their arrest at the Milvian Bridge, and it was here that the Senate had been hastily convened to discuss the matter. Now Cicero had emerged from within and was addressing the crowd from the top of the steps leading into the temple. Beside him, conspicuous for its gleaming newness and the splendor of its workmanship, was a massive bronze statue of Jupiter. The Father of the Gods sat upon his throne, magnificently muscled and heavily bearded, a bundle of thunderbolts grasped in one hand, a sphere cradled in the other, with rays of lightning emanating from his brow. Beside him, Cicero looked quite small and mortal, but his voice was as thunderous as ever.

"Romans! To be rescued from danger, to be snapped from the jaws of certain doom, to be lifted up from a sea of destruction—is there any experience more joyful, more exhilarating? You have been rescued, Romans! Your city has been rescued! Rejoice! Praise the gods!

"Yes, rescued, for under the entire city, beneath every house and temple and shrine, the kindling for the holocaust had been secretly prepared. The flames were flickering—but we stamped them out! Swords were raised against the people, pressed against your very throats—but we knocked those swords aside and blunted them with our bare hands! This morning, before the Senate, I revealed the truth of the matter. Now, fellow citizens, I shall briefly convey the facts directly to you, so that you may know for yourselves the danger that was bravely faced and fended off. I shall tell you how, in the name of Rome and by the grace of the gods, this danger was detected, investigated, uncovered, and cut short.

"First of all, when Catilina broke out of town some days ago, or more precisely, when I drove him away—yes, I proudly take credit for running him off, no longer afraid you will censure me for doing so; more worried, in fact, that you will blame me for letting him leave with his life—when Catilina left, it was my hope that he would take all his foul associates with him and we would be rid of that scum for good! Alas, more than a few of these odious intriguers stayed behind, intent on acting out their criminal designs. Your consul has kept a constant watch since then, fellow citizens; indeed, I have hardly allowed myself to sleep, or even blink, knowing that sooner or later they would strike. But even I have been taken aback at the enormity of their madness. You would hardly believe it yourselves if I did not have the proof to show you. But believe it you must, for the sake of your own self-preservation!

"It came to my ears that the praetor Publius Lentulus— yes, citizens, 'Legs' Lentulus; save your laughter until you've heard the worst!—was trying to corrupt the envoys of the Allobroges, hoping to set off an insurrection beyond the Alps. These envoys were to set off for Gaul yesterday, with letters and instructions, accompanied by one of Lentulus's henchmen, Titus Volturcius, who was also given a letter addressed to Catilina.

"By Hercules, I thought, the chance had come at last, the opportunity I prayed the gods would send—a way to prove once and for all the depth of these men's degeneracy and their hatred for Rome, irrefutable proof that I could lay before the Senate and the people. Yesterday, then, I summoned two valiant and loyal praetors, Lucius Flaccus and Gaius Pomptinus, and explained the situation. Being men of irreproachable patriotism, they accepted my orders without hesitation. As night fell, they made their way secretly to the Milvian Bridge, divided their forces into two detachments on either side of the Tiber, and hid themselves in the nearest houses. Then they waited.

"In the early hours of this morning their patience was rewarded. The envoys of the Allobroges reached the bridge, accompanied by Volturcius and a retinue of his traitorous

companions. Our men burst upon them and encircled them.
Swords were drawn, but the praetors wielded the advantage
of surprise, and when the Allobroges unexpectedly drew aside
rather than join in their defense, Volturcius and his men lost
heart and surrendered. The letters were handed over to the
praetors with their seals intact. Volturcius and his men were
taken into custody and delivered to my doorstep just as dawn
was breaking. I immediately summoned those men whose
seals were upon the letters, or who were otherwise most
deeply implicated, among them that notorious hothead Gaius
Cethegus and, of course, Lentulus, who arrived a slow last,
despite the reputation of his legs. Perhaps he was sleepy from
staying up late, writing incriminating letters!

"Many of our leading statesmen called upon me during the
morning. They advised me to go ahead and open the sealed
letters myself, so that if I was mistaken as to their contents,
I would be spared any embarrassment. But I insisted that they
should be unsealed and read before the Senate, and if I was
embarrassed, so be it; there is no shame in being overzealous
in defense of freedom! So I hastily convened an emergency
meeting of the Senate, here in the Temple of Concord. Remember the significance of this temple and what it commem-
orates: the harmony of the orders, the happy coexistence and
cooperation of the classes, for it is all Romans—plebeians
and patricians, rich and poor, freedmen and freeborn alike—
who have been saved this day from the calamity that menaced
all Rome.

"First Volturcius was summoned to testify before the Senate. The man was in such a panic he could hardly speak. To
loosen his tongue, he was given a promise of immunity—he
was only a mere messenger boy, after all, though a knowl-
edgeable one, as it turns out. This stumbling footman comes
from Croto, down in the toe of Italy. Oh, but a canker on the
toe was enough to cripple the schemes of 'Legs' Lentulus!"

I took a breath and looked around me. The crowd was
laughing, as they laughed at all of Cicero's word games. Even
in the more sophisticated arena of the Senate, it was said that
he could never resist a pun, no matter how awful, especially
if it contained an insult for his enemies. Even Eco was smiling, I noticed, though Meto was not. His face was tightly

drawn and his eyes narrowed, as if he wrestled with a deeper and darker puzzle than Cicero's wordplay.

"What did Volturcius reveal? I will tell you: first, that Lentulus had given him messages and a letter for Catilina, urging him to mobilize an army of slaves and march on Rome." At this the crowd's laughter ceased and there were cries of anger and dismay. I remembered Catilina's analogy of the thunderbolts and how Cicero used them to manipulate the crowd, and I found myself looking not at Cicero but at the gleaming new statue of Jupiter, and at the credulous faces around me. "Within the city their plan was to set the seven hills aflame— yes, with each conspirator taking charge of igniting a given area—and to massacre great numbers of citizens. Catilina was to intercept and slaughter those who fled and then unite his slave army with his loyal forces in the city."

A wave of anger passed through the crowd, as palpable as a hot wind. Slaves and fire: these two things are dreaded most by free Romans. Both are tools to be bent to their will and to give comfort, but either may run out of control and wreak terrible havoc. For any man to turn them loose upon his fellow Romans is an act of unforgivable betrayal, and in a single breath Cicero had managed to accuse Catilina and his friends of plotting to use both.

"Next, the Allobroges were brought before the Senate. They declared that they had been made to swear an oath and been given letters from Cethegus and Lentulus, and moreover had been ordered to send cavalry across the Alps to assist in their planned uprising. Imagine an army of slaves, Gauls, and outlaws, marching on the city in flames! To secure their alliance, Lentulus had declared to them that soothsayers and the Sibylline oracles had foretold that he would be the third of the Cornelii, after Cinna and Sulla, to rule over Rome—or what remained of it, for he also declared his belief that this is the year preordained for the destruction of Rome and its empire, being the tenth year after the acquittal of the Vestal Virgins and the twentieth year after the burning of the Capitol." Cicero shook his head to show his disgust with such blasphemy.

"The Allobroges also informed us of discord within the ranks of these intriguers. It seems that Lentulus, typically lazy, wanted to wait until seventeen days from now and commence their carnage under cover of the festivities of the Saturnalia—the holiday when masters trade places with their slaves. But the bloodthirsty Cethegus, insensitive to such delicate irony, was eager to begin the massacre right away.

"It was time to confront these scoundrels directly. Each of them was called forward and shown the letters that had been intercepted. We showed Cethegus his letter. He agreed that the seal was his. The thread was cut. Written in his own hand and addressed to the leaders of the Allobroges, the message reiterated the plot exactly as I have already described it. Earlier, upon information from the Allobroges, I had sent one of the praetors to Cethegus's house, where a great cache of swords and daggers had been uncovered and confiscated. When I confronted him about this, Cethegus had answered sarcastically that he was merely a collector of fine weaponry! But now that his letter had been read aloud and his wickedness exposed, he collapsed with shame and fear and fell silent.

"Another of the letter writers, Statilius, was brought in. Again, the breaking of the seal, the reading of the letter, the stuttering confession of guilt.

"Then came Lentulus. His letter was read. It reiterated what we already knew, but Lentulus declined to break down and confess like the others. I offered this man—currently serving as a praetor and once a consul of the Roman people—an opportunity to speak on his own behalf. He refused, and instead demanded that Volturcius and the Allobroges be called into his presence, so that he might confront his accusers. This was done; and thus was Lentulus undone, for as our informers resolutely recited the occasions on which they had met with him, he began to crumble, and when they brought up the business of the Sibylline oracles, those of us present witnessed what the exposure of guilt can do to a man. The magnitude of his crime and the glaring absurdity of his delusions suddenly came crashing down on him and robbed him of his wits, and instead of continuing to deny the allegations, which he might easily have done, Lentulus surprised us all by blurting out his confession. He did so in a whimpering voice that none of us had heard before; when he needed them most, his famous oratorical skills and even his notorious sarcasm deserted him completely.

"Volturcius was then called on to produce the single remaining unopened letter. Seeing it, Lentulus blanched and began to tremble; nevertheless, he acknowledged that the seal and the handwriting were his, though the letter itself was unsigned. I will read it to you now." Without turning from the crowd, Cicero held out his hand. From behind him, his secretary Tiro appeared and placed the document into his master's palm. Cicero unrolled it and snapped it stiff between his hands. " 'You will know who I am from the man who brings this to you. Remember that you are a man; consider your situation; take steps to do whatever is necessary. Recruit the aid of all, *even the lowest*.' "

Cicero thrust out his arm, as if the document had an odor, and Tiro relieved him of it.

"Letters, seals, handwriting, confessions—citizens, these might seem to be the most compelling possible evidence against these men. But even more conclusive was the furtive look in their eyes, the pallor of their faces, their stupefied silence and the way they gazed at the floor, ashamed to look up, or else glanced cringingly at one another. Their own guilty appearance was the most incriminating testimony against them.

"Acting on the evidence we have gathered, the Senate unanimously voted to put under arrest the nine men most intimately involved in this conspiracy—only nine, despite the alarming number of traitors among us, because the Senate in its leniency believes that the punishment of these nine alone may recall the others to their senses.

"Thus have the foul schemes of Catilina met with abject failure. Had I not had the foresight to eject him from the city, it might not have been so. For while there was never any real danger, so long as I was vigilant, from lazy Lentulus or the wild-eyed Cethegus, Catilina is another matter. His skill at swaying the hearts of men, his personal attention to every detail of his vast plans, his cunning, his great strength and physical endurance—all these made him the most formidable of Rome's enemies, *so long as he was in our midst*. He would never have made such a stupid mistake as sending off incriminating letters with his own seal upon them! Had he remained, even with myself to watch his steps and counter his designs, we would have had a bitter fight on our hands, a struggle to the death."

Cicero paused. He clasped his hands before him and bowed his head for a moment, then with a deep breath raised his eyes to the statue of Jupiter beside him and stepped closer to it. "In my conduct of these affairs, fellow citizens, I feel very strongly that I have been guided every step of the way by the will of the immortal gods. Such a conclusion is obvious, for human initiative alone could scarcely be credited with directing these matters to such a fortuitous end. Indeed, throughout these dark days, so persistently have the gods made known their will that they have virtually been visible before us. Word of their portents has already spread among you, so that I scarcely need mention all the manifestations—the flames seen in the sky by night, the tremblings of the earth, the strange patterns of lightning. By such signs the gods foretold the outcome of this struggle. I will not enumerate them all, but there is one incident so compelling that I must not pass over it.

"Cast your minds back two years ago, to the consulship of Cotta and Torquatus. In that year the Capitol was struck repeatedly by freakish lightning, which jarred the images of the gods from their pedestals, struck down the statues of our ancestors, and melted the brazen tablets of the law. Even the image of our founder Romulus was struck, that gold-covered statue that shows him suckling the she-wolf. Soothsayers, who had gathered from all over Etruria, prophesied slaughter and conflagration, the overthrow of the law, civil war, and the end of Rome and her empire—unless the gods could be persuaded to alter the course of destiny. In accordance with these dire warnings, ceremonial games were held for ten consecutive days, and nothing that might appease the gods was left undone.

"The soothsayers commanded that a new statue of Jupiter should be made and that it should be placed in a lofty spot facing the dawn and overlooking the Forum and the Senate House. With the image of the Father of the Gods turned upon our mortal activities, any grave threat to the safety of Rome would be brought to light and made manifest to the Senate and the people. So slowly did the construction of this massive, magnificent statue proceed that only now has it been completed—and it was not ready to be installed in its lofty place beside the entrance to the Temple of Concord *until this very day*!

"No man here is so blind that he cannot see how the entire universe, and most specifically this chosen city, is guided and governed by the will and the majesty of the gods. Two years ago we were warned, by those who interpret the signs of the gods, of impending catastrophe and civil chaos. Not all believed the signs, but wisdom prevailed and the gods were placated. Now the time of crisis arrives and—who would dare call it coincidence?—the statue of Jupiter is ready! So timely is the benign intervention of great Jupiter that at the very hour the conspirators were being conducted through the Forum to the Temple of Concord, the engineers were just completing the statue's installation! And now, with Jupiter's terrible gaze upon us, this plot against your safety and the very survival of Rome has been revealed and brought into the bright, harsh light of day.

"Harsher than ever, then, should be your hatred and punishment of these men who have dared to spread the flames of destruction not only to your homes but to the shrines of the gods as well. How proud I would be to assert that their apprehension and arrest is all due to me, but it is not so; it was Jupiter himself who thwarted them. Jupiter wishes for the Capitol to be saved, and for the temples and this city and all of you to be saved as well. In that divine wish I have been his vessel.

"The Senate has decreed a thanksgiving to the gods. Their decree was issued in my name—the first time that such an honor has ever been bestowed upon a civilian. It is framed in these words: 'because he saved the city from flames, the citizens from massacre, and Italy from war.' Yes, citizens, raise your voices in thanksgiving, but not to me; render your loving praise to the father who has saved you all, to the destroyer of Rome's enemies, to Jupiter Almighty!"

Cicero raised his arms to the gleaming statue beside him and stepped back. Cheering erupted throughout the crowd, so precisely on cue that I wondered at first if Cicero had seeded his partisans among the crowd. But the ovation was too over-whelming to be false, and why not? It was not Cicero, the mere vessel, whom they were cheering, but the Father of the Gods, who gazed out at us from beneath his thunderous brow. Even so, as he backed away into the shadows, Cicero wore a smile of utter triumph, as if the cheering were entirely for him.

THIRTY-SIX

"THIS means the end of Catilina," said Eco that night, re-clining on his dining couch. The meal was finished. The food and utensils had been cleared away and only a pitcher of watered wine remained. Diana was fast asleep in her bed, and Bethesda and Menenia had retired to another room.

"Until today," Eco went on, "no one in Rome was certain what would happen. There still seemed a very real chance of an uprising in the city, successful or not. You could feel it in the streets—the anger, the resentment, the restlessness, the longing for any sort of change at any cost. It was as if people were hoping that the sky would open and reveal a whole new pantheon of gods looking down from the heavens."

"Is this what you meant in your letter to me, when you said you could speak more frankly face to face?" I said.

"Well, I could hardly express such ideas in a letter, could I? Look what's become of Lentulus and Cethegus for putting their incriminating thoughts onto parchment! Not that I sym-pathize with them, but everyone has to be very careful these days—what one says, to whom one talks . . ."

" 'The eyes and ears of the consul are everywhere,' " I said.

"Exactly."

"And his eyes watch even one another."

"Yes."

"Then it's too bad all Cicero's cross-eyed spies haven't

tripped over their own feet!" said Meto suddenly, with a vehemence that surprised us. He had been sitting quietly on his couch, drinking watered wine and listening.

Eco looked at his brother, confused. "What do you mean, Meto?"

"I mean—I'm not sure what I mean, but I thought Cicero's speech today was sickening." His voice was infused with the fervent passion of those who are very young, very earnest, very angry. "Do you think there was a word of truth in it?"

"Of course there was," said Eco. Meanwhile I kept quiet, leaned back, and listened to them debate. "You don't suppose Cicero concocted those letters himself?"

"No, but who concocted the scheme in the first place?"

"What scheme?"

"The idea for the conspirators to discredit themselves by dealing with the Allobroges."

"Lentulus came up with the scheme, I suppose, or one of the other—"

"Why not Cicero?" said Meto.

"But—"

"I was listening to some men talking in the Forum after the speech was over and the crowd was breaking up. These men were saying that the Allobroges are unhappy with Roman rule, and not without reason. The Roman officials in Gaul are corrupt and greedy, like Roman officials everywhere. That's why the envoys came to Rome, seeking redress from the Senate."

"Exactly," agreed Eco. "And knowing their discontent, Lentulus saw an opportunity to suborn them."

"Or was it Cicero who saw an opportunity to use them for his own ends? Don't you see, Eco, it's just as likely that it was the Allobroges who approached Catilina's supporters, that the idea came from them, acting secretly at Cicero's behest. He said in his speech today that he was desperate for a way to expose his enemies, to draw them out. Desperate enough to engineer this whole affair himself! Lentulus and Cethegus were set up, and like fools they took the bait. Now Cicero has them in his net, and they'll never get out."

Eco leaned back, looking pensive. "Men were saying this in the Forum?"

"Not too loudly, as you can imagine, but I have good ears."

"It makes sense, I must admit, but it's mad."

"Why? We all know that Cicero prefers to operate in secrecy, with trickery and deceit. Do you think he's above stage-managing the whole incident? It's so simple, so clear. The Allobroges come seeking favors, and the Senate ignores them. Cicero is the most powerful man in Rome; he can get them what they want, if anyone can. He makes them promises, but in return they must act as his agents. So they approach Lentulus and Cethegus, claiming to seek an alliance. Without Catilina to guide them, Lentulus and Cethegus and the rest are getting nowhere on their own, so they eagerly take up the offer. But the Allobroges want an agreement in writing—only that will satisfy Cicero—and the fools give it to them. The envoys pretend to leave for their homeland. Acting on information from Cicero, two praetors stage a dramatic mock ambush on the Milvian Bridge."

"Why 'mock'?" said Eco.

"Because, while the praetors thought the ambush was real, the men they ambushed were expecting them and put up no resistance. Why? Because the informant Volturcius, who was accompanying the Allobroges, was also in on the game, another of Cicero's agents."

"Were they saying that, too, in the Forum?"

"No," said Meto, with a hint of a smile softening his outrage. "The part about Volturcius is my idea."

"But not unlikely," I said, sitting up and rejoining the conversation. "We know that Cicero's spies are everywhere."

"Even in this room," whispered Meto, so low that I barely heard him.

"Still," said Eco, shaking his head, "even if what you say is true, and Cicero set a trap for the conspirators, they needn't have stepped into it. They allied themselves with foreign subjects and plotted war against Rome."

"Yes," I said, "and Meto is right to call them fools for doing it. The Roman people might forgive a plot to bring down the state from within—many of them might even join in such an insurrection, if only for the chance to plunder—but for Romans to plot with foreigners against the state is unforgivable. It turns them from rebels into traitors. I think you're right, Eco, when you say that Catilina can never recover from this. Really, it's no wonder Cicero gave thanks to the gods at the end of his speech—Jupiter himself couldn't have devised a more foolproof way to discredit Catilina and his followers."

Meto covered his ears. "Please, Papa, no talk about gods! You know how Cicero really feels about religion; he makes quite a show among his intellectual friends of having no belief in the gods at all. He says it's all nonsense and superstition. Yet when he talks to the people in the Forum, he turns as pious as a priest and calls himself Jupiter's vessel. Such hypocrisy! And can you believe that nonsense about the statue of Jupiter being an omen? Don't you find it more likely that Cicero chose the day for the 'ambush' on the Allobroges to coincide with the installation of the statue, so that he could exploit the coincidence? That proves, more than anything else, that he must have masterminded the whole affair and timed it to his liking."

Eco opened his mouth to say something, but Meto wouldn't be stopped. "Do you know what else? I'm not even sure that Lentulus and Cethegus were plotting to torch the city. What evidence do we have for that, except the word of Volturcius the informer—Cicero's hired spy? Perhaps Lentulus and Cethegus were stupid enough to have come up with such a plot, or perhaps Cicero simply made up the part about fire to frighten people, just as he made up the stories about Catilina's wanting to lead a slave revolt. Nothing frightens people more than those two things, fire and slaves, running out of control. The rich fear the vengeance of slaves, and the poor fear fire, which can claim all they own in an instant. Even the poorest, who look to Catilina as a savior, would turn their back on any man who plotted arson."

"Thunderbolts, cast into the crowd!" I murmured.

"What did you say, Papa?" said Eco.

"An idea I got from Catilina. Vestal Virgins and sexual debauchery; arson, anarchy, slave revolts; conspiring with foreigners; the will of Jupiter—Cicero seems to have made a science of the words and phrases that will manipulate the masses."

"Don't forget his watchfulness," said Meto. He stood up

and put down his cup. His hands were trembling. "At least I can say something no one else in this room can say: I've never served as the consul's eyes or ears." With that he abruptly turned and left us.

Eco stared after him. "Papa, what on earth has happened to my little brother?"

"He's become a man, I suppose."

"No, I mean—"

"I know what you mean. Ever since his birthday celebration here in Rome, he's become more and more as you see him now."

"But these wild ideas, and the depth of his anger against Cicero—where does it come from?"

I shrugged. "Catilina has slept under my roof several times. I think Meto may have had some private conversations with him while I was elsewhere. You know Catilina's notorious effect on the young."

"But such ideas are dangerous. If Meto wants to brood on the farm, that's one thing, but here in the city I hope he knows enough to keep his mouth shut, at least in public. I think you should have a talk with him."

"Why? Everything he says makes perfect sense to me."

"Yes, but aren't you worried?"

"I suppose. But when he left the room just now, it wasn't worry that I was feeling. I was feeling rather proud of him, actually—and a little ashamed of myself."

There are moments in the theater when the characters and events upon the stage seem to become more real than reality itself. I speak not of bawdy Roman comedies, though sometimes even those attain the phenomenon I'm thinking of; I speak more of those sublime tragedies of the Greeks. One knows that mere actors reside behind the masks, and one knows that the words they speak come from a script, and yet when Oedipus is blinded one feels an anguish more vivid than physical pain and a terror that seems to well up from the deepest recess of the soul. Gods hover in the air: one knows they are merely men suspended from a crane, and yet one experiences an awe that transcends all reason.

The days that followed Cicero's speech in the Forum were

colored with the same sense of vivid, compelling unreality. There was something grand and theatrical, but at the same time grubby and absurd, about the inevitable progression toward the destruction of the men who had fallen into Cicero's power. Ultimately it was not Cicero who decreed their annihilation, but the Senate. Whether that august body acted legally or not is a controversy which I doubt will be resolved in my lifetime.

Roman law does not give to either the consuls or to the Senate the right to put a citizen to death; that right is reserved for the courts and for the people's Assembly. Because the courts are slow and cumbersome and the Assembly is dangerously volatile, neither institution is of much use in an emergency. It might be argued that the Extreme Decree, by which the Senate had empowered the consuls to take any steps necessary to preserve the state, superseded other restrictions and allowed for a penalty of death against Rome's enemies within. Even so, was it right, legal, or honorable to put to death men in captivity, who had laid down their arms and given themselves into custody, and thus posed no immediate threat to anyone? These were some of the arguments that occupied the Senate over the next two days.

Self-professed hater of politics that I was, I should have left the city at once, but I did not. I could not. Like every other citizen I endured the passing hours in nervous, spellbound suspense, feeling the dread of something awful hanging over the city and its people. Everyone felt it, no matter what his political stripe, or his opinion of Cicero, or his belief in the righteousness or wickedness of the men in custody. The dread was like an ache that had settled into every joint of the body politic, a fever that addled the collective mind. We wished to be rid of our illness. We also feared that our physicians in the Senate would resort to some drastic cure that would not only break the fever but also kill the patient.

On the day after Cicero's speech the city became a vast whirlpool of rumors, with the Temple of Concord, where the Senate continued to meet, at its ravenous center. The news that one of Catilina's supporters had implicated Crassus sent a panic through the commodity traders in the Forum; men wrung their hands, wondering what would happen if Crassus should be arrested and his fortune immobilized or confiscated, while others said that Crassus would never allow such a thing and would instead join Catilina in civil war. In fact, a certain Lucius Tarquinius had come before the Senate to state that Crassus had sent him to Catilina to carry news of the arrests and to advise Catilina to march on Rome at once. The senators' reaction, after some consternation, was to shout the man down. Even if the story was true, no one particularly cared to draw Crassus into the affair so long as he remained publicly loyal to the Senate. After a brief debate, those present recorded a vote of confidence in their richest member. It was also decided that Lucius Tarquinius would not be allowed to give any further testimony until such time as he was willing to reveal who had bribed him to give false and slanderous testimony against a man of such indisputable patriotism as Marcus Crassus. Some believed that Tarquinius had set out to implicate Crassus in order to moderate the punishment of those already in custody, since with Crassus among them the Senate would shrink from taking drastic measures. Others thought that it was Cicero who put Tarquinius up to it, in order to silence Crassus and keep him from influencing the debate. Lucius Tarquinius nevertheless stood by his original story and, disqualified from further testimony, was effectively gagged. The matter of Crassus's loyalties was not raised again, but he also removed himself from actively debating the fate of the arrested men.

Caesar was also the subject of scrutiny and suspicion. Had Volturcius and the Allobroges implicated him as well? And had those charges been suppressed by the Senate and censored by Cicero in his speech, because they did not want a confrontation with Caesar? Or were these assertions merely rumors circulated by Caesar's enemies? Whatever the truth of the matter, the rumors against Caesar were widespread. So strong did feelings run among the armed men assigned to protect the Temple of Concord—all equestrians and partisans of Cicero—that when Caesar was leaving the building that afternoon they shouted threats and brandished their swords at him. According to those who were there, Caesar's dignity never faltered, and once he was clear of the cordon he quipped, "What a foul mood these dogs are in; has their master not fed them lately?"

That day the senators voted on the treasonable conduct of the prisoners, and after a brief debate pronounced them all guilty. Whether or not this constituted a legal trial was a question that would loom large for years to come. The senators also voted to give substantial rewards to the Allobroges and to Volturcius.

In the shops and taverns and open squares, details began to circulate about the uprising that had allegedly been scheduled to coincide with the Saturnalia. The entire Senate was to be killed along with as many citizens as possible in an indiscriminate slaughter; only the children of Pompey were to be taken alive, as hostages to keep the great general at bay. A hundred men had been recruited to set fires all over the city and to demolish the aqueducts, so that the fires would burn unchecked; anyone bearing water to extinguish the blazes was to be slain on the spot. Which of these details was authentic and which fantastic? It was impossible to tell, for as soon as one heard a rumor, another arose to contradict it. A silver merchant near the Forum told me he had seen with his own eyes the enormous cache of newly sharpened swords and incendiary material that had been discovered in the house of Cethegus, and that Cethegus's household consisted of a fierce coterie of highly trained gladiators; a few steps away and a few moments later, a wine merchant who claimed to have visited Cethegus only two days before his arrest said that the only weapons at the house were a collection of harmless ceremonial heirlooms, that he kept only a handful of bodyguards (like every senator), and that his house contained no more kindling and brimstone than any other.

Fresh rumors asserted that Lentulus and Cethegus and the rest were planning to escape. The captives had been put under house arrest in the custody of various senators. But Lentulus's freedmen were said to be scouring the streets, trying to incite workmen and slaves to rise up and free their patron, and Cethegus's purported army of gladiators was attempting to join forces with the city's hired gangs to storm the house where he was being kept. Accordingly, the consul ordered more troops from the garrison to surround the nine houses where the accused were incarcerated. The presence of so many armed men in the streets set even more rumors into motion.

At sundown Cicero was banished from his house on the Palatine for reasons that had nothing to do with the crisis. It was the night of the annual rite of the Good Goddess, Fauna, a state ceremony traditionally presided over by the wife of the consul and attended by the Vestal Virgins. Because men are excluded from the rite, Cicero spent the night in the home of his brother Quintus. Among the Vestals in attendance was Cicero's sister-in-law Fabia, who had been tried and acquitted ten years before for consorting with Catilina; according to Bethesda, the chief topic of gossip among the women of Rome centered on what Fabia must be feeling on such a night. I myself was more curious about Cicero's wife, Terentia. Whether or not she had any more belief in Fauna than did her husband in Jupiter, she was just as canny at perceiving omens; when the flame dedicated to the goddess was thought to have gone out and then suddenly sprang up again, Terentia sent a message at once to her husband, advising him that the Good Goddess had sent a sign for him to show no mercy to the enemies of Rome.

The Nones of December dawned bright and cold. A coterie of armed men gathered before the Temple of Concord. One by one the senators arrived, leaving their entourages behind in the milling throng while they mounted the stairs beneath the stern countenance of Jupiter and disappeared within the temple to decide the fate of the conspirators. Crassus was conspicuously absent, as were a great many senators of the populist party, but Caesar attended, making his way through the Forum with a large body of followers.

While the Senate met, the nervous crowd in the Forum awaited the outcome. Men speculated wildly about the debate being staged within, and mad rumors circulated—that Lentulus had escaped, that Cethegus had already been strangled in the night, that Crassus had committed suicide, that Catilina and a huge army were crossing the Milvian Bridge, that parts of the city were in revolt and had been set on fire, that Caesar had been attacked and killed inside the Temple of Concord. This last bit of gossip set off a small riot among Caesar's partisans, who began to storm the temple and were brought under control only when Caesar himself appeared on the steps to show himself alive and whole.

I found myself wishing that Rufus could have smuggled us inside, as he had done on Meto's birthday, so that we could hear the speeches for ourselves. Instead I learned of the details afterward, largely from Rufus but also from reading the speeches themselves; for Cicero, with his mania for surveillance, who in his first speech against Catilina had proclaimed, "Let every man's political views be written on his brow for all to see," actually stationed an army of secretaries among the senators to record the entire debate, something that had never been done before. These secretaries had been trained by Tiro himself in the method called Tironian "shorthand," by which whole words and phrases are recorded with a single stroke. Using this new invention, they were able to take down every word, and thus the sentiments of every senator were put on record in Cicero's files.

The consul-elect Silanus began the debate with a fiery condemnation of those who would have plunged Rome into the ruins of civil war; he conjured up images of children torn limb from limb before their horrified parents, of wives raped in front of their castrated husbands, of boys and girls brutally ravished, temples plundered, homes burned to the ground. No course would satisfy the gods, he argued, except that the prisoners should suffer "the supreme penalty."

Subsequent speakers agreed and seemed bent on outdoing one another with expressions of outrage, until the proposal was countered by Caesar, who pointed out that Roman law permits a convicted citizen to go into exile rather than face execution. He did not argue that the convicted men deserved to live, but rather that the law should be scrupulously adhered to, for the sake of tradition. "Consider the precedent you establish, for all bad precedents originate from measures good in themselves. You would inflict an extraordinary penalty on guilty men who doubtless deserve it. But what happens when power passes into the hands of men less worthy than yourselves, and they wish to inflict death upon men who do not deserve it? They will point to your precedent and no one will be able to stop them." Thus did Caesar, whom many thought to be connected with the conspirators, manage to argue for clemency without actually arguing on their behalf. Instead of executing them, he proposed instead that their property should be confiscated and that they should be banished to distant towns and kept under guard until Catilina had been defeated in battle or the crisis had otherwise passed.

Cicero spoke against this proposal, saying that the only safe period of imprisonment for such men would be imprisonment for life, for which there was no precedent at all, and that the laws that protect the lives of citizens no longer applied to the men in question, "for a man who is a public enemy cannot be regarded any longer as a citizen."

Nevertheless, so persuasive was Caesar that Silanus himself equivocated, saying he had never meant to advocate death for the prisoners, for in the case of Roman senators such as Lentulus and Cethegus "the supreme penalty" meant imprisonment. This was met with guffaws and cries of disdain from all sides.

More speeches followed, and it appeared that those present were deeply split between execution and banishment. Tiberius Nero drew cries of assent when he argued that no action as drastic as execution should be taken in the heat of the moment, and that to follow Caesar's course was best; nothing should be done without strictly legal trials, he said, and no clear judgments could be rendered until after Catilina had been either driven into exile for good or defeated in the field.

At this point Marcus Cato rose to speak. Though the transcripts do not record it, one can imagine a collective groan from the assembly. Marcus Cato was the self-styled conscience of the Senate, ceaselessly admonishing his fellows to uphold those stern moral principles he inherited from his famous great-grandfather.

"Many a time have I spoken before this body," he began, "and many a time have I reproached my fellow citizens for their spinelessness, their self-indulgence, their indolence and greed. By doing so I have made many enemies, but, as I have never excused myself for my own failings, I find no reason to excuse the failings of others. You know my sentiments. You have heard them many times before, and I see your eyes rolling up even now at the prospect of hearing them again.

Men do not like being told that they have lost the virtues of
their ancestors, especially when it is true. Our forefathers built
this empire by hard work, just rule abroad, and integrity
within this chamber. Today you pile up riches for yourselves
while the state is bankrupt. Posts of honor that should be
awarded for merit are sold to ambitious schemers. In your
private lives you are slaves to pleasure, and here in the Senate
you are mere tools for money and influence. The result?
When an assault is made upon the Republic, there is no one
here to defend it! Everyone stands around, trembling and confused, waiting for someone else to act!

"Over the years you have taken little notice of my admon-
ishments. You have shrugged me off and held fast to your
reckless course. Fortunately, thanks to the sound foundation
laid by our ancestors, the state has withstood your wayward-
ness and has even prospered. Now, however, the issue at stake
is not a question of morality, or whether our empire should
be even grander and richer than it is. The issue is whether
our empire is going to remain our empire or whether we shall
lose it to our enemies! In such a crisis, what fool dares to
speak to me of clemency and compassion?

"For a long time now we have ceased to call things by
their proper names. Giving away other people's property is
called generosity; seditious ideas are called innovations; criminal daring is applauded as courage. No wonder we've come
to such a pass! Very well, let us be liberal at the expense of
those who pay taxes, and merciful to those who plunder the
treasury. But must we make a gift of our lifeblood to those
who would murder us? Must we spare a handful of criminals,
only to let them destroy good, honest men?

"We are advised to bide our time, to let our passions cool,
to wait for a clearer perspective—while staring into the jaws
of an abyss! We are urged to adhere to the letter of the law,
to await a formal trial, to allow convicted men the option of
exile—while the kindling is being stacked up around our
houses! Other crimes can be punished after they have been
committed, but not this crime. Nip it in the bud, or else it's
too late. Let these traitors take over, and you can forget about
invoking the law. When a city is captured, its defeated inhabitants lose everything. *Everything!*

"If you cannot be stirred to patriotism, then perhaps you can react to self-interest. Let me address myself to those of you who have always been more concerned for your expensive villas, artwork, and silver than for the good of your country. In Jupiter's name, men, if you want to keep those precious possessions that mean so much to you, wake up while there is still time and lend a hand to defend the Republic. We're not talking here about misappropriated taxes, or wrongs done to subject peoples. Here and now it is *our* lives and liberty that are at stake!

"We may react to this crisis with either strength or weakness. To show weakness would be the most dangerous course, for any mercy you show to Lentulus and the other prisoners is a clear signal to Catilina and his army. The harsher your judgment, the more their courage will be shaken. Show weakness, and like a pack of dogs they will swarm over you and tear you apart. Once that happens, forget about calling upon the gods for help. The gods help those who help themselves!

"Banishment? Imprisonment? What absurd half-measures! These men must be treated exactly as if they had been caught in the act of the offenses they contemplated. If you came upon a man setting fire to your house, would you stand back and debate your reaction—or would you strike him down? As for the senator who argues for a lesser punishment—well, perhaps *he* has less reason to be afraid than the rest of us!"

This was a clear implication that Caesar was somehow connected to the conspirators, and those who sat around Caesar reacted with loud booing and catcalls, until Caesar himself stood up and engaged Cato in a heated debate on the merits of his proposal. Nothing new was said, and no memorable insults were exchanged until, while Cato was speaking, Caesar was handed a letter by one of his secretaries. He began to pore over it, drawing it close to his chest as if it contained a great secret. Cato, apparently thinking it was a note from someone involved in the conspiracy, stopped what he was saying and demanded that Caesar read the letter aloud. Caesar demurred, but Cato vehemently insisted until Caesar handed the slip of parchment to his secretary and sent it across the aisle, saying, "Read it yourself, out loud if you must."

Cato snapped the letter away from the secretary's hand,

held it up, and hurriedly scanned it. While the whole Senate watched, he blushed a purple to match the stripe on his toga. Caesar is said to have barely registered a smile while Cato, sputtering with rage, crumpled the parchment in his fist and hurled it back at Caesar, shouting, "Take it back, you filthy drunkard!"

In the midst of a debate over life and death and the future of the Republic, Caesar had received a lascivious love letter from Cato's own half-sister, the wayward Servilia, a perennial source of embarrassment to the great moralist. Was this scene contrived by Caesar to discombobulate his opponent in the midst of the deliberations? Or did Servilia, pining away in her house on the Palatine and blithely unconcerned about the crisis that had paralyzed the whole city, simply happen to crave Caesar's attentions with an unusual intensity that afternoon? Even the most outlandish writer of comedies would never have dared to compose a scene of such pungent absurdity.

In the end, it was Cato, discombobulated though he may have been, who carried the day. The Senate voted to exact the supreme penalty on five of the nine prisoners. These included the two senators, Lentulus and Cethegus; two men of equestrian rank, Lucius Statilius and Publius Gabinius Capito; and a common citizen, Marcus Caeparius.

The senators feared that nightfall might bring an attempt to free the prisoners, and no time was wasted in carrying out the sentence. While praetors went to fetch the others, Cicero himself, flanked by numerous senators and an armed bodyguard, went to fetch Lentulus from the house on the Palatine where he was being kept. The senators formed a moving cordon as Cicero escorted the former consul through the middle of the Forum. I was among the crowd, holding my breath, listening to the pounding of my heartbeat, alert for the first signs of a riot, my ears pricked for cries of insurrection. But the crowd was hushed and made only a dull, wordless roar like the surging of the sea. I have never seen a crowd in the Forum so subdued. I looked at the men around me, and on their faces I saw that awe which overcomes men when they witness some terrible spectacle. The solemn ritual of death

held them spellbound. I thought again of the theater, with its
strange power to remove men from reality and yet bring them
face to face with something vaster than themselves. The Senate of Rome was enacting its will, and there was no power
on earth that could stop it.

Eco and Meto were with me. I was content to hang back,
but Meto wanted to work his way closer to the procession.
Beyond the shields and upraised swords of the bodyguard,
through a brief opening in the sea of purple-striped togas, I
caught a glimpse of Cicero. One arm was at his side; the other
was raised to his chest to clutch the hem of his toga. His chin
was held high. His eyes looked straight ahead.

Beside him walked another, older man in senatorial garb,
whose posture and expression were exactly the same. Lentulus showed no trace of that irascible sarcasm that had earned
him his nickname, nor did he bow his head in shame or tremble with fear. Had I not known which was the consul and
which the prisoner, by their bearing alone I could not have
told them apart. Then Lentulus chanced to turn his face in
my direction. I caught a glimpse of his eyes and knew that I
saw a man approaching his end.

Close by the Temple of Concord, built into the hard stone
of the Capitoline Hill, is the ancient state-prison of Rome.
The prison was built in the days when kings ruled the city,
as a place to put their enemies. Once Rome became a republic, the prison became a place to keep Rome's conquered foes.
Its most famous inhabitant in my lifetime had been King Ju-
gurtha of Numidia; after being dragged through the streets of
Rome in chains, he and his two sons were taken to the prison
and cast into a lightless, airless pit twelve feet underground,
reached only through a hole in its stone roof. There they lingered for six days without food or water before being strangled by their jailers.

Lentulus did not have so long to wait. Inside the prison,
where the four other prisoners had already been brought, he
was stripped of his toga, then escorted to the same pit where
the King of Numidia had met his end. As befitted his rank,
Lentulus was the first to be lowered through the hole. As soon
as his feet touched the ground, executioners strangled him

with a noose. One by one the four other condemned men were lowered into the pit to join him in death.

When it was over, Cicero emerged from the prison and announced to the hushed crowd, "They have lived their lives"—the traditional way to speak of death without saying the ill-omened word itself, so as not to tempt the Fates or raise the lemures of the unquiet dead.

Once the executions were over, a great tension lifted from the city, as when the final words of a tragedy are spoken and the actors leave the stage. Night was falling. The crowd began to disperse. Cicero, surrounded by his bodyguard, made his way across the Forum. Sudden cries of acclamation filled the air. Men rushed toward Cicero, calling him the savior of the city. As he left the Forum and walked through the luxurious neighborhood of the Palatine toward his house, rich matrons rushed to their windows to see him and sent slaves to put lamps and torches in their doorways, so that his path was brightly lit. He no longer wore a grim face, but smiled, and waved to the crowd as generals do in their triumphal parades.

Thus ended the Nones of December, Cicero's greatest day. To watch the crowd hail him as he ascended the Palatine, one might have believed his triumph was endless and absolute. But when we returned to Eco's house on the Esquiline, we saw no celebrations in the Subura. In its dirty, unlit streets, a sullen silence reigned.

THIRTY-SEVEN

THE year dwindled and the winter grew harsher. Cold winds blew from the north. Sleet pelted the shutters at night. Frost covered the earth, and days seemed to grow dark before they had even begun.

The shortage of hay on the farm grew acute. "We should begin to favor the younger, healthier animals," Aratus told me, "and to consider slaying some of the others to eat, or else try to sell them at market, even at a loss, rather than see them wither and grow weak. Underfed animals will fall prey to a hard winter. They'll die of illness if not starvation. Better to get some use from them than to watch them slowly die."

From time to time we saw troops marching up the Cassian Way toward the north, dressed in battle gear and wrapped in their marching blankets. The Senate's forces were gathering strength for a confrontation. One day, when a troop of legionnaires was passing by, I came upon Meto and Diana up on the ridge. He was pointing to the ranks of soldiers passing below and telling her the names and uses of their various weapons and pieces of armor. When he realized that I was behind him, he fell silent and walked away. Diana ran after him, then turned back. She cocked her head and frowned at me. "Papa," she said, "why do you look so sad?"

Eco sent messages from the city to keep me informed of developments. He continued to hear news of uprisings as far away as Mauritania and Spain, but following the executions in Rome a great many of Catilina's supporters abandoned him at once. Still, there were those who persevered in their loyalty, and even within families there had been great upheavals. Most terrifying was the story of a senator's son, Aulus Fulvius, who had left Rome to join Catilina. His father sent a party of men after him. Aulus was apprehended, brought back to Rome, and put to death by his father.

The Saturnalia came and went without bloodshed. The midwinter holiday was celebrated in Rome as a day of deliverance. Cato declared to the throng in the Forum that Cicero should be saluted as the Father of the Fatherland. The crowd took up the cry without hesitation, and the Senate later passed such a resolution into law. When he began his year as consul, could Cicero have foreseen in his wildest dreams that he would attain such glory?

The first sour note was struck at the beginning of the new year, when Cicero was obliged to lay down his office. Tradition demanded that he should take an oath proclaiming that he had been faithful in his service to Rome, and then be allowed to deliver a valedictory address from the Rostra in the Forum. What a speech Cicero must have been planning! Having once spent several days in his house while Cicero composed his defense of Sextus Roscius, I could imagine him in his opulent library, pacing back and forth, trying out this phrase and that, sending Tiro after various books so as to get every quotation right, polishing and repolishing what was to be the supreme oration of Rome's greatest orator, his declaration to posterity of all his magnificent accomplishments as consul.

But it was not to be. Two of the new tribunes, who had already taken office, used their power to block Cicero from delivering his farewell speech, citing a technicality of the law and saying that a man who had put Roman citizens to death without due process of law could not be allowed to deliver a valedictory address. They occupied the Rostra and would not allow him to mount the platform. Finally they relented, but only to let him pronounce the oath of leaving office. While the tribunes watched, ready physically to remove him, he began the oath—and then quickly improvised: "I swear . . . that I did truly save my country and keep her great!"

Cicero may have had the last word that day, but his bitterness at being deprived of his valedictory must have been great. Some say Caesar and the populists were behind the incident. Others say it was Pompey's faction, who were already tired of hearing Cicero proclaim that his execution of the traitors was as great an achievement as Pompey's conquest of the East, and thought that Senator Chickpea needed to be put in his place.

I was not surprised when Meto came to my library one frosty morning, and said, with his eyes averted that he wished to leave the farm for a while and go to stay with his brother in the city.

I considered this request for a long moment. "I suppose, if Eco is amenable . . ."

"He is," said Meto quickly. "I know, because I already asked him, when we were in Rome last month."

"I see."

"I'm not really needed here. You have all the help you need."

"Yes, I suppose we can manage without you. Diana will miss you, of course."

"Perhaps I won't be gone for long." He sighed and threw

up his hands. "Oh, Papa, can't you see I simply need to get away?"

"Yes, that much is clear. You're right, it would probably be a good thing for you to be in the city. You're a man now. You need to find your own way. And I know that we can trust Eco to look after you. Which of the slaves will you take with you?"

He averted his eyes again. "I was thinking that I would go by myself."

"Oh, no, not with the countryside in such turmoil. You can't travel alone. Besides, I can't send you to Eco without sending along a slave to compensate for the extra burden on his household. How about Orestes? He's strong and young."

Meto merely shrugged.

He left almost at once, having already packed his things the night before. Bethesda waited until after he was gone to start crying. She thought that Meto and I must have had a great row, and pestered me for the details. When I denied this and tried to comfort her, she shoved me from the room and closed the door in my face.

"Perhaps I should flee to Rome myself," I muttered under my breath.

It was turning out to be a very hard winter.

The next day I took a long walk around the periphery of the farm, thinking that exertion and fresh air might help relieve my depression. I struck out toward the Cassian Way and walked along it toward the north until I came to the low stone wall that separated my land from that of Manius Claudius. What a peculiar fellow he had turned out to be, I thought, remembering the scene he had made at Meto's party. Stealing bits of food to take home with him, and then daring to insult me in my son's home! He was probably in Rome now. Claudia had said that he preferred the city, especially in the colder months.

The slaves had done a good job of repairing the wall during the summer, but already the rains and the ice were taking a toll; I noticed several small cracks here and there in the mortar. I looked across the open fields that gradually rose toward my house, from which the smoke of wood fires rose into the still air. From such a distance, with the ridge behind it, it looked the very picture of a rich man's peaceful retreat from the city.

I came to the stream and turned south. Except for the evergreens, all the foliage along its course had been stripped naked by the winter, and the stream had frozen over, locking the waterwheel in place until the thaw. Someday, I thought, the controversy over the stream would be settled for good, and I could visit its banks without thinking of lawyers, law courts, and the sour countenance of Publius Claudius. A hill obscured my view of his property, but I could see a plume of smoke rising from his house. What was my neighbor doing on such a day? Probably keeping warm with his little Dragonfly, I thought. The memory of my brief visit to his house caused me to shiver.

Following the stream, I came to the thicket at the southwestern corner of the farm, the secret place where I had buried Nemo. Amid the denuded branches it was not hard to find his stele. Who had he been, after all—a pawn of Cicero's, or Catilina's, or of Marcus Caelius? Not far away we had buried the body of Forfex. Though we knew his name, I had buried him as a slave, with only a stone to mark the place.

I climbed the ridge and looked down over all. The view was pleasing, even to a melancholy eye, with its muted shades of gray and umber. I would have stayed longer on the hill, but the cold in my fingers and toes drove me back to the house.

Aratus met me at the door. "Master," he said in a low voice, "you have a visitor, waiting for you in your library."

"From the city?" I said, feeling a prickle of dread.

"No, Master. The visitor is your neighbor, Gnaeus Claudius."

"What in the name of Jupiter can he want?" I muttered.

I shrugged off my cloak and headed toward the library. I found Gnaeus seated in a backless chair, looking bored and fingering the little tag attached to a scroll tucked away in its pigeonhole, as if he had never seen a written document before. He raised an eyebrow when I entered but did not bother to stand.

"What do you want, Gnaeus Claudius?"

"Bitter weather we're having," he remarked in a conversational drawl.

"Beautiful weather in its way, if a little harsh."

"Yes, harsh, that's what I meant to say. Like country living in general. It's a hard life, running a farm, especially if you don't have a home in town to retreat to. People from the city read a few poems and imagine it's all butterflies and fauns lurking in the woods. The reality is quite different. All in all, I gather you've had a very harsh year here on cousin Lucius's old farm."

"From where did you gather that idea?"

"So my cousin Claudia says."

"And what concern is that of yours?"

"Perhaps I could help you."

"I don't think so, unless you have hay to sell me."

"Of course I don't! You know there are no decent fields on the mountain for growing hay!"

"Then what are you talking about?"

His sudden vehemence slowly faded into a smile. "I should like to make an offer to buy this farm."

"It's not for sale. If Claudia told you so—"

"I merely assumed you might be ready to give it up and go back where you belong."

"This is where I belong."

"I think not."

"I don't care what you think."

"This is Claudian land, Gordianus. It has been Claudian land since—"

"Tell that to the spirit of your late cousin. It was his will that I should have this land."

"Lucius was always different from the rest of us. He had more money and took everything for granted. No appreciation of his status; no understanding of the importance of keeping plebeians in their place. He'd have left this land to a dog if a dog had been his best friend."

"I think you should go, Gnaeus Claudius."

"I came here prepared to make a serious offer. If you're worried that I'll try to cheat you—"

"Did you come by horse? I'll have Aratus fetch it from the stable."

"Gordianus, it would be best for all concerned—"
"Go now, Gnaeus Claudius!"

I was still brooding over Gnaeus's visit the next day when a
messenger arrived with a letter from Eco. Whatever the news,
it would brighten my outlook to hear his sweet, gruff voice
in my mind. Perhaps Meto had attached a note as well, I
thought. I retired to the library and hastily broke the seal.

> Dearest Papa,
>   Your slave Orestes has arrived with no real explanation
> for being here. He claims that he set out from the farm with
> Meto the other day, but that Meto soon turned back, ordering
> him to go on to Rome without him and to tell me that you
> were making a gift of him to the household. It seems that
> Orestes originally thought that he was accompanying Meto to
> Rome, but at any rate he says that you did intend for him to
> stay with me for good. (He's strong as an ox, I grant, but not
> very bright.) Can you explain?
>   The mood in the city continues to oscillate wildly. I do
> not think there can be any return to normalcy until Catilina
> is soundly defeated. At times this seems inevitable, only a
> matter of days; then one hears rumors that Catilina's forces
> now include thousands of runaway slaves and his army has
> grown larger than that of Spartacus at its peak. It is hard to
> know what to believe from day to day. There even appears to
> be a kind of backlash against Cicero, at least among those
> who are not busy proclaiming him to be the greatest Roman
> who ever lived. . . .

I continued to read long after the words stopped making sense
to me. At length, when I put down the letter, I noticed that
my hand was trembling.

If Meto was not in Rome, then where was he?

The moment I let myself ask the question, I knew the
answer.

"How far away are they? How long will you be gone?" Bethesda demanded.

"How far? Somewhere between here and the Alps. How long? There's no way of knowing."

"You're sure he's gone to join Catilina?"

"As certain as if he had told me so aloud. What a fool I've been!"

Bethesda did not contradict me. As I hurriedly gathered the things I would need, she watched me from the doorway, her arms crossed, her back straight, but with a lurking wildness in her eyes that indicated she was secretly distraught and struggling to hide it. I had seldom seen her so upset; to look into her eyes unnerved me. "What will we do here without you, and without Meto? There could be danger, from runaway slaves, from soldiers. Perhaps Diana and I should go to Rome—"

"No! The roads are too dangerous now. I don't trust the slaves to protect you."

"But you trust them to protect us here in the house?"

"Bethesda, please! Eco will come. I've already written to him. He could be here as soon as the day after tomorrow, or even late tomorrow night."

"You should stay until then, to make sure he gets here."

"No! Every moment that passes—the battle could already be taking place, this very minute—you want Meto to come back, don't you?"

"And what if neither of you comes back?" Her voice was suddenly shrill. She pressed the back of her hand against her lips and shuddered.

"Bethesda!" I clutched her and pressed her hard against me.

She began to sob. "Ever since we left the city, nothing but trouble . . ."

I felt a sudden tugging at my tunic and looked down to see Diana's immense brown eyes staring up at me. "Papa," she said, somehow oblivious of her mother's anguish, "Papa, come see!"

"Not now, Diana."

"No, Papa, you *must* come see!" Something in her voice compelled me. Bethesda heard it, too, for she drew back, holding in her sobs.

Diana ran ahead of us. We followed her through the atrium

and out the front door. She paused in front of the stable, waved for us to catch up, and ran on ahead. My heart began to pound.

We came to the far side of the stable and turned the corner, out of sight of the house. Empty barrels were stacked against the wall. Diana stood beyond them, pointing at something we could not yet see. I took another step. Beyond the barrels, on the ground against the stable wall, I saw two naked feet.

"Oh, no." Another step, and I saw the legs as well. "No, no, *no!*" Another step, and I saw a white, bloodless torso. "Not now, not here, not again—*impossible!*" I took another step and saw all there was to see.

It was a naked corpse, and it had no head.

I buried my face in my hands. Bethesda, oddly, seemed to gain composure from the hideous sight. She took a deep breath. "Who can it be, I wonder?"

"I have no idea," I said.

Diana, her mission accomplished, reached up to hold her mother's hand. She looked at me with an expression of mild accusation and disappointment. "If Meto were here," she said, "*he'd* figure out who it was!"

THIRTY-EIGHT

THE man who travels alone has a fool for a companion," runs the ancient proverb, but in the heat of my urgency to reach Meto I felt oddly invincible, as if no ordinary obstacle on the road, no waylaying team of bandits or desperate gang of escaped slaves, could stop me.

This was an illusion, of course, and a dangerous one, and the wiser part of me knew it, but it gave me the fortitude to leave behind the slaves I might have taken as bodyguards, to protect the farm instead. If I could trust them to do so! There was supposed to have been a slave keeping watch atop the stables the night before, and if he had been there he might have seen how the headless body was delivered, and by

whom. Saying the night had grown too bitterly cold, with
tears in his eyes the slave told me he had abandoned his post
and begged me not to let Aratus beat him. What else should
I have expected? The man was a slave, not a soldier. Even
so, I left his punishment to Aratus, whom I charged with
making certain there were no such lapses in my absence, or
else I would sell him to the mines. I was angry when I said
it, and must have sounded convincing; Aratus turned the color
of chalk. As for the new corpse which Diana had discovered,
I was able to learn nothing significant from a cursory inspec-
tion. I told Aratus to keep the body until Eco arrived; perhaps
he would be able to make some sense of it.

It is a strange experience, to travel alone through a countryside braced for war in the dead of winter. The fallow fields
on either side were empty and abandoned, and so was the
highway. There normally should have been some traffic despite the cold, especially with the sky clear and no prospect
of rain, but for hours at a stretch I saw no one. The farm-
houses I passed had their doors shut and their windows shuttered, with all the animals put away in barns or in pens hidden
from the road. There were not even any dogs to bark a greeting or a warning as I passed. The only signs of life were the
unavoidable plumes of smoke that rose from hearth fires. The
inhabitants wanted to show no signs of wealth or provisions
or even occupancy to anyone passing on the road. They were
like the ostriches one sees sometimes at spectacles in the Circus Maximus, digging a hole in the sand and then burying
their heads, thinking to hide themselves from the roaring
crowd. Had I been any different, thinking I could escape
Rome by hiding on my farm? It had certainly not worked for
me. Nor, I thought, would it work for these nervous country
folk if a ravaging army should happen to pass through. Yet
what choice remains to a bird who has wings but cannot fly—
unless, I thought, he should summon up the will to fight.

The towns through which I passed sometimes seemed as
abandoned as the farms, with all the houses shut up tight and
no one in the streets. Yet each town had a tavern or two, and
it was in these that all the life seemed to have concentrated.
Inside these establishments there was no end to the arguing
and debate of the locals who congregated to assure one an-

other that all the battles would be fought elsewhere and all the troops would requisition their provisions from some other hapless town. They were eager to press for news from a stranger passing through, though I had little to give them. And though I was passing through a region where Catilina could claim his greatest support, I heard few words spoken in his favor. Those most enthusiastic for his cause would have gone to join him already, I thought, or else had done so once but had now abandoned him and fled back to where they came from.

I made the journey by long, hard stages, stopping over in towns whose names I never knew, always seeking word of Catilina's movements. Since the executions in Rome, his army had moved back and forth between the Alps and Rome, evading confrontation with the regular armies sent to engage them. At one time his forces were thought to have numbered two full legions, or twelve thousand men, but after the executions and the failure of a general uprising in Rome, the opportunists and adventurers had quickly deserted. Exhausted by forced marches, left hungry by lack of provisions, even those most devoted to its cause began to abandon the rebel army, until there remained only those for whom there could be no turning back. "I don't think you'll find Catilina and Manlius with more than five thousand men, if that, and many of them poorly armed," a tavern keeper in Florentia told me. He also said that the Roman army under Cicero's fellow consul Antonius had passed through only a few days earlier, pursuing Catilina northward.

I found them encamped in the foothills of the Apennines, outside a small town called Pistoria. Antonius's much larger force was only a few miles away. In order to reach Catilina, I had to make a great circuit on side roads and across open country, avoiding Antonius's men.

I feared that I might be challenged and attacked as I rode in plain sight down the rocky hillside toward the village of camp fires and tents, but no one took much notice of a lone man on horseback, wrapped in a heavy cloak and wearing no armor. Once within the camp I found myself surrounded by many men who looked no more like soldiers than I did, whose only weapons appeared to be hunting spears and carving knives or even sharpened stakes. Some were younger than I, but many were older. Among these were Sulla's veterans, many of whom wore ancient armor that might have fit them once but no longer did. Mixed with the ragtag bands were groups of men in decent legionary dress, well-armored and well-armed, who had the look of disciplined troops.

The mood was less grim than I had expected. The atmosphere was colored by that sense of shared resignation that makes even strangers seem blood kin. Men laughed and smiled, stood next to blazing fires to warm themselves, and talked to one another in low voices. Their faces were weary and somber, but their eyes were bright. They appeared hopeless but not despairing—hopeless in the sense of having come to a place beyond hope, which is to say beyond false dreams or vain ambition. They had followed Catilina to this place willingly, and their faces bore no resentment.

I searched their faces for the one I sought, suddenly at a loss. Among these thousands of men, how was I to find Meto, if indeed he was here at all? I was weary and had come to the end of a long journey and suddenly seemed to have no energy left. But even as I felt gripped by uncertainty, I found that my feet had taken me to the center of the camp, toward a tent that stood out from the others. Red and gold pennants were posted at its corners, and before it, mounted atop a tall standard, was the silver eagle Catilina had carried with him from Rome. In the cold, bright sunlight it looked almost alive, like the eagle that had come to earth on the Auguraculum on the day of Meto's manhood.

Two soldiers in legionary regalia barred my way. "Tell Catilina I want to see him," I said quietly. They looked skeptical. "Tell him my name is Gordianus the Finder."

They looked at each other sourly. Finally the more senior officer shrugged and stepped inside the tent flap. After a long wait he opened it and gestured for me to enter.

The interior of the tent was crowded but orderly. Sleeping cots had been pushed out of the way to make room for small folding tables, upon which maps had been unrolled, with weights to hold down the corners. Leather satchels lay about, stuffed full of documents. Carefully laid out on a table, as if on display, were the ceremonial axes and other insignia that by rights can be carried into battle only by a duly elected magistrate; Catilina must have brought them from Rome, thinking that by such signs he could instill in his men a sense of legitimacy, or perhaps to convince himself of the same.

Among the small circle of men who sat and conferred at the center of the tent, I first recognized Tongilius, who saw me and nodded. He was resplendent in a shining coat of mail and a crimson cape; with his tousled hair pushed carelessly back from his face, he looked like a young Alexander. Other faces turned to glance at me, and among them I recognized several of the young men with whom I had weathered the howling storm in Gnaeus's mine. There was also a broad-shouldered boulder of a man with white hair and a white beard. His round, ruddy face reminded me of Marcus Mummius. He could only be Manlius, the grizzled centurion who had organized the disgruntled Sullan veterans and was now their general.

These men glanced at me for only a moment, then returned their attention to the man who sat with his back to me, speaking to them in a low voice: Catilina. I looked around and suddenly noticed another figure who sat by himself on a sleeping cot at a far corner of the tent, bent over a piece of armor that he was furiously polishing. Even from the back I knew him at once, and my heart leaped into my throat.

There was a sudden burst of acclamation from the group of men around Catilina, who had finished his address. The men stood up and quickly filed out of the tent. Tongilius smiled at me as he passed.

Catilina turned around in his chair. His drawn cheeks and feverish eyes made him look more striking than ever, as if the strain of recent days had refined and purified his handsome features. He gave me a quizzical smile. I stiffened the muscles in my jaw to keep from smiling in return.

"Well, Gordianus the Finder. When the guard whispered your name in my ear, I could scarcely believe it. Your timing is impossibly exquisite. Have you come to spy on me? Too late! Or in your own perverse manner, have you finally decided to cast your lot with me at the last possible moment?"

"Neither. I've come for my son."

"I fear you may be too late," said Catilina quietly.

"Papa!" Intent on his work, Meto had not heard Catilina speak my name, but at the sound of my voice he put down the armor he had been polishing and turned his head. A succession of emotions animated his face until he abruptly stood and walked stiffly out of the tent.

I turned to follow him, but Catilina gripped my arm. "No, Gordianus, let him go. He'll come back in his own time."

I clenched my fists, but the wiser part of me listened to Catilina and obeyed. "What is he doing here? He's only a boy!" I whispered.

"But he wants so desperately to be a man, Gordianus. Can't you see that?"

A terrible feeling of dread swept over me. "None of that matters! I refuse to let him die with you!"

Catilina sucked in his breath and looked away. I had spoken the ill-omened word.

"Oh, Catilina! Why didn't you flee to Massilia, as you said you would? Why did you stay in Italy instead of accepting exile? Did you really think—"

"I stayed because I wasn't allowed to leave! The way was blocked. The Senate's forces in Gaul cut off every pass through the Alps. Cicero had no intention of letting me escape with my life. He wanted a final confrontation. I had no choice. Outmaneuvered," he said, dropping his voice to a hoarse whisper. "Outmaneuvered at every turn. And my so-called compatriots in Rome—what a pack of fools, letting themselves be duped into that scandal with the Allobroges! That was the end of it. After that . . . But you were there, weren't you? As was Meto. His report to me was astonishingly vivid. Your son understands everything that's happened. He's incredibly wise for his years. You should be proud of that."

"Proud of a son I can't understand, who defies me this way?"

"How can you not understand him, Gordianus, when he's exactly like you? Or like you once were, or could have been, or might still be. Brave, as you are. Compassionate, as you are. Committed to a cause, as you might be if you'd allow yourself. Hungry for all that life has to offer, as you must have been once."

"Please, Catilina, don't tell me that you've seduced him, too."

He paused for a long moment then smiled wistfully. "All right, I won't."

I walked blindly to the cot where Meto had been sitting. I picked up the breastplate he had been polishing. For a moment I studied my reflection, distorted amid the hammered flourishes of lions' heads and griffins, then threw the breastplate across the tent. "And now you have him polishing your armor, like a slave!"

"No, Gordianus, that's not my armor. It's his. He wants it to be very bright, for the battle."

I stared at the various pieces on the cot—the greaves to protect his shins, the plumed helmet with its visor, the short sword tucked into its scabbard. The pieces were a hodgepodge that normally would have belonged to men of different ranks; even I could see how makeshift it all was. I tried to imagine Meto wearing it, and could not.

"Speaking of fashion," said Catilina, "I understand that in my honor the whole Senate staged some sort of ceremony to put off their normal togas and put on special clothing for the duration of the crisis, and have admonished the populace to do likewise. Is that true?"

"Eco mentioned something about it in a letter," I said dully, staring at the bits of armor. I suddenly felt lightheaded.

"Imagine that! Well, they're always coming up with these ancient ceremonies and customs that no one alive can remember. Some are rather ridiculous, but I rather like this one. I've always been called an arbiter of fashion, and this proves it; I've gotten even stodgy Cato to change his outfit!"

I lifted my eyes and stared at him. He shook his head.

"No, Gordianus, I'm not mad. But an epigram always relaxes me before a battle."

"A battle?"

"Within the hour, I imagine. Manlius and Tongilius are gathering the troops to hear me speak. You arrived just in time. Imagine, if you had missed my speech—you'd never be able to forgive yourself! Even so, if you wish to take your leave beforehand, so as to have a head start on eluding the carnage, I won't hold it against you."

"But here, now—"

"Yes! The moment has arrived. I had hoped to postpone it once again, to buy a little more time. It was my intention to cross these mountains and somehow get to Gaul, taking back roads to evade battle, fighting our way through the passes if we had to, surviving the snowstorms if we could. But when we reached the pass up above, what do you think we saw waiting for us on the other side? Another Roman army. I decided to come back down and face this one. It's commanded by the consul Antonius, you see. He was once sympathetic to my cause. I hear that Cicero bought him off by giving up the governorship he was due at the end of his consulship and letting Antonius have it instead. Still, you never know; Antonius might decide to join me at the last moment. Yes, Gordianus, I know that's impossible, but don't say so aloud! No more ill omens within the tent, if you please. But look here, just as I said: your son returns."

Meto stood at the entrance. "I've come to put on my armor," he said.

"Here, help me with mine first. It will take only a moment." Catilina stood and raised his arms while Meto fitted a breastplate around him and tightened it, then attached a long crimson cape. He picked up a gilded helmet with a splendid red plume and placed it on Catilina's head.

"There!" said Catilina, observing his reflection in a burnished plate. "Don't tell Tongilius I let you dress me; he'll be jealous of the honor." He took his eyes from the mirror and looked at each of us in turn, a long, steady gaze such as one gives to friends before leaving on a long journey. "I'll leave you alone now. Don't be long."

Meto watched him depart, then walked to the cot where his armor lay.

"Meto—"

"Here, Papa, help me. Would you bring my breastplate? Somehow it ended up across the tent."

I picked it up and went to him. He lifted his arms.

"Meto—"

"It's simpler than it looks. Line up the leather laces with the buckles and fasten the top pair on either side to begin with."

I did as he said, as if I moved in a dream.

"Forgive me for deceiving you, Papa. I couldn't think of any other way."

"Meto, we must leave this place at once."

"But this is where I belong."

"I'm asking you to come home with me."

"I decline."

"And if I command you as your father?"

His breastplate fully fastened, Meto drew back and looked at me with an expression at once sad and rebellious. "But you are *not* my father."

"Oh, Meto," I groaned.

"My father was a slave I never knew, as I was a slave."

"Until I freed you and adopted you!"

One at a time he put his feet on the cot to fasten his greaves into place. "Yes, the law calls you my father, and by law you have the right to command me, or even to kill me for disobeying you. But we both know that in the eyes of the gods you're not really my father. I have none of your blood in my veins. I'm not even Roman, but Greek, or some mongrel mixture—"

"You're my son!"

"Then I'm a man as well, a free citizen, and I've made my own choice."

"Meto, think of those who love you. Bethesda, Eco, Diana—"

From without we heard a trumpet blast.

"That's the signal for Catilina's speech. I have to be there. You should probably leave now, while you still have time, Papa—" He bit his tongue, as if to take back what he had called me, then quickly finished outfitting himself. When he was done, he looked at himself in the burnished plate and seemed gravely pleased. He turned to face me. "Well, what do you think?" he said, with a trace of shyness.

You see, you *are* my son, I thought; why else do you seek my praise? But out loud I snapped at him, "What does it matter?" He lowered his eyes and his cheeks turned red, and now it was my turn to bite my tongue; it would have been worse if I had told him what I truly thought, for as I looked at him dressed in his gleaming, mismatched armor, what I saw was a little boy outfitted in a make-believe costume, pretending to go to war. The idea that others could look at him and see a real soldier, fit to be killed if they could manage it, sent a chill through my heart.

"I can't miss the speech," he said, walking quickly past me. I followed him out of the tent and across the camp, to a place where a depression in the rocky hillside formed a natural amphitheater. We worked our way through the dense crowd until we were close enough to see. There was a blare of trumpets to quiet the crowd, and then Catilina stepped forward, resplendent in his armor and wearing a somber smile on his face.

"No speech from a commander, no matter how rousing or eloquent, ever made a coward brave, or turned a sluggish army into a keen one, or gave men who had no cause to fight a reason to do so. Yet it is the custom for a commander to give his troops a speech before a battle, and so I will.

"One reason for a speech, I suppose, is that in many armies, most of the soldiers have seldom laid eyes on the man who supposedly leads them, much less have spoken to him or been spoken to by him, and so a speech is thought to establish a certain bond. That justification for a speech does not apply here today, for I doubt there is a single man among you whom I haven't personally greeted and welcomed to the ranks of this army, or with whom I haven't shared some moment of hardship or triumph in this struggle. Yet it is the custom for a commander to give his troops a speech before a battle, and so I will.

"I said before that mere words cannot put courage into a man. Every man has a certain degree of boldness, I believe, either inborn or cultivated by training; so much, and no more, does he generally exhibit in battle. If a man is not already stirred by the prospect of glory or by immediate danger, then it is merely a waste of breath to exhort him with rhetoric; fear in the heart makes deaf the ears. Yet it is the custom for a commander to give his troops a speech before a battle, and so I will."

How peculiar, I thought, for a Roman orator to begin a speech by deriding its importance, to satirize an oration even while orating it, to be unabashedly honest before a crowd of listeners!

Catilina's expression became somber. "I will set before you as plainly as I can the prospect we face together, and the stakes for which we fight.

"You know how our allies in Rome have failed us, what a lack of judgment and enterprise was shown by Lentulus and his friends, and how disastrous it has been for themselves and for us. Our present predicament is as obvious to all of you as it is to me. Two enemy armies now bar our way, one between us and Gaul, the other between us and Rome. To remain where we are is impossible, for we have run short of grain and other supplies. Whichever path we decide to take, we must use our swords to cut our way through.

"Therefore I counsel you to be resolute and to summon up whatever measure of courage you have. When you go into battle, remember that riches, honor, glory, and, what is more, your liberty and the future of your country are held in the hand that wields your weapon. If we win, we shall obtain all we need to continue; towns will open their gates to us with thanksgiving and we shall be showered with supplies. New recruits will join us, and we shall grow again in strength and numbers. The tide that flows against us will be turned and will carry us to glory. But if fear causes us to flinch, the whole world will turn against us: no one will shield a man whose own arms have failed to protect him.

"Keep in mind that our adversaries are not impelled by the same necessity as we are, nor by as just a cause. For you and me, country, justice, and liberty are at stake. They, on the other hand, have been ordered into battle to protect a ruling elite for which they can have little love. We have chosen our glorious course; we have endured exile and hardship; we have proclaimed to the world that we will not return to Rome with our heads bowed in shame, willing to live out our lives as the cringing subjects of unworthy rulers. The men we are to face, on the other hand, have already submitted to the yoke of their masters and closed their eyes to any other course. Which of these armies will show the more spirit, I ask you— those whose eyes are meekly cast down or those whose eyes are on the heavens?"

To this question Catilina received a great cheer, and among the other voices Meto's rang in my ears, crying out the name of his commander. The din went on and on. Swords were beaten against shields to produce a deafening clang. The noise died down, only to spring up again in a great roar that covered my arms with gooseflesh. At last Tongilius stepped forward and raised his arms for silence so that Catilina could go on.

He had begun his speech in a dry, sardonic tone, as if by his own brash example he could lend spirit to his men. But I think he was moved by their accolades, for he ended with a quaver in his voice. "When I think of you, soldiers, and consider what you've already achieved, I have high hopes for victory. Your boldness and valor give me confidence. We will fight upon a plain. To our left are mountains, and to our right is rough, rocky ground. In this confined space, the enemy's superior numbers cannot encircle us. We shall face them man to man, with courage and just cause as our strongest weapons. But if, in spite of this, Fortune robs your valor of its just reward, do not sell your lives cheaply. Do not be taken and slaughtered like cattle! Fight like men: let bloodshed and lamentation be the price that the enemy must pay for his bitter victory!"

Another cheer went up, echoing between the hills on either side. It was ended by blaring trumpets, calling for the troops to take up their battle formations. All around us men began to move with quick determination. Meto seized my arm with a bruising grip.

"Go now! If you take your horse, you may be able to escape the way you came, or else head up toward the pass and find some trail to lead you back down again when the battle's over."

"Come with me, Meto. Show me the way."

"No, Papa! My place is here."

"Meto, the cause is hopeless! Never mind Catilina's speech. If you could have heard the way he spoke to me in the tent—"

"Papa, there's nothing you know that I do not. My eyes are open."

And fixed on the heavens, I thought. "Very well, then. Can you equip me with some sort of armor?"

"What?"

"If I'm to stay here and fight beside you, I'd like to have something more suitable than the dagger in my belt, though many of these wretches don't appear to have anything better."

"No, Papa, you can't stay!"

"How dare you say that to me! Would you stand your ground and deny me the same honor?"

"But you've given it no thought—"

"No, Meto, on the journey here I had many hours to think. I imagined this moment long before it came. In my imagination it sometimes turned out considerably more to my liking, but sometimes it turned out much worse—I thought I might find you dead without ever seeing you again, or find only a pit filled with dead bodies, with nothing to show me which was yours. This is better than that, and not as bad as I had feared. For one thing, I'm not as frightened as I thought I would be, at least not yet. No, Meto, this is my deliberate and premeditated choice, to fight beside my son."

"No, Papa, it must be for Catilina, for what he represents, if it's to mean anything!"

"That is *your* cause, Meto; but very well, I'll fight for Catilina. Why not? The truth, Meto: if I had the power of Jupiter I'd wave a thunderbolt and give Catilina everything he wants. Why not? I'd resurrect Spartacus from the dust and let him have his way as well. I'd roll back time and see that Sulla was never born, or Cicero for that matter. I'd change the world in the blink of an eye, for better or worse, merely to see it changed into something different. But I cannot do those things, and neither can anyone else. So why not take up a rusty sword and run screaming into battle beside my son, for the glory of what he loves with all his foolish young heart?"

Meto looked at me for a long time with an unreadable expression in his eyes. He must believe I'm mad, or lying, or both, I thought. But when he finally spoke, he said: "You *are* my father."

"Yes, Meto. And you're my son."

Men ran madly around us. Horses neighed, metal clanged on metal, officers shouted, trumpets blared. At last Meto took my arm. "Come, hurry, I think there's enough spare armor in

Catilina's tent to put something together for you!"

And so at the age of forty-seven I became a soldier for the
first time in my life, outfitted in scraps of cast-off armor,
wearing a coat of mail with half the scales missing and a
much-dented helmet shaped like a hewn-off pumpkin, wielding a blunted sword for a hopeless cause under a doomed
commander. I felt I must be approaching the very heart of the
Labyrinth; I could almost smell the Minotaur's hot breath
upon my face.

There is not much I can do to describe the battle, as I never
knew quite where I was or quite what was happening. It
seems that Catilina arrayed his forces in three parts, with
Manlius on one side, another commander on the other, and
himself in the center surrounded by his ardent young followers and a picked body of well-armed fighting men, along with
Meto and myself. We marched forward with Tongilius carrying the eagle standard until Catilina chose the spot where he
would make his stand, and there Tongilius planted the standard in the ground. There was no cavalry, only infantry, for
before the battle Catilina saw that all the horses were driven
back toward the mountains. By doing this he showed his men
that their commanders could not flee, and that their danger
was shared by all alike.

The danger approached like a great crimson and silver tide,
drawing toward us with a roar unlike anything I had ever
heard. I know now how it must be for the enemies of Rome
when they see their doom approaching. I was awed and horrified, and yet not frightened. Fear seemed pointless in the
face of such catastrophe. Why should a simple man cringe
with fear for his simple life, when the whole world was about
to end in screaming madness?

I felt no regret, but I did feel something of a fool, for I
could not help thinking to myself: stupid man, Bethesda will
never forgive you for this. And it was that I feared, more than
the jagged wall of steel bearing down on us.

I stayed close beside Meto, who stayed close beside Catilina. There was a great deal of running, sometimes from one
side to the other, sometimes forward, but never back. I remember an arrow that whirred by my ear and struck a man

behind me with a sickening thud. I remember soldiers, men I had never seen before, rushing toward me with swords in their hands and murder in their eyes; it all seemed so unlikely that I only wanted the nightmare to end. But the sword in my hand seemed to know what to do, so I followed it blindly.

I remember foaming blood sprayed upon my face like the pounding surf of the ocean. I remember seeing Catilina, his face contorted into a terrible grimace, his sword arm slashing, with an arrow projecting from his left shoulder and blood spilling down his glistening breastplate. I remember seeing Meto rush to Catilina's side with grim determination on his face, hewing a path with his sword as if he had been doing such things all his life. I hurried after him but tripped over something solid and fleshy. As I spun around, I glimpsed Tongilius in the throng behind me, bringing up the eagle standard, for with Catilina leading we had cut our way deep into the enemy's line. I gained my footing again and looked frantically for Meto, who had disappeared in the chaos.

Then, from the corner of my eye, I saw the spear approaching. I remember watching, transfixed, as it came hurtling straight toward my forehead. It seemed to move very slowly, and everything in the world, including myself, came to a sudden stop awaiting its arrival; so slowly did it approach that I felt like a man on a pier waiting for a boat to arrive. It drew closer and closer, and when it was very, very close the world abruptly jerked back into frantic motion. The absurd thought struck me that I really should be doing more than I was to get out of the thing's way—then the spear struck its target with a peculiar sound of crumpled metal and all at once I was flying backward through the air. Behind or above me—direction lost all meaning—I caught a glimpse of the eagle banner as it wavered and tottered and went crashing to the ground like myself, and then the bloodred world turned darkest black.

THIRTY-NINE

I sat on a hard rock surrounded by rough-hewn walls of black stone, with black stone underfoot and above my head. I thought at first that the place was a cave, but the walls were too angular to be natural, and the air was warm, not cold and clammy. Perhaps it was the old silver mine up on Mount Argentum, I thought, but that was all wrong. I was in the famous Labyrinth of Crete, of course, for peering at me from around a corner, its horns making a vast shadow on the wall beyond, was the Minotaur itself.

The thing was quite close to me, so close that I could see the glistening flesh of its great black nostrils and the glint in its great black eyes. I should have been mad with fear, but strangely I was not. All I could think was that the beast's nostrils, moist and porous and sprouting a few coarse hairs, looked very delicate and sensitive, and that its eyes were rather beautiful in a bovine way. It was a living creature, and amid so much hard, bloodless stone anything made of living flesh seemed precious and rare, something to be cherished, not feared. Even so, as the beast stepped from around the corner and drew closer, its two hooves clicking on the stone, I was a bit unnerved at the sight of a bull who walked upright and had a human torso. I noticed also that its tall, curving horns had very sharp points and were marked by a stain the color of rust.

The Minotaur snorted, spraying steam from its dripping black nostrils. It stopped a few steps away and cocked its head. When it spoke, it was in a voice that seemed somehow disguised, for it sounded hoarse and unnatural. "Who are you?" it said.

"My name is Gordianus."

"You don't belong here."

"I came here to find something."

"That was foolish. This is a maze, and the purpose of a maze is to mislead."

"But I've found my way to you."

"Or did I find my way to you?"

I felt a quiver not of fear but of uncertainty, so profound that it made my head ache. I closed my eyes for a moment. When I opened them again, I felt that something had changed, and realized that the stone walls around me had faded away. Even so, it was still quite dark. I was atop a high hill beneath starlight, looking down on a country scene—a stream with a water mill, a stone wall in the distance, a road, a farmhouse. It was my farm, I realized, though I was seeing it from an unfamiliar angle. I seemed to be on a ridge, though not the ridge I was used to. The view was oddly tilted and askew.

We were no longer alone. I turned and saw three naked, headless bodies seated on tree stumps in a row with their hands in their laps, like spectators at a play, or judges at a trial.

"Who are they? What are they doing here?" I asked the Minotaur in a hushed, confidential tone, though the others were clearly deaf, blind, and dumb. "You know, don't you?"

The Minotaur nodded.

"Then tell me."

The Minotaur shook its head.

"Speak!"

The beast snorted through its great, black, steaming nostrils and said nothing. It raised a human arm and pointed at something on the ground beside me. I looked down and saw a sword. I picked it up and weighed it in my grip, pleased by the way it gleamed beneath the starlight. "Speak, or I shall make you join them," I said, pointing with the sword to the three headless witnesses.

The Minotaur remained mute. I stood and brandished the blade. "Speak!" I said, and when the beast refused, I swung the sword with all my strength and cut clear through its great bullish neck. As its head tumbled away, I saw that the Minotaur was hollow inside; its body was only a costume, and its head a mask. The true head began to emerge from within. I stepped back, my temples aching from the suspense.

Then I knew the truth . . .

*   *   *

And then I awoke, with a hammering, blinding pain in my head. Someone touched my shoulder and spoke in a low voice. "It's all right, don't move. You're safe. Can you hear me?"

I opened my eyes and shut them against the brutal light. If I kept still, the pain receded. I caught my breath and heard myself groan. I put my hand over my face and cautiously opened my eyes again, not to harsh sunlight as I had thought, but to the soft, filtered light of a tent. For a moment I thought I was back in Catilina's tent, and wondered how I had got there. If his tent still stood, if his camp was intact, then—

I lowered my hand and saw a face so unexpected that I was cast into utter confusion. A shock of red hair, a spangling of freckles across a handsome nose, and a pair of bright brown eyes looking into my own: my friend the augur, Marcus Valerius Messalla Rufus.

"Rufus?"

"Yes, Gordianus, it's me."

"Are we in Rome?"

"No."

"Then where?"

"Far to the north, near a town called Pistoria. There was a battle—"

"Are we in Catilina's camp?"

He sighed in such a way that I knew no such place existed any longer. "No. This is the camp of Antonius."

"Then—"

"You're very lucky to be alive, my friend."

"And Meto?" My chest constricted.

"It was Meto who saved you."

"Yes, but—"

"He lives, Gordianus," said Rufus, seeing my fear.

"Thank the gods! Where is he?"

"He'll be here soon. When I saw you were stirring, I sent a man to fetch him."

I sat up, clenching my teeth at the pain in my head. My limbs and torso appeared to be intact. I looked around and saw that there was no one in the tent but Rufus, unless one counted the clucking chickens who inhabited the cages stacked near the tent flap. Looking at them suddenly made me feel hungry.

"How long since the battle?"

"That was yesterday."

"How did I get here?"

"Your son is a very brave young man. When he saw you had fallen, he rushed to you and carried you out of danger, behind the lines, beyond the camp, up among the boulders in the foothills. He must have been utterly exhausted. Can you imagine how much you both weighed, wearing that armor? And you a dead weight? And of course he was bleeding from his own wounds—"

"His wounds?"

"Never fear, Gordianus, they were minor. He made sure you were far from the danger; then he must have collapsed from exhaustion. He was found unconscious beside you."

"By whom?"

"After the battle Antonius's reserves were sent to scour the hills. They were ordered to take any man prisoner who was willing to give himself up, and to offer battle only to those who offered it first. Do you know how many prisoners they came back with? Exactly two: yourself and Meto, both unconscious. Of all Catilina's army, only you two survived— such a curious omen that it was thought an augur should come to see it. I was summoned, and once I saw who it was, I put you under my protection and had you brought to my tent. When he awoke, Meto explained to me how you both came to be in Catilina's camp. He went out just a short while ago to look for something to eat."

"Then I hope he brings something back with him," I said, clutching my stomach. "I don't know which feels emptier, my stomach or my head! Only we two, you say; then Catilina—"

"Gone, with all the rest. To a man, they died bravely, and took many lives with them. All morning the soldiers here in camp have been talking about it, saying they never before encountered so much resistance from such an outnumbered foe. Catilina's commanders all died in the front ranks. Each position was held fast until every man defending it was dead, and all their wounds were in front. They exacted a terrible toll: before it was over, all of Antonius's best fighters were dead or severely wounded."

"And Catilina? How did he die?"

"He was found far from his own men, deep within enemy ranks among the bodies of his adversaries. His garments and armor and flesh were all the same color, soaked red with blood. He was pierced by more wounds than could be counted, yet he was still breathing when they found him. They called me to hear his testament if he should speak; he never opened his eyes or uttered a word. But by his face you could see that he was himself to the end. Until his final breath he wore that expression of haughty defiance that caused so many men to hate him."

"And made others love him," I said quietly.

"Yes."

"I know that expression. I should like to have seen his face."

"You still may," said Rufus. Before I could ask him what he meant, from outside we heard a sudden wail of grief so wrenching that it froze my blood. "That's been going on all morning," sighed Rufus. "No cries of jubilation and victory, only lamentations. Men have been wandering about the battlefield, some to strip armor from the dead, others to see the scene by the next day's light, as men like to do in places where they've fought. They turn over the mangled corpses of the enemy and what do they find? The faces of friends and relatives and boys they grew up with. This has been a terrible and bitter victory."

"Why did you come, Rufus?"

"To serve as augur, of course. To take the auspices before the battle."

"But why you?"

"The Pontifex Maximus appointed me to do so," he said, then looked at me shrewdly. "Which is another way of saying that I came at Caesar's behest."

"To be his eyes and ears."

"If you like. As augur I can be privy to all that happens without staining my own hands with Roman blood. I sit in on the councils of war, but I do not make war. I only interpret the mood of the heavens."

"In other words, you're here as Caesar's spy."

"If a man can be a spy when everyone knows his role."

"Does the intrigue never end?"

"*Nunquam,*" he said, gravely shaking his head. *Never.*

"I don't suppose Antonius ever showed the slightest hesitation about destroying his old colleague. Catilina had hoped he might waver."

"He did, in his way. He was struck by a bad case of gout just before the battle, and put one of his lieutenants in charge. During the actual fighting Antonius was in bed with his tent flap tied shut. No one can say he failed to pursue his old friend Catilina, as he was charged to do by the Senate; nor can anyone say, strictly speaking, that he took part in Catilina's destruction. Soon the old goat will be off to enjoy the lucrative governorship in Macedonia he finagled from Cicero, and Rome will have one less hypocrite to clutter up the Forum."

I shook my head, then winced at the lightning behind my eyes. "My head feels like an overripe gourd."

"And looks like one, too." Rufus smiled. "You have a knot on your forehead the size of a walnut."

There was a noise at the tent flap. I turned my head too quickly and fell back against the cot, groaning. The sound must have been more alarming than the actual pain, for Meto was quickly at my side, clutching me and asking Rufus through clenched teeth, "Is he—"

"Your father is well except for the pain in his head."

I opened my eyes and saw Meto for only an instant before his image was blurred by tears. The tears seemed to carry away some of the ache behind my eyes, which was good, for I had many tears to spill. But tears would never make Meto the way he had been before. Rufus had said his wounds were minor, and by the scale of suffering around us he was correct, for Meto still walked and breathed and had all his parts. But the blade that had sliced away a bit of his left ear and cut a gash all the way to the corner of his mouth would leave him with a scar that he would carry forever.

It was impractical and inadvisable for Meto to speak, because the movement of his jaw pulled at the torn flesh of his wound.

Rufus had fashioned for him a simple bandage to tie around
his head, which kept his mouth shut and also covered the cut.
When I first saw him, he had removed the bandage for a while
to take a little food and water.

It was hardly easier for me to speak, or listen for that
matter, because of the throbbing in my head. Perhaps it was
just as well, for words could only have obscured the feelings
that passed between us as he sat beside my cot, holding my
hand.

I did manage to tell him about the new corpse which had
appeared just before I left the farm, and also of my dream
about the Minotaur, and what I had surmised from it. I knew
now who had left the bodies on the farm, and why, and with
whose assistance. Meto was taken aback at first, disbelieving,
and questioned me through clenched teeth, but as I laid before
him the bits of evidence that came to my mind, he was compelled to agree with what the dream had told me.

I longed to go home. Now that Meto was safe, I brooded
over the safety of Bethesda and Diana, whom I had left at
the mercy of the Minotaur. Had Eco come, as I asked him
to? Even if he had, bringing Belbo and a dozen bodyguards
with him, I feared that he might fail to protect them, not
knowing what to protect them from. The Minotaur was growing more desperate and more devious. But when I stood up
and attempted to dress myself, I barely managed to stagger
back to the bed. Riding a galloping horse would have been a
torture impossible to bear.

Rufus offered me nepenthes for my pain and also to help
me sleep. I refused him, telling him that there must be
wounded men in the camp in far more agonizing pain than I
was, who could use the same draft of forgetfulness to ease
their release into death. Still, I think he must have put some
poppy juice in the wine he brought me later, for despite my
pain and the turmoil of my worries, I slipped into a fretless,
healing sleep unhaunted by Minotaurs or any other monsters.

I woke only once in the night, to a darkness lit by a single
small lamp and the sound of two voices quietly conversing.

"But the eagle at the Auguraculum, and Catilina's eagle—"
I heard Meto say, his voice constricted by the bandage around
his head.

"Yes, I agree, these were signs and you read them rightly," said Rufus. "It was the will of the gods that you should fight beside Catilina."

"But I should have stayed with Papa! I only ended up taking him away from Bethesda and Diana when they needed him most—when they needed both of us to protect them. If something terrible has happened on the farm—"

"You can't blame yourself, Meto. There are forces greater than ourselves that drive us through this world, just as winds drive sailing ships or make feathery seeds go dancing on the air. To submit to the wind that brought you here was not a folly."

"But if that was my destiny, I should have died fighting beside Catilina! It was what I thought would happen. I was ready; I didn't fear it. But when I saw Papa fall, I had to go to him. When I saw he was still alive, I couldn't leave him there. I left the battle and carried him to safety, meaning to return, but my strength deserted me and the enemy found me unconscious. I should fall on my sword in shame!"

"No, Meto. You told me something earlier, about the eagle standard. You said that just before you went to your father, you saw the standard totter and fall."

"Yes, Tongilius was struck in the eye by an arrow. The standard fell and there was no one to pick it up."

"Don't you see? An eagle appeared to us all at the Auguraculum, to signal the beginning of your manhood. When you first saw Catilina's silver eagle, you recognized it as an omen and followed it all the way here and into battle. But when that eagle fell, not to rise again, you were released. You had done what you were meant to do. It was the gods' way of telling you to leave Catilina, whom the gods themselves could no longer help, and to go to your father, whom you alone could help. You did the right thing."

"Do you really think so, Rufus?"

"I do."

"And I'm not just a coward or a fool?"

"To follow a dream is never the act of a coward; to lay that dream aside in the fullness of time is the opposite of foolishness. To carry a man over your shoulders across a battlefield is not the act of a coward; to do so for the sake of your father marks you not as a fool but as a Roman, Meto. Ah, your father seems to be stirring. Gordianus? No, I see he's still asleep. But look, he's smiling; his pain must have eased, for him to be having such pleasant dreams."

The next morning I felt remarkably better. Long hours of sleep and the draft of nepenthes must have sorted out the jumbled humors in my head, and the walnut on my forehead had miraculously shrunk to a chickpea. Rufus fretted that I was not yet ready to travel, but when I insisted, he said he would supply horses for us.

"We're not prisoners, then? We're free to go?" I said.

Rufus smiled. "Certain privileges are allowed to an augur who represents the Pontifex Maximus himself. Let us say that, like nepenthes, I have been able to induce forgetfulness. Officially neither of you ever existed. No prisoners were taken at the battle of Pistoria; every one of Catilina's men died in combat. So the Senate will be told, and so the historians will record it. You're both remarkably lucky, not just to be alive but to have each other. Fortune smiles on you, Gordianus."

"Then I pray she continues to smile," I said, thinking of the farm and what might have transpired in my absence.

No one took any notice of us as we mounted our horses and made our way through the makeshift lanes and thoroughfares that threaded among the tents and bonfires. A somber mood prevailed, but there was also that hint of anarchy that enters such encampments when the battle is won and danger has departed. Men sat about in groups, drinking wine, arguing over details of the battle, gambling and haggling over the loot they had stripped from the dead.

Toward the rear of the camp our route took us by the commander's tent. Was Antonius still hiding inside, crippled by gout? I smiled at the thought, but the smile stiffened on my face when I saw the trophy erected on a spit outside the tent. Meto must have seen it in the same instant, for I heard him suck in his breath through clenched teeth.

Now I knew what Rufus had meant when he had said that I might see Catilina's face again.

They had saved it so that it might be taken to Rome and shown to the Senate and the people as proof of his demise.

Those who had feared him would have their fears allayed; those who had wished for his triumph would see their wishes shattered; those who might want to emulate him would be given a vivid warning. "I see two bodies, one thin and wasted, but with a swollen head, the other headless, but big and strong," he had told the Senate. "What is there so dreadful about it, if I myself become the head of the body which needs one?" But now the head of Catilina, bloody and torn at the neck, was mounted on a stake outside the tent of his conqueror, of no more use to anyone. The expression of haughty disdain frozen upon his features was wasted on the impervious flies which buzzed about his eyes and lips.

I swallowed hard. Beside me Meto made a peculiar sound, a great sob stifled by the bandage that kept his jaw shut. We paused for a long moment, gazing upon Catilina for the last time. It was Meto who turned away first, snapping his reins and kicking his horse to a gallop. He raced through the camp and I followed, past startled soldiers who shook their fists and cursed, and slaves who stooped to pick up their scattered burdens. Meto did not slow his steed until he was well out of the camp and onto the open road, where the cold gray sky and the naked hills seemed to offer a kind of solace.

FORTY

TRAVELING south, I found the mood of the countryside no different from when I had traveled north, for we were ahead of the news that Catilina had been defeated and killed. I had no wish to be the bearer of tidings, welcome or not, and kept my mouth shut at the places where we stopped. This was hard to do when I heard men speak of the glorious future that Catilina would bring, or heard others make the same weary jokes about the ruining of a Vestal Virgin, or heard others rant against his vile habits and mad schemes. I feared that Meto would feel compelled to shout and argue, and might reopen his wound, but he bore all that was said about Catilina with the taciturn, hard-jawed stoicism of a true Roman.

On the morning of our return, when we at last drew near
the farm and the countryside grew more familiar, I felt my
spirits lift. A light mist covered the earth, muting the subtle
colors of winter and softening the world's sharp edges. The
air in my lungs was cold and invigorating. We were almost
home. What was done was done, and life could begin again.
Of course there was the matter of confronting the Minotaur,
but so long as nothing terrible had taken place in my absence,
I almost looked forward to the meeting. At least it would
mean an end to the mounting collection of unwanted corpses
on my property, and an end to my ongoing displays of wrong-
headed deduction.

Meto was glad to be home, too. When we turned off the
Cassian Way onto the dirt road, he broke into a gallop, and
so did I. A slave was posted on the roof of the stable and
stood up to scrutinize us as we approached. Good, I thought;
a close watch was being kept even in daylight, just as I had
ordered. When the slave recognized us, he began to call out,
"The Master! And young Meto!"

As we were dismounting in front of the stable, Eco stepped
out of the house. I smiled at him, but he did not smile back.
He must have noticed Meto's bandage, I thought, and was
worried by it. But then Bethesda came running after him. She
could not yet have seen Meto's bandage, but her face was red
from crying. She ran past Eco, who was walking toward us
as if every step caused him pain. She clutched my arms so
hard that I thought her nails would tear the sleeves of my
tunic.

"Diana!" she said, in a voice hoarse from crying. "Diana
is gone!"

Everything changed in an instant, as if night had fallen in
the blink of an eye, or the air had somehow frozen solid.

"Gone?" I said. "Do you mean—"

"Missing," said Eco.

"For how long?"

Bethesda spoke in a rush. "Since yesterday. I was with her
all morning, and at midday she ate, but after that—it wasn't
until the middle of the afternoon that I realized she must be
gone. I took a nap—oh, if only I hadn't. When I woke up I

couldn't find her. I called for her everywhere, I shouted until I was hoarse, until long after it was dark, but there was no answer and she never came. How could she be lost? She knows every part of the farm, and she knows better than to go wandering beyond it. I don't understand—"

I looked at Eco. "The well?" I said.

He shook his head. "I looked there, and in every other place I could think of where she might have fallen or hurt herself. The slaves have combed the property from end to end, more than once. There's no sign of her."

"Meto!" cried Bethesda suddenly, seeing his bandage for the first time. She stepped away from me and put her arms around him.

"And the neighbors?" I said to Eco.

"I've gone to see all four of them. They all claim complete ignorance, but who knows? If I had cause to blame one of them, I'd gladly burn down his house to make him tell the truth."

"Who saw Diana last?"

"She wasn't satisfied with her midday porridge and wanted more. Bethesda was asleep, so Diana took it on herself to go into the kitchen for another helping. Congrio says he teased her about being such a glutton, but gave her another bowl. She ate it there in the kitchen, and then she ran outside to play. But no one seems to have seen her—"

"Meto!" cried Bethesda as he tore himself from her arms and ran toward the house.

"Come, Eco, hurry, before he kills him!" I cried, running after Meto.

By the time I reached the kitchen, Congrio had already been knocked to the floor. He was on his back, a look of surprised panic in his eyes, with his hands raised to shield his face. Meto wielded a heavy iron poker from the furnace and was swinging it without restraint. The metal made a curiously pleasant sound as it connected with the soft flesh that padded Congrio's body. "Where is she? Where is she?" Meto kept growling through clenched teeth, while Congrio wailed and screamed.

"Meto, I've already questioned him!" protested Eco, who made a move to stop the beating, then jumped back as Meto

swung the poker wildly. With Eco out of the way, Meto resumed the beating, striking the plump cook again and again.
I didn't have to see his face to know the satisfaction he felt
by giving in to such unchecked violence, for I felt it, too. All
his despair and bitterness was being vented against the helpless body that kicked and screamed on the floor.

"Papa, stop him! He'll kill the poor slave!" cried Eco.

"As well he might, but not before we find out what he
knows," I said. "All right, Meto, enough. Enough!" Holding
my hands before my face, I managed to intervene and grab
Meto's arm as he raised it to deliver another blow. He fought
against me for a moment, then clumsily transferred the poker
to his other hand, as if he meant to go on beating Congrio,
but Eco was able to wrest the weapon from him, and I was
able to hold his arms at his sides long enough for him to gain
control of himself. Congrio, meanwhile, lay blubbering and
gasping on the floor.

"Torture him, Papa! Make him talk!" snarled Meto.

"Yes, I will if I have to." I turned toward Congrio, intending to deliver the hardest kick I could manage, but the
sight he presented was so pathetic I refrained.

"Please, Master, don't hurt me!" he wept, and when Meto
moved menacingly toward him he shrieked. "I know nothing!"

"Liar!" I couldn't resist kicking him then. His squealing
reaction gave me a taste of Meto's joy. "Liar! I know about
you already. You'll be lucky if I let you live after what you've
done. Now tell me what's become of Diana, or by Jupiter I'll
torture you until you do!"

Congrio was very forthcoming after that.

"We mustn't give ourselves away too soon," I cautioned Meto
and Eco as we guided our horses off the Cassian Way. Belbo
was also with us, along with ten other slaves, most of them
burly strong-armers whom Eco had brought when he came
up from Rome, and all of them armed with daggers. Ahead
of us, mostly hidden beyond a copse, was the little farmhouse.
A plume of smoke rose from the house, which meant that our
quarry was probably still about and had not fled to Rome or
elsewhere. Diana, I prayed, was also within the house, but

the thought of how we might find her caused my chest to tighten and made my stomach twist into knots.

"Since you were already here yesterday asking questions, Eco, perhaps they won't be too surprised to see you again. The important thing is to get inside, and then to move very quickly."

"Don't worry, Papa, we talked about all this before we left the house," said Meto. "We know what to do."

In the copse, hidden by the dense, naked branches, the slaves dismounted and tied their horses. Meto, Eco, and I rode on alone. It was the quiet hour after midday, and no one was stirring outside. When we reached the house we dismounted and Eco rapped on the door. An old slave woman with silver hair opened it. "Ah, you," she said, recognizing Eco, then squinting past him to scrutinize Meto and me.

"My father and brother, just returned from a long journey," Eco said. "They've come to ask about my sister, as I did. For their own satisfaction, you understand."

The slave woman nodded uncertainly. "Ah, yes. Well, let me go and tell—"

"Eco, is that you again?" crooned a familiar voice from within. A dim figure appeared inside the dark house and approached us. "Oh, my dear boy, I wish I had news for you, but I fear that nothing—oh, and your father as well. And Meto, wearing an awful bandage!" she said, stepping into the light of the doorway, pushing a handful of frazzled red hair from her face.

"Yes, Claudia, we've come to ask for your help," I said.

"Then poor Diana is still missing?"

"Yes."

"Oh, dear, and I had so hoped that she would turn up at your house before darkness fell last night. You must be so terribly worried."

"We are."

"Especially Bethesda. I've never known a mother's joys myself, nor a mother's sorrows, but she must be utterly distraught! But I'm afraid I have nothing new to tell you. I had my slaves scour the property, just as you asked, Eco, but they found no trace. If you wish, you could send over some of your own slaves to search—just to satisfy yourselves. I can understand that."

"You would allow that, Claudia?"

"Of course."

"Would you let us search inside your stable and your out-buildings?"

"If you wish. I don't see how she could have gotten inside any of those places without my slaves knowing, or how she could stay unseen, unless she's intentionally hiding for some reason—but search if you wish."

"And would you let us search even inside your house, Claudia?"

Her mask slipped a bit. "Well . . ."

"In your private rooms, in your bedroom, for instance? In places no outsider would ordinarily see?"

"I'm not sure what you mean, Gordianus. The child could hardly be in my house without my knowing it, could she?"

"No, I don't imagine she could."

For an instant her eyes grew hard and glittering, then Claudia drew her brows together and pressed her mouth into a sweetly indulgent pout. "Oh, Gordianus, how distraught you must be to be talking like this. Certainly, search wherever you wish! Do it right now, to set your mind at ease, so that you can get on with your searching elsewhere."

"We shall," I said, and as swiftly and smoothly as I could, as if I were taking her in my arms to kiss her neck, I spun her around and put my dagger to her throat. She opened her mouth and distended her throat to make a noise, but cringed at the touch of the sharp blade and choked instead. I pulled her out of the house into the cold sunlight, while Meto ran inside and Eco called for the slaves.

We met no resistance. The elderly door slave screamed in alarm, and Claudia's slaves came running, some with daggers or clubs, but when they saw their mistress's predicament they drew back and watched dumbly as my men ransacked the stable and the wine press, the tool sheds and the slave quarters, and then searched the house.

"You're making a horrible mistake," said Claudia.

"The horrible mistake will be yours if you've done anything to harm her," snapped Eco, running into the house to join the others in the search.

"The child is not here."

"But she was brought here," I said. "It's no use lying, Claudia. Congrio has betrayed you. Go ahead, stamp your foot and struggle; if you cut your throat it'll be your own fault."

She growled, and I felt the vibration of her throat against the blade. "It has nothing to do with me if your cook has been lying to you!"

"Not a lie but the truth, Claudia. Yesterday you sent one of your men to my house, a kitchen slave, ostensibly there to trade some of your goods for mine, something that happens all the time, something so common that no one even notices the man coming and going. But in reality he was there to plot your next design with Congrio, something that's happened several times before. According to Congrio, your latest scheme has something to do with poison. That was too much for Congrio and he wanted nothing to do with it, or so he claims, and so your man proceeded to argue with him. No one else was in the kitchen, Eco was out of the house and Bethesda was napping, so they spoke freely in hushed voices, until they suddenly looked down to find that Diana had been standing no less than a foot away, listening to them for who knows how long.

"They panicked. Congrio stuffed her mouth with a rag and they wound her in a long cloth. Your man had arrived with a handcart. They carried her outside and managed to fit her inside it and tie her down, and then he left as quickly as he could. My watchman claims he saw the man leave, but I think he's lying to keep from being punished, unless he's deaf and half-blind; even bound and with her mouth stuffed, I imagine Diana must have been able to make some noise and to shake the cart. Even so, the man got away without anyone's noticing. My slaves hardly even remembered his being there, he's become such a regular visitor. Your agent, Claudia, conspiring with my cook! So you see, I know the truth, or enough to have tracked Diana to your door. Now where is she?"

"Ask Congrio," she cried. "The lying slave! Don't you see he's done something unspeakable with your little girl and he won't admit it? Instead he makes up this ludicrous story. How dare you suspect me?"

"How dare you go on lying!" I said, barely able to keep from drawing the blade across her throat.

"If you think she's here, then find her. Go on, search to your heart's content. Your daughter is not here. You'll find nothing, I tell you."

I suddenly realized that she must be telling the truth. Diana had been brought here, of that I had no doubt, but had she remained here? No, Claudia was too clever and cautious to risk having Diana found on her property. Where then? Where would she hide a child—or a child's body?

In my abstraction I must have loosened my grip, for she suddenly slipped free. When I tried to seize her, she bit my hand. I cried out and Meto and Eco came running out of the house, but too late to catch her. She dashed into the midst of her slaves, who made a circle around her and held up their weapons.

Eco called out and his men came running. "We can take them, Papa. Her slaves will scream and run at the first drop of blood."

"Attack me and I won't be responsible for what follows, Gordianus," said Claudia, breathing hard. "Do you really want a blood feud with the Claudii?"

"Say the word, Papa!" said Meto, gripping his dagger so hard that his knuckles turned white.

"No, Meto! No bloodshed! Retribution can wait. The only thing that matters now is finding Diana, and I think I know where she is. Eco, stay here with your men. Make sure that Claudia stays where she is until we return. Meto, mount your horse and come with me."

Claudia must have known of the mine all her life. As a place of remote concealment, it would have come to her mind at once. So I reasoned as we went thundering up the Cassian Way. So I hoped, and dreaded.

We rode past the hidden trail Catilina had used. It would be too slow, and I had no cause for concealment. Instead we took the open way onto Gnaeus's land, up into the foothills and the woods, past the house of the goatherds where poor

Forfex had dwelled, past Gnaeus's gloomy villa, where his hounds stirred and howled to announce our passage.

We came to the end of the road, tethered our horses and proceeded on foot. Neither of us spoke a word. Our thoughts were too close, and what we were thinking we did not dare to say aloud.

The stream above the waterfall flowed quick and cold. The water came to our knees. When I stepped onto the farther bank, my feet were numb with pain, but I forgot it quickly enough as we rushed up the grueling series of switchbacks and then across the flank of the mountain.

What if she wasn't there? My heart was pounding too hard and my breath was too labored to think of what we would do next. And what if she was there? Surely she could have survived a single night, I told myself. She could go without eating, and she would have been out of the wind, shielded from the worst of the cold. But in what condition had they left her, and what sort of terrors had she faced alone in the darkness? What if she had gone wandering, and stepped over an abyss—

Every step I took became a greater and greater torment, until I could no longer tell whether the anguish came from exhaustion or dread. Meto ran on ahead of me. For a moment I wanted to drop to my knees, to wait passively, to let him find what there was to find and come back to tell me. But to stop now was impossible. I trudged on, cursing Claudia, hating the gods and whispering prayers to Fortune.

At last the entrance to the mine came in sight. Meto was not to be seen. He must have already scrambled over the wall that had been built to keep out wandering goats and that would easily keep a little girl prisoner inside. I began to run, though I thought my chest would explode. You've become an old man and a fool, I told myself. You turned your back on the world, and look how the world struck back at you! Everything you love has been brought to the edge of disaster through your own neglect and your stubborn refusal to see clearly. Your vanity overwhelmed your judgment, and now you pay the price. You laid down your wits like a gladiator laying down his weapons; but a gladiator has no choice but to fight or else die, and you have no choice but to go on

finding your way through the deceits of this vicious world or
else be destroyed. What folly, fleeing from Rome, when this
is where the flight led you. Diana!

I came to the wall. I wanted to shout out her name, and
Meto's, but I was afraid of the answer. I reached the top of
the wall and fell against it, too tired to pull myself over. I
took a deep breath and hoisted myself to the top. On the other
side I looked down on Meto, holding something in his arms.
He turned his face up to me, and I saw tears glittering in his
eyes.

"Oh, no, Meto!" I wailed.

"Papa, Papa, you've come for us! I knew you would!" The
thing in Meto's arms began to wriggle wildly until Diana
freed herself from his embrace and reached up to me. I
dropped from the wall and fell to the ground, holding her.

"I told them you'd come, I told them!" she cried. I held
her away from me to have a look at her. She was filthy and
her clothes were torn, but there was nothing wrong with her.
I held her close to me and sat back against the wall, my face
covered with tears, so weary and relieved that I thought I
might melt into the stone.

"I told them, I told them," she kept saying, until I asked
her whom she meant.

"The others!" she said.

"Others?"

"The other little boys and girls." In the gloomy twilight of
the mine, she pointed to a collection of skulls carefully
stacked against one wall, the remains of long-dead slaves.

"I don't remember seeing them stacked up like that when
we were here with Catilina, do you, Meto?" I said, puzzled.

"No," he whispered.

"I did it," said Diana. "I gathered them all up."

"But why?" I asked.

"Because they were lonely, and so was I. I was cold last
night, Papa, but imagine how cold they must have been, without their skins."

I looked at her carefully. "Who do you think they are,
Diana?"

"The other little boys and girls, of course. The ones that
the wicked king brought for the Minotaur to eat. Look, he ate

them all up and left only the bones! Poor little boys and girls. When Claudia's slaves brought me here yesterday, I knew this must be the Labyrinth. They dropped me over the wall and wouldn't help me back over, even though I screamed and told them they'd be sorry. Do you suppose they thought the Minotaur would eat me?"

"Oh, Diana," I said, holding her tight, "you must have been so frightened!"

"Not really, Papa."

"No?"

"No. Meto probably would have been frightened, because Meto would have been afraid of the Minotaur, but not me."

"Why not, Diana?"

"Because the Minotaur is dead!"

"How did you know that?"

"Because you told me so, Papa. Don't you remember?"

"Yes. Yes, I do remember," I said, thinking back to a hot summer day when Diana had come to fetch me because an unexpected visitor had arrived from Rome, and we fell to talking about the Minotaur because Meto had been teasing her. "I told you that a hero named Theseus slew the Minotaur."

"Exactly. And that's why I wasn't frightened, only cold, and a little lonely, because the other poor children couldn't talk to me. And hungry. Papa, I'm so hungry. Can't we get something to eat? But not from Congrio—Congrio wants to poison us. . . ."

FORTY-ONE

METO was of the opinion that we should carve Congrio into filets and make a banquet of him. I pointed out that the dinner would be much too fatty; besides, he might contrive to poison himself first and thus poison us when we ate him. Bethesda thought we should drop him down the well and watch him slowly starve day by day. But why pollute the well again?

Eco, ever practical, suggested we choose an enemy of the family and offer to sell Congrio to the unsuspecting party, knowing how treacherous he was. Now there was an idea, I thought, but whom did we dislike that much?

As for Claudia, no punishment could be severe enough. Numerous ideas were bandied about. Most of these elaborate fantasies began with kidnapping her in the middle of the night and ended with visions of exquisite cruelty and horror to rival the worst abuses of Sulla. Bethesda was especially creative in devising torments, which I thought odd, for the Egyptians are a relatively civilized and easy-going people compared to the Romans. She was truly a Roman matron now, plotting the destruction of another Roman matron, as surely as Meto had proved himself a Roman soldier on the battlefield of Pistoria. We were all Romans now; and so, I argued, why not take recourse in that great Roman institution, the law?

This suggestion met with no enthusiasm at all. We had defeated the Claudii in the courts once, Eco conceded, but that was with a will on our side and Cicero's help. We couldn't be certain of winning against them again, and besides, look at the sluggishness of the courts in dealing with the dispute over the stream. Roman courts and Roman justice had become mere tools for powerful men to attack one another with, more amenable to bribery and intimidation than to demands for truth and justice. As in the days before the Republic, men were being driven to take matters into their own hands if they wanted satisfaction, which is what we would have to do if Claudia was to suffer for what she had done.

There was, of course, the matter of the other Claudii, I pointed out, who surrounded us like an enemy army. None of them struck me as likely to sit idly by if we harmed Claudia, no matter what our justification. They hated us enough already; what would they do if Claudian blood was spilled? Were we to spend the coming years killing and kidnapping one another? What sort of life was that?

It was a good thing to let everyone shout and throw up their arms and goad each other to devise more and more terrible torments for the guilty. After the fight we had suffered, we all needed such a shared release. It also bought me time, for after Diana was found they had all been eager to take drastic action at once. But I wanted that night and at least another day and night to pass before we proceeded on any course. While our anger cooled and left us with clearer heads, Claudia could spend a couple of sleepless nights wondering what we were up to.

On the second morning after Diana had been rescued, having heard all their arguments and cries for action, I exerted my prerogative as father of the household and announced that I would handle the matter in my own way. My decisions would be final and beyond appeal. Having made this clear, I retired to my library and wrote a brief note, then dispatched a slave to carry the message, telling him he would be wise to approach Claudia's house with his hands in the air and an announcement that he was armed only with a letter:

> Claudia:
>   There are matters we must discuss in private, and on neutral ground. Meet me at midday at our usual place on the ridge. I will come alone and unarmed, and I vow by the memory of my father to cause you no harm. Your presence there will indicate that you come under the same conditions. There is nothing to be gained by further acrimony, and I believe that we can come to terms of mutual acceptance. That is the earnest hope of your neighbor,
>
>   Gordianus

The day was cloudless, and there was no wind on the ridge-top, as I had feared there might be. All in all, it was a mild day for the end of Januarius, a month that had already seen enough turmoil for the whole year to come.

I sat on a stump and looked out over the farm, such a placid scene that it was hard to believe so much deceit and wickedness could lurk among the innocent grapevines and the cold, gurgling stream. The sun at its zenith was low in the sky and seemed to hang motionless while I waited. It was a long time, so long that I thought my guest had refused the invitation. Then I heard a rustling among the branches nearby and Claudia emerged from the bushes.

She looked as she usually looked: sausage-fingered, plum-cheeked, and cherry-nosed, with a careless clump of frazzled orange hair atop her head. She was wearing a long woolen tunic with a heavy cloak wrapped around her. She approached without a word, took a seat on the neighboring stump, and joined me in studying the view. I looked at her face, but she did not look back at me. I noticed a few horizontal cuts on her throat, where I had pressed too hard with my blade. She reached up from time to time to touch the marks.

After a moment she said, "Where shall we begin?"

"At the beginning. Before we say anything else, I want you to tell me the truth: did you have anything to do with the death of your cousin Lucius?"

This caused her to turn her head and look into my eyes, but only for a moment. "How could you even think—"

I held up my hand. "No pretty protests, Claudia. The question requires only a simple answer: yes or no."

"Did I murder Lucius? What a question! No, of course not. He died in the Forum, with hundreds of people around, clutching at a pain in his chest. Men die that way every day. It's perfectly natural."

"You did nothing to help nature along? A bit of poison . . ."

"Gordianus, no!"

I studied her profile while she stared fixedly down on the farm. "I believe you. I had no particular reason to think that you might have murdered poor Lucius, but I wanted to know for sure. He was my friend, you know. It would matter to me if someone had caused his death."

We both gazed at the view for a while in silence. It was clear that I would be asking the questions and that she would be answering. I was in no hurry.

"When I lent you Congrio to help cook for your family gathering," I finally said, "that was when you suborned him, wasn't it?"

She shrugged. "It wasn't hard to do. Congrio doesn't like you, and he despises your wife. Some slaves can't stand working for an ex-slave; Congrio hated it, simply on principle. Pride comes with talent, which he has in abundance, as I'm sure you'll agree. He had worked all his life in the respectable household of a patrician master, then suddenly found himself the property of—well, Gordianus, your ancestry is hardly worth mentioning, is it?"

"I'd prefer that *you* didn't mention my ancestors, true enough. So you told Congrio that if he would go along with your schemes, you could set everything right and become his new mistress. He agreed to become your agent in my household."

"Something like that."

"Would you believe that for a long time it was Aratus I suspected of betraying me?"

"Aratus?" said Claudia. "You should have known better. Lucius always said he was the most unwavering and loyal slave he had ever owned. A man couldn't hope for a better foreman to run a farm."

"So I've gradually come to realize. But back to Congrio: when the first headless body appeared in my stable, it was Congrio who placed it there, wasn't it?"

"Why ask me? You must have gotten the story from him already."

"Some of the story. Other bits I've worked out for myself, but there are some things only you could know for certain, Claudia. Well, then, it started on the day that we burned the first batch of blighted hay. There were a lot of fires on my land and a lot of smoke going into the air. One of your slaves showed up, ostensibly to deliver a gift of figs from your farm, in exchange for which I sent you some fresh eggs. I thought the man was there to see what the smoke was about; in reality, he was there to confer with Congrio and make plans for the delivery of the body. I remember he stayed a long time in the kitchen; I thought he was merely tasting Congrio's custard.

"The next day a wagon arrived, full of provisions. Congrio said it came all the way from Rome and that he'd had to go over Aratus's head to order the things he needed. That made me angry at Aratus, and took my mind away from Congrio. Still, I wondered why he insisted on unloading the wagon himself. Now I know: there was a dead body amid the pots and pans. The wagon came from your farm, not from Rome. Congrio unloaded the body, as your agent had instructed the day before. He managed to conceal it in the kitchen and then put it in the stable later. No wonder he was sweating and trembling; I merely thought he was out of breath and angry at Aratus." I spread my hands on my lap. "So I know how the body arrived and who assisted. But who was Nemo?"

"Nemo?"

"That was what I called the headless corpse, having no name for him. From his body, it was hard to tell whether he was freeborn or a slave. If a slave, he wasn't engaged in hard labor and didn't work outdoors. Nemo was your cook, wasn't he?"

Claudia looked at me sidelong. "How did you know that? I never even told Congrio."

"You told me yourself, but I wasn't listening at the time. Do you remember the note you sent back with Congrio, thanking me for lending him to you?" I pulled the scrap of parchment from within my tunic. "I saved it. I don't know why, except that you were so effusive in your gratitude that you called it 'a promissory note' which I could use to call on you for repayment. It was sentimental of me to set much store by it, I suppose, but I was touched by your gratitude. In the note you also said something else. Let me read it to you: 'Greetings neighbor, and my gratitude for the loan of your slaves,' et cetera, et cetera, 'especially your chief of the kitchen, Congrio, who has lost none of his skill since the days when he served my cousin Lucius. I am doubly grateful because my own cook fell ill in the midst of preparations, whereupon Congrio proved to be not merely a great help but utterly essential.' So, your head cook was ill. Later he died."

"How did you know?"

"You told me! It was here on the ridge, over on the eastern side. We were all watching the Cassian Way, you and Meto and I, and you fed us honey cakes. 'My new cook baked them fresh this morning,' you said. 'He's no Congrio, I fear, but he does make fine sweets.' Your *new* cook, Claudia, because the old one, the ill one, had died and you replaced him. And because you hate waste so very much—not even a morsel of a honey cake could you stand to waste!—you even found a use for your dead cook's body, thinking it could be a tool to frighten me off my farm, or at least make a beginning. So Nemo wasn't murdered, was he? He died of an illness, and after he was dead you had his head cut off so that no one would know him when he appeared on my farm. One of the kitchen slaves I lent you just might have seen the man, after all, and thus might have recognized the dead man's face."

"You comprehend everything, Gordianus. And did the appearance of the body not frighten you at all?"

"It frightened me very much, but at the time I had reason to think I knew who had left it, and why, and it had nothing to do with my neighbors or whether I should stay on the farm. I hid the incident from the slaves, including Congrio. Was it maddening when Congrio had nothing to report to your man the next time he came?"

"Quite."

"Meanwhile, I had every reason to think that I could trust you, if anybody, because the kitchen slaves I lent you returned with glowing reports of how you stood up for me to your cousins. It was you who planted the idea that I could use those slaves as spies on your family gathering. You joked about my having them poison your cousins; well, I would never do that, but I could tell my slaves to keep their ears open. And so they simply happened to 'overhear' you defending me to Gnaeus, Manius, and Publius. But you meant for those words to be overheard, didn't you? I was to think you were my only ally, and so when awful things began to happen on my farm, I might suspect anyone and everyone else, but never you. And if the time ever came when I was ready to sell the farm in desperation—well, I would turn to the one neighbor who had stood by me, wouldn't I?"

Claudia shifted on her hard seat. "Something like that," she said quietly.

"The first headless body appeared in the middle of Junius. Then, for a while, nothing untoward happened. Misunderstanding the signal and its origin, I thought this was because I had complied with certain demands made on me against my will. In fact, those days were uneventful because of your absence. You left for Rome to oversee some work on the house on the Palatine, which you inherited from Lucius, so you weren't around to make mischief.

"The second body didn't appear until after the middle of Quinctilis, when we returned from Rome after Meto's birthday and the elections. You had planned to stay in Rome all that time, but you came back early, before we did; you told me at Meto's party that you were about to leave for home. You also made sure that I met your charming cousin Manius, with predictably appalling results that once again portrayed you as my friend and ally. You came back early, and so you were here when your cousin Gnaeus killed his poor slave Forfex in a rage. Perhaps you had no intention of leaving a second body on my land, but when the opportunity presented itself like a gift from the gods, once again you couldn't let a good corpse go to waste. You had the body stolen from where Gnaeus's slaves had interred it along the rocky stream bank. Once again, the corpse was delivered by your slave, visiting Congrio, probably carrying it in a handcart. The man had been dealing with Congrio so regularly, exchanging food-stuffs every now and again, that no one ever took any notice of him.

"You knew that I had met Forfex, and so once again it was, necessary to remove the head, to obscure the corpse's identity. You should have removed the hands as well, but how could you have known that Meto would recall the triangular birthmark on the back of Forfex's left hand? That led me to Gnaeus. He admitted killing Forfex, which was his right as the slave's master, but he denied having dropped the body down my well. He seemed to know nothing about it."

"He didn't," acknowledged Claudia.

"So I thought. Once again, I had cause to suspect someone else, but the connection with Gnaeus left me uncertain and confused. I went about the business of running the farm, de-spite the blighting of the hay, despite the deliberate pollution of my well. I proceeded with building the water mill—"

"That absurd contraption!" Claudia snapped.

"Yes, I realize now how frustrating it must have been for you whenever you'd sneak up here on the ridge to look down on my farm, greedy for it, imagining that it could be yours, despising me for having it, doing what you could in your own craven way to drive me off, and all the while watching the construction of the mill go on day by day, the tangible symbol of my firm intention to stay and make this property my own. How you must have hated it when I invited you to have a look at it after it was completed! How clearly I could sense your loathing, but I thought it was merely for the mill itself. You hid your true feelings well."

"A woman learns to hide her feelings if she's to get what she wants, without a father or a husband to give it to her and without sons to defend her!" said Claudia.

The bitterness in her voice was startling, and all at once I saw a flint-eyed woman so profoundly different from the jolly, good-natured matron I had known that I was almost frightened, as when a pretty mask drops to reveal a hideous face beneath. For two sleepless nights I had puzzled over the riddle of how Claudia could have been behind such atrocities. Now I saw another woman behind the one I thought I knew, who proceeded by guile and deceit and kept her anger and appetites hidden. How else could a woman alone have made her way in such a family and in such a world? For the first time I felt the reality of Claudia's guilt.

"I was confused again when Gnaeus offered to buy my property," I said, "though now I see it was you who put him up to that. He even said so in an oblique way, saying you had told him I was having a hard winter, but I thought that was merely gossip among cousins. In fact you were using him to feel me out before you made your next move, seeing if I'd had enough yet of headless corpses and poisoned water and the harshness of the winter. After his surly offer to relieve me of the farm, I grew suspicious of Gnaeus all over again, especially when, the very day after I ordered him out of my house, a third corpse appeared behind my stable. I was just setting out on a journey; there was no way I could stay to sort it out. That was just as well, perhaps, or I might have attacked Gnaeus without cause.

"The third headless corpse was another of your slaves, wasn't it? You didn't kill Nemo, who died of an illness. Nor did you kill Forfex; Gnaeus did that. But this slave you murdered, didn't you, Claudia?"

"Why do you say that?" she said, casting me a sullen glance.

"Because you needed someone on whom to test your poison. You had already tested it once, on a poor old slave of mine named Clementus. He was a witness of sorts on the night that Congrio dropped the body of Forfex down my well.

His recollection was vague and muddled, but to a slave like Congrio, guilty of conspiring against his master, even old Clementus must have seemed a terrible threat. Congrio had to get rid of him simply, quietly. You supplied him with a poison—strychnos, the deadly nightshade. That accounts for the blue lips, the vomiting, and the slurred speech that afflicted Clementus before he died. I always suspected he had been hurried along. Now I know for certain, for Congrio has confessed everything.

"Still, a poison that kills a doddering old slave may not work on a strong man of forty-seven, so you tried it out on one of your hapless slaves, didn't you, Claudia? How did you pick the poor fellow? Had he been showing signs of laziness, or was he weakened by bad joints, or had he offended you somehow? Or was he simply a good match for me, of about the same size and age, so that you could make sure of an adequate dosage to finish me off?"

She stared into the distance but made no answer.

"Wretched slave, to have such a mistress! Once you'd killed him with your poison—well, there was no use wasting the corpse, was there? Send another signal to Gordianus! A warning of things to come! Again, you removed the head to avoid any possibility of having him recognized, and delivered him via Congrio. Like Nemo, he was discovered by my daughter. Does that make you feel nothing, to know that you gave such a shock to a little girl? I suppose not, knowing what monstrosities you've shown yourself capable of committing."

Claudia abruptly stood. "I didn't come here to be judged, by you or anyone else. Your message said you wanted to come to some resolution and indicated that you had a proposition for me. Make it now and spare me your accusations and hand-wringing."

"Sit down, Claudia. It's a poor murderess who can't bear to hear her crimes recited."

"Poisoning a slave is not murder!"

"Ah, but kidnapping a freeborn child must surely be a crime."

"That's enough!" she said, and turned to go. I seized her shoulders and pushed her down onto the stump.

"You swore you wouldn't hurt me!" she shrieked, and pulled out a long, thin dagger. I knocked it from her hand and she covered her face. I looked hurriedly around, but saw no one in the bushes. She had come armed, but alone.

"Yes, Claudia, I swore it and I meant it, though neither gods nor men would object if I were to strangle you here on this spot! You can drop your haughty demeanor; it doesn't suit you. You'll listen to all I have to say, and together we'll arrive at the truth. Nothing can proceed without that, so don't deny it when I say you intended to poison me. Congrio has confessed! You grew impatient. Months passed, intimidation had failed to move me, and so you were finally ready to resort to the murder of a freeborn citizen—ah, but only an upstart plebeian! Did you think that with me gone you could more easily pressure Bethesda and Eco to sell the farm to you? Or would you have poisoned them as well?

"You wanted Congrio to poison me. Your agent kept pestering him, but Congrio resisted. That was a little too much for him, a little too dangerous. Clementus he had poisoned for his own protection, but to murder his master was too grave a sin. And then disaster—Congrio and your agent were indiscreet and let a little girl overhear them. You know the rest. What I don't know is what you could have been thinking when you sent your men to leave Diana in the mine. Were they meant to strangle her and leave her body there? Were they to abandon her alive and let her slowly starve to death? Or would you have rescued her in time and sold her into slavery, sending her to some foreign city on a ship out of Ostia while her parents mourned her for dead?"

Claudia's eyes darted wildly. I stepped closer, making it impossible for her to bolt. "I said that I wouldn't harm you, Claudia, and I meant it, though at this moment I regret the promise. You should be punished, Claudia—for your duplicity, for your arrogance, for murder, for kidnapping my daughter and making my wife mad with worry. But where would it end? Your cousins have too much bile in them and too much idle time; I should never feel safe if I exacted my just revenge on you. If only one could trust the gods to strike the balance against creatures such as yourself! But I've seen too much of the world to trust justice, human or divine. We make

our own justice in our own way, just as you and I are going
to strike a bargain, here and now."

"A bargain?"

"An agreement, Claudia, from which we shall move forward and never look back. My sons won't be satisfied. They
think you should be destroyed, like a wild dog. Nor will Bethesda be happy. She would like to pluck out your eyes and
make you swallow them. But they will abide by my decision.
And my decision is that you should have this farm."

She looked at me with such a blank expression that I
thought she hadn't heard me. Then she looked out at the farm
and I saw a glimmer in her eyes. "Is this a trick, Gordianus?"

"Not a trick, a bargain. You shall have the farm, just as
you wanted. We shall go down to Rome, to the place in the
Forum where the records are kept, and I shall sign over the
deed to you. And in return . . ."

She turned her head and looked at me sharply.

"In return, you shall give me the house on the Palatine,
which you inherited from Lucius, complete with all its furnishings."

"Absolutely not!"

"No? What use do you have for the house? It means nothing to you."

"It's a splendid house, worth a considerable fortune!"

"Yes, probably worth more than my farm, considering all
the statuary that Lucius collected, and the fine marble he installed, and the elegant furniture in each room, and the prime
location on the Palatine. A valuable house, indeed. I'm sure
that you don't think a mere nobody like me has any business
living in such a house, any more than I had inheriting Lucius's farm, but the fact is that Lucius meant for me to have
a legacy from him, and I will. He intended it to be the farm,
because he thought the farm would please me. It has pleased
me, but it has also brought me much grief.

"You, on the other hand, must want the farm very badly
to have schemed so doggedly to take it from me. You'll double your holdings and have land on both sides of the ridge.
You shall be the envy of your cousins, though, knowing your
cousins, I shouldn't care to have their envy. So you see, the

trade is equitable. Can you devise any other solution to the pass we've come to?"

She sat gazing out at the farm and began to tremble. "You condemn me for scheming against you, Gordianus, but how can you know how much this land means to me? I've wanted it ever since I was a little girl. I used to daydream for hours that it was mine. But the land went to Lucius. Every year that passed without his marrying and having a son, I rejoiced, for there was always the chance that he would leave it to me, if only I outlived him. Patience, patience! But then Gnaeus began complaining in the family councils about his lot, and it was tacitly decided that he should be put ahead of anyone else in our wills. Even so, there was always a chance that the land would come to me in time. Patience and hope! Then, when Lucius died and left the property to a stranger from the city—oh, you can't imagine the shock! It had slipped away from me forever! But now . . ."

"Then you accept the bargain."

She took a deep breath. "You say you want me to leave everything at the house on the Palatine intact. You'll do the same with the farm?"

How easily she slipped from nostalgia to hard dealing, I thought. "Of course. What would I do with farm implements in the city?"

"What about the slaves? Do they come with the farm?"

"Except for the house slaves I brought with me. Yes, you'll get the field slaves."

"Including Aratus?"

How I hated to leave him in the hands of such a mistress! But what would Aratus be without the farm he had been running for so many years? "Yes, Aratus will remain."

"And what about Congrio?"

I stared at the cloudless sky. "By rights I should put him to death," I said quietly.

"No one would blame you," said Claudia, pensively studying her cuticles. "Though I know it would be hard for you to kill him. It goes against your nature."

"I wouldn't have to commit the deed myself. Congrio's betrayal was unthinkable—conspiring against his master, kidnapping his master's daughter. If I advertised his crime, I imagine I could gather a great number of citizens who would be happy to join in stoning such a slave to death, as an example to others. But of course that would mean advertising your involvement, as well."

Claudia bit at one of her cuticles uneasily.

"Or I might sell him, simply to be rid of him," I said. "A cook of such skill would bring a great price. But how could I let loose such a viper into another man's household without warning him, and what man would buy such a slave if he knew the truth? No, I thought the matter through last night, while I was deciding on my proposition to you. Congrio comes with the farm, whether you want him or not."

Her eyes lit up. Could she actually eat Congrio's cooking again, knowing the treachery of which he was capable? Then let her have him! Let the vipers nest together!

"Do you accept my offer, Claudia?"

She breathed in deeply and exhaled. "I accept."

"Good. Then take one last look and go back to your own house. The property isn't yours yet, and until it is I want you to stay away from me and my family, and tell your cousins to do the same. We shall let our advocates settle the matter. I never want to see your face again."

She stood, slowly surveyed the view, then turned and began to walk away, but after a few steps she stopped and turned back, not quite enough to show her face. "Gordianus, do you believe in the gods? Do you believe that Fortune decrees whether we prosper or suffer, and the Fates determine the hour of our death?"

"What are you talking about, Claudia?"

"When I was a girl, barely old enough, I had a baby. Never mind by whom, or how it came about. My father was furious. He said that no one must ever know, so he hid me away, and when the child came he himself tore it from me and carried it up to a wild, hidden place on Mount Argentum and left it there. I wept and screamed, because I was young and in pain and hardly understood what was happening. I told him he had killed my baby, but he said that he had only exposed it to the gods, and that if it died it was by their will.

"I won't apologize for anything I've done to get the thing I want most in the world. My apologies would mean nothing to you, Gordianus, and nothing to me, either. But I want you to know that I would never have killed your daughter outright. When that fool Congrio sent her to me, what was I to do? I decided to send her up on the mountain and to put her in the mine."

"Where she might have fallen to her death!" I said. "Or starved, or died from the cold."

"Yes, but none of those endings would have come from my own hand. Don't you see? I left it up to the gods. And this is how it turned out. Your daughter is safe, and you shall have a fine house in Rome, and I shall have the farm. I did the right thing, after all."

"Claudia," I said, taking a deep breath and clenching my teeth, "I think you should go from here very quickly, or else I shall break my vow, and your neck along with it!"

FORTY-TWO

"PAPA, there's a man to see you at the front door!" said Diana, out of breath from running.

I put down the scroll I was reading. "Diana, how many times must I tell you that we have a slave who answers the door? I don't want you doing it yourself. Here in the city—"

"Why not?"

I sighed. At least her bad experience with Congrio had not made her timid. I yawned, stretched my arms above my head, and looked at the statue of Minerva on the far side of the garden. Made of bronze, she was painted so realistically that I often thought I could see her breathing. She was the only female in the household who never talked back to me, though like the others she never seemed to listen, either. Lucius must have paid a great sum for her.

"Besides, Papa, I recognize the man. He says he's a neighbor."

"Great Jupiter, surely not one of our old neighbors from

the farm." I imagined one of the Claudii standing at my front
door and felt a tremor of alarm. I got up from my chair and
crossed the garden with Diana at my heels.

The man at the front door turned out to be two men, accompanied by a retinue of slaves. The one whom Diana had
recognized was Marcus Caelius. I calculated the months in
my head and realized it was almost exactly a year since he
had come to the farm and called on me to pay back my debt
to Cicero. How Diana had recognized him I didn't know, for
Caelius was clean-shaven now and his hair had an ordinary
cut; the look made fashionable by Catilina and his circle the
year before was not to be seen anywhere in Rome that summer.

The citizen beside him was Cicero. The former consul had
gained a bit of weight since I had last seen him walking across
the Forum in triumph after putting the conspirators to death.

"You see," said Diana, pointing at Caelius, "I told you I
knew the man."

"Citizens, excuse my daughter's manners."

"Nonsense," said Cicero. "Never have I been greeted by
anyone more charming. May we come in, Gordianus?"

While their retinues remained outside, Cicero and Caelius
followed me to the garden. A slave brought cups and a clay
bottle, and as we sipped the wine I watched the two men
appraise their surroundings. Cicero's gaze lingered on the
statue of Minerva. I knew that he also had a statue of the
goddess in his house, but mine, I suspected, was considerably
more valuable. I smiled at the thought.

"Your new house is quite impressive," said Cicero.

"Quite," echoed Caelius.

"Thank you."

"So you gave up the farm," said Cicero. "After I worked
so hard to make sure you got it."

"Your work wasn't wasted, Cicero. The farm became this
house, as the caterpillar becomes the butterfly."

"You must explain that to me sometime," said Cicero.
"Meanwhile, welcome back to the city. How you ever thought
you could stand to leave it, I don't know. We're neighbors
now, if you can imagine that. My house is just over that way."

"Yes, I know. From the terrace off my bedroom upstairs

I have a splendid view of it, with the Capitoline Hill behind."

"And I'm your neighbor as well," remarked Caelius. "I've just taken an apartment in a building around the corner. The rent is exorbitant, but I've come into a bit of money lately."

"Really?" I said, thinking it would be impolitic to inquire where his money came from.

"What a beautiful garden," said Cicero. "And what a fine statue of the goddess. If you should ever wish to part with it, I'm sure I could offer you—"

"I think not, Cicero. Like this house, it came to me by way of a very dear, departed friend."

"I see. Of course." He sipped his wine. "But we didn't just come to admire your good fortune, Gordianus. I have a small favor to ask of you."

"Do you?" I said, feeling a chill despite the warm summer sun.

"Yes." He looked vaguely distressed. "Ah, but first, I wonder if the private facilities are as impressive as the more public ones?"

"You'll find a privy down that hall," I said. Cicero excused himself.

Caelius leaned forward. "Dyspepsia," he said confidentially. "And loose bowels. It's been worse than ever in the last year. Do you know, I sometimes wonder how Cicero manages to finish a speech before the Senate."

"Thank you for sharing that confidence, Marcus Caelius."

He laughed. "Actually, his digestion improved considerably for a while after the Senate passed that bill in the spring."

"What bill?"

"The one that pardoned everyone concerned in putting the conspirators to death."

"Ah, yes, I wasn't yet back in the city when that happened. But my son wrote me with the details: 'To all members of the Senate and to all magistrates, witnesses, informers, and other agents involved in any violations of law which may have been committed in relation to the execution without trial of Publius Cornelius Lentulus Sura, Gaius Cornelius Cethegus, *et alii*, the Senate of Rome grants permanent immunity against prosecution.' In other words, the Senate rather sweepingly let everyone off the hook."

"And a good thing for Cicero. For a while he was truly afraid he might be brought to trial for murder."

"And why not? The executions were completely illegal."

"Please, Gordianus, don't say such a thing when Cicero returns! Or at least wait until I'm gone."

"Leaving, so soon?"

"I can't stay. I have to see a man in the Street of the Weavers about buying some rugs for my new apartment. He uses a new dye that no one else has. It duplicates exactly the green of the eyes of a certain widow I'm trying to impress."

"You've always had such refined taste, Marcus Caelius—"

"Thank you."

"—that I'm left puzzled by your choice of loyalties. Knowing both of them as well as you must have, and having wavered between them, how did you ever come to choose Cicero over Catilina?"

"Gordianus, really! You show your own lack of good taste in asking such a question."

"Because it impugns your youthful idealism?"

"No, because it impugns my common sense. Why would I have chosen to be on the losing side in such a conflict? Oh, yes, I know what you mean about Catilina, and about Cicero. But sometimes, Gordianus, expediency wins out over good taste." He sipped his wine. Keeping an eye on the door through which Cicero had departed, he leaned forward and spoke in a confidential tone. "But if you want to know the truth of the matter, the real truth—"

"As opposed to the false truth?"

"Exactly. The fact of the matter is this: all during the last year I was serving neither Catilina nor Cicero, though both of them believed me to be their man."

"Neither of them? Who, then?"

"My old mentor, Crassus." When he saw the look of disbelief on my face, Caelius shrugged. "Well, he needed someone to keep an eye on both Cicero and Catilina and to report back to him on anything that might concern him; I was able to do both jobs at once. Do you think that Cicero is the only man who keeps spies all over Rome? And Crassus pays considerably better."

"As you should know, if all three of them were paying

what no one has, is a copy of the speech that Catilina delivered to his troops. Forget my talk of a favor; I should gladly reward with silver the man who could recall that speech for me."

"Does this have something to do with your memoirs, Cicero?"

"Perhaps. Why not? Catilina's conspiracy against the state was one of the most crucial events in the whole history of the Republic. As for the part I played in suppressing it, there are those who go so far as to say that in the hours when I wielded absolute power I fulfilled Plato's vision of the philosopherking. Perhaps they exaggerate, but still—"

"Please, Cicero!" Now it was I who felt dyspeptic.

"What I want from you, Gordianus, is a transcript of Catilina's speech, for posterity. Taken down at your convenience, however you like. You could make notes at your leisure, or I could send over Tiro to take your dictation."

"In his famous shorthand?"

"If you speak that fast."

I wrinkled my nose at the idea of putting Catilina's last public words into the hands of his destroyer. And yet, why should I let those words be lost forever? What other legacy of him would survive? No statues of Catilina would ever be erected in Rome; no histories would ever be written to glorify him; he had left no son to carry on his name or his cause. In a few years all that would remain of Catilina would be a series of speeches vilifying him before all the world.

There was also, of course, the water mill. It was Lucius Claudius who had inspired it and Catilina who had solved the riddle of its design. The mill was my private memorial to them both. Before I handed the farm over to Claudia I had seriously considered burning the mill, thinking she was unworthy to possess it. I even went so far as to equip the slaves with torches and hammers one day, intending to demolish it. But the sight of its wheel elegantly turning in the water caused me to desist. I chose to leave it standing as a memorial to all of us who had a hand in creating it.

The sound of Cicero clearing his throat called me back to the present. "Even if I was present at Pistoria," I said, "and

even if I wanted to help you, Cicero, what makes you think
I could remember Catilina's speech?"

"I'm certain that you could, Gordianus. Your memory for
such things is very keen. It's your nature and your vocation
to remember fine details, especially words. I've often heard
you quote word for word from arguments and statements
made years before."

"True enough, Cicero. A man can't escape his memory.
Do you know what I happened to remember a moment ago,
when I saw you on my doorstep? Words spoken years ago
by a man long dead. Yes, it was a little over eighteen years
ago, in your old house over by the Capitoline Hill, on the
night after the trial of Sextus Roscius. Do you remember? We
arrived at your house, you and I and Tiro, and found Sulla's
bodyguards and lackeys outside, and the dictator himself was
waiting for us in your library."

Cicero drew in a breath, as if the encounter still unnerved
him. "Of course I remember. I thought we were all going to
have our heads cut off and mounted on stakes."

"So did I. But for a monster who had just stubbed his toe,
Sulla was surprisingly gracious, though not particularly flattering. He said that I was a dog that went digging up bones,
and asked if I never got tired of getting worms and mud in
my snout."

"Did he say such a thing? I vaguely remember."

"When poor Tiro spoke out of turn, Sulla said he was
hardly good-looking enough to be allowed such liberties and
suggested that you beat him."

"That sounds like Sulla."

"And do you remember what he said about you?"

Cicero's face stiffened. "I'm not sure I know what you
mean."

" 'Stupidly daring or madly ambitious, or maybe both,' he
said. A clever young man and a splendid orator, just the sort
of fellow he'd like to recruit to his ranks, but he knew you'd
never accept such an offer, because your head was still too
full of republican virtue and scorn for tyranny. And then he
said—let me see if I can quote him word for word: 'You
have delusions of piety, delusions about your own nature. I'm
a wily fox and my nose is still keen, and in this room I smell

another fox. I tell you this, Cicero: The path you've chosen in life leads to only one place in the end, and that is the place where I stand. Your path may not take you as far, but it will take you nowhere else. Look at Lucius Sulla and see your mirror.' "

Cicero fixed me with a gelid gaze. "I recall no such words."

"No? Then perhaps you shouldn't trust my recollection of Catilina's speech."

His gaze thawed a bit. "What were you doing in Catilina's camp, anyway?"

"Retrieving a lost lamb who turned out to be a lion cub. But don't you know the details already, from your spies?"

"Some things my spies can't tell me, such as what resides unspoken in a man's heart. Oh, Gordianus, had I known you would be so susceptible to Catilina's corruption, I would never have sent Caelius to ask for your help. I thought that you would see through him in an instant. Instead, I think he must have seduced you, after all. Though not literally, I hope," he added, laughing.

I gazed across the garden at the statue of Minerva. Her bland silence had a way of calming me; detachment from anger is one part of wisdom. "Do you have no regrets about your year as consul, Cicero?"

"None at all."

"No nagging doubts about the precedents you set for the future of this frayed and fragile republic? No secret wish that you could have broken free of the Optimates and struck a blow for change?"

He shook his head and smiled condescendingly. "Change is the enemy of civilization, Gordianus. What is the point of innovation, when things are already in the hands of the Best People? What you might consider progress can only be decay and decadence."

"But, Cicero, you're a New Man! You rose from an unknown family to become consul. You stand for change."

"To be sure, a newcomer of outstanding gifts may sometimes rise to join the Best, just as a high-born patrician like Catilina may fall into ruin and disgrace. Such is the balance of the gods—"

"The gods! How can you be an atheist one day and declare yourself the vessel of Jupiter the next?"

"I was speaking metaphorically, Gordianus," said Cicero patiently, as if my literal-mindedness were an eccentricity to be indulged.

I took a deep breath and gazed at Minerva, but my equanimity was at an end. "I think I must be alone now, Cicero."

"Of course. I'm sure I can find my way to the door." He stood up but did not turn away. Instead he looked down at me expectantly.

"Very well," I finally said. "Send Tiro around tomorrow morning, if you like, with his writing materials. I shall duplicate Catilina's speech from memory as best I can." Cicero nodded and turned to go with a smile on his lips. "And perhaps Tiro will recall Sulla's words more clearly than you do," I added, and saw Cicero's shoulders stiffen almost imperceptibly.

EPILOGUE

FOUR years have now passed since Cicero's visit to my new house on the Palatine.

I thought then that the story was finished, as much as such matters can ever be finished. But it seems to me now that recent events have transpired to give a more fitting ending. Like the statue of Jupiter that took years to put in place, it was simply a matter of time.

The intervening years have seen the continued ascendancy of Caesar, who two years ago formed a coalition (or triumvirate, as they call it in the Forum) with Crassus and Pompey, and who last year was elected consul, at the age of forty-one. Now Caesar is off to Gaul, putting down a troublesome tribe called the Helvetii. I wish him well in his military endeavors, if only because my son is with him.

Shortly after our return to Rome, Meto enlisted under the charge of Marcus Mummius, but he didn't care for Pompey, and now serves under Caesar. His choice of a military career baffles me, but I long ago accepted it. (He has always been inordinately proud of the battle scar he received at Pistoria.) In his latest letter, posted from the town of Bibracte in the land of the Aedui, Meto writes of going into battle against the Helvetii with an account that makes my hair stand on end. How did the winsome little boy I adopted ever grow so inured to the sight of blood and gore? Before the engagement began, Meto writes, Caesar had all the horses sent out of sight, beginning with his own, thus placing every Roman in equal danger—a gesture familiar to me from my one experience of battle under a less fortunate commander. Meto assures me that Caesar is a military genius, but this is hardly reassuring to a father who would prefer a son humble and alive to one covered with glory and dead.

I write to him often, never knowing if my letters will reach him. The battle at Pistoria made us closer in a way, even as it widened the gulf between us. It is easier to open my heart to him in a letter, addressing myself to the image of him I conjure up from memory, than to speak to him face to face. My greatest fear is that I may be writing words to a young man already dead, without my knowing it.

I append copies of two of my letters to him written some months apart, the first from the month of Aprilis:

To my beloved son Meto, serving under the command of Gaius Julius Caesar in Gaul, from his loving father in Rome, may Fortune be with you.

The night is warm, and made even warmer by the heat radiating from the flames which shoot up from a burning house nearby.

Let me explain.

A little while ago I was minding my own business, reading in the garden by the last of the daylight. I noticed that the darkening sky had an oddly reddish tinge, but this I attributed to a florid sunset. I was about to call for a lamp when a slave came to say that I had a caller, and our neighbor Marcus Caelius burst into the garden asking if I could see the fire from the terrace upstairs. Together we rushed to my bedroom, where Bethesda already stood transfixed on the terrace, watching Cicero's house go up in flames.

A few days ago Cicero fled into exile, hounded out of the city by the populist tribune Clodius. The reaction against Cicero has been building for some time. There are still those who praise his virtue and his service to Rome, but even many of his staunchest supporters have grown sick of hearing him go on and on about how sharp and fearless he was in putting down Catilina, in such overblown terms that it's become something of a joke. And then of course his over-weening vanity and rudeness have become legendary. Crassus despises him, Pompey barely tolerates him, and you know the sentiments of your beloved commander, Caesar. And of course there are a great many people of all classes who sympathized with Catilina without ever joining him, who are rankled by Cicero's constant boasting and his vilification (beyond the grave!) of a man they respected.

As tribune, Clodius has been a genius at organizing the people (the Master of the Mob, they call him) and at cowing (even terrorizing) the Optimates. They say his feud with Cicero began as a personal matter (incited by Cicero's wife Terentia, who accused Clodius's sister of trying to break up her marriage by going after Cicero—imagine!), but soon enough Clodius found he could whip up a firestorm of popular support by making public attacks on Cicero. To elicit sympathy, Cicero let his hair grow and went about the city dressed in mourning, but Clodius and his mob followed him everywhere, jeering at him and pelting him with mud, and the hordes of sympathizers Cicero expected to rush to his defense never materialized. What had become of the masses who had hailed him as Father of the Fatherland only a few years before? The mob is fickle, Meto.

Cicero grew so fearful for his life that he fled from the city, whereupon Clodius got the people's Assembly to pass an edict condemning Cicero to exile "for having put Roman citizens to death unheard and uncondemned" and forbidding anyone within five hundred miles of Rome to give him shelter. (Never mind the law the Senate passed promising everyone immunity after the conspirators were executed.) Further, it was decreed that anyone agitating to bring Cicero back from exile should be regarded as a public enemy, "unless those whom Cicero unlawfully put to death should first be brought back to life." Clodius has a dry sense of humor.

So now, with Cicero headed for Greece, Clodius is on a rampage, and Cicero's lovely house on the Palatine is going up in flames. I write to you not by lamplight, but by the bright, flickering flames that illuminate my bedroom and would make it impossible to sleep, even if I were so inclined.

Now, can you tell me a story of fighting the Helvetii as hair-raising as that?

Where all this chaos will lead I do not know, but I doubt that we have seen the last of Cicero; foxes have a way of slinking back to their lairs once the hunters have moved on.

I wish you every blessing of Fortune in your service under Caesar, and each day I pray for your safe return.

Finally, this letter, which bears today's date, the Ides of Sextilis:

To my beloved son Meto, serving under the command of Gaius Julius·Caesar in Gaul, from his loving father in Rome, may Fortune be with you.

I have just returned from a trip up north to Arretium. How wonderful to come home to Rome, to the welcome of Bethesda and your little sister Diana, who in a few days will celebrate her twelfth birthday. They send their love, as do Eco and Menenia and the twins, who have become quite uncontrollable. (I should have become a grandfather in my thirties or forties like most men; now I fear I'm too old for it!)

But I must tell you what I discovered on my trip to the countryside. I had not been north on the Cassian Way in years; I have avoided that road, not wanting to pass by the farm again, but a bit of business involving a lost necklace and an adulterous wife compelled me to go to Arretium. (If you want to know the details, you shall have to give up soldiering, come home, and take up your father's profession!)

On the way up I was so rushed that I merely rode by the farm at a quick pace. Mount Argentum, the ridge, the farmhouse, the grape arbors and orchards and fields—I felt a pang of nostalgia, which lingered long after I had pressed on. On the way home I had more time, and so when I came to Mount Argentum and the farm, I slowed my horse to a walk.

The first thing I noticed was that the stone wall at the northern end of the farm was in the process of being demolished. The earth was hazy with heat and dust, but I could see the farmhouse and the other buildings clearly enough. Squinting beyond them, toward the stream, I could not see the water mill at all, until I was able to pick out its ruined foundation. The mill was gone.

I was almost tempted to go riding up to the farmhouse. Instead I simply stopped in the road and stared. A little while later an oxcart driven by a single slave set out from the stable, heading toward the highway. As he drew closer, I saw that he was not one of the slaves we had owned, so I asked him if he belonged on the farm.

"Yes," he said. His manner was cowed, and he would not look in my eyes.

"Then perhaps you can tell me when your mistress started tearing down the wall up north."

"That wasn't the mistress's idea," he mumbled, looking perplexed at such a suggestion. "It was the master's."

"The master?" I said, wondering if Claudia could have married. "What is his name?"

"Manius Claudius. He started tearing down the wall as soon as he inherited the property, which was a year ago. And quite a job it is, breaking up all that stone and carting it off! Now that he owns all the land as far as the eye can see on both sides of the ridge, he says he has no use for the wall."

"But what happened to Claudia?"

"Ah, the master's cousin, who left him the land. She died—a year ago."

"How did she die?"

"It happened quite suddenly. They say it was quite awful. She went into convulsions, and her tongue turned black. They say it must have been something she ate."

I was quiet for some time, absorbing this. "And the water mill—why was it demolished?"

"That was also at the order of my master Manius. He said, 'Such an abomination is an insult to the institution of slavery!' "

"I see."

"Pardon me," the slave said, looking at the ground, "but you must be the old master, the one who was here before Claudia."

"That's right."

"The old hands speak of your time as a Golden Age."

"Do they? Golden Ages have a way of being overrated. And they never seem to last. Tell me, is Aratus still the foreman?"

"Yes, and a better one I've never worked for. A steady hand in good times and bad."

"So he is, and I hope your master appreciates him. And tell me, is Congrio still the cook?"

"He was, until shortly after the master inherited the farm. Then the master made Congrio a free man and let him go off to the city with a bag of silver on his belt. Can you imagine that?"

"Yes," I said, "I think I can."

From this story, you may draw your own conclusions.

Recounting this tale, putting it into words as if you were here, makes me miss you very much, my son. I worry for your safety. I long for your companionship. Though we have had our differences, there are things we two understand that no one else knows of, and so you are precious to me. Without you, there would be no one else to remember and bear witness to certain incidents that still confound and haunt me.

Seeing the farm again has unleashed many memories, which circle my head like harpies. To whom but you could I ever speak of my feelings about Catilina? What a waste, I sometimes think, to have spent my precious time with him suspecting and resisting him! But another part of me says: What if you had supported him, given yourself to him heart and soul—toward what end? And an even more skeptical part still doubts everything about Catilina and suspects he was nothing more than a very charming and very desperate charlatan, no different from the rest.

To my knowledge there is no god of regret, or of doubt; why should there be when a Roman is not supposed to feel such things? And so there is no altar upon which I can lay these feelings, see them purified by flame and turned to ash. Instead I live with doubt and regret, sustained by the love of those close to me, bemused by such ironies as Cicero's exile and Claudia's fate, and I continue to ponder, as I know you must, Catilina's riddle.

AUTHOR'S NOTE

FEW figures in history have attracted more controversy than Lucius Sergius Catilina. A generation after his death he was already being portrayed as a damned soul by Virgil in the *Aeneid*. Over the centuries he has alternately been held up as a hero or villain, often in extreme terms. Two works published hundreds of years and thousands of miles apart illustrate the dichotomy by their titles alone: compare *Patriae Parricida: The History of the Horrid Conspiracy of Catiline Against the Commonwealth of Rome*, published by an anonymous pamphleteer in London in 1683, and Ernesto Palacio's *Catilina: Una Revolucion contra la Plutocracia en Roma*, published in Buenos Aires in 1977. Which is it to be: Catilina the depraved insurrectionist, or Catilina the heroic revolutionary? The destroyer of decency, or the champion of the underclass?

Ben Jonson adhered faithfully to the classical sources hostile to Catilina to produce *Catiline his Conspiracy*, a tragedy first performed in 1611 by the players of King James and revived in the Restoration; its antirevolutionary themes would please a monarch. Voltaire made Cicero an exemplar for the Age of Reason and Catilina an agent of chaos in his play *Rome Sauvée, ou Catilina*, which grossly distorts the historical record; Caesar is sent into the field to fight the conspirators! (From Gaston Bossier's *La Conjuration de Catilina* of 1905 we learn that Robespierre was called *le Catilina moderne*.) In 1850 Isben delivered a radical revisionist *Catilina* which portrays the conspirator as a sort of Hamlet struggling with his conscience to take a stand against tyranny.

The problem with Catilina lies in the primary sources, which are severely biased against him. Cicero's four famous orations against Catilina are models of invective, and Sallust, who was a partisan of Caesar, had his own agenda when he wrote his book-length history of the *Bellum Catilinae*. The venom in these accounts must be taken with a grain of salt. One finds evidence from his own writings that before and after the conspiracy Cicero found much to admire in Catilina, and Sallust, while repeating every vile rumor about Catilina and his followers like a dutiful tabloid reporter, nevertheless provides compelling evidence to justify their actions.

Many modern historians seem content to accept the negative portrait of Catilina at face value, even knowing that it was painted by his enemies. Others follow revisionist lines that seek to look behind Cicero's rhetoric and Sallust's melodrama. In general, the clearest revelation to emerge from most historical reconstructions is of the particular historian's personal politics and point of view; Catilina becomes merely a prop. Even more distressing are those historians who insist on having the "last word" on a subject for which there can be no last word, short of the invention of time travel or communication with the dead.

Fortunately, the first-person novelist, liberated from any pretense of omniscience, can adhere scrupulously to historical evidence even while allowing for the development of a subjective interpretation. The essential details in *Catilina's Riddle*, including the speeches and the various political maneuverings, are authentic. Nevertheless, the reader is ultimately free to question Gordianus's perceptions and his conclusions, as does Gordianus himself. It has not been my aim to rehabilitate Catilina, as Josephine Tey sought to rehabilitate Richard III in *The Daughter of Time*. Catilina remains today what he must have been in his own time: *ænigma*, which is to say, a riddle.

Books beget books, and I should acknowledge the one that first made me think that a novel about Catilina was dramatically feasible, *The Conspiracy of Catiline* by Lester Hutchinson (Barnes and Noble, 1967), which remains my favorite book-length reconstruction. Among shorter works, "In Defense of Catiline" by Walter Allen, Jr. (*Classical Journal* 34, 1938) provided unique insights. I should also acknowledge Arthur D. Kahn's *The Education of Julius Caesar* (Schocken Books, 1986); the very title of his chapter "The Conspiracy